FRENCH SHORT STORIES OF THE 19TH & 20TH CENTURIES

SELECTED, WITH AN INTRODUCTION, BY

F. C. GREEN, M.A., PH.D.

Professor of French in the University of Edinburgh

LONDON J. M. DENT & SONS LTD
NEW YORK E. P. DUTTON & CO INC

Made in Great Britain
at the
Aldine Press · Letchworth · Herts
for
J. M. DENT & SONS LTD
Aldine House · Bedford Street · London
First published in this edition 1933
Last reprinted 1961

INTRODUCTION

NEXT to the play, it is hard to conceive a form of art more suited to the French literary genius than the short story. Indeed, if we consider the qualities that distinguish the writings of the French from those of any other race, the unique contribution made by them to the development of the short story appears less astonishing than inevitable. Three attributes which are indispensable in this branch of letters they have long treasured and fostered as part of a general, cultural heritage: a profound respect for form, an instinct for clarity and conciseness, and an unerring *flair* for the truly dramatic situation. Obviously the presence of such elements alone will not endow a short story with immortality, but without them assuredly no short story can hope to rise above the mediocre.

A good short story, like a good play, is a miracle of condensation. It leaves the reader with that sense of intellectual happiness which comes only from the contemplation of the finished work of art. Yet the aesthetic pleasure afforded by this sense of formal completeness is but a prelude to enjoyment of a far richer sort. The short story, because of its concise, condensed nature, stimulates the imagination swiftly and suddenly, almost like a shock. It does not, of course, illuminate such a vast zone as that of the novel, but what it loses in range it gains by its intensity. The focus of interest, the centre of irradiation in all perfect short stories is deliberately limited, and to achieve this the author must have the intellectual courage to make ruthless sacrifices to his *amour-propre*, and also the artistic sense to strike a final choice from amongst several situations and traits of character, all of which the novelist might have incorporated in his general scheme. As in drama, in the short story discipline is of paramount importance. There must be no synonyms or phrases: the dialogue must be tense, tingling, and subservient to the action, which it carries along with imperceptible swiftness. The crisis, too, must offer the illusion of a gradual, inevitable ascent. But the real stumbling-block is the *dénouement,* that final tap which closes the arch, the paragraph or sentence that fills the reader with admiration, solves his immediate problem, and unlocks vistas through which fancy may wander at her ease. Relatively unimportant in the novel, the *dénouement* in a short story is a thing of supreme moment. Madame Bovary might easily have run off with a gamekeeper instead of taking prussic acid, but De Maupassant's *The Necklace* simply had to conclude with Madame Forestier's devastating phrase.

Here, it seems, we encounter a fundamental difference between the novel and the short story. This difference is not merely technical: it is integral, since it springs from a divergence in the nature and object of these respective genres, however alike they may be in other respects. And if, as sometimes happens, this difference ceases to be discernible, it is because the author is trying to exercise a purely quantitative condensation, to compress a novel into the dimensions of a *conte*—always a fatal proceeding, like reducing an epic to the stature of a sonnet!

If we compare the endings of *Madame Bovary* and of *The Necklace,* each of which is a perfect example of its particular kind of art, the essential difference referred to is startlingly obvious. But for the particular conclusion imagined by De Maupassant, one cannot possibly experience the story or grasp its pregnant philosophy. The true enjoyment of the tale begins, so to speak, at the end, whereas in the case of Flaubert's work this illumination has been a gradual, cumulative process which is practically complete before we learn of Emma's suicide. Moreover, without offending probability or compromising the integrity of his creations, Flaubert, as we have seen, might quite conceivably have chosen two or three other conclusions all equally consonant with reality.

By way of illustration let us examine the function of the *dénouement* in three stories taken at random from our collection: *A Night with Cleopatra, Fanfarlo,* and *The Match.* In each case there is the same effect of sudden and retrospective illumination, a like impression of completeness and inevitability. To remain credible, Cleopatra had to speak the final phrase attributed to her by Gautier. And if we were to savour fully the acid flavour of Baudelaire's criticism it was absolutely essential that Samuel should crash through the coloured hoop of Romanticism into the sawdust of bourgeois philistinism.

In *The Match*, Charles-Louis Philippe presents the only possible *dénouement* when he makes Létang the author of his own salvation. Any outside intervention, however probably contrived, would have destroyed the essence of the tale, which is contained in the dramatic conflict between the forces of panic and self-preservation operating in the soul of a very ordinary man. Here again, full realization of the situations and emotions adumbrated in the body of the story comes only at the end. The criminal, the man with the brilliant eyes, maintains his dreadful silence: only at this point do we really become aware of Létang's agony.

The peculiar importance assumed by the ending in the short story results necessarily from its condensed, circumscribed nature. It is the author's only chance of lending density and significance to characters and situations which, owing to the limitations of his cadre, could only be etched in the severest outline. The novelist, working under no such self-imposed discipline, is, on the contrary, free to build as he advances, digressing at will until, as has been indicated, the question of how he should end his novel becomes relatively unimportant. Relatively, because although it would be a gross artistic blunder to make Grandet die in the odour of sanctity leaving his money to the Church, or to present Des Grieux respectably married to Manon Lescaut and Mayor of New Orleans, yet both Balzac and Prévost could quite possibly have imagined other endings. Nor can it really be argued that what ultimately happens to their characters inspires us with the feeling that only then do we understand their psychology or taste their experience. Now, both Balzac and Prévost are dramatic novelists, endowed, that is to say, with a strong architectural sense. But if we turn to writers like Marivaux, Fielding, Lesage, or Smollett or Sterne who have not that sense, the cleft between the novel and short story becomes very evident indeed.

If only for this reason, then, a short story is anything but a short novel. And it is rare to find the two forms of art practised with equal success by the same author. De Maupassant's novels cannot bear comparison with his *contes*. Balzac at times, and Zola always, in their short stories are ill at ease. The great English and French novelists as a rule fight shy of the short story. Flaubert, Anatole France, and Hardy are notable exceptions, since in both genres they have produced fine work. The reason is that all three display in their novels, to a marked degree, qualities which we have noted as peculiar to the art of the short story. All are imbued with a profound respect for form. Hardy, indeed, sometimes strains probability to achieve symmetry: one remembers Proust's acute remarks about his 'parallelism'. Flaubert's veneration for form needs no elaboration, and the prose of Anatole France reveals a like regard for balance, word values, and purity of line. All three, too, in the construction of their novels display a strong, dramatic penchant: their works rise in a sweeping curve to a well-defined crisis. It is curious that Stendhal, who also had these qualities, never gave us a good short story. *Vanina Vanini*, his best, is poor stuff. The explanation is, I think, that Stendhal, like Marivaux, cultivated the art of psychological analysis with a delicacy for which the limited cadre of the short story offers no scope. By no *tour de force*, for instance, could complex and darkly fascinating creations like Julien Sorel or the Duchess Sanseverina ever be condensed to fit the dimensions of a *conte*.

Here one perceives another difference in the two forms of fiction. The characters in a novel are always more highly individualized than those of the short story. The latter, like the persons we meet in classic French Comedy, tend, as a rule, to represent general social types or categories. That is why it is exceedingly difficult to evoke a character from one of De Maupassant's tales as, for instance, we can recall a Bovary, a Charlus, or a Coignard. Nearly always they sink their individuality in the general idea which they represent—be it the cunning of the peasant, the gross materialism of the petty bourgeoisie, the stupid vanity of mankind, or the inveteracy of the great human instincts. If their psychology tends to be that of a class rather than of an individual, it is because the author has not the time at his disposal to reveal the subtle play of emotion, the nuances of sentiment, the obscure motives, that govern behaviour. For this we need the leisurely art and the peculiar genius of a Stendhal or a Proust.

The object of the great short story writer is to suggest rather than to exhibit the complexity and the beauty of life. His interpretation of human behaviour is tinged with the hue of a secret ideal which, however, he communicates with more reluctance than the novelist. For his method of interpretation is different. In all the great novels the course of destiny is clearly charted, but the short story can portray but an incident in the journey. What came before and is yet to pass ere that journey be over can only be suggested. Everything, therefore, depends on the significance of that incident; on the choice of the exact moment of the narrator's intervention. With the novelist we slowly climb to the mountain tops and gradually he shows us the windings of the stream from source to estuary: the short story writer is like a chance acquaintance on a moving train who knows that at a certain point there is a gap in the trees affording a momentary glimpse of the river's course. And how often, alas! does he miss the gap, leaving us puzzled and irritated because of this broken promise! Yet, when he has accurately timed his moment, how complete the impression left by that fleeting view. The great artist, like De Maupassant, has the secret of keying one up to a pitch of intense expectation and awareness, for this instant of revelation. And in this process he achieves, as I have said, miracles of condensation, for we must never suspect that the pace of the narrative is being forced. On the contrary, the best short stories leave us always with the certainty that they are much longer than they actually are. In two thousand words De Maupassant can make us experience in all our senses the glory of spring in Normandy, plunge us into the life and character of its peasants, at the same time developing a dramatic situation which illuminates the depths of an individual soul.

What Fielding calls 'that quick and sagacious penetration into the true essence of all the objects of our contemplation' the great story writers possess to an almost incredible degree. And in greater or less measure this power of penetrating, isolating, and formulating the radioactive elements hidden in the dross of life will be found in all the authors whose works are here translated. Few, of course, dig so deep or so surely as De Maupassant, but even the most superficial in his burrowings gets beneath the tuff with which time and habit have crusted over the rich earth of human nature.

Midway between the play and the novel, the short story holds a unique, interesting situation. Whilst partaking somewhat of the nature of both these genres it yet possesses all the individual marks of an independent art form. The *conteur*, like the dramatist, is, as a rule, content to exploit a single situation, employing a limited number of characters. So his work acquires a degree of tension and tempo unattainable by the novelist. On the other hand, by availing himself of the latter's peculiar privileges he is able to introduce his characters and to situate them in their appropriate *ambiance* with a rapidity and completeness beyond the power of the cleverest playwright. To understand this fully, compare a tale like Anatole France's *Crainquebille* with its dramatized version written by the same author.

Here, clearly, the playwright has been forced by the nature of his craft to sacrifice the very elements that compose the essential charm of the short story, and to introduce matter foreign to the art of the latter. *Crainquebille* in its dramatic form is provided with a stage *dénouement* which effectively robs it of that bitter-sweet and penetrating aroma of philosophic resignation which charges the whole atmosphere of the short story.

A short story cannot be dramatized or expanded into a novel without suffering a mortal injury. No doubt the three artists—novelist, playwright, and *conteur*—dispose of the same raw materials; but each has his peculiar alchemy, his individual creative process. A situation like that composing the whole interest of De Bernard's *A Consultation* seems dramatic, yet a playwright could do little with it because it is not dramatic at all, but merely complicated. At no point does it offer a chance for that clash between character and situation which would be the dramatist's chief concern. It is simply a fascinating jig-saw puzzle with human beings as pieces: they click into place and our curiosity ends. De Bernard knew its limitations.

Similarly, Barbey d'Aurévilly was too experienced an artist to write a novel based on Don Juan's life. Such a work, he was aware, would be as monotonous as the memoirs of Casanova. So he crystallized his material into a superb short story. The hero's life is condensed into one vivid impression and our attention cleverly focused on the one incident in that life most calculated to fire our imagination, to set us brooding on the strange complexity of human nature. For what could be stranger than the momentous touching of two destinies so utterly unlike; what more suggestive than this fleeting contact of the extremes of vice and innocence? Illuminated thus in retrospect, the character of Don Juan acquires a new and more vital meaning. Yet imagine that incident related in a novel, chronologically, as it were, and indeed as it must have occurred in what we call reality, preceded and followed by the amorous experience which formed the tissue of Don Juan's existence. Its relative significance would have been lost. But Barbey, employing the art of the *conteur*, rescues the incident from mere temporal reality and invests it with a reality which is much truer. He isolates it, places it in balance against the rest of Don Juan's life, thus projecting both on the screen, not of time, but of eternity. That is great art, but it is not the art of the novelist.

The short stories assembled here were published during the space of nearly a century. Viewed *en bloc* they offer a greater variety both of theme and composition than do the novels of the same period. This is because the short story, owing to its more limited objective, is more flexible than the novel. Very good short stories, witness those of De Bernard and Mérimée, can be created out of mere situation, whereas of course only the most inferior type of novel, the so-called 'thriller', can exist on situation alone. Again, in short stories that portray extraordinary characters—*Fanfarlo* is an excellent example—the *conteur* has again a clear advantage over his brother artist. No novelist could make Samuel a convincing hero: the limits of his credibility are those of a short story and Baudelaire has very nicely judged his point of saturation. Diluted, the character of Samuel would lose its pungency.

De Maupassant, by employing the short story form, was able to handle situations and characters so slight, so ordinary, almost so commonplace, that no great novelist would have exploited them. Some of the lesser Naturalists, it is true, attempted to do so with unfortunate results. That was because they were not even writers of talent, which is a recognition not simply of one's own limitations but of those imposed by one's medium. De Maupassant, being a genius, was at once unconscious of any limits to his own creative powers and instinctively aware that they were not those of the novelist. He discovered that in order to write perfect short stories it is not necessary to imagine queer situations for ordinary people, or queer people in ordinary situations. By portraying quite ordinary people in contact with very ordinary situations, he found that he could all the more convincingly interpret, throw into relief the essential queerness, not of things or people, but of life itself. This is surely what he meant by that passage in *Un Soir* where he refers to 'certain encounters, certain inexplicable combinations of things' which 'without appearing in the slightest degree exceptional, assuredly contain a greater quantity of life's secret quintessence than that dispersed through the ordinary run of events'. Such material, he knew, does not readily lend itself to the art of the novelist, for very few memorable novels have been written about ordinary people in ordinary situations. Yet think what De Maupassant extracts from his drab people, their dingy *milieux* and their everyday, domestic situations; from those wretched clerks, shopkeepers, peasants and their squalid money-grubbing; from the frowsy little ambitions and amours of their women-folk. What inoffensive, uninteresting ingredients are these till properly combined by the cunning of the artist and detonated by the spark of his genius!

F. C. GREEN.

ACKNOWLEDGMENTS

THE translation of 'The Desire to be a Man' from *Sardonic Tales* of Villiers de l'Isle Adam, and of 'The Greatest Love of Don Juan' from Barbey d'Aurévilly's *Les Diaboliques* are reprinted by permission of and special arrangement with Messrs. Alfred A. Knopf Inc., the authorized publishers; the translations of 'Sylvie' by de Nerval and of 'Leviathan' by Julian Green are reprinted by permission of Messrs. William Heinemann; Winifred Stephens' translation of 'Crainquebille' is reprinted by permission of Messsr. John Lane, the Bodley Head, Ltd., and Messrs. Dodd, Mead and Co.; permission to make the translation of 'The Match' by Charles-Louis Philippe is due to the Librairie Gallimard, while permission covering the American market for 'Leviathan' has been given by the American publishers, Messrs. Harper Brothers.

The editor has ventured to include the translations of the Daudet stories without obtaining proper permission. Both he and the publishers have made unsuccessful efforts to trace Mr. Edward Harris or his representatives, and it is hoped that this explanation and acknowledgment will, in some measure, justify the liberty taken.

CONTENTS

NOTE.—All translations have been especially provided for this edition by Mrs. Mary Balairdie Green unless otherwise acknowledged at the end of a story.

FACINO CANE

H. de Balzac

I once used to live in a little street which probably is not known to you—the Rue de Lesdiguières. It is a turning out of the Rue Saint-Antoine, beginning just opposite a fountain near the Place de la Bastille, and ending in the Rue de la Cerisaie. Love of knowledge stranded me in a garret; my nights I spent in work, my days in reading at the Bibliothèque d'Orléans, close by. I lived frugally, I had accepted the conditions of the monastic life, necessary conditions for every worker, scarcely permitting myself a walk along the Boulevard Bourdon when the weather was fine. One passion only had power to draw me from my studies; and yet, what was that passion but a study of another kind? I used to watch the manners and customs of the Faubourg, its inhabitants, and their characteristics. As I dressed no better than a working man, and cared nothing for appearances, I did not put them on their guard; I could join a group and look on while they drove bargains or wrangled among themselves on their way home from work. Even then observation had come to be an instinct with me; a faculty of penetrating to the soul without neglecting the body; or rather, a power of grasping external details so thoroughly that they never detained me for a moment, and at once I passed beyond and through them. I could enter into the life of the human creatures whom I watched, just as the dervish in the *Arabian Nights* could pass into any soul or body after pronouncing a certain formula.

If I met a working man and his wife in the streets between eleven o'clock and midnight on their way home from the Ambigu Comique, I used to amuse myself by following them from the Boulevard du Pont aux Choux to the Boulevard Beaumarchais. The good folk would begin by talking about the play; then from one thing to another they would come to their own affairs, and the mother would walk on and on, heedless of complaints or question from the little one that dragged at her hand, while she and her husband reckoned up the wages to be paid on the morrow, and spent the money in a score of different ways. Then came domestic details, lamentations over the excessive dearness of potatoes, or the length of the winter and the high price of block fuel, together with forcible representations of amounts owing to the baker, ending in an acrimonious dispute, in the course of which such couples reveal their characters in picturesque language. As I listened, I could make their lives mine, I felt their rags on my back, I walked with their gaping shoes on my feet; their cravings, their needs, had all passed into my soul, or my soul had passed into theirs. It was the dream of a waking man. I waxed hot with them over the foreman's tyranny, or the bad customers that made them call again and again for payment.

To come out of my ways of life, to be another than myself through a kind of intoxication of the intellectual faculties, and to play this game at will, such was my recreation. Whence comes the gift? Is it a kind of second sight? Is it one of those powers which when abused end in madness? I have never tried to discover its source; I possess it, I use it, that is all. But this it behoves you to know, that in those days I began to resolve the heterogeneous mass known as the People into its elements, and to evaluate its good and bad qualities. Even then I realized the possibilities of my suburb, that hotbed of revolution in which heroes, inventors, and practical men of science, rogues, and scoundrels, virtues and vices, were all packed together by poverty, stifled by necessity, drowned in drink, and consumed by ardent spirits.

You would not imagine how many adventures, how many tragedies, lie buried out of sight in that Dolorous City; how much horror and beauty lurks there. No imagination can reach the Truth, no one can go down into that city to make discoveries; for one must needs descend too low into its depths to see the wonderful scenes of tragedy or comedy enacted there, the masterpieces brought forth by chance.

I do not know how it is that I have kept the following story so long untold. It is one of the curious things that stop in the bag from which Memory draws out stories at haphazard, like numbers in a lottery. There are plenty of tales just as strange and just as well hidden still left; but some day, you may be sure, their turn will come.

One day my charwoman, a working man's wife, came to beg me to honour her sister's wedding with my presence. If you are to realize what this wedding was like, you must know that I paid my charwoman, poor creature, four francs a month; for which sum she came every morning to make my bed, clean my shoes, brush my clothes, sweep the room, and make ready my breakfast, before going to her day's work of turning the handle of a machine, at which hard drudgery she earned ten sous. Her husband, a cabinetmaker, made four francs a day at his trade; but as they had three children, it was all that they could do to gain an honest living. Yet I have never met with more sterling honesty than in this man and his wife. For five years after I left the quarter, Mère Vaillant used to come on my birthday with a bunch of flowers and some oranges for me—she that had never a sixpence to put by! Want had drawn us together. I never could give her more than a ten-franc piece, and often I had to borrow the money for the occasion. This will perhaps explain my promise to go to the wedding; I hoped to efface myself in these poor people's merry-making.

The banquet and the ball were given on a first floor above a wineshop in the Rue de Charenton. It was a large room, lighted by oil lamps with tin reflectors. A row of wooden benches ran round the walls, which were black with grime to the height of the tables. Here some eighty persons, all in their Sunday best, tricked out with ribbons and bunches of flowers, all of them on pleasure bent, were dancing away with heated visages as if the world were about to come to an end. Bride and bridegroom exchanged salutes to the general satisfaction, amid a chorus of facetious 'Oh, ohs!' and Ah, ahs!' less really indecent than the furtive glances of young girls that have been well brought up. There was something indescribably infectious about the rough, homely enjoyment in all countenances.

But neither the faces, nor the wedding, nor the wedding-guests have anything to do with my story. Simply bear them in mind as the odd setting to it. Try to realize the scene, the shabby red-painted wineshop, the smell of wine, the yells of merriment; try to feel that you are really in the faubourg, among old people, working men and poor women giving themselves up to a night's enjoyment.

The band consisted of a fiddle, a clarionet, and a flageolet from the Blind Asylum. The three were paid seven francs in a lump sum for the night. For the money, they gave us, not Beethoven certainly, nor yet Rossini; they played as they had the will and the skill; and every one in the room (with charming delicacy of feeling) refrained from finding fault. The music made such a brutal assault on the drum of my ear, that after a first glance round the room my eyes fell at once upon the blind trio, and the sight of their uniform inclined me from the first to indulgence. As the artists stood in a window recess, it was difficult to distinguish their faces except at close quarters, and I kept away at first; but when I came nearer (I hardly know why) I thought of nothing else; the wedding party and the music ceased to exist, my curiosity was roused to the highest pitch, for my soul passed into the body of the clarionet player.

The fiddle and the flageolet were neither of them interesting; their faces were of the ordinary type among the blind—earnest, attentive, and grave. Not so the clarionet player; any artist or philosopher must have come to a stop at the sight of him.

Picture to yourself a plaster mask of Dante in the red lamp-light, with a forest of silver-white hair above the brows. Blindness intensified the expression of bitterness and sorrow in that grand face of his; the dead eyes were lighted up, as it were, by a thought within that broke forth like a burning flame, lit by one sole insatiable desire, written large in vigorous characters upon an arching brow scored across with as many lines as an old stone wall.

The old man was playing at random, without the slightest regard for time or tune. His fingers travelled mechanically over the worn keys of his instrument; he did not trouble himself over a false note now and again (a *canard*, in the language of the orchestra), neither did the dancers, nor, for that matter, did my old Italian's acolytes; for I had made up my mind that he must be an Italian, and an Italian he was. There was something great, something too of the despot about this old Homer bearing within him an *Odyssey* doomed to oblivion. The greatness was so real that it triumphed over his abject position; the despotism so much a part of him, that it rose above his poverty.

There are violent passions which drive a man to good or evil, making of him a hero or a convict; of these there was not one that had failed to leave its traces on the grandly-hewn, lividly Italian face. You trembled lest a flash of thought should suddenly light up the deep sightless hollows under the grizzled brows, as you might fear to see brigands with torches and poniards in the mouth of a cavern. You felt that there was a lion in that cage of flesh, a lion spent with useless raging against iron bars. The fires of despair had burned themselves out into ashes, the lava had cooled; but the tracks of the flames, the wreckage, and a little smoke remained to bear witness to the violence of the eruption, the ravages of the fire. These images crowded up at the sight of the clarionet player, till the thoughts now grown cold in his face burned hot within my soul.

The fiddle and the flageolet took a deep interest in bottles and glasses; at the end of a country-dance, they hung their instruments from a button on their reddish-coloured coats, and stretched out their hands to a little table set in the window recess to hold their liquor supply. Each time they did so they held out a full glass to the Italian, who could not reach it for himself because he sat in front of the table, and each time the Italian thanked them with a friendly nod. All their movements were made with the precision which always amazes you so much at the Blind Asylum. You could almost think that they can see. I came nearer to listen; but when I stood beside them, they evidently guessed I was not a working man, and kept themselves to themselves.

'What part of the world do you come from, you that are playing the clarionet?'

'From Venice,' he said, with a trace of Italian accent.

'Have you always been blind, or did it come on afterwards——?'

'Afterwards,' he answered quickly. 'A cursed gutta serena.'

'Venice is a fine city; I have always had a fancy to go there.'

The old man's face lighted up, the wrinkles began to work, he was violently excited.

'If I went with you, you would not lose your time,' he said.

'Don't talk about Venice to our Doge,' put in the fiddle, 'or you will start him off, and he has stowed away a couple of bottles as it is—has the prince!'

'Come, strike up, Daddy Canard!' added the flageolet, and the three began to play. But while they executed the four figures of a square dance, the Venetian was scenting my thoughts; he guessed the great interest I felt in him. The dreary, dispirited look died out of his face, some mysterious hope brightened his features and slid like a blue flame over his wrinkles. He smiled and wiped his brow, that fearless, terrible brow of his, and at length grew gay like a man mounted on his hobby.

'How old are you?' I asked.

'Eighty-two.'

'How long have you been blind?'

'For nearly fifty years,' he said, and there was that in his tone which told me that his regret was for something more than his lost sight, for great power of which he had been robbed.

'Then why do they call you "the Doge"?' I asked.

'Oh, it is a joke. I am a Venetian noble, and I might have been a doge like any one else.'

'What is your name?'

'Here, in Paris, I am Père Canet,' he said. 'It was the only way of spelling my name on the register. But in Italy I am Marco Facino Cane, Prince of Varese.'

'What, are you descended from the great *condottiere* Facino Cane, whose lands won by the sword were taken by the Dukes of Milan?'

'*È vero,*' returned he. 'His son's life was not safe under the Visconti; he fled to Venice, and his name was inscribed on the Golden Book. And now neither Cane nor Golden Book are in existence.' His gesture startled me; it told of patriotism extinguished and weariness of life.

'But if you were once a Venetian senator, you must have been a wealthy man. How did you lose your fortune?'

'In evil days.'

He waved away the glass of wine handed to him by the flageolet, and bowed his head. He had no heart to drink. These details were not calculated to extinguish my curiosity. As the three ground out the music of the square dance, I gazed at the old Venetian noble, thinking thoughts that set a young man's mind afire at the age of twenty. I saw Venice and the Adriatic; I saw her ruin in the ruin of the face before me. I walked to and fro in that city, so beloved of her citizens; I went from the Rialto, along the Grand Canal, and from the Riva degli Schiavoni to the Lido, returning to St. Mark's, that cathedral so unlike all others in its sublimity. I looked up at the windows of the Casa Doro, each with its different sculptured ornaments; I saw old palaces rich in marbles, saw all the wonders which a student beholds with the more sympathetic eyes because visible things take their colour of his fancy, and the sight of realities cannot rob him of the glory of his dreams. Then I traced back a course of life for this latest scion of a race of condottieri, tracking down his misfortunes, looking for the reasons of the deep moral and physical degradation out of which the lately revived sparks of greatness and nobility shone so much the more brightly. My ideas, no doubt, were passing through his mind, for all processes of thought-communications are far more swift, I think, in blind people, because their blindness compels them to concentrate their attention. I had not long to wait for proof that we were in sympathy in this way. Facino Cane left off playing, and came up to me. 'Let us go out!' he said; his tones thrilled through me like an electric shock. I gave him my arm, and we went.

Outside in the street he said, 'Will you take me back to Venice? will you be my guide? Will you put faith in me? You shall be richer than ten of the richest houses in Amsterdam or London, richer than Rothschild; in short, you shall have the fabulous wealth of the *Arabian Nights*.'

The man was mad, I thought; but in his voice there was a potent something which I obeyed. I allowed him to lead, and he went in the direction of the Fossés de la Bastille, as if he could see; walking till he reached a lonely spot down by the river, just where the bridge has since been built at the junction of the Canal Saint-Martin and the Seine. Here he sat down on a stone, and I, sitting opposite to him, saw the old man's hair gleaming like threads of silver in the moonlight. The stillness was scarcely troubled by the sound of the far-off thunder of traffic along the boulevards; the clear night air and everything about us combined to make a strangely unreal scene.

'You talk of millions to a young man,' I began, 'and do you think that he will shrink from enduring any number of hardships to gain them? Are you not laughing at me?'

'May I die unshriven,' he cried vehemently, 'if all that I am about to tell you is not true. I was one-and-twenty years old, like you are at this moment. I was rich, I was handsome, and a noble by birth. I began with the first madness of all—with Love. I loved as no one can love nowadays. I have hidden myself in a chest, at the risk of a dagger thrust, for nothing more than the promise of a kiss. To die for Her—it seemed to me to be a whole life in itself. In 1760 I fell in love with a lady of the Vendramin family; she was eighteen years old, and married to a Sagredo, one of the richest senators, a man of thirty, madly in love with his wife. My mistress and I were guiltless as cherubs when the *sposo* caught us together talking of love. He was armed, I was not, but he missed me; I sprang upon him and killed him with my two hands, wringing his neck as if he had been a chicken. I wanted Bianca to fly with me; but she would not. That is the way with women! So I went alone. I was condemned to death, and my property was confiscated and made over to my next-of-kin; but I had carried off my diamonds, five of Titian's pictures taken down from their frames and rolled up, and all my gold.

'I went to Milan, no one molested me, my affair in no wise interested the State.—One small observation before I go further,' he continued, after a pause; 'whether it is true or no that the mother's fancies at the time of conception or in the months before birth can influence her child, this much is certain, my mother during her pregnancy had a passion for gold, and I am the victim of a monomania, of a craving for gold which must be gratified. Gold is so much a necessity of life for me, that I have never been without it; I must have gold to toy with and finger. As a young man I always wore jewellery, and carried two or three hundred ducats about with me wherever I went.'

He drew a couple of gold coins from his pocket and showed them to me as he spoke.

'I can tell by instinct when gold is near. Blind as I am, I stop before the jewellers' shop windows. That passion was the ruin of me; I took to gambling to play with gold. I was not a cheat, I was cheated, I ruined myself. I lost all my fortune. Then the longing to see Bianca once more possessed me like a frenzy. I stole back to Venice and found her again. For six months I was happy; she hid me in her house and fed me. I thought thus deliciously to finish my days. But the Provveditore courted her, and guessed that he had a rival; we in Italy can feel that. He played the spy upon us, and surprised us together in bed, base wretch! You may judge what a fight for life it was; I did not kill him outright, but I wounded him dangerously.

'That adventure broke my luck. I have never found another Bianca; I have known great pleasures; but among the most celebrated women of the court of Louis XV I never found my beloved Venetian's charm, her love, her great qualities.

'The Provveditore called his servants, the palace was surrounded and entered; I fought for my life that I might die beneath Bianca's eyes; Bianca helped me to kill the Provveditore. Once before she had refused flight with me; but after six months of happiness she wished only to die with me, and received several thrusts. I was entangled in a great cloak that they flung over me, carried down to a gondola, and hurried to the Pozzi dungeons. I was twenty-two years old; I gripped the hilt of my broken sword so hard, that they could only have taken it from me by cutting off my hand at the wrist. A curious chance, or rather the instinct of self-preservation, led me to hide the fragment of the blade in a corner of my cell, as if it might still be of use. They tended me; none of my wounds were serious. At two-and-twenty one can recover from anything. I was to lose my head on the scaffold. I shammed illness to gain time. It seemed to me that the canal lay just outside my cell. I thought to make my escape by boring a hole through the wall and swimming for my life. I based my hopes on the following reasons.

'Every time that the gaoler came with my food, there was light enough to read directions written on the walls—"Side of the Palace", Side of the Canal", "Side of the Vaults". At last I saw a design in this, but I did not trouble myself much about the meaning of it; the actual incomplete condition of the Ducal Palace accounted for it. The longing to regain my freedom gave me something like genius. Groping about with my fingers, I spelt out an Arabic inscription on the wall. The author of the work informed those to come after him that he had loosened two stones in the lowest course of masonry and hollowed out eleven feet beyond underground. As he went on with his excavations, it became necessary to spread the fragments of stone and mortar over the floor of his cell. But even if gaolers and inquisitors had not felt sure that the structure of the buildings was such that no watch was needed below, the level of the Pozzi dungeons being several steps below the threshold, it was possible gradually to raise the earthen floor without exciting the warder's suspicions.

'The tremendous labour had profited nothing—nothing at least to him that began it. The very fact that it was left unfinished told of the unknown worker's death. Unless his devoted toil was to be wasted for ever, his successor must have some knowledge of Arabic, but I had studied Oriental languages at the Armenian Convent. A few words written on the back of the stone recorded the unhappy man's fate; he had fallen a victim to his great possessions; Venice had coveted his wealth and seized upon it. A whole month went by before I obtained any result; but whenever I felt my strength failing as I worked, I heard the chink of gold, I saw gold spread before me, I was dazzled by diamonds. Ah! wait.

'One night my blunted steel struck on wood. I whetted the fragment of my blade and cut a hole; I crept on my belly like a serpent; I worked naked and mole-fashion, my hands in front of me, using the stone itself to gain a purchase. I was to appear before my judges in two days' time. I made a final effort, and that night I bored through the wood and felt that there was space beyond.

'Judge of my surprise when I applied my eye to the hole. I was in the ceiling of a vault, heaps of gold were dimly visible in the faint light. The Doge himself and one of the Ten stood below; I could hear their voices and sufficient of their talk to know that this was the Secret Treasury of the Republic, full of the gifts of Doges and reserves of booty called the Tithe of Venice from the spoils of military expeditions. I was saved!

'When the gaoler came I proposed that he should help me to escape and fly with me, and that we should take with us as much as we could carry. There was no reason for hesitation; he agreed. Vessels were about to sail for the Levant. All possible precautions were taken. Bianca furthered the schemes which I suggested to my accomplice. It was arranged that Bianca should only rejoin us in Smyrna for fear of exciting suspicion. In a single night the hole was enlarged, and we dropped down into the Secret Treasury of Venice.

'What a night that was! Four great casks full of gold stood there. In the outer room silver pieces were piled in heaps, leaving a gangway between by which to cross the chamber. Banks of silver coins surrounded the walls to the height of five feet.

'I thought the gaoler would go mad. He sang and laughed

and danced and capered among the gold, till I threatened to strangle him if he made a sound or wasted time. In his joy he did not notice at first the table where the diamonds lay. I flung myself upon these, and deftly filled the pockets of my sailor's jacket and trousers with the stones. Ah, Heaven! I did not take the third of them. Gold ingots lay underneath the table. I persuaded my companion to fill as many bags as we could carry with the gold, and made him understand that this was our only chance of escaping detection abroad.

'"Pearls, rubies, and diamonds might be recognized," I told him.

'Covetous though we were, we could not possibly take more than two thousand livres weight of gold, which meant six journeys across the prison to the gondola. The sentinel at the water-gate was bribed with a bag containing ten livres weight of gold; and as for the two gondoliers, they believed they were serving the Republic. At daybreak we set out.

'Once upon the open sea, when I thought of that night, when I recollected all that I had felt, when the vision of that great hoard arose before my eyes, and I computed that I had left behind thirty millions in silver, twenty in gold, and many more in diamonds, pearls, and rubies—then a sort of madness began to work in me. I had the gold fever.

'We landed at Smyrna and took ship at once for France. As we went on board the French vessel, Heaven favoured me by ridding me of my accomplice. I did not think at the time of all the possible consequences of this mishap, and rejoiced not a little. We were so completely unnerved by all that had happened, that we were stupid, we said not a word to each other, we waited till it should be safe to enjoy ourselves at our ease. It was not wonderful that the rogue's head was dizzy. You shall see how heavily God has punished me.

'I never knew a quiet moment until I had sold two-thirds of my diamonds in London or Amsterdam, and held the value of my gold dust in a negotiable shape. For five years I hid myself in Madrid, then in 1770 I came to Paris with a Spanish name, and led as brilliant a life as may be. Then in the midst of my pleasures, as I enjoyed a fortune of six millions, I was smitten with blindness. I do not doubt but that my infirmity was brought on by my sojourn in the cell and my work in the stone, if, indeed, my peculiar faculty for "seeing" gold was not an abuse of the power of sight which predestined me to lose it. Bianca was dead.

'At this time I had fallen in love with a woman to whom I thought to link my fate. I had told her the secret of my name; she belonged to a powerful family; she was a friend of Mme. du Barry; I hoped everything from the favour shown me by Louis XV; I trusted in her. Acting on her advice, I went to England to consult a famous oculist, and after a stay of several months in London she deserted me in Hyde Park. She had stripped me of all that I had, and left me without resource. Nor could I make complaint, for to disclose my name was to lay myself open to the vengeance of my native city; I could appeal to no one for aid, I feared Venice. The woman put spies about me to exploit my infirmity. I spare you a tale of adventures worthy of Gil Blas. Your Revolution followed. For two whole years that creature kept me at the Bicêtre as a lunatic, then she gained admittance for me at the Blind Asylum; there was no help for it, I went. I could not kill her; I could not see; and I was so poor that I could not pay another arm.

'If only I had taken counsel with my gaoler, Benedetto Carpi, before I lost him, I might have known the exact position of my cell, I might have found my way back to the Treasury and returned to Venice when Napoleon crushed the Republic——

'Still, blind as I am, let us go back to Venice! I shall find the door of my prison, I shall see the gold through the prison walls, I shall hear it where it lies under the water; for the events which brought about the fall of Venice befell in such a way that the secret of the hoard must have perished with Bianca's brother, Vendramin, a doge to whom I looked to make my peace with the Ten. I sent memorials to the First Consul; I proposed an agreement with the Emperor of Austria; every one sent me about my business for a lunatic. Come! we will go to Venice; let us set out as beggars, we shall come back millionaires. We will buy back my estates, and you shall be my heir! You shall be Prince of Varese!'

My head was swimming. For me his confidences reached the proportions of tragedy; at the sight of that white head of his and beyond it the black water in the trenches of the Bastille lying still as a canal in Venice, I had no words to answer him. Facino Cane thought, no doubt, that I judged him, as the rest had done, with a disdainful pity; his gesture expressed the whole philosophy of despair.

Perhaps his story had taken him back to happy days and to Venice. He caught up his clarionet and made plaintive music, playing a Venetian boat-song with something of his lost skill, the skill of the young patrician lover. It was a sort of *Super flumina Babylonis*. Tears filled my eyes. Any belated persons walking along the Boulevard Bourdon must have stood still to listen to an exile's last prayer, a last cry of regret for a lost name, mingled with memories of Bianca. But gold soon gained the upper hand, the fatal passion quenched the light of youth.

'I see it always,' he said; 'dreaming or waking, I see it; and as I pace to and fro, I pace in the Treasury, and the diamonds sparkle. I am not as blind as you think; gold and diamonds light up my night, the night of the last Facino Cane, for my title passes to the Memmi. My God! the murderer's punishment was not long delayed! *Ave Maria*,' and he repeated several prayers that I did not heed.

'We will go to Venice!' I said, when he rose.

'Then I have found a man!' he cried, with his face on fire.

I gave him my arm and went home with him. We reached the gates of the Blind Asylum just as some of the wedding guests were returning along the street, shouting at the tops of their voices. He squeezed my hand.

'Shall we start to-morrow?' he asked.

'As soon as we can get some money.'

'But we can go on foot. I will beg. I am strong, and you feel young when you see gold before you.'

Facino Cane died before the winter was out after a two months' illness. The poor man had taken a chill.

Translated by Ellen Marriage

A CONSULTATION

Charles de Bernard

In the beginning of last autumn, among the people assembled in Doctor Magnan's waiting room there was a man of about forty, fair-haired, lank, livid, a little bent, in a word with so sickly an aspect that it would have been enough to look at him, to guess that this was a doctor's office. When he came in, this puny individual sat himself down with a careworn expression in a corner: he stayed there patiently until all the other patients had been interviewed by the doctor, who, after giving his last consultation, came towards him with a cordial smile.

'Good-day, Bouchereau,' said the doctor, 'a thousand apologies for having kept you waiting so long: you know that my time belongs in the first place to my patients, and I hope you haven't any claim to that title?'

'The soul's sufferings are worse than the body's,' the man answered stifling a sigh.

'What 's the matter?' inquired the doctor. 'You are all upset! Can it be Madame Bouchereau who is ill?'

'My wife has a cast-iron constitution,' replied Bouchereau, and he accompanied those words with a smile full of bitterness.

'Then tell me the cause of the agitation I see you in. It 's an affair of the soul, did you say? If you don't speak, how do you think I can guess what passes in your soul? Let 's see: what use can I be?'

'My dear doctor,' answered the other, sitting down with an air of dejection, 'we have known each other for more than twenty years. I look on you as one of my best friends, and I have a boundless confidence in you.'

'Let 's leave out the compliments.'

'They are not compliments: I am speaking my inmost thoughts. Besides, the strange confession that I have resolved to make to you will bear witness of the esteem I have for your character.'

'Let 's get on to the facts,' said the doctor, with a little impatience.

'The fact is a sad one for me, and it may even appear ridiculous: that 's why I am hesitating to broach it; but, first promise me to reveal to nobody in the world what I am going to tell you.'

'The secret of the confessional is as sacred for a doctor as for a priest,' said Dr. Magnan in a serious voice.

Bouchereau sighed again, then bit his lips and raised his eyes to the ceiling.

'You know Pelletier?' he said at last, watching the man he was speaking to mournfully.

'The captain of the general staff? That 's all I know. A sanguine temperament, a short neck, more shoulders than brains, the organization of an ox! I predicted long ago that he 'd die of apoplexy.'

'God grant it!'

'You astound me: I thought you were friends.'

'Friends!' repeated Bouchereau, and indignation was mixed with irony in his voice.

'What the blazes! Speak clearly or not at all. I am not an Oedipus to guess your riddles.'

The impatience that gleamed in the doctor's black eyes prevented his suffering friend from avoiding the main point of the confession any longer.

'Well, my dear Magnan, here 's the fact in two words,' he said in a moved voice, 'Pelletier is making advances to my wife.'

The doctor pushed out his lower lip to hide a smile, and nodded his head several times with affected seriousness.

'Think of that!' he said then, 'I wouldn't have believed that that lump of a Pelletier would have had such good taste. But are you quite sure of what you are saying? Usually husbands are the last to know about matters like that.'

'I am only too sure: you 'll see how. My wife went to spend some days at her mother's at Fontainebleau. The day before yesterday, poking about by chance in my bedroom, I noticed that the key of my desk fitted her wardrobe as well. Mechanically I opened that bit of furniture, and in a rather mysterious back drawer, I found several letters from Pelletier.'

'By Jove! But all the same, why open a bit of furniture belonging to your wife?'

'I was within my rights: besides, suspend your judgment. Because of the very tenor of those letters, I got proof of Virginia's complete innocence; she had nothing more to reproach herself with than having kept this correspondence a mystery from me. She had never encouraged him, I am practically sure of it. So I am much less annoyed with her than with Pelletier: but as to him, I feel that I will never pardon him. A man I opened my house to! an old comrade of Sainte-Barbe! a friend, in fact; at least I thought him one!'

'Are you forgetting that a man is betrayed only by his friends?'

'Yesterday I went to see him.'

'Ah!'

'I reproached him with his unworthy conduct; do you know what he answered?'

'He denied it.'

'At first. But at the sight of his letters, he realized that all denials would be useless. "My dear Bouchereau," he said to me then, with that impertinent air of his which you know, "since you are so well informed, I won't take the trouble to tell lies about it. It is quite true that I am in love with your wife; I have already told her so, and I do not promise not to say it to her again, because, in all probability, I would not keep my oath. I understand perfectly that this proceeding displeases you and hurts you; but you are not ignorant that I am a man of honour, and that I am in the habit of taking the responsibility for my acts and deeds. If, then, you are insulted, I am at your service, ready to give you satisfaction, where, when, and as you please."'

'That 's cheek for you!' said the doctor, forcing himself to keep serious. 'What! he dared to say that to you?'

'In so many words.'

'And what did you answer?'

'That he 'd hear from me soon. And then I came away, for it was beneath my dignity to go on any further with a conversation like that. That 's how things stand.'

The doctor's face took on a grave expression. He took a turn up the room, his head down and his hands behind his back; then, approaching his visitor again:

'Now, what do you think of doing?' he said to him, looking at him intently.

'What do you advise?'

'I acknowledge that such a proceeding seems hard for you to endure. On the other hand I would be vexed to see you engaged in a duel with this swashbuckler Pelletier.'

'A swashbuckler!' cried Bouchereau, whose eyes seemed to grow bigger. 'It 's a professional duellist, it 's an assassin you ought to say, a man who spends all his mornings at Lepage's shooting gallery, or in the fencing school, and who has a fight on hand regularly every three months!'

'And you yourself,' said the doctor with a piercing look, 'you have had an affair sometimes?'

'Never,' answered the married man, more livid than ever in that moment, 'not that I haven't had an opportunity several times, but a duel is against my principles. The idea of shedding blood revolts me; it is a barbarous custom, which has always appeared to me to constitute a monstrous anomaly amidst our police-guarded habits.'

'In short, you have no ardent desire to meet him on the field?'

'If I were positively insulted, if I had to avenge a mortal injury, perhaps the voice of passion would speak to me more loudly than that of humanity; for, in certain conjunctures, the wisest man cannot answer for himself. But here, since things have not been pushed to the extreme, if Pelletier, instead of adopting an arrogant tone, had offered me some kind of apology or other, to which I believe myself entitled, and if he had bound himself to behave better in future, it seems to me that then—in everybody's interest—to avoid a scandal—don't you think like me, that it would have been possible and honourable——'

'Not to fight? Certainly,' interrupted Magnan. 'If you meet him on the field, it 's ten to one that Pelletier will bleed you like a chicken, and that 'll be nasty for you.'

'Doctor, you don't understand me properly.'

'Absolutely, on the contrary. And the proof is, that you will not fight, and that the captain will make a satisfactory apology to you. Isn't that what you want?'

The doctor's perspicacity caused a feeble blush to dawn on the cheeks of the peace-lover.

'Pelletier is a bear,' went on the doctor, as if speaking to himself. 'Usually staff officers have more *savoir vivre* than that. To want to please the women, that 's all right; but to challenge the husbands, that 's a total disregard of all the rules of good breeding.'

'You advise me, then, to let some settlement be made?' asked Bouchereau in an insinuating voice.

'Yes, certainly,' answered the doctor laughing, 'and, more than that, I 'll undertake the negotiations. I tell you once again! to-morrow Pelletier will withdraw his provocation; he will make you a formal apology, and will swear to seek no more to trouble your conjugal repose. That is my business; the rest is your affair.'

'The rest?'

'To promise and to keep one's word aren't the same thing, you know that; it will be, I think, on your part, highly prudent to make it easy for the captain to keep his oath, by means of a little voyage which will separate him from Madame Bouchereau for some months. His position keeps him in Paris; you are free. What hinders you from going to spend the winter in the south: at Nice, for instance?'

'I had already considered the expediency of a trip, and I am pleased to find you of the same mind in this matter. But why Nice rather than any other town?'

'I mean that the climate is very healthy, especially for people who have rather delicate chests.'

'But I have an excellent chest—at least I suppose so,' interrupted Bouchereau, and he questioned the doctor's eye with a sort of uneasiness.

'Doubtless; I am not saying the contrary,' the doctor went on in a serious tone, 'on that side I have no positive motive for the advice I am giving you. But precautions never do any harm, and it 's better to prevent the evil than to wait for it.'

'You believe me, then, threatened with a chest complaint?' said the worried man, turning pale. As could be seen, he professed the utmost attachment to his own person.

'I have not said a word of that,' answered Dr. Magnan, who had the air of reproaching himself internally for having said too much, 'do you want to know why I pronounced the name of Nice? It is through egotism. It is possible that I am going there myself to spend a part of the winter; and if you were there, and your wife as well, my stay would certainly seem much more agreeable.'

'Well we 'll see about that; the matter could be arranged,'

answered Bouchereau, and he left the doctor's house even more anxious than he had entered it, for to the uneasiness which the prospect of a duel caused him, had just been added the no less lively fear of an often fatal illness, which he had not dreamt of until then.

At six o'clock in the evening, Dr. Magnan entered the Café Anglais where he was almost sure of meeting Pelletier. The captain of the general staff was already there in fact, seated all alone at a little table, and dining with a very good appetite, without watering his wine. He was a big, stout, vigorous fellow, square in the shoulders, slim in the haunches, with a firm eye, a shining moustache, a warmly coloured complexion, a muscular wrist: one of those men of martial bearing, who, if they are not soldiers, seem to have missed their vocation, and whose look alone imposes on the most forward of men some kind of restraint and modesty.

Other men than the livid Bouchereau would have regarded the fact of having a bone to pick with a lion like that as a veritable catastrophe.

The doctor and the officer greeted each other cordially, and, after having exchanged a few complimentary phrases, they dined, each at his own side. They left the table at the same time, met at the door, and, simultaneously offering each other an arm, they walked down the Boulevard on the side of the Madeleine.

'Well, doctor,' said Pelletier playfully, 'have you found me what I 've asked you for at least ten times; an amiable lady (maid or widow, dark or fair, little or big, it 's all the same to me), who would consent to make my happiness in joining her lot to mine. I only ask a hundred thousand crowns of dowry: deuce take me, I think I 'm modest.'

'Too modest! You are worth more than that.'

'You 're laughing at me.'

'Not at all: besides, the time would be ill-suited for joking, for I must consult with you about a serious matter, while we 're waiting for the fiancée with a hundred thousand crowns. Bouchereau has charged me to speak to you.'

'And you call that a serious matter?' said the captain laughing disdainfully.

'Every matter seems so to me when it can end in blood,' said the doctor with an affected gravity.

'Ah! M. Bouchereau is thirsting for my blood?' Pelletier went on with a louder laugh; 'up to now, I 'd believed him herbivorous, rather than carnivorous. And with what sauce does he propose to eat me? with the sword or the pistol?'

'He leaves you the choice of arms,' said Dr Magnan, with an imperturbable seriousness.

'It 's all the same to me, I 've told him so already. Let 's see: to-morrow I 'm lunching with some of my comrades; it 's a sort of corps dinner, and I 'd be sorry to miss it; but I 'm your man for the morning of the day after. Does that suit you?'

'Perfectly. The day after to-morrow at seven o'clock in the morning at the entrance of the Vincennes wood.'

'Agreed,' said the captain, as he clapped his large hand familiarly on his companion's arm. 'Oho, doctor, you 're taking a hand in a duel, then? All the same, that 's a rival that ought to inspire you with antipathy!'

The doctor replied to this superannuated joke by a malicious smile which he repressed at once.

'You have just put your finger on one of my sore points in jest,' he said after a moment's silence. 'Shall I confess to you an odd thought, I might say a monstrous thought, which strikes me at the moment?'

'Tell me! I 'm quite fond of monstrous thoughts!'

'I was saying to myself that, in the interests of my reputation, I would have cause for hoping that the meeting the day after to-morrow would have a fatal result for Bouchereau.'

'Why that?' demanded the officer in surprise.

'I mean, that, if you do not kill him, before a year 's over, it is I who will pass for having killed him.'

'I don't understand. Do you want to fight with him as well?'

'Not at all; but I am his doctor, and, as such, responsible for his existence in the eyes of many people, who require of the medical art that it preserve for its patients the health that nature has refused them. Now, as Bouchereau, according to all appearances, has only a year to live——'

'What disease has he got, then?' cried Pelletier, opening his big eyes.

'Chest trouble!' answered the doctor with a compassionate accent, 'a chronic disease, without cure! I was going to send him to Nice. You know, we doctors, when we don't know what else to prescribe our patients, send them to drink the waters, or to the south. If nothing happens to him the day after to-morrow, he 'll go. Will he return? God knows!'

'Chest trouble! a man who is always livid like Bouchereau!'

'The colour has nothing to do with it.'

'And you think him in danger?'

'I do not give him a year to live, not six months, maybe.'

The two speakers walked on some time in silence, gravely.

'Yes, captain,' said the doctor, 'you can look on poor Bouchereau as a lost man, even putting aside the danger that your sword is going to make him run. Quite certainly, before a year, his wife will be able to think of remarrying. That 'll be a very seductive little widow, by Jove, and she won't wait for adorers.'

Pelletier threw a sidelong glance at his companion. The doctor's air of good-fellowship destroyed the sort of mistrust which his words had excited.

'If Bouchereau died, his wife would be rich?' said the captain, half under his breath, but with an interrogative accent.

'Gracious!' answered the doctor, 'this time it wouldn't be by one hundred thousand, but by two hundred thousand that you would have to count the crowns of the dowry.'

'You are exaggerating,' cried the captain whose eyes shone with a sudden brilliance.

'The calculation is an easy one to do,' responded Dr. Magnan with an assured air. 'Madame Bouchereau has inherited from her father one hundred thousand francs; she is expecting one hundred and fifty thousand from her mother: and her husband will leave her at least three hundred and fifty thousand: add them up.'

'Then he has left her everything by his marriage settlement?' asked Pelletier, whose emotion had grown at each figure articulated by his companion.

'Everything,' answered the doctor in a solemn voice.

This powerful monosyllable was as good as a long discourse. With a companion whose intelligence he could have esteemed, Dr. Magnan would not have added a single word. But finding the captain richer in shoulders than brain, as he had said of him some hours before, he was not afraid to insist a little heavily on an idea from which he expected a magic result.

'You who have the matrimonial bump well developed,' he went on with an air of pleasantry, 'there 's a match that would suit you; a young woman, pretty, amiable, and a fortune of six hundred thousand francs. It is true that to bring an affair like this safely to harbour, one wouldn't need to begin by killing the husband.'

Pelletier affected to laugh, though his face had taken an instant ago a dreamy expression. Certain of having attained his end, the doctor alleged a visit, and quitted his companion, whom he left at the Boulevard, smitten to the heart by the six hundred thousand francs of the presumptive widow.

All at once, and with the furious rapidity of a wounded boar, the captain went from the Madeleine to the Bastille without a bus: at the Porte Saint Martin, his decision was made.

'Without being aware of it,' he thought, 'the doctor has given me excellent advice: fight with Bouchereau! I 'm not such a fool; I would kill him; my hand is so unlucky! Then how would I dare to appear before Virginia? The little lady doesn't look on me with an indifferent eye; by good luck, in courting her these three months, I 've taken the initiative, so that, when the great day does arrive, she 'll not be able to suppose that I love her for her fortune. Kill Bouchereau? That would be stupid. Let him die his own fine death, the dear man, I 'll make no objections. According to all appearances I shall have enough opportunity to fight with my rivals when his wife 's a widow. Six hundred thousand francs! There 'll be a crowd of them: but let the others look out for themselves. I 've got my name down first, and I 'm not the man to let anybody walk over my body.'

Next morning, the captain entered Dr. Magnan's house well before the hour reserved for consultations.

'Doctor,' he said to him with an air of military frankness, 'what you said to me yesterday about Bouchereau's illness, has made me reflect seriously. It seems to me that, in all good faith, I can hardly fight with a man who has no more than six months to live. Suppose that I wound him. A sword cut, of which another man would get better, would perhaps be fatal to him, considering his condition; and then I would reproach myself all my life for having killed an old friend for a stupid trifle. Did he tell you the cause of our quarrel?'

'No,' said the doctor, who, in his quality of negotiator, thought he had the right to tell lies.

'Some rather high words exchanged on either side,' went on

the officer, deceived by the doctor's candid air, 'to tell the truth I quite believe it was I who was in the wrong. You know I am hot-headed: apropos of some trifle or other I bullied poor Bouchereau, and I 'm sorry for it now. In short, I have fought enough duels to be able to arrange one now pacifically without any one thinking that I 've got cold feet. So then, if you 'd like to advise Bouchereau to let matters drop, I give you a free hand. Between ourselves, I think that the proposition won't displease him.'

'You might be mistaken, captain,' answered the doctor, who kept his gravity admirably; 'yesterday Bouchereau appeared to be exasperated. Although he is of a peaceful disposition, he becomes a tiger when his blood boils. It appears that in your altercation you hurt him seriously, and unless you offer him a formal apology——'

'Don't let that be a stumbling-block,' interrupted Pelletier; 'apologies are scarcely in my line; this will be the first time that such a thing has happened to me; but, with an old friend, one doesn't look at things so closely. Besides, I 'd rather make concessions than have, in the end, to reproach myself. What about us going together to see Bouchereau?'

'Let us go,' said the doctor who could scarcely refrain from smiling at seeing to what extent his own interests were making this duellist by profession humane, sensitive, and considerate.

When he saw the doctor, followed by the general staff officer, entering his room, Bouchereau, who had not been able to close an eye all night, experienced an emotion comparable to that of a condemned man to whom the gaoler reads out the sentence containing the death penalty.

The first words of the interview restored fluidity to the blood which was ready to congeal in his veins. The captain formulated the most explicit and formal apologies, and retired immediately after exchanging a handshake with his old friend, who in his joy at being quit of his terrors, didn't dream of showing himself unreasonable.

'Doctor, you are a sorcerer!' cried Bouchereau, when he was alone with the doctor.

'That 's a bit in my way of business,' the latter said laughing, 'so here 's this terrible affair almost arranged: my share is done, will you do yours? When do you set out for the south?'

The satisfaction imprinted on Bouchereau's features disappeared in a moment, and gave place to an anxious and sombre expression.

'Doctor,' he said in an altered voice, 'you must tell me the truth. I have some strength of mind; I will know how to listen to my sentence: my chest is affected, isn't it?'

'You mean your brain.'

'My brain too!' cried Bouchereau, and he got paler.

'You are mad,' went on the doctor, shrugging his shoulders, 'I would be very glad to change my chest for yours.'

'You are deceiving me; I can't get your words yesterday out of my head. I 've coughed all night, and between my shoulders I feel a pain that I 've never noticed up till now.'

'Imagination.'

'I feel what I feel,' continued Bouchereau in a lugubrious voice, 'I do not fear death; but, I admit, it is not without regret that, in the flower of my manhood, I shall see myself forced to say an eternal farewell to my wife and my family. It is my duty to look after myself for their sakes, if I do not do it for my own. Instead of writing to Virginia to return here, I shall pick her up in passing at Fontainebleau and we will start at once for Nice.'

'Go,' said the doctor, 'this voyage cannot do you any harm.'

'But do you think that it will do me good?'

'Doubtless.'

'And that there is still time to fight this fearful disease?'

'Yes, we shall pull you through that,' said Magnan with a mocking gravity. 'Before six months are gone, I shall be myself in Nice; so you are sure of being looked after by a doctor in whom you have confidence, if, contrary to all appearances, your condition gets worse.'

The two separated, the doctor laughing at the fears of his client, while the latter believed he felt death in his breast, and asked himself if, peril for peril, it might not have been better to face Captain Pelletier's terrible sword, than to go maybe to die, in the prime of life, on a foreign soil. In two days Bouchereau, pursued by this funereal vision, had taken out his passport, set all his affairs in order, and finished his preparations for departure. He got immediately into a post chaise, and fell like a bomb on Fontainebleau, where he was not expected. Using his marital authority more than he had ever dared to do until that day, he carried off his wife, stupefied by so novel a proceeding, and very annoyed at having to leave Paris, for the languorous epistles of the captain of the general staff had for some time past rendered her residence in that town more pleasant than usual. At the end of the week, the husband and wife, the one trembling for his life, the other regretting her love affairs, arrived at Nice, where, towards the end of autumn, they were joined by Dr. Magnan who showed a scrupulous exactitude in fulfilling his promise.

In the following April, *Horace* was being played at the Théâtre Français. Thanks to the youthful talent of Mademoiselle Rachel even more than to the old genius of Corneille, the theatre was full. In the centre of the right-hand balcony, Captain Pelletier, accompanied by several gay dogs of his own kidney, was speaking in a loud voice, laughing in the same tone, criticizing the actors, passing the women in review, and annoying everybody in his neighbourhood, without any one daring to call him to order, so powerful in certain cases is the prestige of an insolent look, a ferocious moustache, and the build of an elephant.

By dint of staring through his opera glasses at every corner of the theatre, from the side boxes to the highest tier, the captain perceived in a box in the second row, a group which instantaneously absorbed his attention. There were first, in the front row, Monsieur and Madame Bouchereau, and, in the rear, Dr. Magnan seated behind the young woman. The attitudes of these three people were characteristic. His face pallid and his physiognomy doctored as usual, his eyes adorned by blue glass spectacles, a new grace which he owed to an imaginary ophthalmia, the peace-loving husband held in his hand the theatre programme which he read between the acts, and he listened conscientiously to the tragedy even when Corneille had for interpreters Monsieur Arsène and Monsieur Fonta. Madame Bouchereau was trifling with a most lovely bouquet, whose perfume she frequently sniffed, and whose purple flowers set off so well the whiteness of her complexion that it was allowable to believe that this manœuvre, executed with an air of carelessness, was not altogether exempt from coquetry. Negligently leaning on the back of her seat, the young woman sometimes turned her head half round, the better to hear the words that the doctor addressed to her, speaking in an undertone and smiling, without the husband taking part in this conversation or appearing to notice its intimate and confidential nature.

'Who is it then you 've been looking at for the last quarter of an hour?' one of the captain's neighbours asked him. 'Is it your old flame Madame Bouchereau? I thought you 'd given up thinking about her a long time ago.'

'I didn't know that she 'd come back from Nice,' answered Pelletier reservedly.

'She 's been in Paris ten days.'

'Don't you think that Bouchereau looks very ill? It doesn't seem as if the climate of the south has done him much good. He 's twice as livid as before he left. Poor Bouchereau!'

'Ah! ah!' said the other, 'you 're for giving him a chest trouble too? That would be too funny.'

'What would be too funny?' asked the captain brusquely.

'The trick that that rogue Magnan played on Bouchereau and on you, for, if I can trust your dumbfounded look, you 've an equal share in the mystification.'

'Berton, you are abusing my patience,' said Pelletier in a gruff voice.

'Dog doesn't eat dog,' went on Berton laughing, 'so let 's speak without losing our tempers. This is the story: all Paris, except you, has been laughing at it all last week. It appears that, on the one hand and without any one suspecting it, the aforesaid Magnan was in love with Madame Bouchereau, and that, on the other, since he had suffered from his chest for some time, he had judged it wise to go and spend the winter in a milder climate than this. What does my gay spark do? He persuades the innocent Bouchereau that it was he, Bouchereau, whose chest was weak; he gets him to set out for Nice, as well as his amiable wife; then at his leisure, without any hurry, he goes to join them. The picture that they all three make just now, leaves no doubt as to the denouement of the story: merely from the look of them one can guess that, without libel, one could hang on the front of their box the title of one of Paul de Kock's latest novels, *The Husband, the Wife, and the Lover.* This Magnan is a witty fellow, and he has ingenious ideas. Fearing doubtless that the husband might see too clearly what was going on, he persuaded him to wear blue glasses, threatening him with an ophthalmia. Isn't it a good trick, and isn't it an amusing adventure?'

'Charming, delicious,' answered the captain, smiling in a fashion to make one believe he was grinding his teeth.

The tragedy was just finishing. Dr. Magnan left his box, Pelletier at once followed his example. A moment afterwards the two men found themselves face to face in the foyer.

'Doctor, a word with you,' said the captain with a serious air.

'Two, if you want, captain,' answered Magnan in a jovial tone.

'It appears that, in spite of your prognostications, Bouchereau is in splendid health.'

'Would you want the man to *die*?' asked the doctor, parodying with comic emphasis the accents of Joanny who had just filled the role of the Father of the Horatii.

'I know that you make the most ravishing jokes,' Pelletier went on with a resentment that was beginning to turn into anger: 'but you ought to know that I am not accustomed to serve as a butt. Will you be good enough to answer me. Seriously, is it true that Bouchereau has never been in danger?'

'In great danger, on the contrary. Hadn't he got to fight with you?'

'And so, when you sent him to Nice——'

'It was to prevent this duel. As a doctor I am accustomed to watch over the health of my patients, and my duty was to preserve Bouchereau from your sword, which is renowned as being a terrible disease.'

'A disease for which you will perhaps have to treat yourself before very long,' said the captain whom the doctor's coolness had finished by exasperating. 'Let that fool Bouchereau die of fear or of any other cause, I certainly won't do him the honour of being concerned in it; but you, my dear sir, you who make such fine jokes, I would be very pleased to see if you have as much courage as wit.'

The role of the unhappy and mystified rival is so very humiliating that, through vanity, Pelletier during this discussion had carefully avoided mentioning his real grievance, and pronouncing the name of Madame Bouchereau. The doctor imitated a reserve, which, beside, for him in his position of favoured lover, was almost a law. He received the challenge of the general staff officer with the impassive smile which up to then had hovered constantly on his lips.

'My dear captain,' he said to him, 'I see that at present it would be particularly agreeable to you to pierce my side with your good blade, or to put a ball in my thigh (I suppose that by reason of our old friendship you would spare my head), and that is a fancy that you can indulge if you are absolutely set on it. But if you kill me, who will arrange your marriage with Mademoiselle Nanteuil?

Pelletier looked at his adversary with a stupefied air which redoubled the other's good humour.

'Who is this Mademoiselle Nanteuil?' he said then, in a tone that was involuntarily softened.

'An amiable heiress whose doctor I am, though she enjoys excellent health; she has two hundred thousand francs cash, and, if an intelligent friend were to take the negotiation in hand, she would consent, I think, to make a fine fellow of your stamp happy.'

'That scamp Magnan!' said the captain, taking the doctor's arm, 'it 's impossible to get annoyed with him.'

A NIGHT WITH CLEOPATRA

THÉOPHILE GAUTIER

I

ABOUT eighteen hundred years ago from the moment we write these lines, a cange[1] magnificently gilded and painted came down the Nile with all the rapidity which can be got from fifty long flat oars crawling on the scratched water like the feet of a gigantic scarabæus beetle.

This cange was narrow, elongated in shape, tilted at the two ends in the form of a crescent moon, slim in its proportions, and marvellously fashioned for speed; a ram's head surmounted by a golden ball armed the point of the prow, and showed that the craft belonged to a personage of royal rank.

In the centre of the boat was erected a cabin with a flat roof, a kind of *naos*, or tent of honour, coloured and gilded, with a moulding of palm leaves, and four little square windows.

Two rooms, covered in the same way with hieroglyphics, occupied the ends of the crescent; one of them, bigger than the other, had, juxtaposed, a story of less height, like the *châteaux-gaillards* of those quaint galleys of the sixteenth century drawn by Della Bella; the smaller, which served as quarters for the pilot, ended in a triangular poop-rail.

The rudder was made of two immense oars, set on many-coloured posts, and trailing in the water behind the bark like the webbed feet of a swan; heads adorned with the *pschent* and wearing on the chin the allegorical horn, were sculptured by handfuls along those great oars which the pilot manœuvred standing erect on the roof of the cabin.

He was a sunburnt man, fawn-coloured like new bronze, with blue glistening high-lights, his eyes tilted at the corners, his hair very black and plaited into little strings, his mouth wide spread, his cheek-bones prominent, his ears sitting out from his skull, the Egyptian type in all its purity. A narrow

[1] A light boat used on the Nile.—TRANSLATOR'S NOTE.

loin-cloth tied on his hips, and five or six twists of glass beads and amulets, composed all his costume.

He seemed to be the only inhabitant of the cange, for the rowers, bent over their oars, and hidden by the gunwale, only made their presence divined by the symmetrical movement of the oar-blades, opening like the spokes of a fan on each flank of the bark, and falling again into the stream after a slight moment of suspension.

No puff of air stirred the atmosphere, and the big triangular sail of the cange, rolled up and tied with a silken cord along the lowered mast, showed that all hope of the wind rising had been abandoned.

The midday sun discharged its leaden arrows; the ash-coloured ooze on the river's banks gave out flamboyant reflections; a hard light, dazzling and dusty because of its intensity, streamed down in torrents of flame; the azure of the sky was white with heat like metal in the furnace; a blazing reddish haze rose like smoke on the burning horizon. Not a cloud showed on that sky as unvarying and mournful as eternity.

The water of the Nile, dull and lustreless, seemed to be sleeping in its course, and to spread out in sheets of molten pewter. No breath wrinkled its surface, nor swayed on their stalks the flower cups of the lotus, as rigid as if they had been sculptured; only at distant intervals the leap of a bechir or a fahaka inflating the under part of his body, barely mirrored in the water a silver scale, and the oars of the cange seemed to tear with difficulty the fuliginous scum of the stagnant stream. The banks were deserted; a deep and solemn gloom weighed on that land which was never aught else than a mighty tomb, a land whose living inhabitants seemed never to have had any other occupation but that of embalming the dead. A sterile gloom, dry as pumice stone, without melancholy, without reverie, having no pearl-grey cloud to gaze at on the horizon, no secret spring in which to bathe its dusty feet; the gloom of the sphinx wearied with perpetually watching the desert, the sphinx who can never quit the granite pedestal on which it has sharpened its claws for twenty centuries.

The silence was so profound that one would have said that the whole world had become mute, or that the air had lost its power of conducting sound. The sole noise to be heard was the whispering and muffled laughter of the crocodiles, swooning with heat, who wallowed in the reeds of the river; or else some ibis who, tired of standing erect, one foot folded back under its body, his head between his shoulders, quitted his immobile station, and, roughly lashing the blue air with his white wings, went to perch anew on an obelisk or a palm-tree.

The cange shot like an arrow through the water of the river, leaving behind it a silvery furrow which soon closed up; and some bubbles of foam, coming to the surface to burst, were the sole witnesses of the passage of the bark that was already out of sight.

The steep banks of the river, salmon and ochre coloured, opened to the view like strips of papyrus between the double azure of the sky and the water, so alike in tone that the slim tongue of land which separated them seemed a pathway flung over an immense lake, so that it would have been difficult to decide if the Nile reflected the sky or if the sky reflected the Nile.

The spectacle changed every moment: now it was gigantic propylæa that came to mirror in the river their shelving walls, set with large flat panels of quaint figures; pylons with splayed capitals, flights of stairs bordered with crouching sphinxes, caps with fluted lappets on their heads, and crossing over their pointed breasts their black basalt paws; inordinate palaces of which the severe horizontal lines of the entablature jutted out against the horizon, where the emblematic sphere opened its mysterious wings like an eagle with inordinate wing-spread; temples with enormous columns, thick like towers, on which, on a background of dazzling white, processions of hieroglyphic figures stood out conspicuously; all the marvellous creations of an architecture of Titans; now it was countrysides of desolating sterility; hills formed by little fragments of stone that had come from excavations and buildings, crumbs of that gigantic debauch of granite which lasted more than thirty centuries; mountains denuded of foliage by the heat, slashed and barred by black lines like the scars of a forest fire; mounds hunchbacked and misformed, squatting like the criocephalus of the tombs, their misshapen forms showing up against the edge of the sky; greenish clay, reddish ochre, tufa rock of a floury white, and from time to time, some steep slope of old rose-coloured marble in which gaped the black mouths of the quarries.

This sterility was tempered by nothing at all; no oasis of foliage refreshed the gaze; green seemed a colour unknown in this land; only at long intervals a scrawny palm-tree sprawled on the horizon like a vegetable crab; a thorny cochineal fig-tree brandished its steely leaves like bronze gloves; a safflower, finding a little humidity in the shade of a stump of a column, set off with a point of red the general uniformity.

After this rapid glance at the general aspect of the country, let us come back to the cange with its fifty rowers, and without announcing ourselves, let us enter without ceremony into the *naos* of honour.

The interior was painted in white with green arabesques, with nets of vermilion and gold flowers of fantastic shapes; a reed mat of extreme fineness covered the floor; at the end of the room stood a small bed with griffin feet, with a back arranged like a sofa or modern settee, a stool with four steps to ascend into it, and, a luxury singular enough according to our ideas of comfort, a kind of half circle of cedar wood, mounted on a pedestal, designed to encircle the back of the neck and to sustain the head of the person in bed.

On this strange pillow rested a very charming head, the head of a woman adored and divine, one look from whom lost half a world. She was the most complete woman who had ever lived, a type of wonder to whom the poets can add nothing, and whom dreamers find forever at the end of their dreams: there is no need to name Cleopatra.

Beside her Charmion, her favourite slave, waved a large fan of ibis feathers. A young girl sprinkled with a shower of scented water the little reed blinds with which the windows of the *naos* were furnished, so that the air might only enter there impregnated with freshness and perfumes.

Near the couch, in a vase of ribbon-like alabaster, with a slender neck, slim and sinuous in outline, recalling vaguely the profile of a heron, was a bouquet of lotus flowers in water, some of them a celestial blue, others a delicate rose like the finger tips of Isis, the great goddess.

Cleopatra, this day, by caprice or policy, was not dressed in Grecian fashion: she had just been present at a panegyry, and she was returning to her summer palace in the cange, wearing the Egyptian costume that she had been wearing at the festival.

Our lady readers will perhaps be curious to know how Queen Cleopatra was dressed in returning from the Mammisi of Hermonthis, where were worshipped the trinity of the God Mandou, the Goddess Ritho, and their son Harphre; that is a satisfaction we can give them.

Queen Cleopatra had for head-dress a kind of very light gold helmet formed by the body and wings of the sacred sparrow-hawk; the wings, smoothed down fan-wise on each side of her head, covered her temples, and stretched almost to her neck, leaving free at a little opening an ear more rosy and more delicately folded than the shell whence sprang Venus whom the Egyptians name Hathor; the tail of the bird occupied the place where our ladies twist their rolls of hair; its body, covered with feathers imbricated and painted in different enamels, enveloped the top of her head, and its neck, gracefully bent towards the forehead, made up with the head a kind of horn sparkling with jewels; a symbolic crest in the shape of a tower completed this elegant, although bizarre head-dress. Hair, black as that of a night without stars, escaped from this helmet and flowed in long tresses down her fair shoulders, but a collar or gorget, ornamented with several rows of serpentine, of azerodrach, and of chrysoberyl, left, alas! only the commencement of those shoulders in sight; a linen robe with diagonal ribs, a mistlike cloth, woven from air, *ventus textilis* as Petronius says, swayed in white vapour round a beautiful body whose lines it softly shaded. This robe had half sleeves, fitting on the shoulders but cut away towards the elbow like our sabot sleeves, and showing a wonderful arm and a perfect hand, the arm clasped by six circles of gold and the hand adorned by a ring representing a scarabæus. A belt, of which the knotted ends hung down behind, marked the waist of this floating and free tunic; a short cloak with fringes completed the attire, and if some barbaric words do not affright the ears of Paris, we will add that this robe was called *schenti* and the short cloak *calasiris*.

As a last detail, let us say that Queen Cleopatra wore light sandals, very slim, bent back at the point and attached to the ankle like the shoes *à la poulaine* of the châtelaines of the Middle Ages.

All the same Queen Cleopatra had not the satisfied air of a woman sure that she is perfectly lovely and perfectly attired; she turned and twisted on her little couch, and her rather brusque movements deranged each moment the folds of her gauze *conopeum* which Charmion readjusted with inexhaustible patience and without ceasing to wield her fan.

'It is stifling in this room,' said Cleopatra, 'even if Phtha, the God of Fire, had set up his forges here, it wouldn't be hotter; the air is like a furnace.' And she passed over her lips the tip of her little tongue, then stretched out her hand like an invalid who feels about for an absent cup.

Charmion, ever attentive, clapped her hands: a black slave, clad in a straight gown pleated like the skirts of the Albanians, with a leopard skin thrown over his shoulder, entered with the rapidity of an apparition, holding balanced on his left hand a tray laden with cups and slices of water-melon, and in the right a long jug furnished with a spout like a tea-pot.

The slave filled one of the cups, pouring into it from a height with a marvellous dexterity, and put it before the queen. Cleopatra touched the beverage with her lips, put it down beside her, and turning towards Charmion, her beautiful black eyes unctuous and lustrous from the living sparkle of light in them:

'Oh, Charmion,' she said, 'I am bored.'

II

Charmion, foreseeing a confidence, made a face of grievous assent, and came near her mistress.

'I am horribly bored,' went on Cleopatra, letting her arms hang loose as one discouraged and defeated, 'this Egypt destroys me and crushes me; this sky with its implacable blue is more sombre than the deep night of Erebus; never a cloud! never a shadow, and for ever this red, dripping sun which stares like the eye of a Cyclops! See, Charmion, I would give a pearl for a drop of rain! From the enflamed eyeball of this sky of bronze has never yet fallen a single tear on the desolation of the earth; it is a huge tombstone, a dome of a necropolis, a sky dead and dried up like the mummies it covers! it weighs on my shoulders like a too heavy coat! it irks me and distresses me; it seems to me as if I could not rise to my full height without bruising my forehead against it; and then, this country is really a fearful country; everything here is sombre, enigmatical, incomprehensible! Imagination here produces nothing but monstrous chimæras and inordinate monuments; this sort of architecture and art terrifies me; these colossi whose limbs fixed in stone, condemn them to rest eternally seated with their hands on their knees, tire me with their stupid immobility; they obsess my eyes and my horizon. When, then, will the giant come who will take them by the hand and relieve them from their twenty-century-long sentry duty? Granite itself wears out at last! What master do they await to leave the mountain that serves them for a seat, and to rise in token of respect? Of what invisible herd are those mighty sphinxes, crouching like watch-dogs, the guardians, that they never close an eyelid and hold for ever their claws at attention? What is the matter with them, then, that they fix so obstinately their eyes of stone on eternity and infinity? What strange secret do their tightly closed lips lock in their breasts? Right and left, on whatever side one turns, there are only monsters frightful to look on, dogs with men's heads, men with dogs' heads, chimæras begotten of hideous matings in the gloomy depths of the syrinx bushes, Anubises, Typhons, Osirises, sparrow-hawks with yellow eyes that seem to look through you with their inquisitive regards, and to see beyond you things that cannot be told: a family of horrible animals and gods with scaly wings, with hooked beaks, with tearing claws, always ready to seize you and devour you, if you pass the threshold of the temple, and if you raise the corner of the veil!

'On the walls, on the columns, on the roofs, on the floors, on the palaces and on the temples, in the corridors and in the deepest pits of the cemeteries, down to the entrails of the earth where the light does not reach, where the torches go out for lack of air, and everywhere and always, interminable hieroglyphics, sculptured and painted, recounting in unintelligible language things that are no longer known, and which belong no doubt to creations that have vanished; prodigious buried buildings where a whole people is worn out to write the epitaph of a king! Mystery and granite, that is Egypt; a fine country for a young woman and a young queen!

'Only menacing and funereal symbols are to be seen, the *pedum*, the *tau*, allegorical globes, entwined serpents, balances where souls are weighed, the unknown, death, nothingness! For the only vegetation, pillars striped with bizarre characters; for alleys of trees, avenues of granite obelisks; for earth, immense paving stones of granite, so huge that each mountain could furnish only a single flagstone; for sky, roofs of granite; a palpable eternity, a bitter and perpetual sarcasm of the fragility and brevity of life! stairways made for strides of Titan, which the human foot cannot step over and which must be ascended with ladders; columns that a hundred arms could not encircle, labyrinths where one could walk a year without finding the exit! the vertigo of enormity, the intoxication of the gigantic, the inordinate effort of pride which would carve at all costs its name on the surface of the world!

'And besides, Charmion, I tell you, I have a thought that terrifies me; in other countries of the earth they bury their dead, and their ashes are soon mingled with the ground. Here one might say that the living have no other occupation than that of preserving the dead; powerful balms snatch them from destruction; all of them keep their form and their appearance; the soul evaporates, the mortal body remains; under this people are twenty peoples; each city has its feet on twenty layers of tombs; each generation that goes leaves a population of mummies in a city of darkness; under the father, you find the grandfather and the great-grandfather in his painted and gilded box, such as they were in their lifetime; and were you to excavate for ever you would for ever find more of them!

'When I think of those multitudes, swathed in their bands, of those myriads of dried-up spectres which fill the funeral pits and which have lain there for two thousand years, face to face, in their silence that nothing comes to trouble, not even the noise that the worm of the tomb makes in his crawling, and who will be found there untouched after another two thousand years, with their cats, their crocodiles, their ibises, all the things that lived at the same time as they did, spasms of terror seize me, and I feel shudders run up my skin. What do they say to each other, since they still have lips, and since their souls, if the fantasy seized them to return, would find their bodies in the state in which they left them?

'Egypt is truly a sinister kingdom and very little fitted for me who am fond of laughter and folly; everything here encloses a mummy; that is the heart and core of everything. After a thousand detours it is there you finish; the pyramids hide a sarcophagus. All that is nothingness and folly. Rip open the sky with gigantic triangles of stone, you will not add an inch to your corpse! How can one rejoice and live in such a land where one breathes as perfume only the bitter odour of naphtha, and the bitumen that boils in the embalmers' kettles, where the floor of your room sounds hollow because the corridors of the hypogeum and the funeral pits stretch even under your dressing-room? To be the queen of the mummies; to have as gossips those statues in their stiff, constrained poses, that 's a lot of fun! And yet, if to lighten the gloom, I had some passion in my heart, an interest in life, if I were in love with somebody or something, if I were loved! But I am not.

'That is why I am bored, Charmion; with love this sterile, surly Egypt would seem to me more charming than Greece with its ivory gods, its temples of white marble, its oleander woods, and its fountains of spring water. I would not think of the grotesque countenance of Anubis, nor of the terrors of the underground cities.'

Charmion smiled with an air of incredulity. 'That shouldn't cause you much grief; for each of your glances pierces men's hearts like the golden arrows of Eros himself.'

'Can a queen,' went on Cleopatra, 'know if it is the diadem or the brow beneath that is loved in her? The beams of her sidereal crown dazzle men's eyes and hearts; were I to come down from the height of my throne, would I enjoy the celebrity and the popularity of Bacchide or Archenassa, of any chance courtesan from Athens or Miletus? A queen is something so far above men, something so lofty, so separated, so impossible! What presumption can flatter itself with hopes of success in such an enterprise? It is no longer a woman, it is an august and sacred figure that has no longer a sex, a being one adores on bended knees without loving, like the statue of a goddess. Who has ever been seriously in love with Hera of the snowy arms, with Pallas of the sea-green eyes? Who has ever tried to kiss the silver feet of Thetis, and the rosy fingers of Aurora? What lover of those divine beauties has ever taken wings to fly towards the golden palaces of heaven? Respect and terror freeze men's souls in our presence, and to be loved by our equals we must needs descend to the cities of the dead that I was talking of just now.'

Although she put forward no objection to the reasoning of her mistress, a vague smile flitting about the lips of the Greek slave showed that she had no great belief in this inviolability of the royal person.

'Ah,' continued Cleopatra, 'I would like something to happen to me, a strange adventure, something unexpected. The song of the poets, the dance of the Syrian slaves, feasts crowned with roses and prolonged till daybreak, midnight races, Laconian dogs, tame lions, humpbacked dwarfs, members of the fellowship of the inimitable, combats in the circus, and ornaments, robes of byssus, matched strings of pearls, perfumes of Asia, the most exquisite elegances, the most senseless sumptuousness, nothing amuses me any more: everything is indifferent to me, everything is insupportable!'

'It is obvious,' murmured Charmion, 'that the queen hasn't had a lover or killed anybody for a month.'

Tired by such a long outburst, Cleopatra lifted again the cup placed beside her, moistened her lips in it, and, putting her head under her arm with a dove-like movement, settled herself as comfortably as possible to sleep. Charmion undid her sandals, and began softly to tickle the soles of her feet with the feathers of a peacock's quill; sleep did not tarry in flinging its golden powder over the lovely eyes of the sister of Ptolemy.

While Cleopatra is sleeping, let us mount again to the bridge of the cange, and enjoy the wonderful spectacle of the setting sun. A wide band of violet, strongly warmed by reddish tones towards the west, fills all the lower part of the sky; as it meets the azure zones, the violet tint melts into clear lilac, and is drowned in the blue in a half shade of rose; on the side where the sun, red like a buckler fallen from Vulcan's furnace, throws burning reflected light, the shades turn to pale lemon, and produce tints like those of turquoises. The water, rippled by an oblique beam, had the flat radiance of a mirror seen from the foil, or a damascened blade; the windings of the river, the reeds, and all the undulations of the bank stand out in firm black lines, which the whitish reflections throw into strong relief. Thanks to this twilight clarity you will see down there, like a grain of dust fallen on quicksilver, a little brown point which trembles in a network of shining threads. Is it a teal that is diving, a tortoise letting itself drift on the stream, a crocodile raising the end of his scaly snout to breathe the less burning evening air, the stomach of a hippopotamus stretching himself on the water's surface? or else indeed a rock left uncovered by the lowering of the river? for the old Hopi-Mou, Father of the Waters, has indeed need to fill his exhausted urn at the rains of the solstice in the Mountains of the Moon.

It is none of these. By the fragments of Osiris so happily sewn together! it is a man who seems to be walking and skating on the water; now the skiff that bears him can be seen, a real nutshell, a hollowed out fish, three bands of cork fitted together, one for the bottom and two for the sides, the whole solidly tied at the two ends by a cord daubed with bitumen. A man is standing upright, one foot on each side of this frail contrivance, which he guides by a single oar that serves at the same time as rudder, and although the royal cange flies rapidly along under the power of fifty oars, the little black skiff gains visibly upon it.

Cleopatra was wanting some strange incident, something unexpected; this little slim skiff, with its mysterious behaviour, has in our eyes all the appearance of bringing, if not an adventure, at least an adventurer. Perhaps it contains the hero of our story; the thing is not impossible.

It was, in any case, a handsome young man of twenty, with hair so black that it seemed blue, a skin fair as gold, and proportions so perfect that one would have said a bronze of Lysippus; although he had been rowing a long time, he betrayed no sign of fatigue, and on his brow was not a single bead of sweat.

The sun plunged beneath the horizon, and on its jagged disk was drawn the brown silhouette of a distant city that the eye could barely have discovered without this trick of lighting; soon it went down altogether, and the stars, those evening flowering blossoms of the night, opened their golden calices to the azure firmament. The royal cange, followed closely by the little skiff, stopped near a stairway of black marble, each step of which was supported by one of the sphinxes hated by Cleopatra. It was the landing stage of the summer palace.

Cleopatra, leaning on Charmion, passed rapidly like a glittering vision, between a double row of slaves carrying signal torches.

The young man took from the bottom of the boat a large lion skin, threw it on his shoulders, leaped lightly to the ground, drew the skiff up the steep bank, and made his way towards the palace.

III

Who is this young man who, standing on a bit of cork, dares to follow the royal cange, and who can race against fifty rowers of the country of Kush, naked to the waist, and rubbed with palm-tree oil? What motive urges him on and rouses his activity? That is what we are obliged to know in our quality of a poet gifted with the gift of intuition, for whom all men, and even all women, and that is more difficult, should have in their sides the window which Momus craved.

It is maybe not very easy to re-create the thoughts some two thousand years ago, of a young man of the land of Keme who followed the bark of Cleopatra, Queen and Goddess Euergetes, returning from the Mammisi of Hermonthis. We shall attempt it all the same.

Meïamoun, son of Mandouschopsh, was a young man of a strange character: nothing that touched the common run of mortals made any impression on him; he seemed of a higher race, and one might have named him the product of some divine adultery. His look had the radiance and the fixity of the sparrow-hawk's, and serene majesty sat on his brow as on a marble pedestal; a noble disdain arched his upper lip, and swelled his nostrils like those of a spirited steed; though he had almost the delicate grace of a young girl, and though Dionysus, that effeminate god, had not a more rounded or polished chest, he hid under this soft exterior nerves of steel and Herculean strength, that singular privilege of certain ancient natures of uniting the beauty of the woman with the strength of the man.

As to his colour, we are obliged to admit that he was tawny as an orange, a colour opposed to the white and rose idea we have of beauty; but that did not prevent him from being a very charming young man, much sought after by all sorts of women, yellow, red, copper-coloured, swarthy, golden, and even by more than one white Greek.

After that, don't go and imagine that Meïamoun was a lady-killer; the ashes of old Priam, the snows of Hippolytus himself were not more insensible or cold; the young neophyte in his white tunic, getting ready for the initiation to the mysteries of Isis, does not lead a more chaste life; the young girl who passes by in the glacial shadow of her mother has not his fearful purity.

The pleasures of Meïamoun, for a young man of such a shy temperament, were all the same of a singular nature; he set out tranquilly in the morning with his little buckler of hippopotamus hide, his *harpé* or sabre with a curved blade, his triangular bow and his quiver of serpent skin filled with barbed arrows; then he plunged into the desert, and set his mare, with her lean legs, her straight head, her dishevelled mane, to the gallop till he found the track of a lioness; it gave him great enjoyment to go and take the little lion cubs from under their mother's body. In everything he loved only the perilous or the impossible; he delighted in walking by impracticable paths, or swimming in raging waters, and he would have chosen for a bathe in the Nile precisely the spot where the cataracts are; the abyss called him.

Such was Meïamoun, son of Mandouschopsh.

For some time back his humour had become ever more unsociable; he buried himself for months at a time in the ocean of sand and only reappeared at rare intervals. His anxious mother hung vainly over the top of her terrace and questioned the road with a tireless eye. After a long wait, a little cloud of dust eddied on the horizon; soon the cloud burst and revealed Meïamoun covered with dust, on his mare, who was as thin as a wolf, her eye red and bloodshot, her nostrils trembling, with scars on her side, scars which were not the marks of the spur.

After having hung up in his room some hyena or lion skin, he set out again.

And yet no one could have been happier than Meïamoun; he was loved by Naphé, the daughter of the priest Afomouthis, the most beautiful girl in the nome of Arsinœ. One would have to be Meïamoun not to see that Naphé had charming eyes tilted at the corners with an indefinable expression of voluptuousness, a mouth round which sparkled a rosy smile, clear white teeth, arms exquisitely rounded, and feet more perfect than the jasper feet of the statue of Isis; assuredly there was not in all Egypt a smaller hand or longer hair. The charms of Naphé could have been surpassed only by those of Cleopatra. But who could dream of loving Cleopatra? Ixion, who was in love with Juno, clasped in his arms only a cloud, and he turns for ever on his wheel among the shades.

It was Cleopatra that Meïamoun loved!

He had at first tried to subdue this mad passion, he had struggled in hand-to-hand fight against it; but love is not throttled as one throttles a lion, and the most vigorous athletes can do nothing about it. The arrow was stuck in the wound and he dragged it about with him everywhere; the picture of

Cleopatra, radiant and splendid under her diadem with golden points, standing alone in her imperial purple among a kneeling people, glittered in his waking moments and in his dreams; like a rash man who has looked at the sun and who sees always an intangible spot flicker before him, Meïamoun saw always Cleopatra. Eagles can contemplate the sun without being dazzled, but what eyeball of diamond can be fixed with impunity on a beautiful woman, on a beautiful queen?

His life consisted in wandering round the royal dwellings so as to breathe the same air as Cleopatra, so as to kiss on the sand—a felicity, alas! too rare—the half effaced imprint of her foot; he followed the sacred feasts and the panegyries, trying to snatch a beam from her eyes, to steal in passing one of the thousand aspects of her beauty. Sometimes shame came upon him at this senseless existence; he gave himself up to hunting with a redoubled fury, and tried to subdue by fatigue the heat of his blood and the tumult of his desires.

He had gone to the panegyry of Hermonthis, and, in the vague hope of seeing the queen again for an instant, when she disembarked at the summer palace, he had followed the cange in his skiff, without heeding the bitter stings of the sun in a heat enough to melt in lava-sweat the sphinxes panting on their reddened pedestals.

And then he understood that he had come to a supreme moment, that his life was about to be decided, and that he could not die with his secret in his heart.

It is a strange situation to love a queen; it is as if one loved a star, and still the star comes each night to shine in its place in the sky; it is a kind of mysterious rendezvous; you find her there, you see her, she is not angry at you for looking at her! Oh, misery! to be poor, unknown, obscure, seated at the very bottom of the ladder, and to feel your heart full of love for something solemn, sparkling, and splendid, for a woman whose meanest servant would have nothing to do with you! to have your eyes fixed on someone who does not see you, who will never see you, for whom you are nothing but a figure in the crowd like all the other figures, and who would meet you a hundred times without recognizing you! to have, if ever the opportunity for speaking arises, no reason to give for such a crazy audacity, neither a poet's talent, nor great genius, nor superhuman qualities, nothing but love; and in exchange for beauty, nobility, power, all the splendours of your dreams, to bring only passion or your youth, rare things indeed!

These ideas oppressed Meïamoun; lying prone on the sand, his chin on his hands, he let himself be carried away and uplifted on the flood of a never-failing reverie; he sketched out a thousand plans, each more insensate than the other. He realized quite clearly that he was striving for an impossible end, but he had not the courage to renounce it frankly, and perfidious hope came whispering at his ear some lying promise.

'Hathor, powerful goddess,' he said in a low voice, 'what have I done to you that you make me so unhappy! Are you avenging yourself for the disdain that I have for Naphé, the daughter of the priest Afomouthis? Are you angry with me for having repulsed Lamia, the hetaira of Athens, or Flora, the courtesan from Rome? Is it my fault if my heart is susceptible to the beauty of Cleopatra alone, your rival? Why have you sunk in my soul the poisoned arrows of impossible love? What sacrifices and what offerings do you demand? Must I raise a chapel of the rose marble of Syene with columns and gilded capitals, a ceiling in one piece, and hollow sculptured hieroglyphics by the best workmen of Memphis or Thebes? Answer me.'

Like all the gods and goddesses that man invokes, Hathor answered nothing. Meïamoun made a desperate resolve.

Cleopatra, on her side, also invoked the goddess Hathor; she asked of her a new pleasure, an unknown sensation; languidly lying on her bed, she mused that the number of senses is very limited, that the most exquisite refinements are very quickly followed by disgust, and that a queen has really a lot of trouble to fill in her day. Trying poisons on slaves, making men fight with tigers, or gladiators with one another, drinking melted pearls, squandering a province, all that is pointless and ordinary.

Charmion was reduced to her last expedient, and didn't know what to make of her mistress.

All at once a whizzing was heard, an arrow came and planted itself quivering in the cedar facing of the wall.

Cleopatra almost fainted with terror. Charmion rushed to the window, and only saw a flake of foam on the river. A roll of papyrus surrounded the wooden shaft of the arrow; it contained these words written in phonetic characters: 'I love you!'

IV

'I love you,' repeated Cleopatra, twisting between her frail white fingers the bit of papyrus rolled up like a scytale,[1] 'that is the message I was asking for; what intelligent soul, what hidden genius has understood my desire so well?'

And thoroughly aroused from her languid torpor, she jumped down from her bed with the agility of a cat who scents a mouse, put her little ivory feet in her embroidered *tatbebs*, threw her byssus tunic over her shoulders, and ran to the window through which Charmion was still looking.

The night was clear and serene: the moon had already risen and sketched with great angles of light and shade the architectural masses of the palace, standing out boldly on a background of bluish transparency, and freezing to watered silver the water of the river in which its reflection streamed in a gleaming column; a light puff of wind, which could have been taken for the breath of the sleeping sphinxes, fluttered the reeds and set the azure bells of the lotus trembling; the cables of the small boats moored to the banks of the Nile groaned feebly, and the flood complained on its bed like a dove without its mate. A vague perfume of vegetation, sweeter than that of the aromatics that burn in the *anschir* of the priests of Anubis, drifted into the room. It was one of those enchanted nights of the East, more splendid than our most beautiful days, for our sun does not compare with that moon.

'Don't you see down there, almost in the middle of the river, a man's head swimming? Look now, he is crossing the track of light, and is being lost in the shadow: he can't be seen any longer.' And, resting on Charmion's shoulder, she leaned half her beautiful body out of the window to try to find again the track of the mysterious swimmer. But a clump of Nile acacias, of doums and sayals, threw at that spot its shadow on the river and protected the flight of the audacious man. If Meïamoun had had the good wit to turn round, he would have seen Cleopatra, the sidereal queen, looking greedily for him across the night, for him, poor obscure Egyptian that he was, a wretched hunter of lions.

'Charmion! Charmion! bid Phrehipephbour, the chief of the

[1] Staff used in Sparta to send secret dispatches.—TRANSLATOR'S NOTE.

rowers, come, and tell them to launch without delay two boats in pursuit of that man,' said Cleopatra, whose curiosity was excited to the highest degree.

Phrehipephbour appeared; he was a man of the race of the Nahasi, with broad hands, muscular arms, wearing a cap of a red colour on his head, rather like a Phrygian helmet, and clothed in a tight pair of drawers, striped diagonally white and blue. His bust, entirely bare, shone in the light of the lamp, black and polished like a ball of jade. He took the queen's orders and retired at once to execute them.

Two long barks, narrow, so light that the slightest forgetfulness of equilibrium must have capsized them, cleft at once the waters of the Nile, whistling under the strength of twenty vigorous rowers, but the search was useless. After having beaten the river in all directions, after having ransacked the smallest tuft of reeds, Phrehipephbour returned to the palace without any other result but that of having raised some heron, asleep erect on one leg, or troubled some crocodile in his digestion.

Cleopatra experienced such a strong resentment at this rebuff that she had a great desire to condemn Prehipephbour to the grindstone or the beasts. Fortunately Charmion interceded for the wretch, who was all in a panic, paling with fear under his black skin. It was the only time in her life that one of her desires had not been granted as soon as formulated; so she felt an uneasy surprise, like a first doubt of her all-powerfulness.

She, Cleopatra, wife and sister of Ptolemy, proclaimed Goddess Euergetes, reigning Queen of the Lands Below and Above, Eye of the Sky, the Favourite of the Sun, as can be seen on the cartouches sculptured on the walls of temples, to meet an obstacle, to wish a thing that was not done, to have spoken and not been obeyed! One might as well be the wife of some poor paraschist who incised dead bodies, and melt soda in a kettle! It is monstrous, it is exorbitant, and one must be, in truth, a very kind and very clement queen, not to crucify this wretched Phrehipephbour.

You were wanting an adventure, something strange and unexpected; you have got just what you wished. You see that your realm is not so dead as you claimed. It is no stone arm from a statue that has sped that arrow, it is not from the heart of a mummy that these three words which have moved you so have come, you who see with a smile on your lips your poisoned slaves beating with their heels and their heads in the convulsions of agony your beautiful mosaic and porphyry pavements, you who applaud the tiger when he has stoutly buried his jaws in the side of a conquered gladiator.

You will have all that you wish, cars of silver starred with emeralds, four-wheeled chariots of griffins, tunics of thrice dyed purple, mirrors of steel framed with precious stones, so clear that you can see yourself therein as lovely as you are; robes come from the lands of the East, so fine, so thin that they can pass through the ring of your little finger; pearls of a perfect water, goblets wrought by Lysippus or Myron, parrots from India that speak like poets; you will get everything, even if you demand the *cestus* of Venus, or the *pschent* of Isis; but, in very truth, you will not have this evening the man who shot that arrow that trembles still in the cedar wood of your bed.

The slaves who will dress you to-morrow will have no easy task; they will be well advised to have a light hand; the golden toilet pins might well have for sheath the throat of the clumsy hair-waver, and the depilator runs a strong risk of being hung up to the ceiling by her feet.

'Who could have had the audacity to shoot that declaration fitted to an arrow? Is it the monarch Amoun-Ra who thinks himself handsomer than the Grecian Apollo? What do you think of him, Charmion? Or rather Chéapsiro, the commandant of Hermothybria, so proud of his combats in the country of Kush! Wouldn't it rather be young Sextus, the Roman debauchee who puts on rouge, rolls his r's in speaking and wears sleeves in the Persian mode?'

'Queen, it is none of these; although you are the loveliest lady in the world, these men flatter you and do not love you. The monarch Amoun-Ra has chosen an idol to whom he will always be faithful, and that is his own person; the warrior Chéapsiro, thinks only of relating his battles; as to Sextus, he is so seriously occupied with the composition of a new cosmetic that he can think of nothing else. Besides he has received some overcoats from Laconia, yellow tunics embroidered with gold, and some Asiatic children who are absorbing him entirely. None of these fine gentlemen would risk his neck in an enterprise so rash and so perilous; they do not love you enough for that.

'You were saying in your cange that dazzled eyes never dared aspire to you, and that men could only pale and fall at your feet asking pardon, and that there remained for you no other resource than to waken in his gilded coffin some old Pharaoh perfumed with bitumen. Now there is an ardent young heart which loves you. What will you do with it?'

That night Cleopatra had difficulty in sleeping; she turned on her bed, she called long in vain on Morpheus, brother of Death; she repeated several times that she was the most unhappy of queens, that every one made it their business to thwart her, and that her life was unendurable; huge grievances which affected Charmion rather lightly, though she put on an expression of sympathy with them.

Let us leave Cleopatra for a little, seeking the sleep that flies from her, and running over in her conjectures all the nobles of the court; let us go back to Meïamoun. More skilful than Phrehipephbour the chief of the rowers, we shall certainly succeed in finding him.

Terrified by his own hardihood, Meïamoun flung himself into the Nile, and had reached swimming the little clump of doum-palms before Phrehipephbour had launched the two barks in pursuit.

When he had got back his breath, and pushed behind his ears his long black hair, soaked with the foam of the river, he felt calmer and more at ease. Cleopatra had something which came from him. A connection existed between them now; Cleopatra was thinking of him, Meïamoun. Maybe it was a thought of wrath, but at least he had succeeded in arousing in her some sort of feeling, terror, anger, or pity; he had made her recognize his existence. It is true that he had forgotten to put his name on the strip of papyrus; but what more would the name convey to the queen; Meïamoun, son of Mandouschopsch!

A monarch or a slave were equal before her. A goddess does not abase herself more in taking as a lover a man of the people than a patrician or a king; from such a height nothing is seen in a man but his love.

The sentence that had been weighing on his breast like the knee of a bronze colossus, had at length emerged; it had crossed the air, it had arrived as far as the queen, the point of the triangle, the inaccessible summit! In that blasé soul it had set curiosity, an immense progress.

Meïamoun did not suspect that he had succeeded so well, but he was more tranquil, for he had sworn to himself by the mystic Bari, who guards the souls in Amenthi; by the sacred birds, Bennon and Ghenghen; by Typhon and by Osiris; by every formidable name that Egyptian mythology could offer, that he would be the lover of Cleopatra, were it only for a day, were it only for a night, were it only for an hour, though it cost him his body and his soul.

How this love had come upon him for a woman that he had seen only from afar, and to whom he scarcely dared to raise his eyes, he who did not drop them before the yellow eyeballs of the lions, and how this little seed fallen by chance in his soul had sprung up there so quickly and thrown out such deep roots, is a mystery that we shall not explain; we have said above: the abyss called him.

When he was quite sure that Phrehipephbour had gone in with his rowers, he flung himself a second time in the Nile, and made his way again to the palace of Cleopatra whose lamp shone through a purple curtain, and seemed a painted star. Leander did not swim towards the tower of Sestos with more courage and vigour, and yet Meïamoun was not waited for by a Hero ready to pour on his head jars of perfumes to banish the odours of the sea, and the bitter kisses of the tempest. Some shrewd blow of a lance or *harpé* was all that could happen to him at the best, and to tell the truth, it was hardly that of which he was afraid.

He skirted for some time the wall of the palace, whose marble feet bathed in the river, and stopped before a submerged opening, through which the water rushed in whirlpools. He dived two or three times unsuccessfully; at last he was more fortunate, hit on the passage and disappeared.

This arcade was a vaulted canal which led the waters of the Nile to Cleopatra's baths.

V

Cleopatra only fell asleep in the morning, at the hour when the dreams return that have flitted through the ivory gate. The illusion of sleep led her to see all sorts of lovers, swimming across rivers, clambering up walls to reach her, and, in memory of the night before, her dreams were riddled with arrows charged with declarations of love. Her little heels, fluttering in agitation, struck the breast of Charmion sleeping across the bed to serve as her cushion.

When she awoke, a gay sunbeam played in the window curtain, the web of which it pierced with a thousand points of light, and came familiarly to the bed to flit like a golden butterfly round her lovely shoulders which it skimmed in passing with a luminous kiss. Happy sunbeam that the gods might have envied!

Cleopatra asked to get up in an expiring voice like a sick child's; two of her women raised her in their arms and laid her preciously on the ground on a huge tiger skin whose claws were of gold and whose eyes were carbuncles. Charmion wrapped her in a *calasiris* of linen whiter than milk, and put her feet in *tatbebs* of cork on the soles of which had been drawn, in token of contempt, two grotesque figures representing two men of the races of Nahasi and Nahmou, bound hand and foot, so that Cleopatra deserved literally the epithet of 'she who treads on the peoples' which the royal cartouches give her.

It was the hour for the bath. Cleopatra went there with her women.

Cleopatra's baths were built in vast gardens filled with mimosas, carob-trees, aloes, lemon-trees, Persian apple-trees, the luxuriant freshness of which made a delicious contrast with the sterility of the surroundings; immense terraces sustained groves of verdure, and raised the flowers up to the sky by gigantic stairways of rose granite; vases of Pentelic marble spread like huge lilies on the side of each step, and the plants they contained, seemed only their pistils; chimæras caressed by the chisels of the most able Greek sculptors, of a less repulsive appearance than the Egyptian sphinxes with their surly faces and their morose attitudes, were lying at ease on the turf all studded with flowers, like graceful white greyhounds on a drawing-room carpet; there were charming figures of women, their noses straight, their foreheads smooth, their mouths little, their arms delicately rounded, their throats round and pure, with ear-pendants, collars, and ornaments, capricious and adorable, bifurcating into a fish's tail like the woman of whom Horace spoke, unfurling on the wings of a bird, widening into the flanks of a lioness, twisting into a volute of foliage, according to the fantasy of the artist or the suitability of the architectural position: a double row of these delicious monsters bordered the alley that led from the palace to the bath-chamber.

At the end of this alley a large swimming pool was reached with four stairways of porphyry; through the transparency of the chrystalline water the steps could be seen going down to the bottom sanded with powdered gold; women, ending in sheaths like caryatides, spouted from their breasts a stream of perfumed water, which fell into the pool in a silver dew, dimpling the clear mirror with little crackling drops. In addition to this use the caryatides had in addition the other of supporting on their heads an entablature adorned with nereids and tritons in bas-relief and supplied with a bronze ring to which to attach the silken cords of the awning. Beyond the gateway was seen greenery, damp and blue-tinted, shady bowers of coolness, a bit of the vale of Tempe transplanted into Egypt. The famous gardens of Semiramis were nothing compared to these.

We shall not speak of the seven or eight other chambers at different temperatures, with their hot and cold vapours, their boxes of perfume, their cosmetics, their oils, their pumice-stone, their horsehair gloves, and all the refinements of the ancient art of bathing pushed to such a high degree of voluptuousness and luxury.

Cleopatra arrived, her hand on Charmion's shoulder; she had walked at least thirty steps alone! a mighty effort! an enormous fatigue! A slight shade of rose, spreading under the transparent skin of her cheeks, freshened their passionate pallor; on her temples, fair as amber, was seen a network of blue veins; her level brow, low like the brows of the olden times, but perfect in its roundness and form, joined by an irreproachable line to a severe straight nose, like a cameo, intersected by rosy nostrils that palpitated at the least emotion like the nostrils of a tigress in love; the little mouth, round, very close to the nose, had its lip scornfully arched; but an unbridled voluptuousness, an incredible ardour for life, gleamed in the red splendour and the moist lustre of the lower lip. Her eyes had straight lids, the eyebrows narrow and almost without inflection. We shall not try to give an idea of them; it was a fire, a languor, a glittering limpidity, enough to turn the head of Anubis' dog himself; each look of her eyes was a poem finer than that of Homer or Mimnermus; an imperial chin, full of force and domination, worthily finished off this charming profile.

She stood erect on the first step of the pool, in an attitude full of grace and pride; slightly curving backwards, her foot raised like a goddess about to quit her pedestal whose eyes are still in the sky. Two superb folds hung from the points of her bosom, and flowed in a single line of the ground. Cleomenes, if he had been her contemporary, and if he could have seen her, would have broken his Venus in pieces in disgust.

Before entering the water, touched by a new whim, she asked Charmion to change her head-dress of silver net; she wanted rather a crown of lotus flowers and reeds, like a sea goddess. Charmion obeyed, her hair flowed free, and fell in black cascades on her shoulders, and hung in clusters like ripe grapes along her lovely cheeks.

Then the linen tunic, held only by a golden brooch, was loosened, slipped down her marble body, and lay collapsed in a white cloud at her feet like the swan at the feet of Leda.

And Meïamoun, where was he?

Oh, cruelty of fate! So many insensible objects were enjoying favours that would ravish a lover with joy. The wind that plays with perfumed locks or gives to fair lips kisses which it cannot appreciate, the water which is absolutely indifferent to this voluptuousness, and which covers with a single caress the lovely adored body, the mirror which reflects so many charming pictures, the cothurnus or the *tatbeb* which encloses a divine little foot; ah! how many lost happinesses!

Cleopatra dipped her vermilion heel in the water, and descended several steps; the trembling water made her a girdle and bracelet of silver, and rolled in pearls on her breast and shoulders like an unstrung necklace; her long hair, uplifted by the water, spread behind her like a royal mantle: she was queen even in the bath. She came and went, diving and bringing up in her hands from the bottom handfuls of powdered gold which she threw laughing to some of her women; at other times she hung from the balustrade of the pool hiding and revealing her treasures, now letting no more than her polished, lustrous back be seen, now showing herself complete like Venus Anadyomene and varying ceaselessly the aspects of her beauty.

Suddenly she uttered a cry more sharp than that of Diana surprised by Actæon; she had seen through the foliage a burning eyeball gleam, yellow and phosphorescent like the eye of a crocodile or of a lion.

It was Meïamoun who, crouching on the earth, behind a tuft of leaves, more breathless thcn a fawn among the corn, was growing intoxicated with the dangerous good fortune of seeing the queen in her bath. Though he was courageous to the extent of temerity, the cry of Cleopatra entered his heart colder than the blade of a sword: a mortal sweat covered all his body; his arteries beat in his temples with a strident noise; the iron hand of anxiety pressed his throat and stifled him.

The eunuchs ran up, lance in hand. Cleopatra showed them the group of trees where they found Meïamoun, squat and cowering on the ground. Defence was impossible; he did not attempt it, and let himself be taken. They got ready to kill him with the cruel and stupid impassibility which characterizes eunuchs; but Cleopatra, who had had time to wrap herself in her calasiris, signed to them with her hand to stop and to bring the prisoner to her.

Meïamoun could only fall on his knees and stretch out suppliant hands to her as to the altar of the gods.

'Are you some assassin bribed by Rome; and what do you come to do in these sacred grounds where men are forbidden?' said Cleopatra with an imperious gesture of interrogation.

'May my soul be found light in the balances of Amenthi, and may Ymeï, daughter of the Sun and goddess of Truth, punish me if ever I had against you, O Queen, an evil thought,' answered Meïamoun, still on his knees.

Sincerity and loyalty shone on his face in characters so transparent that Cleopatra immediately abandoned this thought, and fixed on the young Egyptian a less severe and irritated look; she found him handsome.

'Well, then, what reason drove you to a place where you could meet nothing but death?'

'I love you,' said Meïamoun in a low voice but distinctly; for his courage came back, as it does in all extreme situations which nothing can make worse.

'Ah!' said Cleopatra, leaning towards him and seizing his arm with a brusque and sudden movement. 'It is you who shot the arrow with the papyrus roll; by Oms, the god of the lower world, you are a very daring wretch! I recognize you now; for a long time I have seen you wandering like a plaintive shade round the spots I inhabit. You were at the procession of Isis, at the panegyry of Hermonthis; you followed the royal cange.

Ah! you must have a queen! You have no mediocre ambitions; you expected doubtless to have your reward at once. Certainly I am going to love you. Why not?'

'Queen,' answered Meïamoun with an air of grave melancholy, 'do not jest. I am out of my wits, it is true. I have deserved death, that is true too; be human, kill me.'

'No, I have the whim to be merciful to-day. I give you your life.'

'What do you expect me to do with life? I love you.'

'Well! you shall be satisfied; you shall die,' answered Cleopatra. 'You have dreamed a strange extravagant dream; your desires have passed in imagination an unapproachable threshold, you thought that you were Cæsar or Mark Antony; you loved the queen! In certain hours of delirium you have believed that in the suite of circumstances that occur only once in a thousand years, Cleopatra would one day love you. Well, what you believed impossible is going to be accomplished; I am going to make your dream a reality; it pleases me, for once, to crown a mad hope. It is my wish to flood you with splendour, with sunbeams and lightning. It is my wish that your fortune be dazzling. You were at the bottom of the wheel, I am going to put you on top, brusquely, suddenly, without transition. I take you from nothingness: I make you the equal of a god, and I replunge you into nothingness; that 's all, but do not come to me and call me cruel, implore my pity; do not weaken when the hour strikes. I am kind, I lend myself to your folly; I would have the right to have you killed at once; but you say that you love me; I shall have you killed to-morrow; your life for a night. I am generous, I buy it from you, I could have taken it. But what are you doing at my feet? Rise and give me your hand to go into the palace.'

VI

Our world is indeed small beside the old world, our feats are shabby beside the fearful sumptuousness of the Roman patricians and the princes of Asia; their ordinary meals would pass to-day for unlicensed orgies, and the whole of a modern city would live for a week on the dessert of Lucullus when he supped with some intimate friends. We, with our miserable habits, have difficulty in conceiving those enormous existences, that realized all recklessness, strangeness, and the most monstrous impossibilities that the imagination can invent. Our palaces are stables where Caligula would not have wanted to stable his horse; the richest of our constitutional kings does not keep up the state of a petty satrap or a Roman proconsul. The radiant suns that shone on the earth are for ever extinguished in the nothingness of uniformity; there rise no more on the black ant-heap of men those colossi in Titan's shape who crossed the world in three steps like Homer's horses; there are no more towers of Lylacq, no more giant Babels scaling the sky with infinite spirals, no more inordinate temples made with quarters of mountains, or royal terraces that each century and each people can only raise one layer higher, whence the prince, leaning meditatively on his elbow, can see the whole face of the world like an unrolled map; no more of those confused cities, composed of an inextricable heap of Cyclopean edifices, with their deep circumvallations, their circuses bellowing night and day, their reservoirs filled with sea water, and peopled with leviathans and whales, their colossal flights of stairs, their superimposed terraces, their towers with the coping bathed in clouds, their giant palaces, their aqueducts, their heaving cities and their gloomy necropolises! Alas, nothing more than hives of plaster are left us on a chequer-board of paving-stones!

People are astonished that men did not revolt against these confiscations of all the wealth and all the living force to the profit of a certain few privileged people, and that such exorbitant fantasies did not meet obstacles on their bloody way. The reason is, that these prodigious existences were the realization under the sun of the dream that all of us dream at night; the personification of the common thought, and that the people saw themselves living in symbol under one of these meteoric names which blaze inextinguishably in the night of the ages. To-day, deprived of this glowing spectacle of the all-powerful will, of this high contemplation of a human soul whose slightest desire is translated into unheard-of actions, into granite and bronze enormities, the world is absolutely and desperately bored; mankind is no longer represented in its imperial fantasy.

The story we are writing, and the great name of Cleopatra which figures in it, have plunged us into those reflections which displease a civilized ear. But the spectacle of the ancient world is something so overwhelming, so discouraging for imaginations that believe themselves unlicensed, and for spirits that imagine they have attained the last limits of fairy-like magnificence, that we could not refrain from registering here our complaints and regrets that we were not contemporary with Sardanapalus, with Tiglath-Pileser, with Cleopatra, Queen of Egypt, or even of Heliogabalus, Emperor of Rome and Priest of the Sun.

We have to describe a supreme orgy, a feast that threw Belshazzar's into the shade, a night with Cleopatra. How, in the French language, so chaste, so glacially prude, shall we describe this frantic outburst, this mighty, powerful debauch that was not afraid to mingle blood and wine, those two purples, and the furious transports of unsatisfied voluptuousness rushing to the impossible; all the fervour of the senses which the long fast of Christianity has not yet subdued?

The promised night must be a splendid one; it was necessary that all the possible joys of a human existence should be concentrated into a few hours; it was necessary to make of Meïamoun's life a potent elixir which he might drain in a single cup. Cleopatra wished to dazzle her voluntary victim, and to plunge him in a whirlpool of heady pleasures, to intoxicate him, to madden him with the wine of the orgy, so that death, although accepted, should come without being seen or comprehended.

Let us carry our readers into the banquet-hall.

Our present-day architecture offers few points of comparison with those immense buildings whose ruins bear more resemblance to the landslip of a mountain than to the débris of houses. It requires all the exaggeration of ancient life to people and fill those prodigious palaces whose rooms were so vast that they could have no other ceiling than the sky; a magnificent ceiling, and one well worthy of such architecture!

The banquet-hall had enormous Babylonian proportions; the eye could not penetrate its incommensurable depth! monstrous columns, short, squat, solid enough to support the pole, spread heavily out their splayed shafts on pedestals covered with many-coloured hieroglyphics, and sustained on their big-bellied capitals gigantic arcades of granite, advancing by layers like steps set upside-down. Between each pillar a colossal sphinx of basalt, topped by a *pschent*, stretched out its head with oblique eyes and horned chin, and cast on the hall a fixed mysterious gaze. On the second story, behind the first, the capitals of the columns, slimmer than the first, were replaced by four heads of women placed back to back, with the fluted lappets and the twists of the Egyptian head-dress; instead of sphinxes, idols with bull heads, impassive spectators of the nocturnal delirium and the orgiastic revels, were seated in seats of stone like patient guests who are waiting till the feast begins.

A third stage of a different order, with bronze elephants shooting scented water from their trunks, crowned the building; above that the sky opened like a blue gulf, and the curious stars leant over the frieze.

Prodigious stairways of porphyry, so polished that they reflected the body like a mirror, rose up and down in all directions and linked these huge masses of architecture together.

We are only tracing here a rapid sketch to give an idea of the composition of this formidable erection with its proportions beyond all human measure. It would require the brush of Martin, the great painter of vanished mightiness, and we have only a thin penstroke in place of the apocalyptic depth of the black style; but the imagination will fill the void; less lucky than the painter and the musician, we can only present objects one after another. We have only spoken of the banqueting-hall, leaving aside the guests: and at that, we have done no more than indicate it. Cleopatra and Meïamoun are waiting us; here they come.

Meïamoun was clothed in a linen tunic studded with stars, with a purple mantle and bands in his hair like an Oriental king. Cleopatra wore a pale sea-green robe, split at the side, and kept together by golden bees; round her bare arms played two rows of large pearls; on her head gleamed the crown with golden points. In spite of the smile on her lips, a preoccupied shadow lightly brooded over her lovely forehead, and occasionally her eyebrows drew together in a feverish movement. What subject was it that could vex the great queen? As to Meïamoun, he had the glowing, shining look of a man in ecstacy or seeing visions; sparkling emanations, radiating from his temples and his brow, made him a golden halo, like to one of the twelve great gods of Olympus.

A grave profound joy shone on all his features; he had grasped his chimæra of the restless wings, and it had not flown away; he had attained the object of his life. He might live to the age of Nestor or Priam; he might see his temples veined and covered with white hairs like those of the high priest of Ammon; he would experience nothing new, he would learn nothing further. He had been satisfied so abundantly beyond his maddest hopes that the world had nothing more to give him.

Cleopatra made him sit beside her on a throne flanked by golden griffins, and clapped her little hands together. Suddenly lines of fire, twinkling ropes, traced out the projections of the architecture: the eyes of the sphinxes emitted phosphorescent lights, a fiery breath came from the idols' jaws; the elephants, instead of perfumed water, spouted out a reddish jet; bronze arms sprang from the walls with torches in their hands; in the sculptured heart of the lotus expanded glittering plumes.

Broad bluish flames quivered in the brass tripods, giant candelabras shook their dishevelled lights in a blazing mist; everything twinkled and glittered. Prismatic rainbows crossed and broke in the air; the facets of goblets, the angles of marbles and jaspers, the cut edges of vases became spangling, gleaming, or darting lights. Light flowed in torrents and fell from step to step like a waterfall on a stairway of porphyry; you would have said it was the reflection of a fire in a river; if the Queen of Sheba had stepped up there, she would have raised the hem of her dress, thinking she was walking on water as on Solomon's floor of glass. Through this shining fog, the monstrous figures of the colossi, the animals, the hieroglyphics seemed to move and live with a factitious life; the black granite rams grinned ironically and shook their golden horns, the idols breathed noisily through their panting nostrils.

The orgy was at its height; dishes of flamingos' tongues and parrot-fish liver, eels fattened on human flesh and prepared with garum, peacocks' brains, boars stuffed with living birds, and all the marvels of ancient feasts tenfold and a hundred-fold, were heaped up on the three sections of the gigantic triclinium. Wines from Crete, from the Massicus and Falernum, foamed in golden bowls crowned with roses, filled by Asiatic pages whose beautiful floating hair served to wipe dry the hands of the guests. Musicians playing on the Egyptian timbrel, on the dulcimer, on the sambuca, and the harp of twenty-one strings, filled the upper balustrades and flung their harmonious rattle into the tempest of noise that floated round the feast; thunder would not have had a voice loud enough to make itself heard.

Meïamoun, his head leaning on Cleopatra's shoulder, felt his reason going from him; the banqueting-hall swayed round him like an immense architectural nightmare; he saw, through his bedazzlement, endless perspectives and colonnades; new zones of porticos were superimposed on the real ones, and soared into the skies to heights to which Babels have never attained. If he had not felt in his hand the soft cool hand of Cleopatra, he would have believed himself transported into a world of enchantment by a Thessalian sorcerer, or a Persian magician.

Towards the end of the repast, humpbacked dwarfs and morions executed grotesque dances and combats; the young Egyptian and Grecian girls, representing the black and the white hours, danced in the Ionian mode, a voluptuous dance performed with inimitable perfection.

Cleopatra herself rose from her throne, flung down her royal mantle, replaced her sidereal diadem by a garland of flowers, adjusted her golden castanets to her alabaster hands, and began to dance before Meïamoun, lost in ravishment. Her lovely arms, rounded like the handles of a marble vase, shook down above her head clusters of twinkling notes, and her castanets prattled with an ever-growing volubility. Raised on the vermilion tips of her little feet, she advanced quickly and came to brush the brow of Meïamoun with a kiss; then she recommenced her manœuvres and flitted round him, sometimes curving backwards, her head thrown back, her eyes half-closed, her arms swooning and dead, her hair unbound and hanging like a bacchante's on Mount Mænalus swayed by her god; sometimes gay, alert, laughing, fluttering, tireless, and more capricious in her meanders than a pillaging bee. The love of the heart, the voluptuousness of the senses, ardent passion, inexhaustible fresh youth, the promise of approaching felicity, she expressed them all.

The shamefast stars looked no longer, their chaste golden eyeballs could not bear such a sight; the sky itself was hid, and a dome of inflamed mist covered the hall.

Cleopatra returned to seat herself near Meïamoun. The night wore on; the last of the black hours was about to fly away; the sky itself was hid; a bluish glimmer entered with perplexed step among this tumult of red lights, like a moonbeam that falls on a furnace: the high arcades grew softly blue; day was appearing.

Meïamoun took the horn vase that an Ethiopian slave of sinister aspect presented to him, a vase which contained a poison so potent that it would have shattered any other vessel. Throwing his life to his mistress in a last look, he carried to his lips the fatal cup where the poisoned liquor boiled and hissed.

Cleopatra grew pale, and put her hand on Meïamoun's arm to stay him. His courage touched her; she was going to say, 'Live on to love me; I desire it——', when the blast of bugles was heard. Four heralds at arms entered on horseback into the banqueting-hall. It was Mark Antony's officers who preceded their master by a few steps. Silently she dropped Meïamoun's arm. A sunbeam came to play on Cleopatra's forehead as if to replace her absent diadem.

'You see that the moment has come; it is the hour when lovely dreams fly away,' said Meïamoun.

Then he drank at a single draught the fatal vase and fell as if struck by lightning. Cleopatra bent her head, and in the cup a burning tear, the only one she had shed in her life, went to join the melted pearl.

'By Hercules! my lovely queen, it was no use my making haste, I see that I have come too late,' said Mark Antony, as he entered the banqueting-hall: 'the supper is finished. But what is the meaning of this body lying on the flag-stones?'

'Oh, nothing,' said Cleopatra, smiling. 'It 's a poison I was experimenting with to be ready for myself if Octavius took me a prisoner. Would it amuse you, my dear lord, to sit beside me and watch these Greek buffoons dance?'

FANFARLO

Charles Baudelaire

Samuel Cramer, who formerly, under the signature of Manuela de Monteverde, was responsible for a few romantic follies—in the hey-day of romanticism—is the contradictory product of a pallid German and dark Chilean mother. Add to this double origin a French upbringing and a literary civilization, and the queer complications of his character will be less surprising to you—if they do not satisfy or edify you. Samuel has a pure and noble brow, eyes as brilliant as drops of coffee, a teasing and mocking nose, impudent and sensual lips, a square despotic chin and pretentiously republican hair. He is at once very lazy, mournfully ambitious, and illustriously unfortunate; for all his life he has scarcely ever had any complete ideas. The sun of his idleness which shines with constant splendour within him, vaporizes and consumes that moiety of genius with which Heaven has endowed him. Among all those demi-great men whom I have known in this terrible Parisian life, Samuel was, more than any other, the man of beautiful abortive works: a sickly fantastic creature, whose poetry shines much more in his person than in his works, and who towards one o'clock in the morning, between the blaze of a coal fire and the tic-toc of a clock, always appeared to me like the God of Impotence—a modern hermaphroditic god—Impotence so colossal and so enormous that it becomes epic.

How can I explain, how can I let you clearly see the depths of that tenebrous nature, striped with vivid lightning flashes, lazy and at the same time enterprising, fertile in difficult schemes and in ridiculous abortions; a mind in which paradox often assumed the proportions of naïveté, yet whose imagination was as vast as absolute solitude and laziness? One of Samuel's most natural foibles was to consider himself the equal of those whom he had contrived to admire. After passionately reading a fine book his involuntary conclusion was: 'Here 's something fine enough to be my own!' and from that to thinking, 'Therefore it is my own', is merely a matter of omitting the inverted commas.

In the world of to-day a character of this type is more common than one thinks; the streets, the public walks, the estaminets, and all the refuges of idlers swarm with creatures of this sort. They identify themselves so completely with the latest model, as to believe almost that they have invented it. To-day you find them painfully deciphering the mystic pages of Plotinus or Porphyry; to-morrow they will admire how well Crébillon the younger has expressed the French and flighty side of their nature. Yesterday they were conversing familiarly with Jerome Cardan; now they are playing with Sterne or wallowing with Rabelais in all the gluttony of hyperbole. Besides, they are so happy in each of their metamorphoses that they are not in the slightest annoyed with all those fine geniuses for having anticipated them in the esteem of posterity. What naïve and respectable impudence! Such was poor Samuel.

By birth a very gentlemanly fellow, and a bit of a rogue for diversion—an actor by temperament—he played, for his private benefit and *in camera*, incomparable tragedies, or rather tragi-comedies. If the wing of gaiety brushed and tickled him, he had, of course, to impress the fact upon himself, so our man used to practise bursting into fits of laughter. Did a tear but well up in the corner of his eye at some memory, he went to the mirror to watch himself cry. If some trollop in a fit of brutal and childish jealousy scratched him with a penknife or a needle, Samuel glorified it into a dagger thrust, and when he owed a few wretched twenty thousand francs he used to shout joyously:

'What a sad and lamentable fate to be a genius harassed by a million of debts!'

By the way, please don't believe that he was incapable of knowing true sentiments, or that passion merely brushed his epidermis. He would have sold his shirt for an almost complete stranger whose hands and countenance he had examined and yesterday made his bosom friend. To the things of the mind and soul he brought the idle contemplativeness of Germanic natures; to matters of passion, the rapid and fickle ardour of his mother; and to the practice of life all the foibles of French vanity. He would have fought a duel for an author or an artist two centuries dead. Just as he had been furiously devout, he was passionately atheistic. He was at once all the artists he had studied and all the books he had read, and yet, despite this protean faculty, he remained profoundly original. He was always the gentle, the fantastic, the lazy, the terrible, the erudite, the ignorant, the Bohemian, the dandy Samuel Cramer, the romantic Manuela de Monteverde. He raved over a friend as over a woman, loved a woman as a comrade. He possessed the logic of all the good sentiments, and the science of all sorts of knavishness, and nevertheless he never succeeded in anything because he believed too much in the impossible. Why should it be astonishing? He was always conceiving the impossible.

Samuel, one evening, hit on the idea of going out; it was beautiful, scented weather. He had, in accordance with his natural taste for the excessive, equally violent and prolonged habits of seclusion and dissipation, and for a long time he had remained faithful to his house. The maternal laziness, the Creole love of doing nothing which flowed in his veins prevented him from finding anything intolerable in the disorder of his room, his linen, and his greasy, excessively tangled hair. He combed it, washed himself, managed in a few moments to recover the dress and aplomb of people for whom elegance is an every-day affair; then he opened the window. The warm golden light rushed into the dusty study. Samuel was astonished to see how quickly and noiselessly spring had come. A mild air, impregnated with sweet odours, made his nostrils twitch. One part of it mounting to his brain filled him with dreaminess and desires, the other naughtily stirred his heart, his stomach and his liver. Resolutely, he blew out his two candles, one of which was still palpitating on a volume of Swedenborg, and the other flickered out on one of those shameful books the reading of which is profitable only to minds possessed of an immoderate taste for truth.

From the height of his solitude, cluttered with documents, paved with old books and peopled with his dreams, Samuel often observed whilst walking in an *allée* of the Luxembourg, a face and form which he had loved in the provinces, at an age when one really loves. Her features, though matured and blunted by some years of use, had the profound and decent grace of the respectable woman; in the depths of her eyes there still shone occasionally a humid, virginal dreaminess. She used to come and go, always escorted by quite a smart maid, whose face and demeanour revealed the confidante and companion rather than the servant. She seemed to seek out the deserted spots, and used to sit down sadly in widow-like attitudes, absently holding in her hand a book which she did not read.

Samuel had known her in the neighbourhood of Lyons, when she was young, alert, sprightly and thinner. By dint of watching her, and so to speak recognizing her, he had revived one by one all the tiny memories which attracted him to her in his imagination: he had recounted to himself, detail by detail, the whole of this youthful romance, which since that time had lost itself in the preoccupations of his life and in the labyrinth of his passions.

On that particular evening he raised his hat to her with more care and ceremony. Passing in front of her he heard behind him this snatch of dialogue.

'What do you think of that young man, Mariette?'

But this was said in such an absent-minded tone that the most malicious observer could have found no fault with the lady.

'Oh, I think he is very nice, madame. Madame knows that it is M. Samuel Cramer?'

And more severely:

'Now how do you happen to know that, Mariette?'

That is why next day Samuel took great care to bring her back her handkerchief and her book, which he found on a bench, and which she had not lost, since she was close at hand watching the sparrows squabbling for crumbs, or seeming to contemplate the inner workings of the vegetation. As often happens between two beings whose souls by a complicity of destiny have been brought into tune with one another, opening the conversation rather abruptly, he had, nevertheless, the good fortune to find a person disposed to listen and to reply to him.

'Is it possible, madame, that I am fortunate enough to be still esconced in a corner of your memory? Have I changed so much that you cannot recognize in me a comrade of your childhood with whom you deigned to play at hide-and-seek, and to play truant?'

'A woman', replied the lady with a half smile, 'has not the right to remember people so easily; that is why I thank you, sir, for being the first to afford me the opportunity of recalling those beautiful and joyous memories. And then—each year of life contains so many events and thoughts—and really it seems to me that it is many years ago?'

'Years,' replied Samuel, 'which for me have been sometimes very slow, sometimes very quick to flee away, but all diversely cruel!'

'And poetry?' said the lady with a smile in her eyes.

'Always, madame!' replied Samuel laughing. 'But what is that you are reading?'

'A novel of Walter Scott's.'

'Now I understand your frequent interruptions. Oh, what a tiresome writer! A dusty unearther of chronicles! A wearisome pile of description and bric-à-brac, a heap of all sorts of old things and costumes: armour, crockery, furniture, Gothic inns and melodramatic castles, through which stalk a few puppets on strings, dressed in motley doublet and hose; hackneyed types which no eighteen-year-old plagiarist will look at in ten years; impossible ladies and lovers completely devoid of actuality, no truth of the heart, no philosophy of the sentiments! How different from our good French novelists, where passion and morality are always preferred to the material descriptions of objects! What does it matter whether the lady wears ruff or panniers or an Oudinot underskirt provided she sobs or betrays properly? Does the lover interest you much more because he carries a dagger in his waistcoat instead of a visiting card, and does a despot in a black coat terrify you less poetically than a tyrant encased in leather and mail?'

Samuel, as you see, was drifting into the category of *intense* people, intolerable and passionate men whose profession ruins their conversation, and for whom every occasion is a good one, even an acquaintanceship struck up under some tree or at some street corner—were it with a rag-picker—obstinately to develop their ideas. The only difference between commercial travellers, roving industrials, hopeful commission agents, and *intense* poets is the difference between advertising and preaching; the latter vice is quite disinterested.

Now, the lady answered him simply.

'My dear Monsieur Samuel, I am merely the public, that is sufficient to tell you that I have an innocent soul. Consequently pleasure is for me the easiest thing in the world to find. But let's talk of yourself: I should esteem myself fortunate were you to judge me worthy of reading some of your productions.'

'But, madame, how does it happen——?' exclaimed the swollen vanity of the astonished poet.

'The proprietor of my circulating library says that he does not know you!'

And she smiled sweetly as if to deaden the effect of this fleeting, teasing thrust.

'Madame,' said Samuel sententiously, 'the true public of the nineteenth century is the women; your support will make me greater than twenty academies.'

'Well, sir, I count on your promise. Mariette, the parasol and the scarf. *Somebody* is perhaps getting impatient at home. You know your master is coming back early.'

She made him a graceful, abrupt little bow, which was not in the slightest compromising, and the familiarity of which was not without a certain dignity.

Samuel was in no wise astonished to discover a former youthful love chained by the conjugal tie. In the universal history of sentiment, that is in order. She was called Madame de Cosmelly and lived in one of the most aristocratic streets in the Faubourg Saint-Germain.

Next day he found her, head inclined, in a graceful, almost studied melancholy, towards the flowers in the border, and he offered her his volume of *The Ospreys*, a collection of sonnets such as we all have written, and all have read in the days when our judgment was so short and our hair so long.

Samuel was very curious to know whether his *Ospreys* had charmed this beautiful melancholy soul, and whether the screams of these nasty birds had disposed her favourably towards him; but a few days later she said to him with despairing candour and honesty:

'Sir, I am only a woman, and consequently my judgment is of little account; but it seems to me that the sorrows and loves of authors have very little resemblance to the sorrows and loves of other men. You address gallantries, excellent no doubt and exquisitely chosen, to ladies whom I esteem sufficiently to believe that they must sometimes be frightened by them. You sing of the beauty of mothers in a style which is bound to deprive you of their daughters' suffrage. You inform the world that you are madly in love with the foot or hand of Madame So-and-so, who, let us suppose for her honour, spends less time in reading you than in knitting stockings and mittens for the feet and hands of her children. By a most peculiar contrast, the mysterious cause of which is still unknown to me, you reserve your most mystic incense for queer creatures who read still less than ladies, and you go into Platonic ecstasies before low-born sultanas who, it seems to me, at the sight of the delicate person of a poet must open eyes as big as those of cattle awakening in a conflagration. Again, I do not know why you are so fond of funereal subjects, and anatomical descriptions. When one is young, and when, like you, one possesses fine talent and all the presumed conditions of happiness, it seems to me much more natural to celebrate health and the joys of decent men than to practise anathemas and talking with *Ospreys*.'

This was his reply to her:

'Madame, pity me, or rather pity us, for I have many brothers of my kind; it is hatred of all the world and of ourselves which led us to those lies. It is from despair at not being noble and beautiful according to natural means, that we have so strangely painted our faces. We were so busy sophisticating our hearts, we have so much abused the microscope to study the hideous excrescences and the shameful warts with which they are covered, growths we arbitrarily magnify, that it is impossible for us to speak the language of other men. They live for the sake of living, and we, alas! we live for the sake of knowledge. There lies the whole mystery. Age changes but the voice, destroying only the teeth and hair: we have altered the accent of nature, one by one, we have eradicated the virginal purities with which our innate decency bristled. We psychologized like madmen who increase their mania by striving to understand it. The years merely distort the limbs, and we have deformed the passions. Woe, thrice woe to the weakly sires who made us rickety and abnormal, predestined as we are to give birth only to still-born offspring!'

'More *Ospreys*!' said she. 'Come, give me your arm and let us admire the poor flowers the spring has made so happy!'

Instead of admiring the flowers, Samuel Cramer, whose phase and period had arrived, began to turn into prose and to declaim a few bad stanzas composed in his first manner. The lady let him run on.

'What a difference there is, and how little is left of the same man, save the memory! But memory is only a fresh suffering. What a beautiful time was that when morning never found us with knees stiff and racked by the fatigue of dreams, when our bright eyes laughed at all nature; when our sighs flowed gently without noise or pride! How many times in the leisure of imagination I have seen again one of those beautiful autumnal evenings when young souls make progress comparable to those trees which shoot up several handbreadths in a thunderstorm. Then I see, I feel, I understand! The moon awakens the big moths; the warm wind opens the petals of the *belles-de-nuit*; the water sleeps in the great fountains. Listen in spirit to the sudden valses of that mysterious piano. The perfumes of the storm come in at the windows; it is the hour when the gardens are full of pink and white dresses that do not fear the rain. The complaisant bushes catch at the fleeting skirts; dark hair and blond curls mingle in a whirling dance. Do you remember, madame, the enormous haystacks, so swift for sliding down, the old nurse so slow to pursue you, and the bell so prompt to call you back to your aunt's watchful eye, in the great dining-room?'

Madame de Cosmelly interrupted Samuel by a sigh, made as if to open her lips, no doubt to beg him to stop, but he had already resumed.

'The most desolating thing of all,' he said, 'is that every love always ends badly, all the more badly the more divine, the more winged was its beginning. There is no dream, however ideal, which one does not rediscover with a greedy brat fastened to its breasts; there is no retreat, no cottage however delightful and secluded which the pickaxe does not raze to the ground. And yet this destruction is quite material: but there is another, more pitiless and more secret, which attacks invisible things. Imagine at the moment when you lean upon the being of your choice and say: "Let us flee together and seek the depths of the sky!" an implacable and serious voice broods over your ear to tell you that our passions are liars, that it is our short-sightedness that creates the beautiful faces, and our ignorance the beautiful souls, and that necessarily there comes a day when the idol, for more clairvoyant eyes, is now a mere object, not of hatred, but of contempt and astonishment.'

'For mercy's sake sir!' said Madame de Cosmelly.

At the same time she was moved; Samuel had noticed that he had thrust the steel into an old wound, and he persisted cruelly.

'Madame,' he said, 'the salutary sufferings of the memory have their charms, and, in this intoxication of grief, one sometimes finds a solace. At this funereal warning, all loyal souls would cry: "Lord, take me hence with my dream intact and pure: I want to give back to nature my passion with all its virginity, and carry elsewhere my unwithered crown". Besides, the results of disillusion are terrible. The sickly children of a dying love are sad debauch and hideous impotence; debauch of the mind, impotence of the heart, the result of which is that the one no longer lives save from curiosity, and the other pines away daily from lassitude. All of us resemble more or less some traveller who has traversed a great country, and each evening watches the sun, which once superbly gilded the beauties of the route, go down in a drab horizon. Resignedly, he sits down on dirty hills covered with unknown litter and says to the perfumes of the heather that it is no use their rising towards the empty heaven; to the sparse and wretched seeds that it is no use sprouting in a dried-up soil; to the birds which think their marriages blessed by someone, that they are wrong to build nests in a country swept by cold and violent winds. Sadly he goes on his way towards a desert which he knows is similar to that just traversed, escorted by a pale ghost called Reason, which, with pale lantern, lights the aridity of his road, and, to quench the ever rising thirst of passion that seizes him from time to time, pours into him the poison of ennui.'

Suddenly, hearing a deep sigh and a repressed sob, he turned again towards Madame de Cosmelly. She was weeping copiously and had no longer the strength to hide her tears.

For some time he considered her in silence, with the most sympathetic and the most unctuous air he could assume: the brutal and hypocritic actor was proud of those beautiful tears; he considered them as his work and his literary property. He was mistaken as to the inward meaning of this grief, just as Madame de Cosmelly, drowned in this candid desolation, was mistaken as to the purport of his look. It was a peculiar play of misunderstandings, as a result of which Samuel Cramer, with a decisive gesture, stretched out both his hands, which she took with tender confidence.

'Madame,' continued Samuel, after some moments of silence, the classic silence of emotion, 'true wisdom consists less in malediction than in hope. Without the truly divine gift of hope, how could we cross the hideous desert of ennui which I have just described to you? The ghost which accompanies us is really a ghost of reason; one can drive him away by sprinkling him with the holy water of the first theological virtue. There is an amiable philosophy which contrives to find consolations in the apparently most unworthy objects. Just as virtue is better than innocence, and as there is more merit in sowing a desert than in carelessly rifling the sweets of a fruitful orchard, so it is really worthy of a choice soul to purify itself and to purify its neighbour by contact. As there is no treachery one does not forgive, there is no fault for which one cannot obtain absolution, no oversight which one cannot remedy; there is a science of loving one's neighbour and finding him lovable, as there is a science of correct living.

'The more delicate a mind is, the more original beauties it discovers; the more tender a soul, the more open to divine hope, the more reasons for love it finds in others, however sullied they may be; this is the work of charity, and more than one traveller, desolate and lost in the arid deserts of disillusionment, has been seen to reconquer faith and fall more deeply in love with what she had lost, and with all the more reason, since she then possesses the knowledge of how to direct her passion, and that of her beloved.'

Little by little Madame de Cosmelly's face had lit up; her sadness shone with hope like a watery sun, and scarcely had Samuel finished his speech than she said to him quickly and with the naïve candour of a child:

'Is it really true that this is possible, and that there are branches so easy to seize for those in despair?'

'But certainly, madame!'

'Ah, what a happy woman you would make me if you would please teach me your recipes!'

'Nothing easier,' he replied brutally.

In the midst of this sentimental marivaudage, confidence had arrived and indeed had joined the hands of the two characters; so much so that after some hesitations and little prudish gestures which to Samuel appeared very promising, Madame de Cosmelly in her turn took him into her confidence, beginning thus:

'I understand everything that a poetic soul can suffer from this isolation, and how quickly a spiritual ambition like yours must consume itself in its solitude; but your griefs, which belong to none but you, come, as far as I have been able to discern through the pomp of your language, from strange and unsatisfied needs which are almost impossible to satisfy. You suffer, it is true; but possibly your suffering constitutes your grandeur, and is as necessary to you as happiness is to others. Now will you deign to listen to and sympathize with sorrows more easy to understand, a provincial grief? M. Cramer, I expect from you, the scholar, the man of wit, the advice and perhaps the help of a friend.

'You know that at the time you knew me, I was a good little girl, already a little dreamy like you, but timid and obedient, that I looked at myself in the mirror less often than you did, and that I always hesitated to eat or pocket the peaches and grapes you went boldly and stole for me in our neighbours' orchards. To me a pleasure was never really agreeable and complete save in so far as it was permitted, and I much preferred kissing a nice boy like you in front of my old aunt than in the middle of the fields. The coquetry and the attention that every marriageable girl ought to pay to her person only came to me later. When I could almost sing a romance at the piano they dressed me with more care, they forced me to stand up straight; they made me do gymnastics and forbade me to spoil my hands planting flowers or bringing up birds. I was allowed to read other things than Berquin and taken in evening dress to the local theatre to hear bad operas.

'When M. de Cosmelly came to the château, I at once took a great liking to him. Comparing his flourishing youth with my grandmother's rather carping old age, I thought he looked noble and upright, and his attitude towards me was one of the most respectful gallantry. Then they talked of wonderful things he had done; his arm smashed in a duel for a rather cowardly friend who had entrusted him with his sister's honour, enormous sums lent to old and penniless comrades, and I don't know what else. He had with everybody a commanding air, both affable and irresistible, which won me over too. How had he lived before leading this château life with us? Had he known other pleasures then than those of hunting with me, or singing virtuous romances on my bad piano? Had he had mistresses? Of that I knew nothing, and I never even dreamed of inquiring. I began to love him with all the credulousness of a girl who has never had time to make comparisons, and I married him, which pleased my aunt very much indeed. When I was his wife in the eyes of the Church and of God, I loved him still more. I loved him far too much, of course. Was I wrong, was I right? Who can tell? I was happy in that love, and I was wrong not to realize that it might be disturbed. Did I know him well before marrying him? Of course not; but it seems to me that one can no more accuse a nice girl who wants to get married for making an unwise choice than an abandoned woman for taking a cad for a lover. Both of us—wretched creatures that we are—are equally ignorant. What these unfortunate victims called marriageable girls need is a shameful education—I mean the knowledge of men's vices. I should like each one of those poor little things, before assuming the marriage tie, to hear in some secret place, without being seen, two men talking together about the things of life and especially about women. After that first and formidable test they could abandon themselves with less danger to the terrible hazard of marriage, knowing the strength and weakness of their future tyrants.'

Samuel did not exactly see what this charming victim was driving at, but he began to find that she was talking too much about her husband for a disillusioned woman.

After a pause of a few moments as if she feared to approach the fatal spot, she resumed thus:

'One day M. de Cosmelly wanted to return to Paris; it was necessary that I should shine in my own light and be in a setting worthy of my merit. A beautiful and clever woman, he said, owes herself to Paris. She must know how to pose before society, and shed some of her reflected light on her husband. A woman of noble mind and good sense knows that she has no glory to expect in the world save in so far as she shares the glory of her travelling companion, serves the virtues of her husband, and above all, that she obtains respect only in so far as she makes him respected. Of course, it was the simplest, surest way of getting himself obeyed almost joyously. To know that my efforts and my obedience would make me more beautiful in his eyes: it did not require even as much as that to decide me to face this terrible Paris, of which I was instinctively afraid, and the black, dazzling ghost of which, looming on the horizon of my dreams, sent a shudder through my poor girlish heart. That then, according to him, was the real reason for our journey. A husband's vanity constitutes the virtue of a loving wife. Perhaps he was lying to himself in a sort of well-meaning way, and cheating his conscience without being aware of it. In Paris we had days reserved for close friends of whom, in the long run, M. de Cosmelly got bored as he had got bored with his wife. Perhaps he had got a little disgusted with her because she was too loving; she kept none of her love back. He got disgusted with his friends for the opposite reason. They had nothing to offer him save the monotonous pleasures of conversations where passion has no share. Henceforth, his activity took another direction. After his friends came horses and cards. The hum and stir of society, the sight of those who had remained unfettered, and who gave endless accounts of the memories of a mad, busy youth, snatched him from his fireside and our long intimate talks. He who had never had any business but his heart, became a busy man. Rich and without profession, he managed to create a crowd of bustling, frivolous occupations which filled all his time. "Where are you going?" "At what time shall I see you again?" "Come back quickly"—these wifely questions I had to thrust back again down into the depths of my heart: for English life—that death of love—the life of clubs and meetings absorbed him completely. The exclusive care he took of his person, and the dandyism he affected, shocked me to begin with; obviously I was not the object of it. I tried to be like him, to be more than beautiful, that is to say to be coquettish, attractive for him as he was for everybody; where formerly I used to offer everything and give everything, now I wanted to be pleaded with. I wanted to rekindle the ashes of my dead happiness by shaking and stirring them; but apparently I am not very clever at deception, and very awkward at vice. He did not even condescend to notice it. My aunt, cruel like all old and envious women, who are reduced to admiring a show in which they were formerly actresses, took great care to let me know, through the interested medium of a cousin of M. de Cosmelly's, that he had fallen in love with an actress who was then the rage. I made them take me to all the plays, and, at the appearance on the stage of every good-looking woman I trembled lest I was admiring my rival. Finally, by the charity of the same cousin, I learned that it was Fanfarlo, an actress as stupid as she was beautiful. You who are an author, you know her of course. I am not very vain or proud of my looks, but I swear to you, M. Cramer, that many a time at night, about three or four in the morning, tired of waiting for my husband, my eyes red with tears and lack of sleep, after long and beseeching prayers for his return to fidelity and duty, I asked God, my conscience, and my mirror, if I was as beautiful as that wretched Fanfarlo. My mirror and my conscience replied "Yes". God forbade me to be proud of it, but did not forbid me to derive a legitimate victory from the fact. Why, then, between two equal beauties, do men often prefer the flower whose perfume every one has inhaled to that which had always kept aloof from passers-by in the darkest walks of the conjugal garden? Why is it, then, that women who are prodigal with their bodies, a treasure of which only one sultan should have the key, possess more adorers than we others, unfortunate martyrs of a solitary love? What is the magic charm which vice sets like a halo on the brow of certain creatures? What awkward and repulsive aspect does virtue lend to certain others? Tell me, you who from your profession must know all the sentiments of life and their various reasons.'

Samuel had no time to reply, for she continued ardently:

'M. de Cosmelly has very grave things on his conscience if the loss of a young and virginal soul interests the God who created it for the happiness of another. If M. de Cosmelly were to die this very evening he would have a great many pardons to implore; for, by his fault, he has taught his wife dreadful sentiments, suspicion of a loved one, and the thirst for revenge. Ah, monsieur, I spend nights of great sorrow and sleepless anxiety: I pray, I curse, I blaspheme. The priest tells me I must bear my cross with resignation, but you cannot teach resignation to insane love and shattered faith. My confessor is not a woman, and I love my husband; I love him with all the passion and all the grief of a mistress beaten and trodden under foot. There is nothing I have not tried. Instead of the dark and simple dresses that formerly pleased his eye, I have worn dresses as crazy and sumptuous as those of actresses. I, the chaste wife whom he had discovered hidden in an old château, I paraded before him dressed like a courtesan. I made myself witty and gay when death was in my heart. I spangled my despair with glittering smiles. I put on rouge, sir, I put on rouge! You see it is a banal story, the story of all unhappy women, a provincial novel!'

Whilst she was sobbing, Samuel looked like Tartuffe in the grasp of Orgon, the unexpected husband who springs from his hiding place, as the virtuous sobs of the lady sprang from her heart, seizing our poet's tottering hypocrisy by the scruff of the neck.

Madame de Cosmelly's extreme self-abandonment, her freedom and confidence had prodigiously emboldened, without astonishing him. Samuel Cramer, who has often astonished the world, scarcely ever was astonished. In his life he seemed to try to practise and demonstrate the truth of that thought of Diderot's: 'Incredulity is sometimes the vice of a fool, and credulity the defect of a man of wit. The man of wit sees far into the immensity of the possible. The fool scarcely ever conceives as possible anything save what actually is. It is that perhaps which makes the one timid and the other bold'. This is the reply to everything. No doubt some scrupulous readers, who love probable truth, will find many objections to this story, in which, however, all I have had to do was to change the names and accentuate certain details; how is it, they will say, that Samuel Cramer, a poet of doubtful tone and morals, can so quickly approach a woman like Madame de Cosmelly? And how can he, apropos of a Scott novel, flood her with a torrent of romantic and banal poetry? How can Madame de Cosmelly, the discreet and virtuous spouse, pour out to him, without shame or mistrust, the secret of her sorrows? To which I reply that Madame de Cosmelly was a simple, beautiful soul, and that Samuel was bold like all butterflies, cockchafers and poets: he threw himself into all sorts of flames and entered all sorts of windows. Diderot's thought explains why one was so abandoned, and the other so brusque and so shameless. It explains, too, all the blunders Samuel committed in his life, blunders which a fool would not have committed. That portion of the public which is essentially pusillanimous will hardly understand the character of Samuel, who was essentially credulous and imaginative, to the point of believing—as a poet, in his public—as a man, in his own passions.

Now he perceived that this woman was stronger, more precipitous than she seemed, and that he must not dash, bull-headed, at this candid piety. Once more he served up his romantic jargon. Ashamed at having been stupid, he tried to be a roué; for a time he still spoke to her in a jesuitical strain of wounds to be closed or cauterized by opening fresh wounds which would bleed freely and painlessly. Anybody who, without possessing the absolutory power of Valmont or Lovelace, has desired to possess a decent woman who was not very interested, knows with what ridiculous and emphatic awkwardness every one says, showing his heart: 'Take my bear'. This will dispense me from explaining to you how stupid Samuel was. Madame de Cosmelly, that amiable Elmire, who had the clear and prudent vision of virtue, saw promptly what advantage she could gain from this novice of a scoundrel, for her own happiness and for her husband's honour. She therefore paid him in the same coin; she let him squeeze her hand; she spoke of friendship and Platonic matters. She murmured the word, vengeance; she said that in these painful crises of a woman's life, one would willingly give to the avenger whatever was left of a heart abandoned by perfidy, and other dramatic sillinesses and marivaudage. In short, she played the coquette for a worthy purpose, and our young roué, who was simpler than a savant, promised to snatch Fanfarlo from M. de Cosmelly and rid him of the courtesan, hoping to find in the arms of the decent woman the reward of this meritorious work. It is only poets who are naïve enough to invent monstrosities of this sort.

A rather comic detail of this story, a sort of intermezzo to the painful drama which was about to be played between these four characters, was the misunderstanding about Samuel's sonnets; for in the matter of sonnets he was incorrigible; one for Madame de Cosmelly, in which he praised, in mystic style, her Beatrice-like beauty, her voice, the angelic purity of her eyes, the chastity of her gait, etc., the other for Fanfarlo, in which he served her up a ragout of gallantries with enough seasoning to sting the most experienced palate, a type of poetry, by the way, in which he was a past master, and in which he had long ago outstripped the most Andalusian of Andalusians. The first morsel went to the creature, who threw this dish of cucumber into her cigar-box; the second to the poor deserted one, who first stared, then finally understood, and, despite her grief, could not help bursting out laughing as in better days.

Samuel went to the theatre and began to study Fanfarlo on the boards. He found her light, magnificent, vigorous, full of taste in her accoutrements, and considered M. de Cosmelly very lucky to be able to ruin himself for such a piece.

He presented himself twice at her house, a villa with velvety staircase, full of portières and carpets, in a new and leafy district, but under no reasonable pretext could he gain admission. A declaration of love was a profoundly useless and dangerous thing. One rebuff would have prevented him from returning. As for getting himself introduced, he learnt that Fanfarlo never received. A few close friends saw her from time to time. What could he say or do in the house of a dancer magnificently salaried and maintained, and adored by her lover? What could he bring her, he who was neither tailor nor dressmaker, ballet master, or millionaire? He therefore took a brutal and simple decision: Fanfarlo must come to him. At this period, critical and eulogistic articles had more value than now. The *facilities* of the feuilleton, as a worthy lawyer recently said in a sadly celebrated case, were much greater than to-day; a few talented artists having sometimes capitulated to the journalists, the influence of these adventurous and hair-brained youths no longer knew any bounds. So Samuel undertook—he who did not know a word of music—the special work of criticizing lyrical plays.

Henceforth Fanfarlo was weekly and savagely slated in the bottom columns of an important paper. It was impossible to say, or even hint that her legs, ankles, or knees were badly shaped; the muscles played beneath the stocking, and every opera-glass would have cried blasphemy. She was accused of of being brutal, common, devoid of taste, of wanting to import to our stage habits from beyond the Rhine or the Pyrenees, castanets, spurs, high heels, not to mention the fact that she drank like a trooper, was too fond of little dogs and her caretaker's daughter, and other dirty linen of private life which is the daily meat and relish of certain little newspapers. With those tactics peculiar to journalists, who insist on comparing dissimilar things, he held up against her an ethereal dancer, always dressed in white, whose chaste movements left every conscience at rest. Sometimes, Fanfarlo shouted and laughed very loudly to the pit when she finished a bound at the footlights; she dared to walk while dancing. Never did she wear those insipid gauzy dresses which show everything and leave nothing to the imagination. She loved stuffs that made a noise, long, crackling, spangled, tinselled dresses, which have to be lifted very high with a vigorous knee, the kind of corsages worn by mountebanks; she danced not with curls, but with ear-rings, I might say candelabras. She would have liked to have tied a crowd of little dolls to the bottom of her skirts, like those old gipsies who tell your fortune with a threatening air, and who are to be met at high noon under the arcades of Roman ruins; drolleries all of which the romantic Samuel, one of the last romantics possessed by France, very much adored.

So much so, that having run down Fanfarlo for three months, he fell madly in love with her, and she finally wanted to know who was the monster, the heart of bronze, the pedant, the half-wit who so obstinately denied the royalty of her genius.

This much justice must be accorded to Fanfarlo; all that actuated her was idle curiosity, nothing more. Had such a man really a nose in the middle of his face, and was he shaped quite like his fellow-beings? When, after having made one or two inquiries about Samuel, and learnt that he was a man like any other, of some sense and some talent, she understood vaguely that there was some mystery, and that this terrible Monday article might very well be only a peculiar sort of weekly bouquet, or the visiting card of an obstinate suitor.

He found her one evening in her box. Two great candles and a big fire made their lights flicker on the motley costumes which littered this boudoir.

The queen of the place, about to leave the theatre, was reassuming the garb of an ordinary mortal and, crouched in a chair, was putting on her shoes, shamelessly revealing an adorable leg; her hands, plumply slender, made the lace of the buskin play through the eyelet holes like an agile shuttle, without a thought of the skirt which should have been pulled down. The leg was already for Samuel an object of eternal desire. Long, slender, strong, plump yet sinewy, it had all the correctness of the beautiful, and all the wanton allure of the pretty. Had it been dissected perpendicularly at its widest place, this leg would have offered a sort of triangle whose apex would have been situated on the tibia, and of which the rounded line of the calf would have furnished the convex base. A regular man's leg is too hard, the women's legs drawn by Devéria are too soft to give you an idea of it.

In this agreeable attitude, her head, bent towards her foot, displayed a proconsular neck, broad and strong, and allowed one to guess at the line of the shoulder-blades covered with brown abundant flesh. The thick, heavy hair fell forward on both sides, tickling her bosom and blinding her eyes, so that at every other moment she had to disturb and toss it back. A petulant, charming impatience, like that of a spoiled child who finds that things are not going fast enough, animated the whole creature and her clothing, and at every instant disclosed new points of view, new effects of line and colour.

Samuel stopped respectfully, or pretended to stop respectfully; for with this confounded fellow the great problem is always to know where the actor begins.

'Ah! there you are, monsieur!' she said to him without disturbing herself, though she had been told a few minutes previously about Samuel's visit. 'You 've something to ask me, haven't you?'

The sublime impudence of these words went straight to poor Samuel's heart; he had chattered like a romantic magpie for a whole week at Madame de Cosmelly's; here he quietly replied:

'Yes, madame!'

And tears came to his eyes.

That had an enormous success. Fanfarlo smiled.

'And what insect has been stinging you, monsieur, that you bite at me so savagely? What a frightful profession——'

'Frightful indeed, madame. The fact is, I adore you.'

'I thought as much,' replied Fanfarlo. 'But you are a monster. These are abominable tactics. Poor girls that we are!' she added laughing. 'Flore, my bracelet. Give me your arm to my carriage, and tell me whether you liked me this evening.'

They went off thus, arm in arm, like two old friends. Samuel was in love, or at least felt his heart beating hard. He was perhaps odd, but certainly, this time he was not ridiculous.

In his joy, he had almost forgotten to warn Madame de Cosmelly of his success, and to bring hope to her deserted home.

A few days afterwards, Fanfarlo was playing the part of Columbine in a huge pantomime created for her by some men of genius. Here, by an agreeable succession of transformations, she appeared in the characters of Columbine, Marguerite, Elvire and Zépherine, and, in the gayest possible way, received the kisses of several generations of personages borrowed from various countries and various literatures. A great musician had not disdained to write a fantastic score appropriate to the queerness of the subject. Fanfarlo was, in turn, respectable, fairy-like, mad, mirthful; she was sublime in her art, as much an actress with her legs as a dancer with her eyes.

In our country the art of dancing is too much despised, let me say in passing. All great nations, first of all those of the ancient world, those of India and Arabia have cultivated it to the same extent as poetry. Dancing is as much above music, for certain pagan temperaments at least, as the visible and created are above the invisible and uncreated: only those can understand me to whom music gives pictorial ideas. Dancing can reveal all the mystery hidden in music, and it has, moreover, the merit of being human and palpable. Dancing is poetry with arms and legs: it is matter, graceful and terrible, beautified by movement. Terpischore is a southern muse; I presume she was very dark, and often shook her feet in the golden wheat; her movements, full of precise cadence, are so many divine motifs for the sculptor. But Fanfarlo, the Catholic, not content with rivalling Terpischore, called to her aid all the art of more modern divinities. Commingled in the mists are forms of fairies and water-sprites less diaphanous and less nonchalant. She was at once a Shakespearean caprice and an Italian drollery.

The poet was delighted; he thought he saw before his eyes the dream of his earliest days. He would willingly have cut ridiculous capers in his box and bumped his head against something in the mad intoxication that possessed him.

A low, close-curtained carriage rapidly carried the poet and the dancer towards the villa of which I have spoken.

Our man expressed his admiration by silent kisses which he fervently showered on her hands and feet. She too admired him very much, not that she was ignorant of the power of her charms, but she had not met a man so odd or a passion so electric.

The weather was black as the grave, and the wind, rocking together masses of clouds, from their joltings drew down a shower of rain and hail. A great tempest shook the attics, and made the steeples moan; the gutter, that funereal bed which swallows up the love letters and orgies of last night, foamingly swept along its thousand secrets to the sewers: mortality swooped joyously down on the hospitals, and the Chattertons and Savages of the Rue Saint-Jacques clenched their frozen fingers over their writing decks, when the most false, the most greedy, the most sensual, the most witty of our friends sat down before a fine supper and a good table in the company of one of the most beautiful women ever fashioned by nature for the pleasure of the eyes. Samuel wanted to open the window to cast a conqueror's glance over the accursed town; then lowering his gaze to the various felicities which he had beside him, he hastened to enjoy them.

In the company of such things he had to be eloquent; so despite his too high brow, his hair like a virgin forest and his snuff-taker's nose, Fanfarlo found that he was almost right.

Samuel and Fanfarlo had exactly the same ideas about cooking and the diet necessary to creatures of the *élite*. Silly meats, insipid fish were excluded from the suppers of this siren. Champagne rarely dishonoured her table. The most celebrated and most perfumed Bordeaux yielded place to the heavy serried battalion of the Burgundies, the wines of Auvergne, of Anjou and the south, and of the foreign wines, German, Greek, Spanish. Samuel was accustomed to say that a glass of real wine should resemble a bunch of black grapes, and that in it there was as much meat as drink. Fanfarlo loved bleeding meats, and wines laden with intoxication. However, she never got drunk. Both professed a sincere and profound esteem for the truffle. The truffle, that secret and mysterious vegetation of Cybele's, that savoury malady which she has hidden in her entrails longer than the most precious metal, that exquisite matter which defies the science of the agronomist, as did gold that of the Paracelsuses; the truffle which marks the distinction between the old and the modern world,[1] and which, before a glass of Chian, produces the effect of several zeros after a figure.

As to the question of sauces, ragouts, and seasonings, a grave question which would demand a chapter as grave as a scientific paper, I can assure you that they were in perfect agreement, especially upon the necessity of calling in the whole pharmacy of nature to the aid of the kitchen. Pimentos, English powders, saffrons, colonial substances, exotic dusts, all would have seemed good to them, nay, even musk and incense. Were Cleopatra alive now, I am certain she would have liked to do up fillets of steak or roebuck with Arabian perfumes. It is certainly deplorable that the *cordons bleus* of to-day are not constrained by a special law to know the chemical properties of matter, and are incapable of discovering, for

[1] The truffles of the Romans were white, of another species.

special cases, like that of an amorous banquet, almost inflammable culinary ingredients swift to invade the organic system, like prussic acid, or to volatilize, like ether.

Curiously enough, this harmony of opinions on the question of good living, this similitude of tastes, formed a strong bond of union; that profound understanding of sensual life which shone in every one of Samuel's looks and words, struck Fanfarlo very forcibly. That speech, now brutal as a numeral, now delicate and perfumed as a flower or a sachet, that strange conversation, the secret of which was known to him alone, completely won for him the good graces of this charming lady. Besides, it was not without deep and lively satisfaction that he recognized, on inspecting the bedroom, a perfect confraternity of taste and sentiments in the matter of furniture and interior arrangements. Cramer hated profoundly, and in my opinion he was perfectly right, the straight line in apartments, and the introduction of architecture into the house. The huge rooms of old châteaux terrify me, and I pity the *châtelaines* for having been forced to make love in great dormitories which looked like cemeteries, in huge catafalques calling themselves beds, or great monuments which used to assume the pseudonym of arm-chairs. The apartments of Pompeii are the size of your hand; the Indian ruins that cover the coast of Malabar reveal the same system. Those great, voluptuous and wise races understood the question perfectly. The intimate sentiments can only be evoked in a very narrow space.

Fanfarlo's bedroom, then, was very little, very low, cluttered up with soft things, perfumed and dangerous to touch; the air, laden with queer miasmas, made one want to expire slowly as if in a hot-house. The light of the lamp played on a confusion of laces and stuffs of a violent but equivocal hue. Here and there, on the wall, it lit up a few paintings full of Spanish voluptuousness; very white flesh-tints against very dark backgrounds. It was in the depths of this delightful hovel, which smacked at once of the bagnio and the sanctuary, that Samuel saw, advancing towards him, the new goddess of his heart in the radiant and sacred splendour of her nudity.

Where is the man who, even at the cost of half a lifetime, would not wish to see his dream, his real dream, pose unveiled before him, and the adored phantom of his imagination drop, one by one, the garments designed as a protection against the vulgar gaze? But here was Samuel, seized by a queer caprice, beginning to shout like a spoiled child: 'I want Columbine. Give me back Columbine! Give her back to me as she appeared to me the evening she made me mad with her fantastic trappings and her mountebank's corsage!'

Fanfarlo, at first astonished, was quite willing to lend herself to the eccentricity of the man she had chosen, and Flore was summoned; it was no use the latter representing that it was three o'clock in the morning, that everything was locked up at the theatre, the concierge asleep, the weather frightful—the storm was still raging; she who herself obeyed, had to be obeyed, and the chambermaid went out. Suddenly Cramer, seized with a new idea, clung to the bell-pull, and shouted in a voice of thunder:

'Hey, don't forget the rouge!'

This characteristic trait, which was related by Fanfarlo herself one evening when her comrades were asking her about the beginning of her liaison with Samuel, in no way astonished me; I well recognized in this the author of the *Ospreys*. He will always love rouge and ceruse, chrysocolla and tinsel of every sort. He would be quite prepared to repaint the trees and the sky, and if God had entrusted him with the plan of nature, perhaps he would have spoiled it.

Though Samuel had a depraved imagination, and perhaps for that very reason, love was with him less an affair of the senses than of the reason. It was, above all, admiration and appetite for beauty; reproduction he regarded as a vice of love, pregnancy a spiderish disease. Somewhere he has written: 'Angels are hermaphroditic and sterile'. He loved a human body like a material harmony, like a fine piece of architecture plus movement; and this absolute materialism was not far removed from the purest idealism. But, as in beauty, which is the cause of love, there were, according to him, two elements: line and appeal—and because all this concerns only line—the appeal for him, at least that evening, was rouge.

So Fanfarlo summed up for him line and appeal: and when, seated on the edge of the bed, in the care-free, victorious tranquillity of the loved woman, her hands delicately resting upon him, Samuel looked at her, it seemed to him that he saw the infinite behind the bright eyes of this beauty, and that gradually his own looked down on immense horizons. Besides, as often happens with exceptional men, he was often alone in his paradise, none being able to inhabit it with him. And if, by chance, he ravished and dragged her thither almost by force, she always lagged behind; consequently in the heaven where it held sway, his love began to be sick and sad of an azure melancholy like a solitary king. However, he never got tired of her; never, on leaving his amorous retreat, walking briskly on a pavement in the fresh morning air, did he experience that selfish cigar and hands-in-pocket enjoyment of which our great novelist[1] somewhere speaks.

If he had no heart, Samuel had a noble intelligence and, instead of gratitude, enjoyment had engendered in him that luscious contentment, that sensual dreaminess which is perhaps better than love as the vulgar understand it. Besides, Fanfarlo had done her best and dispensed her most cunning caresses, having observed that the man was worth the trouble: she had grown accustomed to that mystic language variegated with impurities and enormous crudities. That had for her at least the attraction of novelty.

The dancer's escapade had made its scandal. There were several 'no performances' on the bill; she had neglected rehearsals; many people envied Samuel.

One evening when chance, M. de Cosmelly's ennui, or some complicated manœuvre of his wife's, had brought them together at the fireside; after one of those long silences which occur in household where husband and wife have nothing more to say to each other, or a great deal to conceal; after having made him the best possible tea in a very modest and very cracked teapot, perhaps still the one from her aunt's château; after having sung at the piano a few selections from music in vogue ten years ago; she said to him, with the sweet and prudent voice of virtue anxious to be amiable and afraid of scaring the object of its affections, that she pitied him very much, that she cried a lot, more about him than about herself; that she would have liked at least, in her very submissive and devoted resignation, that he might have found elsewhere than with her the love which he no longer wanted from his wife; that she had suffered more at seeing him deceived than at being herself abandoned; that, besides, she was very much to blame, that she had forgotten her tender, wifely duties in not warning her husband

[1] The author of *La Fille aux Yeux d'Or*.

of the danger; that, besides, she was quite ready to close that bleeding wound, and by herself alone to repair an imprudence committed by both, etc., and all the honeyed words suggested by a cunning authorized by love. She wept, and wept well; the fire lit up her tears and a face beautified by sorrow.

M. de Cosmelly did not say a word and went out. Men caught in the snare of their faults dislike making an offering of their remorse to clemency. If he went to Fanfarlo's he would doubtless find traces of disorder, cigar ends, and newspapers.

One morning Samuel was awakened by the roguish voice of Fanfarlo, and slowly raised his tired head from the pillow where it was resting to read a letter which she handed to him.

'Thanks, monsieur, a thousand thanks; my happiness and gratitude will be noted to your credit in a better world. I accept. I am taking back my husband from your hands and am carrying him off this evening to our estate at C——, where I am going to recover the health and the life I owe to you. Receive, monsieur, the promise of an eternal friendship. I have always believed you to be too fine a man not to prefer one more friendship to any other reward.'

Samuel, wallowing in lace, and leaning over one of the coolest and most beautiful shoulders it is possible to see, felt vaguely that he was tricked, and had some difficulty in marshalling in his memory the elements of the plot, the dénouement of which he had brought about; but he said to himself quietly:

'Are our passions really sincere? Who can know with certainty what he wants, and know exactly the barometer of his heart?'

'What 's that you 're muttering? What is it? I want to see,' said Fanfarlo.

'Oh, nothing,' said Samuel. 'A letter from a nice woman to whom I promised that I 'd make you love me.'

'I 'll make you pay for that,' she hissed.

It is probable that Fanfarlo loved Samuel, but with that love known to so few souls, with spite at the bottom of it. As for him, he had been punished where he sinned. He had so often aped passion, he was forced to know it; but it was not the tranquil, calm and strong love that decent girls inspire, it was the terrible, desolating and shameful love, the sickly love of the courtesan. Samuel knew all the tortures of jealousy, and the degradation and sadness into which we are cast by the consciousness of an incurable, constitutional malady; in short, all the horrors of that vicious marriage which is called concubinage. As for her, she is getting stouter every day; she has become a plump, fresh, shining, and artful beauty, a sort of ministerial tart. One of these days she will take the Easter Communion and will hand out the consecrated bread to the parish. At that period perhaps, Samuel, killed by hard labour, will be *nailed down by the planks*, as he used to say in the good old days, and Fanfarlo, looking like a canoness, will turn the head of some young heir. Meantime she is learning how to have children; she has just been happily delivered of twins. Samuel has given birth to four learned books: a book on the four evangelists, another on the symbolism of colours, a memoir on a new advertising system, and a fourth, the title of which I do not wish to remember. The most frightful thing about the last one is that it is full of verve, energy, and curiosities. Samuel had the nerve to give it the epigraph: *Auri sacra fames!* Fanfarlo wants her husband to get into the Academy, and she is intriguing at the Ministry to procure him the cross.

Poor singer of the *Ospreys*! Poor Manuela de Monteverde! He has fallen very low. I recently learned that he was founding a socialist newspaper, trying to enter politics. Intellectually dishonest! to quote that honest man, M. Nisard.

THE BEAUTY SPOT

ALFRED DE MUSSET

I

IN the year seventeen hundred and fifty-six, when Louis XV, tired of the quarrelling between the magistracy and the Great Council about the two-sous tax,[1] made up his mind to hold a 'Bed of Justice', the members resigned their functions. Sixteen of those resignations were accepted, whereupon there were the same number of exiles.

'But can you,' Madame de Pompadour said to one of the presidents, 'can you watch in cold blood a handful of men resist the authority of a king of France? Wouldn't you give an adverse judgment on that? Put aside your little cloak, Mr. President, and you will see all that as I do.'

It was not only the exiles who suffered for their wrong intentions, but their relations and their friends as well. The *unsealing* of letters amused the king. To save himself from being bored by his pleasures, he used to get his favourite to read all the queer things in his postbag. It is obvious that under the pretext of being himself his own secret police, he got amusement from the thousands of intrigues that passed before him in this way; but whoever was related, closely or distantly, to the heads of the factions, was almost always lost. We know that Louis XV, along with all kinds of weaknesses, had only one driving power, that of being inexorable.

One evening, when he was sitting before the fire, his feet on the chimney fender, in his usual state of melancholy, the marquise, running through a bundle of letters, shrugged her shoulders laughing. The king asked what was the matter.

'I 've found here', she answered, 'a letter with no common sense in it, but it 's a touching story, and makes one feel sorry.'

'What 's at the bottom?' said the king.

'No name: it 's a love letter.'

[1] Two sous in the pound on the tenth of the revenue.

*D 896

'And what 's outside?'

'That 's the funny thing. It 's addressed to Mademoiselle d'Annebault, the niece of my dear friend Madame d'Estrades. Apparently it is in order that I should see it that it has been stuffed in among these papers.'

'And what 's inside?' said the king again.

'But I 'm telling you, love! There 's talk, too, of Vauvert and Neauflette. Are there any gentlemen in those districts? Does your majesty know them?'

The king prided himself on knowing France by heart, that is to say, the nobility of France. He had studied the etiquette of his court and it was not more familiar to him than the coats of arms of his kingdom: a knowledge restricted enough, nothing else counting at all. But his vanity was involved in it, and the hierarchy was in his eyes like the marble staircase of his palace: he wanted to walk up it as master. After brooding a few minutes he frowned as if struck by an evil recollection, then, signing to the marquise to read, he threw himself back in his easy chair, and said with a smile:

'Go on, then, the girl 's a pretty girl.'

Madame de Pompadour, making use of her most sweetly mocking tone, began to read a long letter, all filled with amorous outbursts.

'See then', the writer said, 'how the Fates are persecuting me. Everything seemed disposed to grant my prayers, and you, my dear love, had you not led me to hope for happiness? Yet I must renounce it all, and that for a fault I have not committed. Is it not the extreme of cruelty to have let me glimpse the heavens in order to plunge me in the abyss? When a wretch is condemned to death do we take a barbarous pleasure in leaving before his eyes all that should make him love and regret life? Such, however, is my fate: I have no other refuge, no other hope than the tomb, for, from that moment that I became unfortunate, I can no longer dream of your hand. When fortune was smiling on me, all my hope was that you might be mine: poor as I am to-day, I would shudder at myself if I dared still to hope it, and from the moment I can no longer make you happy, I forbid you to love me, who am myself dying of love. . . .'

The marquise smiled at those last words.

'Madame,' said the king, 'that 's a fine fellow. But what 's keeping him from marrying his lady?'

'Let me continue, sire.'

'This injustice that overwhelms me, comes on me unexpectedly from the hands of the best of kings. You know that my father was asking for me a place as cornet or ensign in the Guards, and that this place would influence all my future life, since it would give me the right to offer myself to you. The Duke of Biron had proposed me: but the king has rejected me in a fashion whose memory is very bitter to me, for if my father has his own way of thinking (I wish this was a fault) ought I all the same to be punished for it? My devotion to the king is as true and sincere as my love for you. The world might clearly see them both if I could draw a sword. It is desperately disappointing that my request should be refused; but that it should be without a valid reason that I am smothered in disgrace like this, that is opposed to the well-known kindness of his majesty——'

'Aha!' said the king, 'this interests me.'

'If you knew how sad we are! Ah, my dear, this domain of Neauflette, this lodge of Vauvert, these copses! I walk alone in them all day. I have forbidden them to be raked; the wretched gardener came yesterday with his steel-shod broom. He was going to touch the sand. . . . The print of your steps, lighter than the wind, is still not effaced. The tips of your little feet, and your high white heels, were still marked in the alley; they seemed to walk before me, while I followed your lovely form, and this charming spirit at times came to life for a moment, as if it poised itself on the fleeting imprint. It is there, it is while walking along by the flower beds, that it was given to me to know you, to appreciate you. An admirable education in an angel's mind, the dignity of a queen with the grace of the nymphs, thoughts worthy of Leibniz with so simple a language, Plato's bees on Diana's lips: all that has shrouded me in a veil of adoration. And all that time those beloved flowers blossomed around us, I breathed them as I listened to you: in their perfume lived your memory. Now they droop their heads: they show me death——'

'That 's bad Jean-Jacques,' said the king. 'Why do you read me that?'

'Because your majesty ordered me to, for love of the beautiful eyes of Mademoiselle d'Annebault.'

'That 's true, she has beautiful eyes.'

'And when I came in from these walks I find my father alone

in the big drawing-room, head on his hand beside a candle, amid those faded gildings that cover our worm-eaten wainscoting. He sees me coming with sorrow—my pain disturbs his own. Athénaïs! at the other end of the room near the window, is the keyboard up which your delicious fingers flitted, fingers which once my lips have touched, while your lips opened sweetly to the notes of most tuneful music—so sweet that your songs were no more than a smile. How happy are they, your Rameau, your Lulli, your Duni, and mayhap many another! Yes, yes, you love them, they linger in your memory, their breath has passed over your lips. I sit me down too at the piano, I try to play one of those airs that please you; how cold and monotonous they seem! I leave them, and hear them die away, while the echo loses itself beneath this sad roof. My father turns and sees me desolate: what can he do? A bed-chamber intrigue, an ante-room plot has shut our gates. He sees me, young, ardent, full of life, asking no more than to take my place in the world: he is my father, and can do nothing.'

'Wouldn't you say', said the king, 'that this lad was going hunting, and that somebody was killing his falcon on his wrist? Who 's he annoyed at, anyway?'

'It is quite true,' continued the marquise, going on with her reading in a lower tone, 'it is quite true that we are near neighbours and distant relations of the Abbé Chauvelin——'

'That 's what it is,' said Louis XV yawning. 'Still another nephew of the Inquests and Requests. My Parlement abuse my goodness: they have really too big families.'

'But if he is only a distant relation!——'

'Even so! that crowd isn't worth anything. That Abbé Chauvelin is a Jansenist. He 's a good chap, but he 's one of the resigned list. Throw that letter in the fire, and don't let me hear about it again.'

II

These last words pronounced by the king were not exactly a condemnation to death, but they were almost a prohibition of going on living. What, in seventeen hundred and fifty-six, could a young man without fortune do, whose name the king didn't like mentioned? Try to be a clerk, or turn philosopher, poet perhaps, but without the dedications, and the trade in that case wasn't worth anything.

Such was not, by a great deal, the vocation of the Chevalier Vauvert, who had just written with tears the letter the king laughed at. At this moment, alone with his father, deep in the old château of Neauflette, he was walking up and down the room with a sad and furious look.

'I want to go to Versailles,' he was saying.

'And what will you do there?'

'I don't know: but what am I doing here?'

'You are keeping me company; it is quite true that that cannot be very amusing for you, and I don't hold you back in any way. But are you forgetting that your mother is dead?'

'No, sir; and I have promised her to consecrate to you the life which you gave me. I will come back, but I must go. I can't stay any longer in this place.'

'What is the cause of that?'

'A mighty love. I am madly in love with Mademoiselle d'Annebault.'

'You know that it is hopeless. It is only Molière who makes marriages without a dowry. Are you forgetting my disgrace too?'

'Ah, sir, your disgrace—might I be allowed, without swerving from the most profound respect, to ask you what caused that? We are not Parlement men. We pay the tax, we do not make it. If the Parlement haggles about the king's revenue, it is their affair and not ours. Why does the Abbé Chauvelin drag us down in his ruin?'

'The Abbé Chauvelin acts like an honest man. He refuses to approve of this tithe because he is disgusted with the waste at the court. Nothing like this would have happened in the time of Madame Châteauroux. She was beautiful, at least, that lady, and she cost nothing, not even what she gave so generously. She was mistress and sovereign, and she declared herself satisfied if the king did not send her to languish in a dungeon when he withdrew his favour from her. But this Étioles woman, this Le Normand, this insatiable Poisson!'

'And what does it matter?'

'"What does it matter?" say you. More than you think. Are you aware of this one fact, that at present, while the king bleeds us to the white, the fortune of his light-of-love is incalculable? She got herself given a hundred and eighty thousand francs a year: but that was only a drop in the bucket, that doesn't count any more now; you can't imagine the fearful sums that the king throws at her head: three months of the year don't go by without her catching in passing, as if by accident, five or six hundred thousand francs, yesterday on the salt tax, to-day on the increases of the Treasury of the Stables; in addition to all the suites that she has in the royal mansions, she buys La Selle, Aulnay, Brimborion, Marigny, Saint-Remy, Bellevue, and as many estates again, houses in Paris, in Fontainebleau, in Versailles, in Compiègne, without counting a secret fortune invested in every country in all the banks of Europe, in case of disgrace probably, or of the king's death. And who pays for all that, if you please?'

'I don't know, sir, but it isn't me.'

'It is you, as well as the rest of us; it is France, it is the people who sweat blood and water, who cry out in the streets, who insult Pigalle's statue. And the Parlement wants no more of that: it wants no more new taxes. When it was a question of war expenses our last crown was ready: we didn't dream of haggling. Our victorious king could see clearly that he was loved by the whole kingdom, see it even more clearly still when he was at death's door. Then all dissension, all faction, all bitterness ceased: the whole of France kneeled at the king's bedside and prayed for him. But if we pay without counting his soldiers or his doctors we do not want any longer to pay his mistresses, and we have other things to do than to entertain Madame de Pompadour.'

'I am not defending her, sir. I wouldn't know whether she was right or wrong. I have never seen her.'

'Doubtless: and you wouldn't be sorry to see her, isn't that the way of it, so that you could have some opinion about it? For at your age the head judges through the eyes. Try them if you think fit: but that pleasure will be refused you.'

'Why, sir?'

'Because it 's foolish: because this marquise is as invisible in her little boudoirs at Brimborion as the Grand Turk in his harem: because all the doors will be shut in your face. What do you want to do? Attempt impossibilities! Seek for fortune like an adventurer?'

'No, but like a lover. I do not claim a favour at all, sir, but I appeal against injustice. I have a definite hope, almost a promise from M. de Biron. I was on the eve of possessing the lady I loved, and that love is not unreasonable; you had not disapproved of it Let me then try to plead my cause. Whether I shall have to do with the king or with Madame de Pompadour I do not know, but I want to go.'

'You do not know what the court is like, and you want to go there!'

'Well, maybe I shall be received more easily, for the very reason that I am unknown there.'

'You, unknown, sir! Do you think that? With a name like ours! We are gentlemen of old descent, sir: you could not possibly be unknown.'

'Well then, the king will listen to me!'

'He will not even deign to hear you. You dream of Versailles, and you think you 'll be there when your postilion stops. Suppose that you get in to the antechamber, to the gallery, to the Œil de Bœuf, you will see between his majesty and yourself, nothing but the leaf of a folding door: there will be an abyss. You will turn around, you will look for subterfuges, for protection, you will find nothing. We are relations of Monsieur de Chauvelin: and how do you think that the king avenges himself? By torture for Damiens, by exile for the Parlement, but for the rest of us, by one word, or even worse, by silence. Do you know what the king's silence is, when, with his speechless look, instead of answering you, he scrutinizes you in passing and annihilates you? After the block and the Bastille there is a certain grade of punishment which, less cruel in appearance, shows just as well the hand of the hangman. The condemned man, it is true, remains at liberty, but he must no longer dream of approaching a lady, nor a courtier, nor a drawing-room, nor an abbey, nor a messroom. Before him on his way all paths are closed or turned aside, and he wanders there without guidance in an invisible prison.'

'I will bustle about so eagerly that I will get out!'

'No more than any one else can. M. de Meynières's son was not more guilty than you. He had, like you, promises, the most reasonable hopes. His father, his majesty's most devoted servant, repulsed by the king, went, grey hairs and all, not to beg, but to try to persuade the light-of-love. Do you know what she answered? Here are her own words, which Monsieur de Meynières sent me in a letter':

"The king is the master: he does not think it fitting to show his displeasure with you personally. He is content with making you feel it in depriving your son of a career: to punish you in another fashion would be starting on a long business, and he does not want that. We must respect his wishes. I am sorry for you, however: I sympathize with your grief. I have been a mother; I know what it must cost you to leave your son without a career."

'That 's the style of that creature, and you want to throw yourself at her feet!'

'They are said to be charming, sir.'

'In faith, yes. She is not pretty, and the king does not love her: that 's common knowledge. He yields, he bends before that woman. To maintain her strange power she must indeed have something else than her wooden head.'

'They say that she is very witty!'

'And has no heart, much good that is!'

'No heart! She who can declaim so finely Voltaire's verses, sing Rousseau's music, she who plays Alzire and Colette! It is impossible. I will never believe it.'

'Go see for yourself, since you want to. I give you advice, not orders, but you 'll get nothing out of it but the expense of your journey. You are deeply in love, then, with Mademoiselle d'Annebault?'

'More than my life.'

'Go, sir.'

III

Some have said that travel is harmful to love because it provides distractions: some have said, too, that it strengthens love because it leaves time for dreaming. The chevalier was too young for such learned distinctions. Tired of the coach, half-way there, he had taken a post nag, and so arrived about five in the evening at the sign of the Sun, an out-of-date inn of the time of Louis XIV.

There was at Versailles an old priest who had been curé near Neauflette; the chevalier knew him and loved him. This curé, simple and poor, had a well-placed nephew, an abbé of the

Court, who might prove useful. The chevalier went then to the nephew, and he, a man of importance, sunk in his clerical neck-cloth, received the new-comer very kindly, and did not disdain to listen to his request.

'But, by Jove,' he said, 'you come just at the right moment. To-night there is an opera at the Court, a kind of birthday party for somebody or other. I am not going there because I am sulking with the marquise, with a view to getting something. But here you are: here 's a line of invitation from my Lord Duke of Aumont that I 'd asked of him for somebody, I don't remember who. You are not presented yet, it 's true, but for the theatre that isn't necessary. Try to place yourself in his way when the king passes through the little lobby. One look and your fortune is made.'

The chevalier thanked the abbé, and, tired out by a disturbed night, and a horseback ride, he dressed himself before the inn mirror, and produced one of those careless effects which are so becoming to lovers. An untrained servant girl helped him as well as she could, and covered his spangled suit with powder. In this fashion he set out on his way to try his luck. He was twenty.

Night was falling when he reached the château. He advanced timidly to the great gate, and asked his way of the sentinel. He was shown the main staircase. There he learned from the Swiss guard that the opera had just begun, and that the king—that is, everybody—was in the hall.[1]

'If my lord marquis cares to cross the courtyard,' added the Swiss guard (just in case, refer to anybody as a marquis), 'he will be at the theatre in a moment. If he prefers to go through the rooms——'

The chevalier did not know the palace at all. Curiosity made him answer at first that he would go through the rooms: then, as a lackey got ready to follow him as guide, a burst of vanity made him add that he had no need of being accompanied. He went on alone, not without a certain thrill.

Versailles was gleaming with light. From ground-floor to attic the candelabras and branched candlesticks, the gilded

[1] The reference here is not to the present-day hall, built by Louis XV, or rather by Madame de Pompadour, but finished only in 1769 and opened in 1770 for the marriage of the Duke of Berri (Louis XVI) with Marie Antoinette. Here the reference is to a sort of movable theatre that could be carried into a gallery or a room, according to Louis XIV's custom.

furniture, the marbles, sparkled. Apart from the queen's rooms, the folding doors were open everywhere. As the chevalier advanced he was struck with a growing astonishment and a wonder not difficult to imagine: for what made the sight spread before his eyes absolutely miraculous was not only the beauty, the glory of the spectacle itself, it was the complete solitude in which he found himself in this sort of enchanted desert.

Indeed, to see oneself alone in a vast enclosure, be it in a temple, a cloister, or a castle, has in it something strange, one might say something mysterious. The building seems to weigh on the man. The walls watch him: the echoes listen to him: the sound of his steps disturbs such a great silence that he feels an involuntary fear, and only dares walk respectfully.

At first the chevalier acted so, but soon curiosity took the upper hand and drew him on. The candelabras in the Gallery of Mirrors, reflecting themselves, shot back their flames. You know how many thousands of cupids, of nymphs, and of shepherds played with each other there along the panelling, hovered on the ceilings, and seemed to entwine the whole palace in an immense garland. Here were vast reception rooms with canopies of velvet strewn with gold, and state arm-chairs that preserved still the majestic stateliness of the great king: here, rumpled ottomans, folding chairs in disorder round a card-table: an infinite suite of drawing-rooms for ever empty, whose magnificence stood out the more, the more useless that magnificence seemed: from time to time secret doors opening on endless corridors, a thousand stairways, a thousand passages crossing as in a labyrinth; columns, stages made for giants; boudoirs disordered like a child's playroom; an enormous canvas of Vanloo's near a porphyry chimney-piece; a beauty-patch box lying forgotten by the side of a grotesque figure from China; at one turn an overpowering grandeur, at the next an effeminate grace; and, everywhere, amidst luxury, prodigality, and indolence, a thousand seductive odours, strange and various, the mingled perfumes of flowers and of fair ladies, an enervating soft warmth, the atmosphere of voluptuousness.

To be in such a place at twenty, amidst marvels like these, and to find oneself there alone, was assuredly reason enough for bedazzlement. The chevalier went on at random, as in a dream.

'A true fairy palace,' he murmured, and in truth he seemed to see realized around him one of those fairy tales in which princes who have lost their way discover enchanted palaces.

Were they really mortal creatures who lived in this peerless dwelling? Were they real women who had just sat in those chairs, whose gracious contours had left on the cushions faint imprints which still breathed of indolence? Who knows? Behind those thick curtains, from the depths of some immense and brilliant gallery, perhaps there was going to appear a princess who had slept for a hundred years, a fairy in hoop petticoats, an Armida in spangles, or some hamadryad of the Court stepping out of a marble column, slipping through a gilded wainscoting!

Dazzled in spite of himself by all those fantasies, the chevalier, the better to dream, had thrown himself on a sofa, and maybe he would have remained there lost a long time if he had not recalled that he was a lover. What, during all this time, was Mademoiselle d'Annebault, his beloved, doing; she who was left behind in an old château?

'Athénaïs!' he cried all at once, 'what am I doing losing my time here? Are my wits astray? Where am I, great heavens, and what is coming over me?'

He rose and continued on his road across this new country, and lost his way, that goes without saying. Two or three lackeys, speaking in an undertone, appeared at the far end of a gallery. He advanced towards them, and asked them the way he should go to the comedy.

'If my lord marquis', one of them answered (always using the same formula), 'would be good enough to give himself the trouble of descending by that staircase, and following the gallery on the right, he will find at the end of it three steps to ascend: he should turn then to the left, and when he has crossed the drawing-room of Diana, that of Apollo, that of the Muses, and that of Spring, he should redescend six steps more: then, leaving the guard room on the right, as if making for the staircase of the ministers, he cannot fail to meet there other ushers who will show him the way.'

'Much obliged,' said the chevalier, 'and with such fine directions it will certainly be my fault if I do not get there.'

He started out again courageously, stopping continually in spite of himself to gaze on one side or the other, then recalled his love afresh; finally at the end of a good quarter of an hour, as he had been informed, he found lackeys again.

'My lord marquis has made a mistake,' they said to him, 'it is through the other wing of the château that he should have gone: but nothing is easier than to find the way again. My lord has only to go down that staircase, then he should cross the drawing-room of the Nymphs, that of Summer, that of——'

'Thanks,' said the chevalier.

'And I am a fine fool', he thought, moreover, 'to go asking questions of servants like a booby. I bring dishonour on myself for no good at all, and even if it happens, by an impossible chance, that they are not making fun of me, what use to me is their nomenclature, and all the pompous designations of those drawing-rooms of which I don't know a single one?'

He made up his mind to go straight before him, as far as that could be done.

'For, after all,' he said to himself, 'this palace is very beautiful, it is very fine, but it has its limits, and even if it were more than three times as long as our rabbit warren, I 'd have to see the end of it some time.'

But it isn't easy in Versailles to go straight before one for a long time, and the rustic comparison of the royal dwelling with a rabbit warren maybe displeased the nymphs of the place, for they began again more cunningly than ever to mislead the poor lover, and, doubtless to punish him, they took pleasure in making him turn and return on his own steps, bringing him back incessantly to the same place, exactly like a countryman astray in a copse. And so they enveloped him in their marble and gold maze.

In Piranesi's *Antiquities of Rome* there is a series of engravings which the artist entitles his *Dreams*, and which are a memory of his own visions during the delirium of a fever. These engravings represent huge Gothic rooms: on the floor are all sorts of engines and machines, wheels, cables, pulleys, levers, catapults, etc. —the expression of enormous power set in action, and of formidable resistance. Along the walls you see a staircase, and on that staircase, climbing, not without difficulty, Piranesi himself. Follow the steps a little higher, they stop suddenly before an abyss. Whatever might happen to poor Piranesi, you think him at least at the end of his labour, for he cannot take another step without falling: but raise your eyes, and you see a second staircase, and on this staircase again, Piranesi on the edge of another precipice. Look up still higher, and another staircase still more aerial rises before you, and again poor Piranesi continuing his ascent, and so on, up to the eternal staircase, and Piranesi disappearing with it into the clouds, that is, into the border of the engraving.

This feverish allegory represents fairly exactly the weariness of a useless labour, and the kind of giddiness which impatience produces. The chevalier, journeying for ever from drawing-room to drawing-room, and from gallery to gallery, was seized by a kind of rage.

'By Jove,' said he, 'this is cruelty. After having been so charmed, so ravished, so enthusiastic about finding myself alone in this wretched palace (it was no longer the palace of the fairies) I won't be able to get out of it. Plague on the idiocy which this idea of coming in here like Prince Fanfarinet with his boots of massive gold inspired me with; instead of telling the first lackey I met to conduct me without more ado to the auditorium!'

When he was experiencing these tardy regrets, the chevalier was, like Piranesi, half up a staircase on a landing, between three doors. Behind the centre door he seemed to hear a murmur so slight, so voluptuous, so to speak, that he could not refrain from listening. At the very moment he walked on, trembling lest he should be lènding an indiscreet ear, the two swing-doors opened. A rush of air, scented by a thousand perfumes, a torrent of light, bright enough to dim the Gallery of Mirrors itself, struck him so suddenly that he recoiled a few paces.

'My lord marquis desires to enter?' asked the usher who had opened the door.

'I want to go to the play,' answered the chevalier.

'It has just finished at this very minute.'

As he spoke extremely beautiful ladies, delicately enamelled in white and carmine, giving, not the arm, nor even the hand, but the tips of their fingers to old noblemen and young noblemen, began to come out of the auditorium, taking great care to walk sideways so as not to spoil their hoop petticoats. All this brilliant company were speaking in hushed voices with a half gaiety, an admixture of fear and respect.

'What 's this?' said the chevalier, not guessing that chance had led him precisely to the little lobby.

'The king is going to pass,' answered the usher.

There is a sort of audacity which feels no qualms, it is only too much at home; it is the courage of those who are ill-bred. Our young provincial, though he was reasonably brave, did not possess this accomplishment. At the very sound of those words: 'The king is going to pass', he stopped motionless and almost terrified.

King Louis XV, who rode on horseback at the hunt a dozen leagues without noticing them, was, as is well known, royally listless. He boasted, not without reason, of being the first gentleman in France, and his mistresses said of him, not without cause, that he was the best built and the most handsome. It was an important business to see him leave his chair and deign to walk in person. When he crossed the lobby, with one arm placed, or rather stretched, on the shoulder of Monsieur d'Argenson, while his red heel slid along the floor (he had made this form of laziness fashionable), all the whisperings ceased: the courtiers inclined their heads, not daring to bow completely; and the fair ladies bending gently back on their flame-coloured garters, amid their immense flounces, risked this coquettish good night that our grandmothers called a *curtsey*, which our generation has replaced by the brutal *handshake* of the English.

But the king concerned himself with none of it, and only saw what he pleased. Alfieri perhaps was there, who narrates thus his presentation at Versailles in his *Memoirs*:

'I knew that the king never spoke to strangers who were not notable. I could not, however, get accustomed to the impassive and supercilious bearing of Louis XV. He eyed the man who was presented to him from head to foot, and he had the air of receiving no impression of him. Yet it seems to me that if you said to a giant: "Here 's an ant that I am presenting to you!', as he looked at it he would smile or perhaps say: "Ah, the little animal!"'

The taciturn monarch passed then through these flowers, these beautiful ladies, and all that Court, preserving his solitude amidst the crowd. The chevalier had no need of long reflections to understand that he had nothing to hope for from the king, and that the story of his love would not win him any success in that quarter.

'Unlucky fellow that I am,' he thought. 'My father was only too right when he said that at two steps from the king I would see an abyss between him and me. Even indeed if I risked asking for an audience, who will protect me? who will present me? There he is, this absolute master who can with one word change my destiny, make my fortune secure, fulfil all my wishes. He is there, before me; by stretching out my hand, I could touch his clothes. And I feel farther from him than if I were still in the depths of my province! How to speak to him? Who will come to my rescue?'

While the chevalier was lamenting himself thus, he saw a young lady enter, rather pretty, with an air full of grace and delicacy. She was dressed very simply, in a white robe, without diamonds or embroidery, with a rose over her ear. She had given her hand to a gentleman 'all in amber', as Voltaire said, and she was speaking quite low to him behind her fan. Now chance willed that in talking, laughing, and gesticulating, this fan happened to slip from her hand and to fall under a chair, precisely in front of the chevalier. He bent at once to pick it up, and to do that he knelt on one knee. The young lady seemed to him so charming, that he presented her fan to her without rising. She stopped, smiled, and passed on, thanking him with a slight inclination of the head: but, at the look she had thrown on the chevalier, he felt his heart beat without knowing why. He was right. This young lady was the little 'd'Étoiles girl', as the malcontents still called her, while the rest, in speaking of her, said, 'the marquise', as one says, 'the queen'.

IV

'That lady will protect me, that lady will come to my aid! Ah! how right the abbé was in telling me that a look would decide my life! Yes, those eyes that are so subtle and gentle, that little mocking delicious mouth, that little foot smothered under its pompom. That 's my good fairy!'

Such were the thoughts, almost uttered out aloud, of the chevalier going back to his inn. Whence came to him this sudden hope? Was it only his youth that was speaking, or had the eyes of the marquise spoken too?

But the difficulty remained always the same. If he no longer dreamed now of being presented to the king, who would present him to the marquise?

He spent a great part of the night in writing to Mademoiselle d'Annebault a letter almost the same as the one which Madame de Pompadour had read.

It would be very little use to repeat that letter. Apart from lunatics there are only lovers who perpetually feel the thrill of novelty as they perpetually repeat the same thing.

When morning came, the chevalier went out and began to walk meditatively about the streets. It didn't occur to him to have recourse again to the friendly abbé, and it would not be easy to say just why he refrained. It was as it were a mixture of fear and audacity, of false shame and romance. And indeed, what would the abbé have answered, if he had told him the story of the night before?

'You happened to be there in the nick of time to pick up a fan: have you managed to profit by it? What did you say to the marquise?'

'Nothing.'

'You ought to have spoken to her.'

'I was excited: I had lost my head.'

'That 's a mistake: a man must always seize his chance. But that can be remedied. Would you like me to present you to Mr. So-and-so? He is a friend of mine. To Madame So-and-so? She is better still. We will try to get you as far as this marquise who frightened you, and this time,' etc.

Now the chevalier was not worrying about anything like that. It seemed to him that in recounting his adventure, it would have been as it were spoilt and deflowered. He said to himself that chance had granted him an unheard-of, an incredible opportunity, and that it ought to be a secret between himself and fortune: to confide that secret to any chance comer, was, in his opinion, to take away all its virtue, and show himself unworthy.

'I went yesterday all alone to the Château of Versailles,' he thought, 'I will go all alone to Trianon' (that was at the moment the abode of the favourite).

Such a way of thinking may appear, nay, even must appear, extravagant to calculating minds, who neglect nothing, and leave as little as possible to chance: but the most austere men, if they have ever been young (everybody is not young even in their youth), can recognize this odd sentiment, weak and venturesome, dangerous and seductive, which pulls us toward our destiny: we feel ourselves blind, and we want to be blind: we do not know whither we go, and we go on. The charm of it lies in this carefreeness, and this very ignorance: it is the pleasure of the artist in his visions, of the lover who spends the night under his mistress's window: it is, too, the instinct of the soldier: it is, above all, that of the gamester.

The chevalier, then, almost without knowing it, had taken the road to Trianon. Without being very well got up, as the saying was, he was not lacking in elegance, nor in that way of carrying himself which prevents a lackey who meets you on the way, from asking where you are going. He found no difficulty, then, thanks to several inquiries he had made at his inn, in arriving at the main gate of the château, if such a name can be given to that chocolate box of marble which was a witness of so many pleasures and so much boredom. Unfortunately the gate was shut, and a big Swiss guardsman, clad in a plain greatcoat, was walking, hands behind his back, in the inside passage like a man who was not expecting visitors.

'The king is here,' said the chevalier to himself, 'or the marquise is not here.' It is self-evident that when the gates are closed and the servants are going walking, the masters are busy inside or have gone out.

What was to be done? Just as he had felt, an instant before, confidence and courage, so he experienced suddenly trouble and disappointment. The thought alone, 'The king is here', frightened him more than had done the evening before those six words, 'the king is going to pass', for then it was only an unforeseen contingency, but now he knew that cold look, that impassible majesty.

'Oh, good God! what a figure I should cut if I tried like a rash fool to get into this garden, if I am going to find myself face to face with this proud monarch, taking his coffee by the side of a brook.'

At once before the lover's eyes loomed the cruel silhouette of the Bastille: instead of the charming image that he had cherished of the marquise passing on smiling, he saw dungeons, secret cells, black bread, and the water of the torture chamber: he knew the story of Latude. Little by little came reflection and little by little hope took flight.

'And all the same,' he said to himself, 'I am hurting nobody —certainly not the king. I am protesting against an injustice: I have never lampooned any one. I was so well received yesterday at Versailles and the lackeys were so polite! What am I afraid of? Of doing something imprudent. I will do other things which will make up for the first.'

He went up to the gate and touched it with his finger: it was not quite shut. He opened it and went in resolutely. The Swiss turned with an air of boredom.

'What do you want? Where are you going?'

'I am going to Madame de Pompadour.'

'Have you an audience?'

'Yes.'

'Where is your letter?'

No longer did he get the title of marquis as on the night before, and no longer had he a Duke of Aumont to fall back on. The chevalier sadly lowered his eyes, and saw that his white stockings and rhinestone buckles were covered with dust. He had made the mistake of coming on foot, in a country where none walked. The Swiss lowered his eyes as well, and scrutinized him not from the head to the feet, but from the feet to the head. The suit seemed right enough to him, but the hat was a little aslant and the hair unpowdered.

'You have no letter? What do you want?'

'I want to speak to Madame de Pompadour.'

'Really! And do you think that that is done like that?'

'I don't know anything about it. Is the king here?'

'Maybe. Go away and let me alone.'

The chevalier didn't want to get angry but, in spite of himself, this insolence made him white.

'I have sometimes told a lackey to go away,' he answered, 'but a lackey has never said that to me.'

'Lackey? Me! a lackey?' cried the Swiss in a fury.

'A lackey, a porter, a valet, a pack of flunkeys, I don't care which, and they 're of no importance to me.'

The Swiss took a step towards the chevalier, his fists clenched and his face on fire. The chevalier, recalled to himself at this show of threatening, raised slightly the hilt of his sword.

'Take care,' he said, 'I am a gentleman, and it costs thirty-six francs to bury a churl like you.'

'If you are a gentleman, sir, I belong to the king's household. I am only doing my duty, and I do not think——'

At this moment the sound of a flourish of trumpets which seemed to come from Satory wood was heard in the distance and lost itself in the echoes. The chevalier let his sword slip into its scabbard, and, not heeding the quarrel that had begun:

'Eh, by Jove,' he cried, 'that 's the king setting out for the hunt. Why didn't you tell me that at once?'

'That is not my business, nor yours.'

'Listen, my dear man. The king isn't there. I have no letter: I have no audience. Here is something to get a drink, let me in.'

He drew from his pocket some gold pieces. The Swiss looked him up and down again with sovereign contempt.

'What 's that?' he said disdainfully. 'Are you trying to get in that way to a royal dwelling? Instead of making you go away, take care I don't shut you up.'

'You, twice scoundrel that you are!' said the chevalier, getting angry again and seizing his sword again.

'Yes, me!' repeated the fat man.

But during this conversation, in which the historian is sorry to have compromised his hero, thick clouds had obscured the sky: a thunderstorm was coming. There was a quick flash of lightning, followed by a violent clap of thunder, and the rain began to fall heavily. The chevalier, who was still holding his gold pieces, saw a drop of water on his dusty shoe, as big as a small crown piece.

'Bother,' he said, 'let 's take shelter. It 's no good letting ourselves get wet.'

And he made his way nimbly to Cerberus's cave, or if you like, the caretaker's house. Then, flinging himself carelessly in the big chair of the caretaker himself:

'Jove, what a nuisance you are!' he said, 'and what an unlucky fellow I am! You take me for a conspirator, and you don't understand that I have in my pocket a petition for his majesty! I am a provincial, but you are only a fool.'

The Swiss for all answer, went to a corner to get his halberd, and stood erect, the weapon in his hand.

'When will you go away?' he cried in a stentorian voice.

The quarrel, alternately forgotten and recommenced, seemed this time to be becoming quite serious, and already the two fat hands of the Swiss were trembling oddly on his pike.

What was going to happen? I do not know, when, turning his head suddenly:

'Ah,' said the chevalier, 'who 's coming here?'

A young page, mounted on a superb horse (not an English one: in those days thin legs were not the fashion), was riding up at full speed and at a triple gallop. The path was soaked by the rain: the gate was only half open. There was some hesitation. The page used his spur: the horse, checked a moment, tried to get into his stride again, missed his footing, slid on the wet earth, and fell.

It is not at all pleasant, indeed almost dangerous, to raise a horse that has fallen. There is no whip that will hold him, the movements of the legs of the beast, who is doing all it can, are extremely disagreeable, above all when the man has himself a leg caught under the saddle.

The chevalier, all the same, came to the rescue without reflecting on the inconveniences, and went about it so adroitly that soon the horse was on his feet again, and the rider extricated. But the latter was covered with mud and could hardly limp along. He was carried, as best they could, into the house of the Swiss, and seated in his turn in the big arm-chair.

'Sir,' he said to the chevalier, 'you are a gentleman, unquestionably. You have rendered me a great service, but you can render me a still greater one. Here is a message from the king to madame the marquise and the message is very urgent, as you see, since my horse and I, in order to go more quickly, have almost broken our necks. You understand that in the state I am in, with a lame leg, I would be unable to carry in this paper. For that, I 'd need to be carried in myself. Will you go in my place?'

At the same time he drew from his pocket a large envelope, gilded with arabesques, accompanied by the royal seal.

'Very willingly, sir,' answered the chevalier, taking the letter. And nimble and light as a feather, he set out, running on the tips of his toes.

V

When the chevalier arrived at the château, a Swiss guard once again was before the peristyle.

'Order of the king,' said the young man, who this time, had no longer any fear of halberds; and showing his letter he entered gaily amidst half a dozen lackeys.

A tall usher, standing in the middle of the vestibule, seeing the order and the royal seal, bowed gravely like a poplar bent by the wind; then, with one of his bony fingers, he touched, smiling, the corner of some wainscoting.

A little swing door, hid by a tapestry, opened at once as if of itself. The bony man made a welcoming movement; the chevalier entered, and the tapestry, which was half open, fell into place softly behind him.

A silent valet showed him then into a large room, then into a corridor, out of which opened two or three little side rooms, then at last into a second drawing-room, and asked him to wait a moment.

'Am I at the Château of Versailles all over again?' the chevalier asked himself. 'Are we going to begin playing at hide-and-seek again?'

Trianon was at the period neither what it is to-day, nor what it had been. It has been said that Madame de Maintenon made Versailles an oratory, and Madame de Pompadour a boudoir. It has been said as well of Trianon that this *little porcelain château* was Madame de Montespan's boudoir. Whatever is the truth about all these boudoirs it seems that Louis XV put them everywhere. The same gallery in which his ancestor had stepped majestically, was at this time quaintly divided into an infinite number of compartments. There were boudoirs of all colours; the king used to flit like a butterfly in those groves of silk and velvet. 'Do you think my little furnished rooms are in good taste?' he asked the beautiful Countess of Séran one day. 'No,' she said, 'I would like them blue.' As blue was the king's colour, this answer flattered him. At their second meeting, Madame de Séran found the room furnished in blue as she had wanted it to be.

The room in which, at the moment, the chevalier found himself alone was neither blue, nor white, nor pink, but full of mirrors. It is well known what advantage a pretty woman who has a pretty figure gains from letting her picture be reflected thus in a thousand aspects. She dazzles, she, so to speak, envelops the man she wants to please. Whatever he looks at, he sees her; how can he avoid it? Nothing remains but to fly or to avow himself subjugated.

The chevalier looked at the garden too. There, behind the arbours and the labyrinths, the statues and the marble vases, was beginning to dawn the pastoral taste which the marquise was going to make fashionable, and which, later on, Madame Dubarry and Queen Marie Antoinette were to push to such a high degree of perfection. Already rustic fantasies were putting in an appearance where bored caprice found a refuge. Already bloated tritons, grave goddesses and learned nymphs, busts with long perukes, frozen with horror in their green niches, saw arise from the earth an English garden amidst the startled yews. Little lawns, little brooks, little bridges were soon to dethrone Olympus, to replace it by a dairy, a strange parody of nature which the English copy without understanding, a real child's game become the pastime of an indolent master, who did not know how to escape from boredom at Versailles in Versailles itself.

But the chevalier was too charmed, too ravished at finding himself there, to permit a single critical reflection to rise to his mind. He was, on the contrary, ready to admire everything, turning the letter in his fingers like a provincial does with his hat, when a pretty chambermaid opened the door and said softly to him:

'Come this way, sir!'

He followed her; after passing again through several more or less mysterious corridors, she introduced him into a big room where the shutters were half closed. There she stopped and seemed to listen.

'Hide-and-seek again,' said the chevalier to nimself.

However, at the end of several minutes, a door opened agam, and another chambermaid, who it seemed must be as pretty as the first, repeated in the same tone the same words:

'Come this way, sir.'

If he had been moved at Versailles, he was moved now in a different fashion, for he understood that he was approaching the threshold of the temple which the goddess inhabited. He advanced with a beating heart: a soft light, delicately veiled by thin gauze curtains, succeeded to shade: a delicious, almost imperceptible perfume was diffused in the air around him: the chambermaid timidly drew aside the corner of a silk curtain, and at the end of a large sitting-room, furnished with the most elegant simplicity, he saw the lady of the fan, that is to say, the all-powerful marquise.

She was alone, seated before a table, wrapped in a dressing-gown, her head leaning on her hand, and she seemed very preoccupied. When she saw the chevalier enter, she rose with a sudden and, as it were, involuntary movement.

'You come from the king?'

The chevalier could have answered, but he could find nothing better to do than to bow profoundly, as he presented to the marquise the letter that he brought her. She took it, or rather she took possession of it, with extreme vivacity. While she was opening it her hands trembled on the envelope.

This letter, written in the king's own hand, was fairly long. She devoured it, so to speak, in the twinkling of an eye, then she read it greedily with profound attention, her brows knit and her lips compressed. She was not beautiful like this, and had no longer any resemblance to the magic apparition in the king's lobby. When she reached the end, she seemed to reflect. Little by little her face, which had paled, flushed to a delicate carnation (at this hour she wore no rouge); not only did her grace return, but a flash of true beauty passed over her delicate features: her cheeks could have been taken for two rose petals. She uttered a half sigh, let the letter fall on the table, and turning towards the chevalier:

'I have made you wait, sir,' she said to him with the most charming smile, 'but the fact is I was not yet dressed, and I am not still! That is why I was forced to bring you here by stealth: for I am besieged here almost as much as I was at home. I would like to send the king an answer. Will it weary you to do my message?'

This time he had to speak: the chevalier had had time to regain a little courage.

'Alas, madame,' he said sadly. 'It is a great honour you do me; but unfortunately I cannot take advantage of it.'

'Why so?'

'I have not the honour of being in the king's household.'

'Then how did you come here?'

'By chance. I met on the way a page who had fallen on the ground and who asked me——'

'What? Fallen on the ground?' repeated the marquise, bursting out laughing. She appeared to be so happy at this moment, that gaiety came to hand without effort.

'Yes, madame, he fell from his horse at the gate. I happened to be there, fortunately, to help him to get up, and, as his suit was much spoiled, he begged me to undertake his message.'

'And by what chance did you happen to be there?'

'Madame, the fact is that I have a petition to present to his majesty.'

'His majesty lives at Versailles.'

'Yes, but you live here.'

'Indeed! So that the fact is that you want to charge me with a message.'

'Madame, I beg you to believe——'

'Don't be afraid, you are not the first. But what is your reason for addressing yourself to me? I am only a woman, like any one else.'

As she said these words with a mocking air, the marquise cast a triumphant look in the letter she had just read.

'Madame,' said the chevalier, 'I have always heard that men exercise power and that women——'

'Dispose of it, eh? Well, sir, there is a queen of France.'

'I know it, madame, and that is what caused me to *happen to be here* this morning.'

The marquise was more than accustomed to compliments like these, although they were only paid her in an undertone; but in the present circumstances, this one seemed to please her in a very singular way.

'And relying on what faith,' she said, 'on what assurance, did you think that you could get entrance here? for you didn't count, I suppose, on a horse falling on the road.'

'Madame, I believed—— I hoped——'

'What did you hope?'

'I hoped that chance would bring about——'

'Always chance! Chance is a friend of yours, as far as I can see; but I warn you, that if you have no others, it is a gloomy recommendation.'

Perhaps Fortune was offended and wanted to avenge herself for this irreverence, for the chevalier, who had been more and more troubled by those last questions, suddenly saw on a corner of the table precisely the same fan that he had picked up the night before. He took it, and, as he had done the previous evening, he presented it to the marquise, bending his knee before her.

'This, madame,' he said to here, 'is the only friend I have.'

The marquise seemed at first astonished, hesitated a moment, looking now at the fan and now at the chevalier.

'Ah, you are right,' she said at length. 'It is you, sir. I recognize you. It is you I saw yesterday, after the play, with M. de Richelieu. I dropped that fan, and you *happened to be there*, as you said.'

'Yes, madame.'

'And very gallantly, like a true chevalier, you gave it back to me. I did not thank you, but I have always been persuaded that the man who can, with sufficient grace, raise a fan, can also at need, raise a glove, and we are rather fond of that, we ladies.'

'And that is only too true, madame, for, when I came here just now I almost had a duel with the Swiss guard.'

'For pity's sake!' said the marquise, overcome with a second burst of gaiety. 'With the Swiss! And for what?'

'He didn't want to let me come in.'

'That would have been a pity. But sir, who are you? what are you asking for?'

'Madame, I am called the Chevalier de Vauvert. M. de Biron had asked for me a place as cornet in the guards.'

'Of course. I remember. You come from Neauflette, and you are in love with Mademoiselle d'Annebault——'

'Madame, who can have told you that?'

'Oh, I warn you that I am much to be feared. When my memory fails, I guess. You are a relation of the Abbé Chauvelin, and were rejected because of that, weren't you? Where is your petition?'

'Here, madame. But honestly, I cannot understand——'

'Why understand? Rise up and put your paper on that table. I am going to answer the king. You will bear to him at the same time your request and my letter.'

'But madame, I thought I had told you——'

'You will go. You entered here on the king's orders, isn't that so? Well, you will enter the king's presence by the orders of the Marquise de Pompadour, lady of the queen's palace.'

The chevalier bowed without saying a word, seized with a sort of stupefaction. Everybody had known for a long time how many discussions, ruses, and intrigues the favourite had set in motion, and what obstinacy she had shown, to obtain this title, which, when all was said, brought her nothing but a cruel insult from the Dauphin. But she had desired it for ten years, she wanted it, she had got it. M. de Vauvert, whom she did not know though she knew of his love affairs, pleased her like a piece of good news.

Standing behind her motionless, the chevalier watched the marquise, who wrote at first with all her heart, passionately. Then she reflected, stopped, and passed her hand over her shrewd little nose. She grew impatient, a witness confused her. At last she made up her mind and made an erasure, we must admit it was nothing more than a scribble.

Opposite the chevalier, at the other side of the table shone a fine mirror of Venetian glass. Our extremely shy messenger hardly dared to raise his eyes. Yet it was difficult not to see in this mirror, over the marquise's head, the charming perplexed face of the new lady of the palace.

'How beautiful she is,' he was thinking. 'It 's a pity I am in love with somebody else, but Athenaïs is more lovely, and besides, it would be such a frightful disloyalty for me——'

'What are you speaking about?' said the marquise. (The chevalier as he often did, had uttered his thoughts aloud without knowing it.) 'What did you say?'

'I, madame? I am waiting.'

'There, that 's done,' answered the marquise, taking another sheet of paper. But with the slight movement she had just made to turn round the dressing gown had slipped from her shoulder.

Fashion is a strange thing. Our grandmothers found it quite all right to go to court with immense robes which left their bosoms almost uncovered, and none saw any indecency in that, but they religiously kept their backs hidden, and the fair ladies to-day display their backs in the opera balcony. It is a newly invented form of beauty.

On Madame de Pompadour's fragile, snow-white, dainty shoulder, there was a little black mark which looked like a fly fallen in the milk. The chevalier, as serious as a blunderer who wants to try to keep himself in countenance, looked at this mark, and the marquise, holding her pen in the air, looked at the chevalier in the mirror.

In this mirror a rapid glance was exchanged, a glance which a woman never mistakes, and which meant on the one side, 'You are charming', and on the other, 'I am not angry'.

Nevertheless the marquise drew up her gown.

'You are looking at my beauty spot, sir.'

'I am not looking, madame. I see it and I admire.'

'Look, here 's my letter, take it to the king along with your petition.'

'But, madame——'

'What is it now?'

'His majesty is hunting. I have just heard the horns in Satory wood.'

'That is true. I wasn't thinking about that. Well, to-morrow, the day after to-morrow, it doesn't matter—— No, this very moment. Go, you will give that to Lebel. Farewell, sir. Try to remember that beauty spot you have just seen; in all this kingdom there is only the king who has seen it. And as to your friend Chance, tell him, if you please, to get the habit of not talking all alone to himself as loudly as he did just now. Farewell, chevalier.'

She touched a little bell, then, tossing up on her sleeve a foamy mass of lace, she extended her bare arm to the young man.

He bowed again, and barely brushed with his lips the rosy finger nails of the marquise. She saw no impoliteness in that, far from it, but just a little too much modesty.

Immediately the little chambermaid reappeared (the big ones were not up yet), and behind them, erect as a steeple among a flock of sheep, the bony gentleman, always smiling, showed him the way.

VI

Alone, sunk in an old arm-chair, shut up in his little room at the Sun inn, the chevalier waited all the next day, then the day after; no news.

'A singular woman! sweet and imperious, good-natured and spiteful, most frivolous and most obstinate! She has forgotten me. Oh, bad luck! She is right. She has all the power and I am nothing.'

He had risen and was pacing the room.

'Nothing at all. I am only a poor wretch. How true were my father's words! The marquise was making fun of me: it is quite simple, while I was watching her, it was her own beauty which pleased her. She was quite content to see in that mirror and in my eyes the reflection of her charms, which, by Jove, are really incomparable! Yes, her eyes are little, but what grace! And Latour, before Diderot, took to paint her portrait the dust of a butterfly's wings. She is not very tall, but her figure is well shaped. Ah! Mademoiselle d'Annebault! Ah! my dear love, could I, too, be one of the men who forget!'

Two or three smart little knocks on the door aroused him from his peevishness.

'What 's that?'

The bony man, dressed all in black, with a fine pair of silk stockings stuffed to stimulate the calves he did not possess, entered and made a low bow.

'This evening, my lord, there is a masked ball at the Court, and madame the marquise sends me to tell you that you are invited.'

'That is all I require, sir, many thanks.'

When the bony man had gone away, the chevalier rushed to the bell. The same serving girl who three days before had assisted him as well as she could to dress, helped him to put on the same spangled suit, trying to turn him out still finer.

After which the young man made his way to the palace, invited this time, and more tranquil as far as looks went, but more nervous and less audacious than when he had taken the first step in this as yet unknown world.

VII

Dazzled, almost as much as the first time, by all the splendours of Versailles, which this evening was not a desert, the chevalier walked in the great gallery, looking on every side, trying to conceive why he should be there, but nobody seemed to think of speaking to him. At the end of an hour, he got tired and was going to go away, when two masked ladies, exactly alike, seated on a bench, stopped him on his way. One of them pointed her finger at him, as if she were holding a pistol; the other rose and came to him.

'It seems, sir,' said the masked lady to him, taking his arm carelessly, 'that you are pretty friendly with our marquise.'

'I beg your pardon, madame, but of whom are you speaking?'

'You know well enough.'

'Not in the very least.'

'Oh! yes, indeed.'

'Not at all.'

'All the Court knows that.'

'I am not of the Court.'

'You are behaving like a child. I tell you that it 's known.'

'That may be, madame, but I do not know it.'

'You know, all the same, that yesterday a page fell from his horse at the gate of Trianon. Were you not there, by good luck?'

'Yes, madame.'

'Didn't you help him to get up?'

'Yes, madame.'

'And didn't you go into the Château?'

'Undoubtedly.'

'And didn't somebody give you a paper?'

'Yes, madame.'

'And didn't you carry it to the king?'

'Certainly.'

'The king was not at Trianon, he was hunting: the marquise was alone, isn't that so?'

'Yes, madame.'

'She had just awakened: she was hardly dressed, except, the story goes, in a big dressing-gown.'

'People who can't be stopped from speaking say whatever comes into their heads.'

'Very good, but it seems that between her head and yours a look passed that didn't displease her.'

'What do you mean by that, madame?'

'That you did not displease her.'

'I know nothing of that and I would be in despair if an act of kindness so sweet and so rare, which I did not expect, and which has touched me to the bottom of my heart, could become the cause of any scandal.'

'You take fire very quickly, chevalier; one would think that you were going to challenge the whole Court: you 'll never succeed in killing so many people!'

'But, madame, if this page fell, and if I carried his message. Permit me to ask you why I am questioned.'

The masked lady pressed his arm, and said:

'Sir, listen.'

'At your service, madame.'

'This is what 's in the air just now. The king is no longer in love with the marquise, and nobody believes that he has ever loved her. She has just committed an indiscretion: she has got the whole Parlement against her with her two-sous tax, and to-day, she is venturing to attack a much greater power, the Company of Jesus. She will be worsted. But she has arms, and before perishing, she will defend herself.'

'Well, madame, what have I to do with it?'

'I am going to tell you. Monsieur de Choiseul is half at loggerheads with Monsieur de Bernis; they are not sure, either of them, what they want to try to do. Bernis is going to leave: Choiseul will take his place: one word from you can decide it.'

'In what way, madame, I ask you?'

'In letting your visit of the other day be talked about.'

'What connection can there be between my visit, the Jesuits, and the Parlement?'

'Write me a line, the marquise is lost. And have no fears but that the most intense interest, the most devoted gratitude——'

'I ask your pardon again, madame, but that is a dastardly action you are asking me to do.'

'Is there any gallantry in politics?'

'I know nothing about that. Madame de Pompadour let fall her fan before me, I picked it up, I gave it back to her: she thanked me, she allowed me, with her distinctive graciousness, to thank her in my turn.'

'A truce to all this ceremony! Time is passing. My name is the Countess d'Estrades. You are in love with Mademoiselle d'Annebault my niece, don't deny it, it 's no use: you are asking a position as cornet——. You will have it to-morrow, and, if Athénaïs attracts you, you will soon be my nephew.'

'Oh! madame, what excessive kindness!'

'But you must speak.'

'No, madame.'

'I was told that you loved this young lady.'

'As much as man can do; but if ever my love can be declared before her, my honour must be there too.'

'You are very obstinate, chevalier! Is that your last answer?'

'It is the last, as it was the first.'

'You refuse to enter the Guards? You refuse my niece's hand?'

'Yes, madame, if that is their price.'

Madame d'Estrades threw a piercing look on the chevalier, a

look full of curiosity: then, seeing on his face no sign of hesitation, she withdrew slowly and was lost in the crowd.

The chevalier, unable to make anything of this singular adventure, went and sat down in a corner of the gallery.

'What does that woman think she 's doing?' he said to himself. 'She must be a little mad. She wants to upset the state by means of a silly slander, and as a way of deserving the hand of her niece, she proposes to me to dishonour myself! But Athénaïs would have no more to do with me, or, if she lent herself to such an intrigue, it would be I who should refuse her. What! try to injure that good marquise, spread stories about her, blacken her good name? Never, no, never!'

Faithful as ever to his distractions, the chevalier, very likely, was going to rise and speak out loud, when a little finger, rose coloured, touched him lightly on the shoulder. He raised his eyes and saw before him the two identical masks who had stopped him.

'Then you don't want to give us a little help?' said one of the masked ladies, disguising her voice. But although their two costumes were exactly alike, and although everything appeared calculated to put him on the wrong scent, the chevalier was not deceived. Neither the look nor the accent were the same.

'Will you answer, sir?'

'No, madame.'

'Will you write?'

'Still less.'

'It is true you are obstinate. Good-night, lieutenant.'

'What are you saying, madame?'

'Here is your commission and your marriage contract.' And she threw him her fan.

It was the fan that the chevalier had already picked up twice. Boucher's little loves played on the parchment, amidst the gilded mother-of-pearl. There was no room for hesitation, it was Madame de Pompadour's fan.

'Good heavens, marquise, is it possible?'

'Very possible,' said she, raising the scrap of black lace from her chin.

'I do not know, madame, how to answer——'

'It isn't necessary. You are a gallant man, and we will see each other again, for you are in our household. The king has put you in the White Guard. Remember that, for a petitioner, there is no greater eloquence than that of knowing how to keep silent at the right time. And forgive me,' she added laughing, and slipping away, 'if, before giving you our niece, we made some inquiries.' [1]

[1] Madame d'Estrades, shortly after this, was disgraced along with M. d' Argenson, for having conspired, this time in earnest, against Madame de Pompadour.

SYLVIE

Gérard de Nerval

I. Leisure Nights

I LEFT the theatre where I sat every evening in a stage box, dressed with the elegance and care befitting my hopes. Sometimes the house was full, and sometimes empty, but it mattered little to me whether my eyes rested upon thirty or forty deadheads in the pit and upon boxes filled with old-time caps and dresses, or whether I found myself part of an enthusiastic audience, crowding every tier with colour and the gleam of jewels. The stage awakened my interest no more than did the house, except, during the second and third scene of the tiresome play, when a vivid appearance illuminated the empty spaces, and, with a breath and a word, summoned the shadowy figures of the actors back to life.

I felt that I lived in her, and that she lived only for me. Her smile filled me with infinite contentment, and the resonance of her voice, now soft, now vibrating with emotion, made me tremble with joy and love. She understood all my enthusiasms and whims; for me she possessed every perfection—radiant as the day, when the footlights shone upon her from below; pale as the night, when the footlights were turned down and the rays of the chandelier showed her simple beauty against a curtain of shadows, like one of the divine Hours carved on the sombre background of the frescoes of Herculaneum.

For a year it had not entered my mind to find out what her life away from the theatre might be, and I was loath to disturb the magic mirror that held her image. I may have listened to idle speculations about her private life, but my interest in it was no greater than in the prevailing rumours about the Princess of Elis or the Queen of Trebizond, for one of my uncles who had lived in the eighteenth century had warned me in good time that an actress was not a woman and that Nature had forgotten to give her a heart. Of course he meant those of his own time, but he recounted so many of his illusions and his deceptions, and he showed me so many portraits on ivory—charming medallions which now adorned his snuff-boxes—so many faded letters and ribbons, each the token of a disappointment, that I had fallen into the habit of mistrusting them all.

We were in the midst of strange years then, years like those that generally follow a revolution or the decline of a great empire. There was none of the noble gallantry of the Fronde, the polite vice of the Regency, or the scepticism and mad orgies of the Directorate; we lived in a confusion of activity, hesitation, and indolence, of dazzling Utopias, of philosophical or religious aspirations, of vague enthusiasms mingled with certain impulses towards a renewal of life, of weariness at the thought of past discord, of unformulated hopes—it was something like the epochs of Peregrinus and Apuleius. We looked for new birth from the bouquet of roses that the beautiful Isis would bring us; and at night the young and pure goddess appeared, and we were stricken with shame for the daylight hours we wasted. But ambition had no part in our life, for the greedy race for position and honours had closed to us all possible paths to activity. Our only refuge from the multitude was that Ivory Tower of the poets which we were always climbing higher and higher. Upon these heights whither our masters led us, we breathed at last the pure air of solitude, we drank forgetfulness from the golden cup of legend, and we were intoxicated with poetry and love. Love, alas! vague figures, tinges of blue and rose, spectral abstractions! Intimacies with women offended our ingenuousness, and it was our rule to look upon them as goddesses or queens, and above all never to approach them.

But there were some of our number nevertheless who thought little of these platonic sublimities, and sometimes amid our dreams borrowed from Alexandria they shook the smouldering torch of subterranean gods, and sent a trail of sparks through the darkness. Thus on leaving the theatre, my soul full of the sadness of a fading vision, I was glad to avail myself of the society of a club where many were supping and where melancholy yielded to the unfailing warmth of certain brilliant spirits whose ardour and passion often rendered them sublime—such people as one always meets during periods of renovation or decadence—people whose discussions often reached a point where the more timid amongst us would go to the windows to make certain that the Huns, or the Turcomans, or the Cossacks, had not arrived at last to put an end to rhetoric and sophism. 'Let us drink, let us love, that is wisdom!' was the only opinion of the youths among them, and it was one of these who said to me:

'I've been meeting you in the same theatre now for a long time, I always find you there. For whom do you go?' For whom? . . . It had never occurred to me that one could go there for another. However, I mentioned a name.

'Well,' said my friend, indulgently, 'there's the happy man who has just taken her home and who, faithful to the laws of our club, will probably not see her again until to-morrow morning.'

Without showing too much interest, I turned and saw a young man of the world faultlessly attired, with a pale, expectant face and eyes full of a gentle sadness. He was sitting at a whist-table, where he threw down his gold and lost it heedlessly.

'What does he matter to me?' I said, 'or any other? There had to be someone, and he seems worthy of her choice.'

'And you?'

'Me? I'm following a likeness, nothing more.'

I went out through the reading-room and instinctively picked up a newspaper; I think I wanted to see how the market was going, for after the wreck of my fortune there remained a considerable sum in foreign shares, and a rumour was afloat that the property was at last going to amount to something. A ministry had just fallen and the quotation was very high; I was rich once more.

Only one thought arose out of this turn in my affairs: the woman I had loved for so long was mine for the asking; my ideal was within reach. Surely I was deluding myself with a mocking misprint? But all the newspapers contained the same quotation, and my winnings rose up before me like the golden statue of Moloch. What would that young man say now, I wondered, if I were to take possession of the woman he had forsaken? . . . I trembled at the thought and then my pride asserted itself. No! at my age one does not put an end to love with money; I will not be a seducer. After all, the times have changed, and how do I know she is mercenary?

My eyes ran vaguely over the newspaper I was still holding, and I read these two lines: '*Fête du Bouquet Provincial.* To-morrow the archers of Senlis will present the bouquet to those of Loisy'. These simple words awakened in me an entirely new train of thought; memories of the province forgotten long ago, distant echoes of the care-free festivals of youth. The horn and the drum sounded far away in the hamlets and in the forests; maidens were weaving garlands, and they sang as they sorted out the bouquets tied with ribbons. A heavy wagon drawn by oxen passed by to receive these gifts, and we, the children of the country, took our places in the procession, knights by virtue of our bows and arrows, unaware then that we were but repeating through the years a druidic festival that would outlive monarchies and new religions.

II. Adrienne

I went to bed but found no rest; and as I lay there between sleeping and waking, memories of my childhood thronged about me. In this state, where the mind still resists the fantastic combinations of dreams, the important happenings of a long period of one's life often crowd themselves into a few moments.

The picture rose up in my mind of a château of the time of Henry IV., with its pointed slate roofs, its reddish front and yellowed stonework, and its wide enclosure edged by elms and lindens whose foliage scattered golden shafts of sunlight upon the smooth green surface. Maidens danced in a ring on the grass, and they sang old melodies, handed down to them by their mothers, with an accent so unaffectedly pure that one seemed to be actually living in that old Valois country where the heart of France beat for more than a thousand years.

I was the only boy at this dance and I had taken Sylvie with me, a little girl from the next hamlet. She was so alive and so fresh, with her black eyes, her clearly cut profile and delicately tanned complexion! . . . I loved no one but her, I had eyes for no one else—until then! . . . I saw a tall and beautiful light-haired girl in the ring where we were dancing, one whom they called Adrienne. All at once, by the rules of the dance, we found ourselves alone in the middle of the ring. We were of the same height; we were told to kiss each other, and the dancing and singing became livelier than ever. . . . I pressed her hand when I kissed her, and I felt the light touch of long golden ringlets upon my cheeks. From that moment a strange uneasiness took possession of me.

Adrienne had to sing that she might have the right to rejoin the dance. We sat in a circle about her and she began at once in the clear and delicately modulated voice peculiar to the young girls of that misty country. Her song was one of those old-time ballads, full of passionate sadness, that always tell of the misfortunes of a princess imprisoned in her tower for having loved. At the end of each stanza the melody passed into one of those quivering trills that young throats can make so much of, when, by means of a restrained shudder, they simulate the trembling voices of their grandmothers.

Twilight came down from the great trees around us as the song drew to a close, and the light of the rising moon fell upon her, alone in the midst of our listening circle; then she stopped and none of us dared to break the silence. A faint white mist spread itself over the lawn and rested upon the tips of the grass; we thought ourselves in Paradise. . . . At last I got up and ran to where there were some laurels planted in tall earthenware vases, and brought back two branches which had been woven into a crown and tied with ribbon. I placed this ornament upon Adrienne's head, and its shiny foliage caught the pale gleam of the moon. She was like Dante's Beatrice smiling at him as he wandered on the borders of heaven.

Then she got up, and making us a graceful curtsey, which showed us her slender figure, she ran across the lawn into the château. They said she was the granddaughter of one of the descendants of a family related to the ancient kings of France; the blood of the Valois ran in her veins. For this day of festivities she had been allowed to join in our games, but we were not to see her again, for she was returning the following morning to her convent school.

Sylvie was crying when I returned to her, and I found that the reason for her tears was the crown I had given to Adrienne. I offered to get her another, but she refused, saying she was unworthy of it. I tried to defend myself, but she did not speak to me again that evening.

When I returned to Paris to continue my studies, my mind was divided between a tender friendship that had come to an end, and a vague, impossible love enveloping me with painful thoughts which a schoolboy's philosophy was powerless to disperse.

But Adrienne triumphed in the end—a mirage of beauty

and nobility, that lightened or shared the severity of my studies. During the next summer's holiday I learned that, in obedience to her family's wishes, she had entered the convent.

III. Resolution

Everything was made clear to me by this half-dreamed memory. This unreasonable and hopeless love I had conceived for an actress, that took possession of me every evening at the time of the play, only to set me free at bedtime, had its origin in the memory of Adrienne, a flower of the night that opened to the pale moon, a youthful apparition, half-bathed in mist, gliding across the grass. The almost-forgotten features were now singularly clear, and it was as though a pencil sketch, dimmed by time, had become a painting; first the master's rough study and then the splendid finished picture.

To love a nun in the guise of an actress! And what if they were one and the same! That possibility leads to madness, but it is an inevitable impulse—the unknown beckons like the will-o'-the-wisp fading through the rushes in a still pool. But we must cling to realities.

Why have I forgotten Sylvie for so long, Sylvie whom I loved so well? She was such a pretty little girl, much the prettiest in Loisy. Surely she is still there, as innocent and as good as she was then. I can see her window now, framed by creepers and roses, and the cage of warblers hanging on the left; I can hear her whirring spindle and she is singing her favourite song:

La belle était assise
Près du ruisseau coulant . . .

She is still waiting for me. Who would have married her? She was so poor! There were only peasants in Loisy and the neighbouring hamlets, rough fellows with toil-worn hands and thin, sunburnt faces, so when I came to visit my uncle who lived near by, she loved *me*, a little Parisian. My poor uncle is dead now and for the last three years I have been lavishly spending the modest legacy he left me, and it might have been enough for the rest of my life. With Sylvie I would have saved it, and now chance brings to my mind this opportunity before it is too late.

What is she doing at this moment? She is asleep—no, she

cannot be, for to-day is the Festival of the Bow, the only one of the year when they dance the night through. . . . She is at the dance.

What time is it now?

I had no watch, and my gaze wandered over the extravagant collection of furniture with which an old-fashioned apartment is usually given its proper atmosphere. My Renaissance clock of tortoiseshell surpassed all the other objects with its quiet richness. A gilded dome, surmounted by the figure of Time, is supported by caryatids of the Medici period upon half-rampant horses, and Diana, leaning upon her stag, is in bas-relief beneath a dial inlaid with enamelled figures of the hours. But I did not buy this clock in Touraine that I might know the time, and, though an excellent one, it has probably not been wound up for two centuries.

I went downstairs, saying to myself that I could get to Loisy in four hours. The porter's clock struck one as I passed out into the Place du Palais-Royal, where there were still four or five cabs waiting, no doubt, for fares from the clubs and gambling houses. I mentioned my destination to the nearest driver.

'And where is that?' he asked.

'Near Senlis, about twenty miles.'

'I will take you to the post-house,' he said, less absorbed than I.

How dreary the Flanders road is at night, until it enters the forest! Always the double rows of trees, monotonous and vague in the mist; meadows and ploughed land to right and left, with the grey hills of Montmorency, Écouen, and Luzarches beyond. And then comes the dreary market town of Gonesse with its memories of the League and the Fronde; but, beyond Louvres, there is a short cut to the villages where I have often seen apple blossoms shining through the darkness like stars of the earth. While my carriage slowly ascends the hill, let me try to call those happy days to life.

IV. To the Island of Venus

Several years had passed, and already my meeting with Adrienne in front of the château was no more than a memory of youth. I had been at Loisy on the patron saint's day and took my accustomed place among the Knights of the Bow. Some young people from the dilapidated châteaux in the neighbouring forests arranged the festival, and from Chantilly, Compiègne, and Senlis joyous companies came trooping to join the rural cavalcade. After the long walk through towns and villages, and when mass was over and the prizes for the sports had been awarded, a banquet for the prize-winners was held on an island, covered with poplars and lindens, in one of the lakes fed by the Nonette and the Thève. Barges adorned with flowers carried us to this island, chosen for its oval temple which was to serve as banqueting hall. There are many of those delicate structures thereabouts, built by rich philosophers towards the end of the eighteenth century. I think this temple must have been originally dedicated to Urania. Three of the pillars had fallen, carrying a part of the architrave with them, but the fragments had been cleared away and garlands were hung between the remaining pillars; such was the restoration of this modern ruin, for which the paganism of Boufflers or Chaulieu was responsible rather than that of Horace.

It may be that the crossing of the lake had been devised to call up the memory of Watteau's 'Voyage à Cythère', and the illusion was complete but for our modern costumes. The great bouquet of the festival was taken from the wagon that carried it and placed in one of the largest barges, the customary escort of little girls in white dresses took seats around it, and this graceful procession, re-created from that of another day, was mirrored in the calm waters that lay between it and the island. The thickets of thorn, the colonnade and the brilliant foliage glowed red in the afternoon sun, and when all the barges had landed and the bouquet had been carried ceremoniously to the centre of the table, we took our places, the more fortunate of the boys sitting next to the girls. To obtain this favour it was only necessary to be known to their families, and I managed to sit by Sylvie, for her brother and I had been together in the procession. He reproached me for never coming to see them, and I spoke of my studies which kept me in Paris, assuring him that this time I had come especially to pay them a visit.

'No, he 's forgotten me,' Sylvie said. 'We 're village people and Paris is so far above us!'

I wanted to close her mouth with a kiss, but she kept on pouting until her brother intervened and she offered me her cheek in a very half-hearted fashion. It was the sort of kiss she had often given to others and I did not enjoy it, for in that old country, where one speaks to everybody, a kiss is no more than a politeness among well-mannered people.

The directors of the festival had arranged a surprise for us, and when the banquet was over, a wild swan rose up out of the depths of the basket where it had been confined beneath the flowers. Wreaths and garlands were lifted upon its strong wings and they fell all about us, and each boy took possession of one of them for the adornment of his companion's brow, while the swan took joyous flight towards the glow of the sinking sun. It was my good fortune to get one of the finest of these wreaths, and this time Sylvie was smiling when I kissed her, so the memory of that other day was blotted out. My admiration of her now was complete, for she had become so beautiful. She was no longer the little village girl whom I had scorned when my eyes fell upon another, taller and more used to the manners of the world. She had improved in every possible way: the spell of her black eyes, so captivating even as a little child, had now become irresistible; there was a gleam of Attic intelligence in her smile when its quick light spread over her calm regular features—a face that might have been painted by an old master. With her white, well-rounded arms, her long delicate hands, and her slender figure, she was no longer the Sylvie I had known, and I could not help telling her how changed I found her, in the hope that she would forget my former faithlessness.

Every circumstance was in my favour; I had the friendship of her brother, the atmosphere of the festival was alluring, and the time and place for this echo of a gay ceremonial of bygone days had been chosen with tasteful discrimination. We escaped from the dance as soon as we could, that we might talk of our childhood, and dream together as we watched the sunlight fading from tne foliage and the still surface of the lake; but Sylvie's brother put an end to our meditations, telling us the time had come to go back to Loisy.

V. The Village

I left them at the old guard house at Loisy, and returned to my uncle with whom I was staying at Montagny. Turning from the road to go through the little wood between Loisy and Saint S——, I soon found myself following the deep path that skirts the forest of Ermenonville, expecting every moment to come upon the convent walls which would cause me to go more than half a mile out of my way. Every now and then the moon was hidden by clouds, and I had great difficulty in avoiding the grey rocks and the tufts of sweet heather on both sides of the way. The path branched neither to the right nor to the left, and great druidic boulders rose up out of the thick forest, where the memory of the sons of Armen, who were killed by the Romans, is still lurking. The distant lakes looked like mirrors set in the misty plain, but I could not tell which one had been the scene of the festival.

The soft air was laden with the perfume of the wood, and I decided to go no farther, but to sleep till morning on a bed of sweet heather. When I awoke, the outlines of my surroundings were just visible. To the left, the walls of the Convent of Saint S—— stretched away into the mist, and across the valley I saw the ridge of the Gens-d'Armes and the jagged remains of the old Carlovingian dwelling. Then came Thiers Abbey, high above the tree tops, its crumbling walls, pierced by trefoils and pointed arches, silhouetted against the sky; and beyond, the moated manor of Pontarmé had just caught the first rays of the sun. To the south rose up the high turret of La Tournelle, and on the first slopes of Montméliant I saw the four towers of Bertrand-Fosse.

My thoughts were held captive by the memory of the day before, and I thought only of Sylvie. Nevertheless, the appearance of the convent forced the idea into my mind that perhaps Adrienne was within. The tolling of the morning bell, which had undoubtedly awakened me, was still in my ears, and I was suddenly possessed by the desire to climb upon the highest rock that I might look into the enclosure, but a moment's hesitation kept me from this as from a profanation. With the fullness of daylight this futile memory vanished from my mind, and I saw only the pink cheeks of Sylvie.

'Why not awaken her myself?' I said, and I started off along the path that skirts the wood towards Loisy: twenty thatched cottages festooned with vines and climbing roses. Some spinners, their hair tied in red handkerchiefs, were already at work, but Sylvie was not among them. Her people were still peasants, but Sylvie had become a young lady now that she was engaged in making fine laces. . . . I went up to her room without shocking any one, and found her already at work plying her bobbins, which clicked gently against the green frame upon her knees.

'You lazy thing,' she said, smiling adorably, 'I believe you 're only just out of bed!'

I told her how I had passed the night, of my wanderings through the woods and among the rocks, and she replied half indulgently, 'I hope you 're not too tired for another ramble, because we 're going to see my great-aunt at Othys.'

I had scarcely time to answer before she gleefully abandoned her work, arranged her hair before a mirror and put on a rough straw hat. Her eyes were bright with innocent pleasure as we set out, first following the banks of the Thève, then through a meadow full of daisies and buttercups and on into Saint-Laurent wood. Every now and then we leapt over streams and broke through thickets in order to shorten our way. Blackbirds whistled in the trees above us, and tomtits darted exultingly from the nearest bushes.

At our feet there was periwinkle, so dear to Rousseau, opening its blue flowers upon sprays of paired leaves, and Sylvie was careful not to crush them, but memories of the philosopher of Geneva did not interest her for she was hunting for strawberries. I spoke to her of *La Nouvelle Héloïse* and recited several passages I knew by heart.

'Is it good?' she asked.

'It is sublime!'

'Better than Auguste Lafontaine?'

'There is more tenderness in it.'

'Oh, well,' she said, 'I must read it then. I 'll tell my brother to get it for me the next time he goes to Senlis.' Then I recited some more passages while she gathered her strawberries.

VI. Othys

As we emerged from the wood we came upon a great clump of purple foxglove, and when Sylvie had picked an armful of it she told me it was for her aunt. 'She loves to have these beautiful flowers in her bedroom.'

There remained only a bit of level field to cross before reaching Othys, and we could see the village steeple against the bluish hills that rise from Montméliant to Dammartin. Now there fell upon our ears the pleasant rustling sound of the Thève flowing in its bed of sandstone and flint. The river was narrow here, for its source, a tiny lake enclosed by gladioli and iris, lay close by in the meadow's sleepy embrace. We soon came to the outskirts of the village where Sylvie's aunt had a little thatched cottage built of rough sandstone blocks hidden beneath trellis work that supported wild grape and hop vines; she lived on the produce of a small piece of land the village people had worked for her since her husband's death. At her niece's arrival the cottage seemed at once to be full of commotion.

'Good-morning, auntie! Here are your children!' cried Sylvie, 'and we 're dreadfully hungry!'

It was only after kissing her affectionately and placing the bunch of foxgloves in her arms that it occurred to her to introduce me: 'He is my sweetheart!' And when I too had kissed her, she said:

'What a fine young fellow—and fair hair too!'

'He 's got nice soft hair,' Sylvie added.

'It won't last,' the old woman said, 'but you 've got plenty of time, and your dark hair goes well with his.'

'We must give him some breakfast,' announced Sylvie, and she brought brown bread, milk, and sugar from the cupboard, and spread out on the table some earthenware plates and platters with flowers and bright-feathered cocks upon them in large design. A Creil bowl of strawberries, floating in milk, went in the centre, and when several handfuls of cherries and currants had been brought in from the garden, Sylvie placed a vase of flowers at either end of the tablecloth. But her aunt, who was not to be outdone, objected: 'This is all very nice, but it 's only dessert. You must let me do something now,' and taking down the frying-pan, she threw a faggot on the fire. Sylvie wanted to help her, but she was firm. 'You mustn't touch this; those pretty fingers are for making lace, finer lace than they make at Chantilly! I know, because you once gave me some.'

'Yes, I know, auntie. But tell me, have you got any old bits? I can use them for models if you have.'

'Go upstairs and see what you can find; perhaps there are some in my chest of drawers!'

'But the keys, auntie!'

'Nonsense! The drawers are open.'

'It 's not true; there 's one that 's always locked,' and while the old woman was cleaning the frying-pan, Sylvie snatched a little key of wrought steel from its place at her belt and waved it at me triumphantly.

Then she ran quickly up the wooden staircase leading to the bedroom, and I followed her. Oh, sacred Youth! Oh, sacred Old Age! Who could have dreamed of such an intrusion into that innermost sanctuary where the memory of a first love lay carefully guarded? At the head of the rough bedstead, a young man with black eyes and red lips smiled down from an oval gilt frame. He was wearing a gamekeeper's uniform of the house of Condé, and his soldierly appearance, rosy cheeks and finely modelled forehead beneath his powdered hair had cast upon this otherwise commonplace portrait the spell of youthful grace and simplicity. Some unassuming artist, invited to the royal hunt, had done the best he could, and upon the opposite wall in a similar frame hung his portrait of the young wife, mischievous and inviting, in her slim, ribbon-laced bodice, coaxing a bird perched upon her finger to come still nearer. This was indeed the same person who was cooking now down there bent over the hearth, and I thought of the fairies at the *Funambules* and the shrivelled masks that concealed soft bright faces of youth until the last scene when they were cast aside and the Temple of Love gleamed beneath the magical rays of a revolving sun.

'Oh!' I exclaimed, 'how pretty she was!'

'And what about me?' said Sylvie, who had finally succeeded in opening the famous drawer. From it she drew a long dress of worn taffeta that crackled when she shook out the wrinkles.

'I must try it on to see if it suits me. Oh! I 'm going to look like an old-fashioned fairy!'

'The Fairy of Legend, for ever young!' I thought to myself; and Sylvie unhooked her printed-cotton frock, letting it fall around her feet. The taffeta dress fitted her slim waist perfectly, and she told me to hook her up.

'Oh, these wide sleeves, aren't they absurd!' she cried; but their loop-shaped openings revealed her pretty bare arms, and her little white throat rose gracefully out of the faded tulle and ribbons of the bodice.

'Do finish it! Don't you know how to hook up a dress?' She reminded me of Greuze's 'Village Bride'.

'You must have some powder,' I said.

'We 'll find some,' and she began to rummage again in the drawers. And the treasures they contained! What delicious perfume! What a glistening of tinsel and brilliant colours: two slightly broken mother-of-pearl fans, some Chinese paste boxes, an amber necklace, and a host of other trinkets from which Sylvie extracted two little white slippers with paste buckles.

'Oh, I must wear these,' she said, 'and there ought to be embroidered stockings to go with them.' A moment afterwards we unrolled a pair of silk ones—delicate pink with green clocks; but the old woman's voice and the rattling of the frying-pan below put an end to our explorations.

'Go on down,' Sylvie commanded, and nothing I could say would persuade her to allow me to help with the stockings and slippers, so I went down to find the contents of the frying-pan already dished up—a rasher of bacon with fried eggs. But I soon had to mount the stairs again at Sylvie's call, and found her costume now complete.

'Dress yourself quickly,' and she pointed to the gamekeeper's wedding-suit spread out on the chest. In a few moments I had become the bridegroom of a past generation. Sylvie was waiting for me on the stairs, and we descended hand-in-hand to meet the astonished gaze and the startled cry of the old woman:

'Oh, my children!' She wept first and then smiled through her tears. It was a vision of her youth, at once cruel and delightful. We sat gravely down beside her, but our gaiety soon returned when she began to recall the pompous festivities of her wedding. She even remembered the old part-songs that had been sung around her bridal table, and the simple epithalamium that had accompanied her return, upon her husband's arm, after the dance. We repeated these, mindful of every hiatus and assonance; Solomon's Ecclesiastes was not more full of colour nor more amorous. And we were husband and wife for that whole lovely summer's morning.

VII. Chaâlis

It is four o'clock in the morning; the road sinks down into a cut, and then rises again. The carriage will soon pass Orry, then La Chapelle. To the left there is a road that skirts the Forest of Hallate, where I went one evening with Sylvie's brother in his cart; I think it was to some sort of festival on Saint Bartholomew's day. His pony flew over the little-used woodland roads as if bound for a witches' sabbath, until we turned through the village street at Mont-l'Évêque and, a few moments afterwards, drew up at the guard house which had once been Chaâlis Abbey . . . Chaâlis, and my mind throngs again with memories.

There is nothing of this ancient refuge of emperors left to admire except the ruins of its cloister of byzantine arches through which one may look out across the lakes—the forgotten relic of a holy edifice upon what used to be known as Charlemagne's farms. The cardinals of the House of Este, owing to their long stay thereabouts at the time of the Medici, had left their mark upon the religion of that country, so far removed from the life and movement of cities, and there is still something noble and poetic in its quality and practice; in the chapels beneath delicately moulded arches, decorated by Italian artists, one breathes the perfume of the fifteenth century. Figures of saints and angels are painted in pink upon the pale blue background of the vaulting, with an appearance of pagan allegory that calls to mind the sentimentality of Petrarch and the fictitious mysticism of Francesco Colonna.

Sylvie's brother and I were intruders that evening at what turned out to be a sort of allegorical spectacle. It had been arranged by the owner of the domain, a person of noble birth, and he had invited some families of the neighbourhood to be his guests. Some little girls from a near-by convent were to take part in the performance, which was not a reproduction of the tragedies of Saint-Cyr, but dated back to those first lyrical experiments brought into France at the time of the Valois: a mystery play of the Middle Ages. The costumes worn by the actors were long robes of azure, hyacinth or gold, and the opening scene was a discourse by the angels upon the destruction of the world. They sang of its vanished glories, and the Angel of

Death set forth the causes of its downfall. A spirit then rose up out of the depths, holding the Flaming Sword in its hand, and bade them bow down in admiration before the Glory of Christ, Conqueror of the regions beneath the earth. It seemed as though I were gazing upon Adrienne, transformed by the spirit's robe as she already was by her vocation, and the gilded pasteboard halo that encircled her head seemed to us quite naturally a ring of light. The range and the power of her voice had increased, and her singing, with its birdlike twitter of gracenotes, gave an Italian flavour to the severe phrasing of the recitative.

As I set down these words I cannot help wondering whether the events they describe actually took place or whether I have dreamed them. Sylvie's brother was a little drunk that night, for we had stopped a few moments at the guard house, where a swan with wings outspread, suspended above the door, impressed me greatly, and there were high cupboards of carved walnut, a grandfather's clock, and some trophies, bows, arrows, and a red and green marksmen's record. An odd-looking dwarf in a Chinese hat, holding a bottle in one hand and a ring in the other, seemed to be urging the marksmen to aim accurately. He was, if I am not mistaken, cut out of sheet-iron. . . . But the presence of Adrienne!—is it as clearly fixed in my mind as these details and the unquestionable existence of Chaâlis Abbey? Yet I can remember that it was the guard's son who took us into the room where the performance took place; we stood near the door and I have to-day a distinct impression of the deep emotion of that numerous company seated in front of us. It was Saint Bartholomew's day, peculiarly associated with the memory of the Medici, whose coat of arms, united with that of the house of Este, decorated the old walls. . . . But perhaps, after all, that cherished appearance was only one of my obsessions, and now, happily, the carriage has stopped at the Plessis road; I emerge from the world of dreams and it is only a quarter of an hour's walk, by a deserted path, to Loisy.

VIII. The Loisy Dance

I arrived at the Loisy dance just at that melancholy but somehow agreeable stage when the lights begin to grow dim at the approach of dawn. The lower outlines of the lindens had sunk into obscurity and their topmost branches were blue in the half-light. The rustic flute strove but faintly now to silence the song of the nightingale, and I could hardly recognize those I knew, scattered through the pale, dishevelled groups. At last I found Lise, one of Sylvie's friends, and she kissed me, saying, 'It 's a long time since we 've seen you, Parisian!'

'Ah, yes, a long time.'

'And you 've come just now?'

'By the post-coach.'

'And not too quickly!'

'I wanted to see Sylvie; is she still here?'

'She never leaves before morning; she adores dancing, you know.'

The next moment I saw her, and though her face looked tired, I noticed that same Attic smile as she turned her black eyes upon me. A youth standing near by withdrew with a bow; she would forgo the quadrille.

It was almost broad daylight as we went out hand-in-hand from the dance. The flowers drooped in the loosened coils of Sylvie's hair, and petals from the bouquet at her waist fell down over the crumpled lace of her frock. I offered to take her home and we set out beneath a grey sky along the right bank of the Thève. Yellow and white water lilies bloomed in the still pools at each bend in the stream, upon a delicately embroidered background of water stars; the meadows were dotted with sheaves and hayricks, and though their fragrance was less intoxicating than the cool scent of the woods and the thickets of flowering thorn, we followed the river path.

'Sylvie,' I said, 'you love me no longer!'

'Ah, my dear friend,' she sighed, 'you must be reasonable; things don't come out in life as we want them to. You once spoke to me of *La Nouvelle Héloïse*; I 've read it now, but the first sentence that met my eyes made me shudder, 'Every girl who reads this book is lost'. However, I went on with it, trusting to my own judgment. You remember the day we dressed up in the wedding clothes at my aunt's. In the book there were engravings of lovers in old-fashioned costumes, and when I saw Saint-Preux I thought of you, and I was Julie. Oh, if you had only been here then! But they told me you were in Italy, and I suppose you saw girls there much prettier than I am.'

'None as beautiful as you, Sylvie, nor with such clear-cut features. You might be a nymph out of some old legend! And our country here; it's just as beautiful as the Italian country; the rocks there are just as high as ours, to be sure, and a cascade falls down over them like the one at Terni, but I saw nothing there that I miss here.'

'And in Paris?'

'In Paris?' I shook my head without replying, and I thought suddenly of that shadowy form that had troubled my mind for so long.

'Sylvie,' I said, 'let's stop here, do you mind?' Then I knelt at her feet, and told her of my indecision and my fickleness, while the hot tears rolled down my cheeks, and I called up the sinister apparition that haunted my life. 'Sylvie,' I sobbed, 'you must save me, for I shall always love you and no one else.'

She turned to me tenderly and was about to speak, but at that moment we were interrupted by a gay burst of laughter from some bushes behind us. It was Sylvie's brother, who, after numerous refreshments at the dance, had come on to join us, in a state of exaltation far beyond the usual limits of country gaiety. He called to Sylvie's admirer, who had remained behind the bushes, but who now came towards us even more unsteadily than his companion. He seemed more embarrassed with me than with Sylvie, and his sincere though awkward deference prevented me from bearing him any ill-will for having been the partner with whom Sylvie had stayed so late at the dance. I thought him not a very dangerous rival.

'We must go home, so good-bye for the present,' Sylvie said, and she offered me her cheek, which did not seem to offend her admirer.

IX. Ermenonville

I hadn't the slightest desire to sleep, so I went to Montagny to see my uncle's house once more. Sadness took possession of me when I caught sight of its yellow front and green shutters; everything was just as before, except that I had to go around to the farmhouse for the key, and then the shutters were thrown open, and I stood among the old bits of carefully polished furniture, all in their accustomed places: the high walnut cupboard, the two Flemish pictures, said to be the work of our artist grandfather, some large engravings after Boucher, and a series of engraved illustrations from *Émile* and *La Nouvelle Héloïse* by Moreau. The stuffed dog on the table had been my companion during his lifetime for many tramps through the woods; he was an Italian pug, perhaps the last of that forgotten race.

'The parrot 's still alive,' the farmer told me, 'I 've got him over at my house.' And I looked out across the garden, a mass of luxuriant weeds; but over in the corner I could still see traces of the little patch that had been my own garden as a child. Trembling with emotion, I entered the study with its little bookcase of carefully chosen volumes, old friends of the man whose memory they evoked, and on his desk I saw the old Roman vases and medallions he had dug up in his garden, a small but greatly treasured collection.

'Let 's see the parrot,' I said, and on entering the farmhouse we could hear him demanding his lunch as stridently as ever. He turned his gaze on me, and his round eye in its circle of wrinkled skin made me think of a calculating old man.

My belated visit to this well-loved spot filled me with gloomy thoughts, and I longed to see Sylvie again. Sylvie was not a memory, she was alive and young, the only person who could keep me in this country of my childhood. At midday I set out along the Loisy road, and since everybody would be sure to be resting after the dance, I decided to walk two miles and a half through the woods to Ermenonville. The sun scarcely penetrated the interlacing branches of the trees above me, and the forest road was as deliciously cool as an avenue in some great park. Scattered among the tall oaks were birches with their white trunks and quivering foliage; no birds were singing, and the stillness was complete but for the tap-tap of a green woodpecker building its nest. The directions on the finger-posts were often quite illegible, and once I very nearly lost my way, but at last, leaving the *Désert* on my left, I came to the dancing-green and found the old men's bench still in existence and I stood before this graphic realization of *Anacharsis* and of *Émile*, beset by memories of an ancient philosophy revived by the previous owner of the estate.

A little farther on when the glistening surface of a lake shone through the branches of the hazels and willows, I knew it was to this spot that my uncle had so often brought me.

Here in a grove of pines stands the Temple of Philosophy, unhappily never completed by its founder. This unfinished structure, already in ruins, resembles the temple of the Tiburtine sibyl, and upon it are the names of great thinkers, beginning with Montaigne and Descartes and ending with Rousseau; graceful strands of ivy hang down among the columns, and the steps are covered with brambles. I remember being brought here as a little child to witness the awarding of school prizes to white-robed maidens. Raspberry and dog-briers have killed the roses now; and have the laurels been cut, as they were in the song of the maidens who would not go into the wood? No, those delicate Italian shrubs could not live in our misty country, but Virgil's privet still blooms as if to emphasize his words inscribed above the door: *Rerum cognoscere causas!* Yes, this temple is falling away like so many others; tired and forgetful men will pass it by unnoticed, and Nature will carelessly reclaim the ground that Art sought to take from her, but a desire for knowledge will persist for ever as the strength-giving incentive to every action.

I turned and saw the island with its grove of poplars, and the tomb of Rousseau which no longer contains his ashes. Ah! Rousseau, we were too weak to avail ourselves of what you set before us; we have forgotten what you taught our fathers, and we have wrongly interpreted your words, those last echoes of ancient wisdom. Still, we must take courage, and, as you did at the moment of your death, turn our eyes to the sun.

I saw the château surrounded by still waters, the cascade splashing down over the rocks, and the causeway joining the two parts of the village with its four dovecots. The lawn stretches away to a great length between steep, shady hills, and Gabrielle's tower is reflected in the flower-starred waters of the artificial lake; little billows of foam press against the rocks beneath the cascade, and there is a monotonous hum of insects. The artificiality of the place repels me, and I hurry away across the sandy heathland, with its bracken and pink heather. How lonely and cheerless all these places are now, without Sylvie, and how delightful her childish joy made them seem to me years ago! I can recall her little cries as she ran here and there among the rocks and heather. With tanned skin and bare feet she was like a young savage, except for the straw hat whose broad ribbons streamed out behind with her black hair. We went to get some milk at the dairy farm, and the farmer said to me, 'How pretty your sweetheart is, little Parisian!'

And she didn't dance with peasants then, you may be sure. She danced with me only, once a year, at the Festival of the Bow.

X. *Curly-Head*

When I reached Loisy, everybody was up and about. Sylvie had quite the air of a young lady, and her clothes were almost entirely in the style of the city. She took me upstairs with all her former artlessness, and her smile was just as captivating as ever, but the prominent arch of her eyebrows gave her a look of seriousness now and then. The bedroom saw still quite simple, though the furniture was modern. The antique pier-glass had gone and in its place there was a mirror in a gilt frame, and above it a picture of a shepherd offering a bird's nest to a pink and blue shepherdess. The four-post bed, modestly hung with old flowered chintz, was now replaced by a walnut bedstead with a pointed canopy, and there were no more warblers in the cage by the window, but canaries. There was nothing of the past in this room, and my one idea was to leave it.

'Will you be making lace to-day?' I asked her.

'Oh, I don't make lace any more, there 's no demand for it here; even at Chantilly the factory is closed.'

'What do you do then?'

For answer she produced from one of the cupboards a steel instrument that looked like a long pair of pliers, and I asked her what it was.

'It 's what they call "the machine"; with it you hold the skin of the glove in order to sew it.'

'Ah, then you make gloves, Sylvie?'

'Yes, we work here for the Dammartin trade, and it pays very well just now. Where d' you want to go? I 'm not working to-day.'

I looked towards the Othys road, but she shook her head and I knew that her aunt was no longer alive. Then she called a little boy and told him to saddle the donkey.

'I 'm still tired from last night, but this will do me good. Let 's go to Chaâlis.'

The little boy followed us through the forest, carrying a branch, and Sylvie soon wanted to stop, so I urged her to rest a while, kissing her as I helped her to dismount. Somehow I could no longer bring our talk round to intimate matters, and was obliged to tell her of my travels and my life in Paris.

'It seems strange to go so far away.'

'To see you again makes me think so too.'

'Oh! that 's easily said.'

'And you must admit that you are prettier now than you used to be.'

'I know nothing about that.'

'Do you remember when we were children, how much bigger you were than I?'

'And I was the naughtiest too!'

'Oh, Sylvie!'

'And we were put in two baskets slung on the donkey's back.'

'Do you remember showing me how to catch crayfish beneath the bridges over the rivers?'

'And do you remember the day when your foster-brother pulled you out of the water?'

'You mean Curly-head! And it was he who told me I could wade across!' Then I hurried on to change the conversation. This incident vividly recalled the time when I had come there dressed in a little English suit, and all the peasants had laughed at me except Sylvie, who thought me magnificent. But I lacked the courage to remind her of her compliment of long ago, and the thought of the wedding clothes we had put on at Othys rose up in my mind, so I asked what had become of them.

'Dear old auntie, she lent me the dress to dance in at the Dammartin Carnival two years ago; she died last year.' And Sylvie wept so bitterly that I did not like to ask her how it was that she had gone to a masked ball. But I understood without asking when I remembered that, thanks to her trade of glove-maker, she was no longer a peasant. Her people were still as they had always been, but she was like an industrious fairy bringing ease and comforts to them all.

XI. The Return

When we came out of the wood we found ourselves among the lakes of Chaâlis. The slanting sun fell upon the little château which had sheltered the loves of Henry IV and Gabrielle, and it glowed red against the dull green of the forest.

'That 's a real Walter Scott landscape, isn't it?' said Sylvie.

'And who told you about Walter Scott? You *have* been reading since I saw you three years ago! I want to forget books, and what gives me real pleasure is to revisit the old abbey where we used to play hide-and-seek together as little children. Do you remember how frightened you were when the keeper told us the story of the Red Monks?'

'Oh, don't let 's talk about that.'

'Then you must sing me the song of the maiden who was carried off while walking by the white rose tree in her father's garden.'

'One doesn't sing that song any more.'

'Have you been studying music?'

'A little.'

'Then I suppose you sing nothing but operatic airs now!'

'And why should you complain of that?'

'Because I love those old melodies and because you will forget how to sing them.'

Sylvie then went through several bars of an air from a modern opera, phrasing them as she sang.

We walked past the pools and soon came upon the smooth green lawn edged by elms and lindens where we had danced so often. My conceit led me to mark out the old Carlovingian walls for her and to decipher the coat of arms of the House of Este.

'And you talk to me of reading! See how much more you have read than I. You 're quite a scholar.' Her tone of reproach was irritating just when I had been waiting for a favourable moment to renew my entreaties of the morning. But what could I say to her, accompanied by a donkey and a very wide-awake little boy who never left us for a second, in order not to miss hearing a Parisian talk? And then I was stupid enough to tell her of that unforgettable appearance of

Adrienne at Chaâlis long ago; we even went into the very room in the château where I had heard her sing.

'If I could only hear your voice here beneath these arches, Sylvie, it would drive away the spirit that torments me, be it divine or the old bewitchment.'

Then she repeated after me:

Anges, descendez promptement
Au fond du purgatoire! . . .

'What a gloomy song!'

'To me it 's sublime; it is probably by Porpora, and I think the words were translated in the sixteenth century.'

'I 'm sure I don't know,' said Sylvie.

We came back through the valley, taking the Charlepont road which the peasants, naturally unversed in etymology, insist upon calling Châllepont. Sylvie, weary of the donkey, was walking beside me, leaning upon my arm. The road was deserted and I tried to speak the words that were in my mind, but somehow nothing but the most vulgar expressions occurred to me, or perhaps a pompous phrase from a novel that Sylvie might have read. Then, as we approached the walls of Saint S——, I surprised her with something quite classic, and fell silent for we were crossing water meadows and our path had to be carefully chosen among the interlacing streams.

'What 's become of the nun?' I said suddenly.

'How tiresome you are with your nun! . . . Well, that affair hasn't turned out very well.' And this was all Sylvie would say about it.

I wonder whether women know when men are not speaking their true feelings? So often are they deceived, that it seems hardly possible, and many men act the comedy of love so cleverly! Though there are women who submit knowingly to deception, I could never bring myself to practise it, and besides, there is something sacred about a love that goes back to one's childhood. Sylvie and I had grown up together, almost as brother and sister, and to attempt to seduce her was unthinkable. Quite a different thought rose up in my mind!

Were I in Paris at this moment, I said to myself, I would be at the theatre. What will Aurelia (that was the actress's name) be playing in to-night? Surely the princess in the new drama, and how pathetic she is in the third act! And the love scene in the second, with that wizened old fellow who plays the hero. . . .

'What are you meditating?' asked Sylvie, and then she began to sing:

> A Dammartin, l'y a trois belles filles:
> L'y en a z'une plus belle que le jour . . .

'Ah, that 's not fair,' I cried, 'you know plenty of those old songs!'

'If you came here oftener I would try and remember them, but it would take time. You have your occupation in Paris, and I have my work here. Don't let 's be too late; to-morrow I must be up at sunrise.'

XII. Father Dodu

I was about to reply by throwing myself at her feet and offering her my uncle's house which I could still buy back, for there had been several heirs and the little estate was as yet undivided, but unhappily we had arrived at Loisy, where supper was being delayed for us. Onion soup proclaimed itself before we entered, and some of the neighbours had been invited to celebrate the day after the festival. I recognized Father Dodu at once, the old woodman who used to tell stories by the fire in the evenings. In his time, Father Dodu had been a shepherd, a messenger, a gamekeeper, a fisherman, and even a poacher, and in his leisure moments he made cuckoo clocks and turnspits. His present occupation was to show Ermenonville to the English, taking them to all the places where Rousseau had sat in meditation, and telling them about the philosopher's last days. It was Father Dodu who, as a little boy, had been employed by him to sort out his plants, and he had gathered the hemlock whose juice was to be squeezed into his cup of coffee. The innkeeper of the Golden Cross would never believe this last detail and consequently the old woodman had always hated him. It had long been grudgingly admitted that Father Dodu possessed several quite innocent secrets, such as curing sick cows by reciting a verse of the Scriptures backwards, and making the sign of the cross with the left foot. But he always disowned them, declaring that, thanks to the memory of his conversations with Jean-Jacques, he had long since abandoned superstitions.

'Have you come here, little Parisian, to corrupt our girls?

'I, Father Dodu?'

'You take them into the woods when the wolf 's not there!'

'You are the wolf, Father Dodu.'

'I was, as long as I could find any sheep; now there are only goats and they can defend themselves. You Paris people are a bad lot, and Jean-Jacques was right when he said, "*L'homme se corrompt dans l'air empoisonné des villes.*"'

'You know only too well, Father Dodu, that men are corrupt everywhere.' Whereupon the old man began a drinking-song which he finished in spite of our outcry against a certain filthy verse that we all knew it contained. We besought Sylvie to sing, but she refused, saying that one did not sing at table nowadays.

I had already noticed the youth who had been so attentive to her the night before, for he was sitting on her left, and there was something in his round face and dishevelled hair that was strangely familiar to me. He got up and came round behind my chair; 'Don't you recognize me, Parisian?' And then the woman who had been waiting on us whispered in my ear. 'Don't you remember your foster-brother?'

'Oh, it 's Curly-head, of course,' I cried, thankful for the timely information, 'and you pulled me out of the water!'

Sylvie burst out laughing at our meeting, and Curly-head continued, after kissing me, 'I didn't know you had a beautiful silver watch in your pocket, and that you were much more anxious at its having stopped than you were about yourself; you said, "The animal's drowned, he doesn't go tick-tack any more! Whatever will my uncle say?"'

'So that 's what they tell little children in Paris!' said Father Dodu. 'Fancy an animal in a watch!'

I thought Sylvie had forgotten me completely, for she started to go up to her room, saying she was sleepy, but as I kissed her good night she said, 'Come and see us to-morrow.'

Father Dodu sat with us for a long time over a bottle of ratafia. Once he paused between two verses of a song he was singing and said, 'All men are the same to me. I drink with a pastry-cook as I would drink with a prince!'

'And where is the pastry-cook?' I asked.

'This young man wants to go into the business.' Then Curly-head blushed, and I understood everything.

I was fated to have a foster-brother in this place made illustrious by Rousseau (Rousseau who reproved the use of wet-nurses!). Father Dodu told me that Sylvie would probably marry Curly-head, and that he wanted to open a confectioner's shop at Dammartin. I asked no more questions, and the next day the Nanteuil-le-Haudoin coach took me back to Paris.

XIII. Aurelia

To Paris! . . . The coach would take five hours, but I only wanted to be there for the evening, and eight o'clock found me in my usual seat. The play, the work of a poet of the day, and faintly reminiscent of Schiller, owed much to Aurelia's inspired reading of her lines, and in the garden scene she was astonishing. She did not appear in the fourth act, and I went out to Madame Prévost's to buy her a bouquet. In it I put a very affectionate letter, signed *Un Inconnu,* saying to myself that I now had something settled for the future. The next morning I started for Germany. And why did I do this? To bring order into the confusion of my thoughts. If I were to write a novel about a man in love with two women at once, what chance would I have of getting it accepted? Sylvie had slipped away from me, and though I had no one to blame for this but myself, it had taken only a day to rekindle my love for her. Now she was for me a statue in the Temple of Wisdom, whose placid smile had caused me to hesitate at the edge of an abyss. And it seemed inconceivable to offer myself to Aurelia, to join that company of commonplace lovers who fluttered like moths into a consuming flame.

We shall see one day, I said, whether she has a heart or not, and it was not long before I read in the papers that Aurelia was ill. I wrote to her from the mountains of Salzburg, but my letter was so full of Germanic mysticism that I hardly expected it to have much success; there could be no answer, for I had not signed my name, and I put my faith in Chance and . . . *l'Inconnu.*

Months went by while I was writing a poetic drama about the painter Colonna's love for Laura, whose family had placed her in a convent, and whom he had loved till the end of his days; there was something in this subject akin to my own perplexities. When I had finished the last line I began to think about returning to France.

What can I say now that will not be the story of most of my fellow-beings? I passed, circle by circle, into the Purgatory which we call the theatre; 'I ate of the drum and drank of the cymbal,' as runs the senseless phrase of the initiates of Eleusis. It means, no doubt, that when the need arises one must go beyond the boundaries of nonsense and absurdity. For me it was a question of achieving my ideal and of making it permanent.

Aurelia accepted the leading part in the drama I had brought back with me from Germany, and I shall never forget the day when she let me read it to her. It was she who had inspired the love scenes, and consequently there was true feeling in my rendering of them. Then I disclosed the identity of *l'Inconnu* of the two letters, and she said, 'You are quite mad, but come and see me again. I am still waiting to find the man who knows how to love me.'

Oh, woman! Is it love you are seeking? And I? The letters I wrote her then must have been more exquisite and more moving than any she had ever received, but her replies did not exceed the limits of friendship. One day, however, her emotions were stirred, and she summoned me to her boudoir to tell me of an attachment from which it would be very difficult to extricate herself.

'If you really love me for myself,' she said, 'you will want me to be yours and yours only.'

Two months later I received an effusive letter, and a few moments after reading it I was on my way to her flat. A friend whom I met in the street gave me this precious bit of information: the young man I had met at the club had just joined the Algerian cavalry.

The next summer Aurelia and her companions gave a performance at the Chantilly race meeting and I made myself as agreeable as possible to the manager. He had played Dorante in Marivaux's comedies and the lover's part in many dramas, and his latest success was in the play after the manner of Schiller, when he looked so wizened. At close range he seemed much younger, and being slender he was able to produce quite an effect in the provinces, for he still had plenty of vivacity. I had succeeded in getting him to give performances at Senlis and Dammartin, for I had become attached to the company as Chief Poet: he was at first in favour of Compiègne, but Aurelia had agreed with me. The following day, while they were dealing with the authorities and obtaining a theatre, I hired some horses and we rode out past the lakes of Comelle to have lunch at the Château of Queen Blanche. Dressed in her riding-habit, and with her hair streaming out in the wind, Aurelia rode through the wood like a queen of bygone days, to the great bewilderment of the peasantry, who had never seen any one, since Madame de F——, so imposing or so gracious. After lunch we went to some neighbouring villages, so like those of Switzerland, with sawmills run by the waters of the Nonette. These places, full of precious memories for me, awakened only a mild interest in Aurelia, and even when I took her to the green lawn in front of the château near Orry, where I had first seen Adrienne, she was unmoved. So I told her how my love had been awakened by that slender figure bathed in mist and moonlight, and how, since then, that love had lived only in my dreams, now to be realized in her. She was gravely attentive, and when I had finished speaking she said, 'You don't love me at all! You 're only waiting for me to tell you that the actress and the nun are the same person. All you want is a drama, and the climax evades you. I 've lost my faith in you completely!'

A flash of the truth came to me as she spoke. This extraordinary passion that had possessed me for so long, these dreams and these tears, this despair and this tenderness, perhaps it wasn't love at all? But then where was love to be found?

Aurelia played that evening at Senlis, and it seemed to me that she showed rather a fondness for the manager, the wizened lover. He was an extremely upright man, and he had been very useful to her. One day she spoke of him to me, 'If you want to see someone who really loves me, there he is!'

XIV. The Last Leaves

Such are the vagaries that beguile and disturb the morning of life, and though there seems to be little order in what I have written here, I know there are those who will understand me. Illusions fall away from us one after the other, and experience is like a fruit that may not be tasted until the skin is removed.

Its flavour is often bitter, but there is something invigorating in bitterness. (I hope these old phrases will be forgiven.)

Rousseau says that to look upon Nature is consolation for everything, and I sometimes go in search of my favourite grove at Clarens, lost in the mists to the north of Paris, but there is nothing there to stir my memory. All is changed.

Ermenonville!—where they still read Gessner's ancient idyl, translated for the second time—no longer will your twofold radiance fall upon me, blue or rose, like Aldebaran's elusive star; now Adrienne, now Sylvie, the two objects of a single passion, an unachieved ideal and a sweet reality. Your shady groves, your lakes, and even your solitudes, what are they to me now? Othys, Montagny, Loisy, your humble neighbours, and Chaâlis now being restored: they have kept nothing of the past. Sometimes the need rises up within me to revisit these places of silence and meditation, and sadly to evoke the fugitive memories of a time when my affectation was to be natural; and I often smile on reading the once admired lines of Roucher cut into the surface of a rock, or a benevolent saying carved on a fountain or above the entrance to a grotto sacred to Pan. The ponds, dug out at such great expense, offer their leaden waters to the swans in vain, and the woods no longer echo with the horns of the Condé huntsmen or flash with the colour of their habits. To-day there is no direct road to Ermenonville; sometimes I go by Creil and Senlis, and sometimes by Dammartin.

I never go to Dammartin until evening, so I spend the night at the *Image Saint Jean*, where they give me a room with old tapestry upon the walls and a pier-glass hanging between the windows. Beneath an eiderdown coverlet, with which one is always provided in that part of the country, I sleep warmly, and in the morning, through an open window framed by vines and roses, I survey with delight a green expanse of twenty-five miles. The poplars look like lines of soldiers, and here and there villages shelter beneath their pointed church towers. First there is Othys, then Ève, then Ver; and I could find Ermenonville in the forest, if it had a tower, but in that retreat of philosophers the church has been neglected. I breathe deeply of this pure upland air, and set forth to the confectioner's shop.

'Hello, Curly-head!'

'Hello, little Parisian!' And after a friendly hand-clasp,

I run upstairs to be welcomed by shouts of joy from the two children and by Sylvie's delighted smile. I say to myself, 'Perhaps this is happiness! Still . . .'

I sometimes call her Lolotte, and though I do not carry pistols, for it is no longer the fashion, she thinks me a little like Werther. While Curly-head is occupied in getting the lunch ready, we take the children for a walk through the avenue of limes that encircles what is left of the old brick towers of the château, and while they are playing with their bows and arrows we read poetry or a page or two from one of those short books that are so rare nowadays.

I forgot to say that I took Sylvie to the performance at Dammartin, and asked her whether she thought Aurelia resembled someone she knew.

'Whom do you mean?'

'Don't you remember Adrienne?'

'What an idea!' she exclaimed, and burst out laughing, but then, as if in self-reproach, she sighed and said, 'Poor Adrienne, she died at the Convent of Saint S—— about 1832.'

Translated by James Whitall.

THE BLUE ROOM

Prosper Mérimée

A young man was walking about agitatedly in the entrance hall of a railway station. He wore blue spectacles, and though he did not have a cold, he raised his handkerchief continually to his nose. In his left hand he carried a little black bag which contained, as I learned later, a silk dressing-gown and a pair of Turkish trousers.

From time to time he went to the door at the entrance, looked into the street, then pulled out his watch, and consulted the station clock. The train did not leave until an hour later; but there are people who are always afraid of being late. This train was not one of those that take people in a hurry: there were few first-class compartments. The time of day was not such as allowed members of the Stock Exchange to set out after business so as to dine in their country houses. When the passengers began to put in an appearance a Parisian would have recognized them from their style of dress as farmers or petty tradesmen from the suburbs. Yet every time that a man came into the station, every time that a carriage stopped at the door, the heart of the young man in the blue spectacles swelled like a balloon, his knees began to tremble, his bag was ready to slip from his hands, and his spectacles to fall from his nose where, to mention it in passing, they were set askew.

It was even worse when, after a long wait, there appeared, through a side door, coming just from the only quarter that was not the object of his continual watching, a woman dressed in black, with a thick veil over her face, who was holding in her hand a brown morocco bag containing, as I discovered later on, a wonderful dressing-gown and bedroom slippers of blue satin. The woman and the young man advanced towards one another, glancing right and left, never in front. They met, touched hands, and remained several minutes without saying a word, panting, gasping, in the grip of one of those poignant emotions for which I myself would give a hundred years of a philosopher's life.

When they found strength to speak:

'Leo,' said the young woman (I have forgotten to say that she was young and pretty), 'Leo, splendid! I would never have recognized you behind those blue spectacles.'

'Splendid!' said Leo. 'I would never have recognized you behind that black veil.'

'Splendid!' she went on. 'Let 's take our seats quickly; if the train were to go without us!' (and she squeezed his arm hard). 'Nobody has the least suspicion. I am at this moment with Clara and her husband, on the way to her country house, where I 'm supposed to say good-bye to her *to-morrow*. And', she added laughing and hanging her head, 'she has gone away an hour ago, and to-morrow—after having spent my *last evening* with her!' (again she squeezed his arm)—'to-morrow in the forenoon, she will leave me at the station where I shall find Ursula, whom I have sent in advance to my aunt's. Oh, I have foreseen everything. Let us get our tickets! It is impossible for any one to guess about us! Oh! if we are asked our names in the inn? I 've forgotten already.'

'M. and Madame Duru.'

'Oh no! Not Duru. There was a bootmaker at the boarding-house called that.'

'Well then, Dumont?'

'Daumont.'

'That 's settled, but we won't be asked.'

The bell rang, the door of the waiting-room opened, and the young woman, still carefully veiled, darted into a coach with her young companion. For the second time the bell rang; the door of the compartment was shut.

'We are all alone!' they cried to each other joyously.

But at the same instant, a man of about fifty, all dressed in black, with a grave preoccupied expression, entered the carriage and settled himself in a corner, the locomotive whistled, and the train began to move. The young people, moving away as far as they could get from their unwelcome neighbour, began to speak to one another in a low voice, and in English, by way of excess of precaution.

'Sir,' said the other traveller, in the same language and with a much purer British accent, 'if you have secrets to tell, you will do well not to tell them in English before me. I am an Englishman. I am dreadfully sorry to embarrass you, but in the other compartment there was a man alone, and I make it my principle never to travel with a man alone—that man there had the face of a Judas. And that might have tempted him.'

He pointed to his travelling bag, which he had thrown down before him on a cushion.

'Anyhow, if I 'm not asleep I 'll be reading.'

In fact, he tried loyally to sleep. He opened his bag, took out of it a comfortable cap, put it on his head, and kept his eyes closed for several minutes; then he opened them again with a gesture of impatience, looked in his bag for his glasses, then a Greek book; finally he began to read with great attention. To get at the book in his bag he had to disarrange a lot of things tossed in haphazard. Among others, he drew from the depths of the bag a fairly fat bundle of English banknotes, put them on the seat opposite him, and before replacing them in his bag he showed them to the young man, asking him if he would be able to change banknotes at N——.

'Probably. It 's on the road to England.'

N—— was the place to which the two young people were going. There is in N—— a tidy enough little hotel where hardly anybody sleeps except on a Saturday night. The rooms are said to be good. The proprietor and his staff are not far enough away from Paris to have this provincial vice. The young man, whom I have already called Leo, had been to see this hotel some time before, without his blue spectacles, and in consequence of the report he had brought of it, his friend had seemed smitten with the desire to visit it.

In any case she was on that day in such a state of mind that the walls of a prison would have seemed to her full of charm, if she could have been shut up there with Leo.

However, the train still went on; the Englishman read his Greek without turning his head towards his companions, who talked so low that only lovers could have heard each other. Maybe I shall not surprise my readers when I tell them that they were lovers in all the senses of the word, and what is deplorable about it is, that they were not married, and that there were reasons which prevented them from becoming so.

The train reached N——. The Englishman got down first. While Leo helped his lady to get out of the coach without showing her legs, a man leaped on to the platform from the neighbouring compartment. He was pale, yellowish even, his eyes hollow and bloodshot, his beard ill-kempt, a sign by which great criminals are often recognized. His suit was clean, but worn threadbare. His frock-coat, formerly black, now grey at the back and the elbows, was buttoned up to his chin, probably to hide a worn-out waistcoat. He went up to the Englishmen, and in a very humble tone:

'Uncle!' he said in English.

'Leave me alone, you wretch,' cried the Englishman, in the same language, and his grey eyes lit up with a flash of anger.

And he took a step to leave the station.

'Don't drive me to despair,' the other went on with an accent at once pathetic and almost menacing.

'Please be good enough to look after my bag a moment,' said the old Englishman, throwing his travelling bag at Leo's feet.

Straightway he took the arm of the man who had accosted him, led him or rather pushed him to a corner where he hoped not to be overheard, and there spoke to him for a minute in a very rude tone, as it appeared. Then he drew from his pocket some papers, crushed them up, and put them in the hands of the man who had called him uncle. The latter took the papers without thanks, and almost immediately walked away and disappeared.

There is only one hotel at N——; it is no matter for astonishment then, if at the end of several minutes all the personages of this true story found themselves together there. In France every traveller who has the good luck to have a well-dressed lady on his arm is sure of getting the best room in any hotel: and so is established the legend that we are the most polite nation in Europe.

If the room which was given to Leo was the best, it would be rash to conclude from that that it was excellent. There was a big walnut bed, with chintz curtains on which was printed in violet the magic story of Pyramus and Thisbe. The walls were covered with a painted wall-paper, representing a view of Naples with many figures; unfortunately, idle and indiscreet travellers had added pipes and moustaches to all the faces, male and female; and a lot of stupid remarks in prose and in verse, written in blacklead, could be read on the sky and on the sea. On this background were hung several engravings; 'Louis Philippe taking his Oath to the Charter of 1830', 'The First Interview of Julie and Saint-Preux', 'The Expectation of Bliss', and 'Regrets', after M. Dubuffe. This room was called the Blue Room, because the two arm-chairs to right and left of the mantelpiece were in Utrecht velvet of that colour; but for many years they had been hidden under covers of grey-glazed cotton with amaranth trimmings.

While the maidservants of the hotel pressed round the new arrival, and offered her their services, Leo, who was not deprived of his good sense although in love, went to the kitchen to order dinner. He had to make use of all his best rhetoric and some means of corruption to obtain the promise of a dinner in private; but his horror was great when he learnt that in the principal dining-room, that is to say, in the room next to his, the officers of the Third Hussars, who were about to relieve the officers of the Third Chasseurs at N——, were intending to join these latter, this very day, in a farewell dinner, at which would reign the greatest cordiality. The host swore by his great gods that, apart from the gaiety natural to all French soldiers, the Hussars and the Chasseurs were known in all the town for their gentleness and good behaviour, and that their proximity would not be awkward in the very slightest for madame; the custom of the officers being to rise from the table before midnight.

As Leo regained the blue room after this assurance, which caused him no little inquietude, he noticed that his Englishman occupied the room next to his. The door was open. The Englishman, sitting before a table on which were a glass and a bottle, was watching the ceiling with deep attention, as if he were counting the flies that walked across it.

'What do the neighbours matter?' said Leo to himself. 'The Englishman will soon be drunk, and the Hussars will go away before midnight.'

When he entered the blue room his first care was to assure himself that the communication doors were fast locked, and that they had bolts. On the side of the Englishman there was a double door; the walls were thick. On the side of the Hussars the partition was thinner, but the door had lock and bolt.

After all, against curiosity, it was a barrier much more efficacious than the blinds of a carriage, and how many people think themselves isolated from the world in a cab.

Assuredly, the most fertile imagination cannot conceive of

felicity more complete than that of those two young lovers who, after a long wait, found themselves alone, far from jealous and curious eyes, ready to recount to each other at leisure their past sufferings, and to taste the delights of a perfect reunion. But the devil always finds means of pouring his drop of wormwood into the cup of happiness.

Johnson has written, but he was not the first, and he had taken it from a Greek, that no man can say to himself: 'To-day I shall be happy'. This truism, recognized at an epoch so far remote by the greatest philosophers, is still unknown to a certain number of mortals, and singularly unknown to the majority of lovers.

While they were having a pretty middling dinner in the blue room of several dishes purloined from the banquet of the Hussars and the Chasseurs, Leo and his lady had much to suffer from the conversation which was being kept up by those gentlemen in the next room. They were treating of subjects foreign to strategy and tactics—subjects which I shall take care not to recount.

It was a succession of bizarre stories, almost all of them very light, accompanied by bursts of laughter, in which it was sometimes rather difficult for our lovers not to take part. Leo's lady was not a prude; but there are things that one does not like to hear, even *tête-à-tête* with the man that one loves. The situation was becoming more and more embarrassing and, as dessert was just about to be taken in to the officers, Leo thought he ought to go down to the kitchen, and beg the host to represent to these gentlemen that there was a lady ill in the room next to them, and that it was expected of their courtesy that they would be good enough to make a little less noise.

The proprietor, as usually happens during these corps dinners, was all in a flurry, and didn't know whom to answer. At the same moment as Leo was giving his message for the officers, a waiter was asking champagne for the Hussars, and a maid-servant port wine for the Englishman.

'I said there wasn't any,' she added.

'You 're a fool. There are always all kinds of wine in my hotel: I 'm going to find him some port! Bring me a bottle of ratafia, a bottle of cheap red wine, and a carafe of brandy.'

After he had manufactured the port in the twinkling of an eye, the host entered the big dining-room, and executed the commission which Leo had just charged him with. It excited first a furious tempest.

Then a bass voice which dominated all the others asked what sort of woman their neighbour was. A kind of silence ensued. The host answered:

'Honour bright, gentlemen, I hardly know what to say. She is very nice and very shy. Mary Jane says she has a wedding ring on her finger. That might mean that she is a bride who has come here for her honeymoon, as happens sometimes.'

'A bride?' cried forty voices. 'She must come and drink a toast with us! We 'll drink to her good health, and show her husband his conjugal duties!'

At these words a great noise of spurs was heard, and our lovers trembled, thinking that their room was going to be taken by assault. But suddenly a voice was raised which stopped the movement. It was obvious that it was a senior officer who was speaking. He reproached the officers for their want of manners, and gave them orders to sit down again, and to speak decently without shouting. Then he added some words too low to be heard in the blue room. They were listened to with deference, but not without exciting all the same a certain restrained hilarity. From that moment there reigned in the officers' room a relative silence, and our lovers, blessing the salutary rule of discipline, began to speak to each other with more abandon. But, after such a disturbance, time was needed to recapture the tender emotions that inquietude, the annoyances of the journey, and above all, the loud joy of their neighbours, had seriously troubled. At their age, nevertheless, the thing is not so very difficult, and they had soon forgotten all the discomforts of their adventurous expedition, and only thought of the most important of its results.

They believed that peace was made with the Hussars; but, alas! it was only a truce. At the moment when they least expected it, when they were a thousand leagues from this sublunary world, blared out eighty trumpets, sustained by several trombones, playing the air well known to French soldiers, 'We ourselves are Victory!' What chance was there of resisting such a tempest? The poor lovers were greatly to be pitied.

No, not so much to be pitied, for at the end, the officers left the dining-room, defiling before the door of the blue room with a loud clatter of sabres and spurs, and crying one after the other:

'Good-night, my lady bride!'

Then all the noise stopped. I am wrong. The Englishman went into the corridor and cried:

'Waiter, bring me another bottle of the same port.'

Calm was re-established in the hotel of N——. The night was balmy, the moon at its full. Since time immemorial lovers have loved to watch our satellite. Leo and his lady opened their window, which looked on a little garden, and breathed with pleasure the fresh air scented by a bower of clematis.

They did not remain there very long all the same. A man was walking in the garden, his head bowed, his arms crossed, a cigar in his mouth. Leo thought he recognized the nephew of the Englishman who liked the good port wine.

I hate useless details, and besides, I do not feel myself obliged to tell the reader anything that he can easily imagine, nor to recount hour by hour all that passed in the hotel of N——. I shall say then that the candle which burned on the fireless mantelpiece of the blue room was more than half consumed when, in the chamber of the Englishman, lately silent, a strange noise was heard, like that which a heavy body makes in falling. To this noise was joined a kind of crackling not less strange, followed by a stifled cry, and some indistinct words like an oath. The two young occupants of the blue room shuddered. Perhaps they had been awakened with a start. On both of them this noise, which they did not try to account for, had made an almost sinister impression.

'It 's our Englishman dreaming,' said Leo, forcing himself to smile.

But he failed to reassure his companion, and he shivered involuntarily. Two or three minutes afterwards a door opened in the corridor, cautiously it seemed; then it was shut very quietly. A slow, ill-assured step was heard which, as far as all appearances went, was trying to pass unnoticed.

'This confounded inn!' cried Leo.

'Ah, it is Paradise!' answered the young woman, letting her head fall on Leo's shoulder. 'I 'm dead sleepy.'

She sighed and fell asleep again almost at once.

An illustrious moralist has said that men are never talkative when they have nothing more to ask. Let no one be astonished, then, if Leo made no effort to renew the conversation, or to discuss the noises in the hotel of N——. In spite of himself he was preoccupied with them, and his imagination linked up with them many circumstances to which, in another mood, he would have paid no attention. The sinister figure of the Englishman's nephew returned to his memory. There was hate in the look he had thrown on his uncle, all the while he spoke to him with humility, without a doubt because he was asking money from him.

What was more easy for a man who was still young and vigorous, desperate besides, than to climb from the garden to the window of the neighbouring room? Besides, he was living in the hotel, since, at night-time, he was taking a walk in the garden. Perhaps—probably—in fact, undoubtedly he knew that his uncle's black bag contained a fat wad of banknotes. . . . And that dull thud, like the blow of a club on a bald head! . . . that stifled cry! . . . that frightful oath! . . . and then those steps! That nephew had the face of a murderer . . . but murders aren't committed in an hotel full of officers. Without a doubt that Englishman had shot his door bolt like a prudent man, especially knowing the rogue to be in the neighbourhood! He distrusted him since he hadn't wanted to speak to him with his bag in his hand. Why give himself up to hideous thoughts when he is so happy?

That 's what Leo was saying to himself in his mind. Wrapped up in his thoughts which I shall refrain from analysing at greater length, and which rose before him almost as confused as the visions of a dream, he had his eyes fixed mechanically on the communication door between the blue room and that of the Englishman.

In France doors shut badly. Between this one and the floor there was a space of at least two centimetres. Suddenly in this space, hardly distinguishable by the reflection of the floor, appeared something darkish, flat, like the blade of a knife, for the edge, struck by the light of the candle, showed a thin, very brilliant line. This moved slowly in the direction of a little blue-satin slipper, thrown down indiscreetly a little distance from the door. Was it some insect like a centipede? . . . No, it was not an insect. It had no fixed shape. Two or three brown tracks, each with its line of light at the edges, have penetrated into the room. They roll down more quickly, thanks to the slope of the floor. They advance rapidly, they come and touch the little slipper lightly. No more doubt! It is a liquid, and this liquid, as one sees the colour distinctly now in the light of the candle, was blood! And while Leo, motionless, watched horror-stricken these terrible tracks, the young woman slept still her tranquil sleep, and her regular breathing warmed the neck and shoulder of her lover.

The care that Leo had shown in ordering dinner immediately on his arrival at the hotel of N——, proves sufficiently well that he had a pretty good head, an educated intelligence, and that he knew how to foresee emergencies. He did not prove false on this occasion to the character we have already recognized in him. He made no movement, and all the power of his wits was strained in the effort to come to some resolution in face of the frightful misfortune which threatened him.

I imagine that the majority of my readers, and above all my lady readers, filled with heroic sentiments, will blame in this conjuncture the conduct and immobility of Leo. He ought, someone will say to me, he ought to have run to the Englishman's room and arrested the murderer; at the very least pulled his bell, and roused by its clamour the people of the hotel. To that I shall answer first, that in French hotels bells are only put in for chamber ornaments, and that their ropes have no relation with any metallic apparatus. I shall add respectfully but firmly that, if it is wrong to let an Englishman die in the next room, it is not praiseworthy to sacrifice to him a lady who is sleeping with her head on your shoulder. What would have happened if Leo had made enough racket to wake the hotel? The police, the imperial prosecutor, and his clerk would have arrived at once. Before asking him what he had seen or heard these gentlemen are, by profession, so curious that they would have said to him first of all:

'What 's your name? Your papers? and madame? What were you doing together in the blue room? You will have to appear at the Assize Court to state that on the so-and-so of such a month, at such an hour of night, you were the witnesses of such an act.'

Now it is precisely this idea of the imperial prosecutor and the minions of justice that was the first to spring up before Leo's mind. There occur sometimes in life cases of conscience difficult to settle: is it better to let an unknown traveller have his throat cut, or to dishonour and disgrace the lady one loves?

It is not agreeable to have to set oneself such a question. I give the cleverest of you ten guesses to find the answer.

Leo did, then, what probably most of us would have done in his place: he did not budge.

His eyes fixed on the blue slipper and the little red brook that touched it, he stayed a long time as if fascinated, while a cold sweat wetted his temples, and his heart beat to bursting in his breast.

A crowd of thoughts and queer horrible pictures obsessed him, and an inner voice called out to him every moment, 'In an hour, all will be known, and it is your fault'. Yet, by dint of saying, 'What business of mine is it in this galley?' in the end he saw some rays of hope. He said to himself at last:

'If we leave this cursed hotel before the discovery of what has occurred in the next room, perhaps we could manage to obliterate our tracks. Nobody knows us here; I have only been seen in blue spectacles, she has only been seen under a veil. We are two steps from a railway station, and in an hour we shall be far away from N——'

Then, as he had studied the time-table at length to organize his expedition, he remembered that a train passed at eight o'clock going to Paris. Soon after, they would be lost in the immensity of that town where hide so many criminals. Who would be able to unearth two innocent people there? But wouldn't somebody go into the Englishman's room before eight o'clock? All the crux of the question was in that.

Quite convinced that there was nothing else to be done, he made a desperate effort to shake off the torpor which had possessed him for so long: but, at the first movement he made, his young companion wakened and embraced him madly. At the touch of his icy cheeks, she let out a little cry.

'What 's the matter?' she said to him uneasily, 'your brow is cold as marble.'

'It 's nothing,' he answered in a shaky voice. 'I heard a noise in the room next door.'

He disengaged himself from her arms, and first of all removed the blue slipper, and placed an arm-chair before the communicating door, so as to hide from his lady the fearful liquid that, ceasing to spread, had now formed a pretty big stain on the floor. Then he half opened the door which gave on the corridor and listened attentively: he even dared approach the Englishman's door. It was shut. There were already signs of movement in the hotel, and from the second floor, an officer came downstairs and his spurs rang. He was going to preside at that interesting task, more agreeable to horses than to men, which in technical terms is called 'Forage the horses'.

Leo returned to the blue room, and, with all the circumspection that love could impart, with a great expenditure of circumlocutions and euphemisms, he set before his lady the situation in which they found themselves.

Danger in remaining: danger in going away too precipitately: still greater danger in waiting in the hotel till the catastrophe in the next room was discovered.

It is useless to tell of the terror caused by this communication, the tears that followed it, the insensate proposals which were brought forward: how many times the two unfortunate lovers threw themselves in each other's arms, crying, 'Forgive me!' Each thought himself the more to blame. They promised to die together, for the young woman had no doubt but that justice would find them guilty of the murder of the Englishman, and, as they were not sure if it were allowable to kiss each other still on the scaffold, they kissed to suffocation, vying in watering each other with their tears. At length, having said lots of absurdities and lots of tender, heartrending words, they recognized, amid a thousand kisses, that the plan thought of by Leo, that is to say the departure by the eight o'clock train, was in reality the only practical one, and the best to follow. But there remained still two mortal hours to pass. At each step in the corridor, they shuddered in all their limbs. Each creaking of boots announced for them the entrance of the imperial prosecutor.

Their little bundle was tied up in the twinkling of an eye. The young woman wanted to burn the blue slipper in the fireplace, but Leo picked it up, and, after having wiped it on the rug, kissed it, and put it in his pocket. He was surprised to find that it smelled of vanilla: his lady used as perfume the bouquet of the Empress Eugénie.

Already everybody was awake in the hotel. They could hear waiters laughing, servant-girls singing, soldiers brushing their officers' clothes. Seven o'clock had just struck. Leo wanted to induce his lady to take a cup of coffee and milk, but she declared that her throat was so contracted that she would die if she tried to drink anything.

Leo, furnished with his blue spectacles, went down to pay his bill. The host asked his pardon, pardon for the noise that had been made, and that he could not even yet account for, as the officers were always so quiet! Leo assured him that he had heard nothing and that he had slept perfectly.

'I warrant you, your neighbour on the other side', continued the host, 'won't have inconvenienced you. He doesn't make much noise, that fellow. I bet he 's still sound asleep.'

Leo leant heavily on the counter to keep himself from falling, and the young woman, who had elected to follow him, hung on his arm, pressing her veil before her eyes.

'He 's an Englishman,' pursued the pitiless host. 'He must always have the best of everything. Ah! a very respectable man! But all the English are not like him. There 's one here who is a skinflint. He finds everything too dear, the room, the dinner. He wanted to pay me down a note for his hundred and twenty-five francs, a note of the Bank of England for five pounds sterling—provided only that it 's good. Wait, sir, you ought to know, for I heard you speaking English with your wife. Is it good?'

As he said this, he handed him a banknote for five pounds sterling. On one of the corners was a little red stain that Leo accounted for at once.

'I believe it 's quite good,' he said in a strangled voice.

'Oh, you have plenty of time,' went on the host. 'The train is only due at eight o'clock, and it is always late. Please take a seat, madame, you seem tired.'

At this moment a fat servant-girl entered.

'Quick, some hot water,' she said, 'for the English milord's tea! Bring me a sponge too! He has broken his bottle, and all his room is flooded.'

At these words Leo dropped on a chair, and his companion did the same. A great inclination to laugh seized them both, and they had some trouble not to let it burst out. The young man joyfully squeezed her hand.

'Certainly,' said Leo to his host, 'we shall not go until the two o'clock train. Get us a nice lunch for midday.'

THE ELIXIR OF THE REVEREND FATHER GAUCHER

Alphonse Daudet

'Sip this, my friend. It would make a dumb man eloquent,' said the minister of Graveson, as he poured out drop by drop, in measured cadence, a thimbleful of the most exquisite nectar that ever gladdened the inner man.

'It is the Elixir of Father Gaucher, the glory, the stimulant divine of our Heaven-blessed Provence. It is made at the Convent of the Prémontré Canons, two leagues from your Mill. The finest of the much-vaunted chartreuses is but small beer in comparison. This Elixir has a history, too piquant, you may think, for the lips of a reverend churchman, but, M. Daudet, even saints have their off-days.'

Then leaning back in his arm-chair, in the snug dining-room of the Parsonage, hung with dainty curtains and with pictures of the Passion, the Abbé commenced the story of the Elixir, apocryphal in parts, and spiced here and there with a dash of profanity in the style of Erasmus and Charles d'Assouci.

'Twenty years ago the Canons of Prémontré, or the White Fathers as we call them in Provence, had fallen on evil days. The convent was tumbling about their ears. The outer walls and the Tower of St. Pacôme were crumbling in pieces. Grass grew in the cloisters, the pillars were cracking, the saints were wasting away in their niches. Not a window, not a door was intact. The wind from the Rhône swept through the court-yards and the chapels, as it sweeps across the waste of Camargue, extinguishing the tapers, breaking the leaded panes, and spattering the holy water. But the most depressing feature of all was the silent clock-tower, tenantless as a deserted dove-cot. No silver convent-bell summoned the Fathers to matins, only the painful parody of almond-wood castanets.

'Oh, poverty-stricken Fathers! I can vividly recall your piteous procession on Corpus Christi Day. Your threadbare cloaks, your pale faces and dejected mien, your frames emaciated with the hermit fare of citrons and water-melons. And your worthy Abbé, the last of the train, his head bent, all too painfully conscious of his tarnished cross and moth-eaten mitre. The sisters wept as the monks filed past, but the coarse, lusty banner-bearers sneered at their miserable plight. Monks, like starlings, grow lean when there 's not enough to go round, so, no longer able to keep body and soul together, there seemed no alternative but to quit the Convent and wander forth into the world in search of new pastures.

'One day, when the situation was being discussed by the Chapter, word was brought to the Prior that Brother Gaucher could disclose an infallible specific for poverty and woe, and was waiting outside for an audience.

'Brother Gaucher, I must tell you, was the cow-herd at the Convent, if the term could be applied to one whose duty consisted in tending two emaciated cows as they cropped the scanty herbage growing in the chinks of the flag-stones of the establishment. He had been brought up by a roving, half-witted woman of Baux, who called herself his aunt. When he was twelve years old the monks took him into the Convent. He was despised as a brainless clod, fit only to drive cattle, and capable, intellectually, only of mumbling the Paternoster in his native patois. Though physically robust, he never rebelled against his superiors, and kissed the rod of contempt with the exemplary meekness of a Christian. Sometimes, however, he saw visions and dreamt dreams. "One of Brother Gaucher's visions will be a diversion," thought the Chapter, so he was ushered in.

'An outburst of derisive merriment greeted his entrance, so grotesque were his unwieldy bulk, his uncouth gestures, his clownish gait. In making obeisance he nearly tripped himself up backwards. But the clown had a sense of humour as fumbling with his beads he naïvely remarked:

'"May it please your Reverences! It 's an old saying, but it 's a true saying, that the emptiest vessels make the most noise. I 've been turning over and over my clod of a pate, and at last drops out a treasure. You know my old Aunt Bégon who took care of me when I was a youngster? Peace to her soul, poor body! But the old hussy could sing a comic song after a sip of her Elixir! Well, the body was always on the tramp, and knew the taste of every stimulating herb on the mountain-side better than the most wide-awake old Corsican blackbird. And she knew how to keep a good thing to herself. Well, after many a year of wandering, picking, tasting, and mixing, she lighted on a concoction of the choicest piquancy. Although it 's many a year since I helped her to cull the herbs, I think that under the guidance of St. Augustine, with the permission of our good Father Abbé, and by taking pains, I could recover the secret of the wondrous Elixir. I should know the taste of it again. You would only have to bottle it and sell it at a fancy price to fill your coffers with golden louis. Then you might hold your heads as high as the haughty Brothers of La Trappe and the Grande Chartreuse!"

'The Chapter leapt to their feet. The Prior threw his arm round Gaucher's neck. The Canons grasped his hands. The Treasurer's gratitude was unbounded—he kissed the tattered hem of the Brother's sackcloth gown. The excitement having subsided and deliberations resumed, the Chapter decided unanimously to hand over the cows to Brother Thrasybulus, leaving Brother Gaucher free to pursue the quest of the Elixir.

'It sufficeth to say that the recipe was found. When, how, where, Gaucher alone knows. History is in the dark. That the Brother was neither dolt nor laggard is decisively proved by the fact that, in less than six months, not a single farmhouse or cottage throughout the Comtat and the region around Arles but could show in the locked pantry cupboard, between the bottles of home-made wine and the jars of picholine olives, a little brown earthenware flagon, its seal stamped with the arms of Provence, its label all-glorious with—a Monk in Raptures on a Silver Ground.

'By the magic succours of Aunt Bégon's Elixir, wealth poured into the Convent Treasury. The crumbling fabric was restored, the monk's penury relieved, the Prior was resplendent in vestments new, and the next Resurrection dawn was ushered in by the strains of virgin bells pealing forth full-throated pæans of thanksgiving.

'The despised lay-brother Gaucher, whose clownish bearing had excited the Chapter's mirth, was buried in oblivion. Were Brother Gaucher asked for at the Convent, it was replied, "There 's no such Brother here—perhaps you mean the Reverend Father Gaucher?"

'"The Father lived apart from the humdrum life of the Cloister, immersed in his distillery, the Superior of thirty monks who scoured the mountain in search of herbs. A disused chapel, standing apart at the foot of the Canon's garden, served as distillery. It was an inviolable sanctum, forbidden ground even to the Prior himself. The unsophisticated Fathers regarded it with fear and tıembling, a place of deep, perhaps unhallowed, mysteries. Should a venturesome, prying brother scale the vine and peep in at the rose window, a moment's glance at the necromantic array took away his breath. There stood the black-bearded Father Gaucher, hydrometer in hand over a steaming furnace. Around were retorts of red-sandstone, gigantic stills, spiral condensing pipes, a bizarre sorcerer-like equipment blazing uncannily through the red panes of the window. Aghast at his own temerity, peeping Tom would scramble down the vine as if the devil were in pursuit.

'At sunset, when the last Angelus was rung, a door in the distillery was cautiously opened, and His Reverence walked forth to Evensong. The Brothers lined up on either side with hushed respect. "He has the secret," was faintly whispered. The Treasurer followed with bent head. As the Father advanced through the awe-struck throng, a wide-brimmed hat encircling the back of his head like an aureole, he fanned his face, looked with serene self-complacency on the courts planted with orange trees, on restored roofs with newly-gilded weather-cocks, on the dazzling whiteness of the Cloister, its elegant columns crowned with carved capitals, on the spick-and-span vestments of the Canons.

'"All these are yours, Gaucher," said His Reverence to himself.

'Yes, he walked with conscious pride. But pride goes before a fall, as is exemplified in the sequel.

'Picture the scene one evening at Vespers when Father Gaucher burst in upon the worshippers, breathless, flushed, reeling, his cowl all awry, plunging into the holy water right up to his elbow. At first the monks thought that, his distillery duties having detained him, he was flustered at finding himself late; but when he turned his back to the High Altar, made obeisance to the organ and galleries, scudded up the nave like a madman, staggered through the chancel, plunged into his stall with a crash, and rocked from side to side, gazing round with sanctimonious serenity, a buzz of pious horror filled the chapel. The monks whispered behind their breviaries:

'"What 's possessed the Father to-night?"

'Twice the Prior struck his crosier on the floor to command silence. The choir continued the chants, but the responses were scarcely audible. In the middle of the *Ave Verum*, Gaucher raised himself in his stall and struck up in stentorian tones one of Aunt Bégon's comic songs:

'There lived a monk in gay Paree,
  Patatin, Patatan, Tarabin, Taraban.
He kissed a nun with golden hair,
  Tarabin, Patatan, Patatin, Taraban.
  Golden hair, golden hair.'

'The congregation were scandalized. They rose in a body amidst shouts of "Turn him out, he has a devil!" The Canons crossed themselves in holy horror. The Prior waved his crosier frantically. Father Gaucher rocked and smiled, blissfully, unconscious of anything wrong. Two sturdy monks rushed forward and hustled the offender out at a side door, the delinquent struggling violently, and vociferating at the pitch of his voice:

'Golden hair, golden hair.'

'The next day—that morrow which chasteneth the night before—was a day of penance.

'At dawn the culprit is seen on his knees in the Prior's oratory making a full confession with streaming eyes.

'"Monseigneur, alas, the Elixir had got me into its grip!" he said, beating his breast.

'The Prior was not a stern man and was deeply moved at the penitent's contrition.

'"My dear Gaucher, be calm! The little incident of last night, well, the impromptu outburst of song could not be ignored, but the morning sun dispels the mists of night. Really, there 's no harm done. The novices were away at the back, and probably thought some recondite ceremonial was being performed, one whose mystery had not yet been revealed to babes and sucklings. But between ourselves I should like to know the real facts. It was the Elixir, of course? Your tasting hand was rather heavy, perhaps? You were running the risk of all scientific pioneers. You 're another Brother Schwartz of gunpowder fame, the victim of your own invention. Be frank, my dear fellow; your life is precious, we owe you everything. Could not some tasting instrument be contrived?"

'"Monseigneur, a gauge can test the strength and temperature, but the subtle bouquet, the velvety softness elude all but the most exquisitely sensitive of human tongues."

'"So far, so good. But—be frank—does your exquisitely sensitive tongue really relish the tasting process, or it is a compelling duty?"

'"Alas, Monseigneur," confessed the much-tried penitent, "on the last two evenings the bouquet, the aroma were quite overpowering. I felt myself in the grip of the Tempter. Now I am resolved at any price to use only the testing-tube, even though the pearl should lose its fineness and connoisseurs reject an inferior brand."

'"Stop!" cried the Prior excitedly, "do nothing rash! We must study our clients. Listen! Keep a watch on yourself. What would you consider a safe maximum dose? Fifteen drops? Make it twenty. Even after twenty the devil would need to rise very early in the morning to catch you napping. But as a precaution against eventualities, I dispense henceforth with your attendance at Evensong. You can observe it privately in the distillery. Now depart in peace, Reverend Father, and—count your drops."

'Alas, the Reverend Father needed all his arithmetic to keep the Tempter at bay!

'Evensong in the distillery was unique.

'All went well during the day-time. The Father heated his furnaces and stills, sorted carefully the herbs, those incomparable herbs of Provence, delicate, intoxicating, serrated, warmed and scented through and through with the meridional sun. But at eventide, when the herbs were infused, and the Elixir simmering in the huge copper cauldrons, the Father's martyrdom began.

'Seventeen, eighteen, nineteen, twenty!

'The drops fell from the pipe one by one into a silver-gilt goblet. "This is the Prior's limit," said Gaucher, swallowing them at a gulp. "Simply insipid," was the verdict. "It 's only when you get to the twenty-first drop that the spirit begins to tickle."

'Oh, the longing after the twenty-first drop!

'"Lead us not into temptation," groaned the Father, as he fell upon his knees at the far end of the distillery, repeating the Paternoster with unctuous vehemence. As the temperature of the liquid rose, its aroma was heightened. As the fumes circled round the head of the kneeling monk, a subtle fascination drew him irresistibly to the steaming cauldrons. He stood spell-bound, with dilated nostrils, as he reverently stirred the scintillating green and gold nectar. He saw in the glittering bubbles dancing on the emerald flood the alluring twinkles of Aunt Bégon's witch-like eyes.

'"Just one more drop," and another, and so on, until the goblet was full to the brim. Then he fell back into a large arm-chair, and, stretched at his ease with half-closed eyes, sipped drop by drop the soul-damning potion, muttering between alternate fits of sinning and repentance:

'"Lost, lost, irretrievably lost!"

'Having drained the last drop, lo and behold, at the bottom of the cup was a complete edition of Aunt Bégon's comic ditties! They were "The Three Little Gossips who went out for a Spree," "The Maid and the Monk who met in the Wood," and of course the immortal "Patatin, Patatan" of the White Monk.

'The next morning he was accosted by his fellow sleepers with:

'"Father Gaucher, you had fairy dreams last night!"

'Then followed tears, despair, fasting, hair shirts, penance. But all to no purpose. Every night the Tempter triumphed.

'The Fathers were inundated with orders. They came from Nîmes, Aix, Avignon, Marseilles. The languishing Convent became a hive of industry. A well-organized division of labour was established. The Brothers became packers, labellers, book-keepers, carters. Fewer beads were told, fewer Masses said. The souls of the departed were left to their Redeemer's keeping, the bodies of the living fortified with the bread of toil.

'On one fine Sunday morning, as the Treasurer was reading his yearly financial statement before a full Chapter, the eyes of the Canons glistening, their ears tingling with joy, their faces wreathed with smiles, Father Gaucher burst into the assembly.

'"I 've done with the Elixir! Let him make it who will! I 'll go back to the cows."

'The Prior was stunned.

'"What do you mean, Father Gaucher?"

'"Mean? Mean that I 'm galloping headlong to perdition! Drinking! drinking! drinking!"

'"But didn't I tell you to count the drops?"

'"And haven't I counted them? Yes, by the cupful! Three bottles a night! No mortal can stand it! Gaucher has washed his hands of the soul-perilling mixture."

'The Chapter looked glum.

'"Would you ruin us?" said the Treasurer, brandishing his ledger excitedly.

'"Would you send me to perdition?"

'The Prior intervened.

'"Reverend Fathers," he said, deprecatingly spreading out his lily-white hand on which glittered the pastoral ring, "I have a way out of the difficulty. It is in the evening, is it not, when the Tempter assails you?"

'"Yes, Monseigneur, in the evening and every evening. As night approaches a clammy perspiration comes over me like that which assailed Capitou's ass when he saw the saddle brought out."

'"Fear nothing, my dear boy! Henceforth at Evensong we will put up on your behalf the orison of St. Augustine, which carries plenary indulgence. Whatever happens you will be safe. Commission and absolution will synchronize."

'"Thanks unspeakable, Monseigneur!"

'Father Gaucher asked no more. He returned to his alembics carolling like a lark.

'Faithful to compact, the officiating priest never failed to put up after Compline an intercessory prayer for the tempted Father who was risking his soul for others' good.

'Looking into the chapel at Evensong, we see the white-hooded monks kneeling in grateful devotion, as the orison steals over their heads like a night-breeze over St. Bernard's snows. And in the stillness there is wafted from the red-lit distillery the sonorous fortissimo of Father Gaucher:

'There lived a monk in gay Paree,
Patatin, Patatan.'

'I 've come to the end of my yarn,' said the Abbé. 'Luckily none of my parishoners have been present.'

Translated by Edward Harris.

THE OLD FOLKS AT HOME

Alphonse Daudet

'Is that a letter, Daddy Azan?'

'Yes, sir, all the way from Paris.'

The patriarch regards everything coming from Paris with awe and wonder, so hands me the note with reverent care.

But I am disillusioned of the glamour of the capital, and looked upon a letter arriving so early in the morning as heralding a visitor, perhaps an infliction, for the day. I was mistaken. The note ran thus:

My dear Daudet—You must shut up the Mill to-day and go on an errand for me to Eyguières. It is only about ten miles from the Mill, just a morning's stroll for a young man [he says nothing about strolling home]. When you get there inquire for the Convent of the Orphans. Next door to the Convent is a small house with grey shutters and a garden plot behind. The door is always open, so go in without knocking. When inside, shout at the pitch of your voice, 'Good-day, my friends, I'm a friend of Maurice.' Then you will see two old, old antediluvian fossils buried in arm-chairs older than themselves. Hug them for me as if they were your own devoted ancestors. Then talk away, they will at once join in, and always on the one inexhaustible topic—Maurice. They will laud your scapegrace friend to the skies. They will never tire of extolling the peerless perfections of this flawless paragon. Another such a paragon never was, or will be. Mind, don't give me away, never hesitate for an answer! Laugh! at the peril of your life! They are my grandparents, my life-long companions until ten years ago. Yes, it is ten years since I left them for Paris, and Paris holds me as in a vice. The frail old relics would fall to pieces on the road if they attempted the journey hither, so, my esteemed miller, do the grand filial for me and give them a vicarious hug. I have already painted your portrait for them at full length, every feature *couleur de rose*, etc.

Thus the letter ran.

Just my luck! This is a perfect day for staying at home and dreaming in a shady nook, and here I am dragged ten miles each way, the sun blazing overhead and the dust blowing in my eyes. But, anything to oblige a friend. I bang the door, turn the key, putting it through the cat's hole, and stroll away with my pipe and stick.

I got to Eyguières a little before two. The village was deserted; everybody was working in the fields. Certainly a donkey was sunning himself in the municipal square, pigeons were flying round the church fountain, and grasshoppers, with as much vivacity as those in the wilderness of Oran, were chirping round the elms of the village green, white with dust. But I could see no living person to direct me to the Orphanage. Suddenly a good fairy came to my rescue. I espied an emaciated hag, crouching in a doorway. I asked her for directions, and, pointing with her withered finger, the convent came into view as by the stroke of a magician's wand. It was a large, ugly, gloomy building, glorying in an old cross of red sandstone, with a Latin inscription over the doorway. Beside it was a small house with grey shutters and garden plot behind. This was my destination, and I entered without knocking.

The picture of that house is graven on my memory for ever. The spotless cleanliness, the hushed quiet of the long corridor, the rose-tinted walls, the vista of the garden flowers fluttering in the breeze behind the light-coloured blind, the wall panels decked with painted violins and flowers, now faded with age. I imagined myself in the house of one of the bailies of the time of Sedaine. I heard through a half-open door the tick-tack of a clock and a child's voice reading aloud, word by word, syllable by syllable: 'Then—Saint—I-rénée—cried—out—I—am—the wheat — of — God — and I — must — be — ground — to — powder — by — the — teeth — of — these — beasts.' I approached on tiptoe and looked in.

Amidst the stillness and veiled daylight I saw an old man, his mouth open, his hands on his knees, sound asleep in an arm-chair. His cheeks were rosy, his flesh wrinkled to the finger tips. At his feet sat a little girl, wearing a long blue shawl and small blue hood—the costume of the orphans. It was she who was spelling out the life of St. Irénée from a book almost as large as herself. The wondrous reading acted as an opiate on the inmates of the room. The old man in his arm-chair, the flies on the ceiling, the canaries in their cage, all slumbered; the grandfather's clock with its tick-tack, a sunbeam streaming through the shutters with its myriads of dancing particles, alone vivifying the room. Amidst the universal drowsiness the child continues her reading with solemn persistence: 'Immed–i–ate–ly — two — lions — rushed — on — her — and — de–vour–ed — her.' I entered the room at this crisis. The raging lions could hardly have caused a greater flutter in the household. The little blue girl dropped her book with a shriek, the canaries and flies woke up, the clock struck, the old man jumped up with a start, quite dazed. I stood on the threshold somewhat embarrassed, but, summoning up courage, shouted:

'Good day, my friend! I 'm the friend of Maurice.'

Maurice acted as a talisman.

The old man flew towards me with open arms, wrung my hands, and rushed about the room, distractedly crying, 'Mon Dieu! Mon Dieu!'

His every wrinkle beamed. His face was crimson with excitement. He stammered:

'Oh, sir! Oh, sir!'

Then he rushed to the door, crying:

'Come, Mamma! quick, Mamma!'

A door in the corridor opened. A pit-a-pat was heard, and Mamma entered.

How sweetly pathetic was the scene! The little old lady in a mutch-cap and a pale brown carmelite dress, carrying an embroidered handkerchief. And how much alike they were! The resemblance was striking. A little change of dress, a cap or so, and grandpa might be taken for grandma, only grandma had many more tear-worn wrinkles. Each had a little orphan girl as protectress—age guarded by infancy. On entering, grandma made me a low curtsy, as in the days of chivalry, but the impatient old man cut short ceremony:

'Mamma, this is the friend of Maurice.'

She quivered like an aspen-leaf, tears ran down her cheeks, she dropped her handkerchief, her face reddened even more than his. The old folks have only one drop of blood in their veins, yet the least excitement crimsons their faces all over.

'Quick, quick! a chair for the visitor,' said the old lady to her little blue girl.

'Open the shutters,' said the old man to his.

Then each taking one of my hands, they toddled with me to the window to survey their guest. The arm-chairs were brought forward, I was installed on a camp-stool between them, the children stood behind, and the inquisition began.

'How is he? How does he spend his time? Why doesn't he come to see us? Is he quite happy?'

And so they plied me with questions for nearly an hour.

I bore up bravely, told them all I knew, inventing, embellishing at a pinch.

'The wall-paper, madame? It 's a lovely cerulean blue, with festoons of roses.'

'Is it really?'—adding, as she turned to Papa, 'Isn't he a fine fellow?'

'Yes, yes, a fine, fine, fellow!'

And during the whole of my agony there were noddings of the snow-white heads, smile-beams on the wrinkled faces, bursts of child-like laughter, the exchange of knowing glances.

And the old man turned to me saying:

'Speak up, she 's rather deaf.'

Mamma retaliated:

'Louder, please, he 's hard of hearing.'

I obeyed. They smiled their thanks, and, smiling, fathomed my eyes, seeking the likeness of their boy. Looking into theirs I beheld dimly, as through a mist, the face of my friend, smiling.

Suddenly raising himself in his chair, the old man exclaimed: 'Mamma, are you dreaming? perhaps he hasn't lunched yet.'

'Not lunched, poor dear!'

As her thoughts were probably dwelling on Maurice, I was hastening to assure her that the dear boy never lunched later than noon.

'Maurice's friend, I mean,' said the old man.

'Oh, sir, a thousand pardons!'

My hunger was rampant, so I did not prevaricate.

'Quick, little blues! Lay the Sunday cloth on the middle table, and bring the best flower-patterned plates. Quick! don't giggle like silly geese; best foot foremost.'

The lunch was ready in a twinkling.

'This is just a small, small repast,' said grandma as she led me to the table. 'Excuse our not joining you, but we lunch before noon.'

When visitors arrived, the old folks had always 'lunched before noon'.

The menu comprised two strips of white of egg, some dates, and a *barquette*, a kind of pastry, quite enough to sustain grandma and her canaries for a week. All eyes were upon me during the meal. The little blues whispered, the canaries twittered: 'Oh, look at that great, greedy glutton; he 's eating up all the *barquette*.'

The great, greedy glutton certainly swept the board, though almost unconsciously, so absorbed was he in contemplating the bright and peaceful room, fragrant with memories of the past.

My eyes were riveted on two small beds, almost like cradles. I pictured them at day-break, still shrouded in their fringed curtains. The clock strikes three, the hour when the old folks awaken.

'Are you asleep, Mamma?'

'No, dear.'

'Isn't Maurice a fine fellow?'

'Yes, yes, a fine, fine fellow.'

Yes, it was Maurice, Maurice, from early morn to dewy eve!

But while I was musing, a drama was being acted at the end of the room. The old gentleman was standing on a chair, making heroic efforts to reach a bottle of preserved brandy-cherries placed on the topmost shelf of a cupboard. The bottle had been undisturbed for ten years, and awaited Maurice's return. In spite of his wife's dissuasions, grandpa was determined to get and open the bottle in honour of his guest. The old man was straining every nerve and muscle, the little blues were clasping the chair, the old lady looked on in fear and trembling with bated breath and arms stretched out to rescue the hero in case of need. One supreme effort, the prize was seized, and handed down to the now beaming grandma. And what a delicious whiff of sweet bergamot came from the linen in the cupboard!

Maurice's little embossed silver mug was brought out and filled to the brim.

Yes, Maurice loved cherries.

As grandpa handed me the mug, his mouth watering with epicurean gusto, he whispered, 'You 're a lucky dog, you don't get the like of this at the mill. His grandmother preserved them.'

However expert grandma might be in preserving cherries, she had fallen short this time. She had forgotten the sugar. Still, one must make allowance for the vagaries of old age. But I rose to the occasion, set my teeth, and gulped them down without blinking, whispering an aside:

'Madame, your cherries are—atrocious!'

As I rose to take my leave, the old folks pressed me to continue my true narrative of the exploits of the paragon, but as the light was failing, and the mill 'only about ten miles' off, it was time to set out.

The old man also rose.

'My coat, please, Mamma. I must see him as far as the Square.'

Mamma remarked on the chilliness of the night air, but did not oppose the old man's whim. As she helped him on with his smart snuff-coloured Spanish coat, with mother-of-pearl buttons, she said in bantering tones:

'Now, dear, you 'll promise, won't you, promise faithfully that you won't stay out late to-night?'

The old man, not to be outdone, replied with an 'I-won't-come-home-till-morning' air:

'Yes! No!'

'Perhaps I will! Perhaps I won't!'

'I don't know! I don't care!'

'Don't wait up, dear! I 've got the key.'

Then they looked into each other's eyes and laughed till they cried. The little blues laughed because they laughed, and the canaries twittered to join in the fun.

Between ourselves, I think the cherry brandy had made every one a little 'breezy'.

It was getting dark when grandpa and I left the house. He was a proud man that evening as he walked through the village arm in arm with the friend of Maurice. How could he be conscious of a little blue protectress following at a distance to bring him home? Grandma, her face beaming, her frame quivering, watched us from the doorstep.

'See, my old man can step out yet!'

Translated by EDWARD HARRIS.

THE GREATEST LOVE OF DON JUAN

J. A. Barbey d'Aurévilly

The Devil's primest fare is innocence.

I

'He is still alive then, that hoary old reprobate?'

'Still alive! I should rather think he was—by God's grace,' I took care to add, remembering Madame's piety, 'and of the most distinguished and aristocratic parish of Sainte-Clotilde—*Le roi est mort! vive le roi!* is what they used to say under the old monarchy, in the days when their fine old piece of Sèvres porcelain was yet unbroken. But Don Juan, in spite of all your democracies, is a monarch they will never break.'

'Yes! yes! no doubt the Devil is among the immortal!' she returned in a self-approving tone.

'As a matter of fact, he . . .'

'Who? . . . the Devil? . . .'

'No! no! Don Juan. He supped, I say, only three days ago in pleasant company. . . . Guess where. . . .'

'At your horrid Maison d'Or, of course. . . .'

'My dear madame! Don Juan *never* goes there now . . . they 've no fish fit to fry for his highness's palate. The Señor Don Juan has always been a bit like Arnold of Brescia's famous monk who, the chronicles tell us, lived only on the blood of souls. That is what he loves to colour his champagne with, and it 's many a long day since it was to be had at the rendezvous of the commonplace *cocotte*!'

'You 'll be telling me next,' she interrupted, in the ironic vein, 'he supped at the Benedictine nunnery with the holy ladies. . . .'

'Yes! ladies of the Perpetual Adoration; why, certainly, madame. For indeed I do think the adoration he has once inspired, our redoubtable Lovelace, seems to last for good and all.'

'And I think that for a good Catholic you are a trifle profane, sir!'—this she said slowly, but not without a touch of irritation—'and I must beg you to spare me the details of your naughty suppers. I suppose this is a new way of telling me about your disreputable lady friends, this harping on Don Juan and his doings to-night.'

'I merely state the facts, madame. The disreputable persons present at the supper in question, if they *are* disreputable, are not *my* friends at all . . . unfortunately . . .'

'Enough! enough!'

'Forgive my modest disclaimer. . . . They were . . .'

'The *mille e tre*? . . .' she interrupted again, thinking better of it, and all but recovering her good temper under the stress of curiosity.

'Oh! not all of them. . . . A round dozen merely. With as many as that, nothing could be more respectable, you know.'

'Or more disreputable,' she put in tartly.

'Besides, you know as well as I do the Comtesse de Chiffrevas's boudoir will not hold a crowd. Everything was done that could be done; but, after all, it 's only a small room, her boudoir.'

'What!'—raising her voice in astonishment. 'They had supper in the boudoir?'

'Yes! in the boudoir. And why not? A battlefield makes a famous place to dine in. They wished to give a very special and particular supper to Señor Don Juan, and it seemed better worthy of his exploits to give it on the scene of his former triumphs, where fond memories bloom instead of orange-blossoms. A pretty notion, at once tender and sad! *'Twas no victims' ball!* it was a victims' supper-party!'

'And Don Juan?' she asked in the tone of Orgon, in the play, saying: 'And Tartufe?'

'Don Juan took it in excellent part, and made an excellent supper,

> . . . He, he alone before them all,

as the poet sings—in the person of someone you know very well indeed—none other than the Comte Jules-Amédée-Hector de Ravila de Ravilès.'

'Comte de Ravilès! Why, yes! He was a Don Juan. . . .'

So saying, the pious lady, case-hardened in her narrow bigotry as she was, and long past the age of day-dreams, lapsed then and there into a fond reverie of which Comte Jules-Amédée was the theme—that man of the old Don Juan breed, to which God has not indeed given 'all the world and glory thereof', but has suffered the Devil to do it for Him.

II

What I had just told the aged Marquise Guy de Ruy was the unvarnished truth. Hardly three days had elapsed since a dozen ladies of the virtuous Faubourg Saint-Germain (rest them easy, I will never damage their noble names!), who, every one, the whole dozen, if we are to believe the cackling dowagers of the quarter, had been 'on the best of good terms' (a really charming old-fashioned locution) with the Comte Ravila de Ravilès, had conceived the idea of offering him a supper—he being the only male guest—in pious memory of . . . well! they did not say of what. A bold thing to do, but women, while timid individually, are as bold as brass when banded together. Probably not one of the whole party would have ventured to invite the comte to a *tête-à-tête* supper at her own house; but all together, each backing up the other, they feared not to weave a chain, like mesmerists round their mystic tub, round this magnetic and most compromising individual, the Comte de Ravila de Ravilès. . . .

'What a name!'

'A providential name, madame.'

The Comte de Ravila de Ravilès, who, by the by, had always lived up to his high-sounding and picturesque title, was the perfect incarnation of all the long line of Lovelaces Romance and History tell of, and even the old Marquise Guy de Ruy—a discontented old lady, with light-blue eyes, cold and keen, but not so cold as her heart, or so keen as her tongue—allowed that in these times, when women and women's concerns grow day by day less important, if there *was* any one who could recall Don Juan, it must surely be he! Unfortunately it was Don Juan in the Fifth Act. The witty Prince de Ligne said he could *not* make himself believe Alcibiades ever grew to be fifty; and here again the Comte de Ravila was to be a true Alcibiades to the end of the chapter. Like d'Orsay, a dandy hewn out of the marble of Michael Angelo, who was the handsomest of men down to his last hour, Ravila had possessed the good looks especially belonging to the Don Juan breed—that mysterious race which does not proceed from father to son, like other races, but appears here and there at recurring intervals in the families of mankind.

His beauty was beyond dispute—of the gay, arrogant, imperial sort, *Juanesque* in fact (the word is a picture, and makes description heedless); and—had he made an unholy bargain with the Devil?—it was his still. . . . Only, God was beginning to exact His penalty; life's cruel tiger-claws already seamed that 'front divine', crowned with the roses of so many kisses, and on his wide and wicked temples appeared the first white hairs that proclaim the impending invasion of the barbarian hosts and the fall of the empire. . . . He wore them, it is true, with the calm insouciance of pride surfeited with power; but women who had loved him would sometimes gaze at them with sad eyes. Who knows? perhaps they had read what hour of day it was for themselves in that whitening brow? Alas and alas! for them as for him, 'twas the hour for the grim supper with the cold white-marble Commendatore, after which only Hell is left —first the Hell of old age, then the other! And this perhaps is why, before sharing with him this last, bitter meal, they planned to offer him this supper of their own, and made it the miracle of art it was.

Yes, a miracle of good taste and refinement, of patrician luxury, elegance, and pretty conceits; the most charming, the most delicious, the most toothsome, the most heady, and, above all, the most original of suppers. How original, just think for a moment! Commonly it is love of merriment, the thirst for amusement, that supply motives for a supper-party; but this one was dedicated only to fond memories and sad regrets, we might almost say to despair—but despair in full dress, despair hidden beneath smiles and laughter, despair that craved just one more merry night, one more escapade, one last hour of youth, one last intoxication—and so an end of it all for ever.

The fair Amphitryons of this incredible supper, so far removed from the timid habits of the society to which they belonged, must surely have experienced something of the feelings of Sardanapalus on his funeral-pyre when he heaped upon it, to perish with him, wives, slaves, horses, jewels, all the splendid trappings of his life. They too collected at this last supper of farewell all the splendid trappings of their past. To it they brought all their stores of beauty, of wit and wisdom, of magnificence and power, to pour them forth once and for all in one supreme and final conflagration.

The hero before whom they wrapped and robed themselves in this garment of consuming fire counted for more in their eyes than all Asia did for Sardanapalus. They flirted with him as never women flirted with any man before, or with any roomful of men; and their keen coquetry was yet further inflamed by jealousy, which is concealed in good society, but which they had no cause to dissemble here, for they all knew that he had been the lover of each and all of them, and shame shared among so many ceases to be shame at all. . . . The sole and only rivalry between them was, which should carve his epitaph deepest in her heart?

That night he enjoyed the rich, sovereign, nonchalant, ruminating pleasure of a father confessor and a sultan. There he sat, monarch and master, in the centre of the table, facing the Comtesse de Chiffrevas, in her boudoir with its peach-blossom hangings—or was it the fruit of the tree of the knowledge of evil?—this has always been a moot point. The fiery gaze of his blue eye—heavenly blue many a poor creature has deemed to her cost, to find it later of quite another sort—was fixed on his fair companions. All twelve were beautiful, all were dressed to perfection; and, seated round the festive board, which glistened with crystal lights and flowers, they displayed, from the scarlet of the open rose to the soft gold of the mellow grape, every nuance of ripe and opulent charms.

Only the crude green of extreme youth was absent, the little girls Byron loathed, smelling of bread and butter, thin, weedy, undeveloped creatures. Fine, full-flavoured summer, rich and generous autumn, these were the seasons represented—full curves and ample proportions, dazzling bosoms, beating in majestic swell above liberally cut corsages, and below the clear modelling of the naked shoulder, arms of every type of beauty, but mostly powerful arms, Sabine biceps, that have struggled against the Roman ravisher, vigorous enough, you would think, to grasp the wheels of the car of life and twine around the spokes and stop its course by sheer force.

I have spoken of happy ideas. One of the happiest at this supper was to have all the waiting done by maidservants, that nothing might disturb the harmony of a celebration where women were the only queens, and did all the honours. . . .

Señor Don Juan then was able to bathe his burning gaze in a sea of living and dazzling flesh, such as Rubens delights to flaunt in his strong, fleshy pictures, but, besides, he could plunge his pride in the ether, more or less transparent, more or less turgid, of all these hearts. The fact is, at bottom, and despite all appearances to the contrary, Don Juan is an ardent idealist! He is like the Devil, his master, who loves men's souls better than their bodies, and actually traffics in the former by choice, the hellish slave-driver!

Witty, high-bred, and aristocratic, but for the nonce as recklessly gay as pages of the household—when there was a king's household and pages of it—they exhibited a scintillating brilliance, a dash, a verve, a *brio*, that were beyond compare. They felt themselves in better form than they had ever been in their most palmy days; they felt a new and mysterious power in their inmost being which they had never suspected the existence of before.

Joy at this discovery, a sensation of tripled intensity in the vital powers, still more the physical incitements, so stimulating to highly strung temperaments, the flashing lights, the penetrating odour of many flowers dying in an atmosphere overheated with the emanations of all these lovely bodies, the sting of heady wines, all acted together. Then the mere thought of this supper, which had just the piquancy of naughtiness the fair Neapolitan asked for in her lemonade to make it perfectly delicious, the intoxicating notion of complicity in this wild, wicked feast—not that it condescended for an instant to any of the vulgar incidents of the Regent's suppers; it remained throughout true to the tone of the Faubourg Saint-Germain and the nineteenth century, and of all these lovely bosoms, with hearts beating beneath that had been under fire and still loved to tempt the fray, not one lost so much as a pin or a knot of ribbon—all these things together helped to tune the magic harp which all of them carried within themselves, and to stretch the strings wellnigh to breaking point, till they quivered again in passionate octaves and ineffable diapasons of emotion. . . . A curious page it will make of his Secret Memoirs this, if Ravila ever writes them! . . . As I told the Marquise Guy de Ruy, I was not at the supper myself, and if I am able to report some of its incidents and the narrative with which it concluded, I owe them to no other than Ravila himself who, faithful to the traditional indiscretion of all the Don Juan breed, took the trouble one evening to tell me the whole story.

III

It was getting late—or, rather, early—and dawn was near. On the ceiling, and at one spot in the pink silk curtains of the boudoir, otherwise hermetically closed, there grew and increased a splash of opalescent light, like an ever-enlarging eye, the eye of day, as if fain to look in through the crevice and see what was doing in the brilliantly lighted room. A certain languor was in the air, assailing these champions of the Round Table, these merry-makers who had been so animated but a moment ago. The crisis is familiar at every supper party, the instant when, wearied with the gaiety and emotional stress of the night, everything seems to languish at once, drooping heads, burning cheeks, reddened or paled by excitement, tired eyes under heavy, darkened lids, even the candles themselves, which seem to quiver and grow larger in the many-branched candelabra, fiery flowers with stems of chiselled bronze and gold.

The conversation, hitherto general and vivacious, a game of shuttlecock, where each had put in her stroke, had grown fragmentary and broken, and no distinct word was now audible amid the general confusion of voices which, with their aristocratic tones, mingled in a pretty babble, like birds at break of day on the confines of a wood, when one of them—a high-pitched voice, imperious, almost insolent, as a duchess's should be—cried suddenly above all the rest to the Comte de Ravila what was evidently the conclusion of a previous whispered conversation between the two, which none of the others, each engaged in talk with her immediate neighbour, had heard.

'You are the reputed Don Juan of our day: well! you should tell us the history of the conquest of all others which most flattered your pride as a ladies' man, and which you judge, in the light of the present moment, the greatest love of your life. . . .'

And the question, no less than the voice in which it was uttered, instantly cut short the scattered conversations that were buzzing round the table, and imposed a sudden silence.

The voice was that of the Duchesse de * * *—I will not lift

the veil of asterisks, but you will very likely know who it was when I tell you she is the fairest of all fair women, both complexion and hair, with the darkest eyes under long golden eyebrows in all the Faubourg Saint-Germain. She was seated, like a saint at God's right hand, at the right hand of the Comte de Ravila, the God of the Feast, a god that, for the moment, waived his right to use his enemies as his footstool; slender and spiritual, like an arabesque and a fairy, in her dress of green velvet, with glints of silver, the long train twining round her chair, no bad imitation of the serpent's tail in which the alluring shape of the sea-nymph Melusina terminates.

'A happy thought!' put in the Comtesse de Chiffrevas, seconding as mistress of the house the wish expressed by the duchess. 'Yes! the love of all loves, inspired or felt, you would most gladly live again, were such a thing possible.'

'Oh, I would be glad to live them all again!' cried Ravila, with the unquenchable gusto of a Roman Emperor, the insatiable craving your utterly *blasé* man of pleasure sometimes retains. And he flourished aloft his champagne glass, the glass our fathers drank from, tall and slender, and called by them a *flûte*, mayhap from the celestial harmonies in which it often bathes our heart! Then he embraced in one sweeping look the whole circle of fair women that wreathed the board so royally. 'And still,' he went on, replacing his glass before him with a sigh that sounded strange from such a Nebuchadnezzar, whose only experience as yet of the grass of the field as an article of diet had been the tarragon salads at the Café Anglais—'and still, how true it is there is always *one* among all the emotions of a lifetime that shines ever in the memory more brightly than the rest, as life advances—one for which we would gladly exchange them all.'

'The brightest diamond of the casket,' murmured the Comtesse Chiffrevas in a dreamy tone, perhaps looking back at the sparkling facets of her own career.

'. . . The legends of my country,' broke in the Princess Jable—who is from the foothills of the Ural Mountains—'tell of a famous and fabulous diamond, rose-coloured at first, but which turns black presently, yet remains a true diamond all the time, and sparkles the more brilliantly for the change. . . .' She said it with the strange exotic charm peculiar to her, this Gipsy Princess. For a true gipsy she is, married for love by the handsomest prince of all the exiled Polish nobility; yet having as much the air of a high-born princess as if she had first seen the light in the palace of the Jagellons.

A regular explosion followed. 'Yes! yes!' they clamoured with one voice. 'Tell us, comte!' they urged in tone already vibrating with a passionate supplication, curiosity quivering in the very curls that fringed the back of their necks. They drew together, shoulder to shoulder; some with cheek on hand and elbow on the board, some leaning back in their chairs, with open fans before their mouths, all challenging him with wide inquisitive eyes.

'If you are bent on hearing the story,' said the comte with the nonchalance of a man well aware how much procrastination adds to the keenness of desire.

'We are, we are!' cried the duchesse, gazing, as a Turkish despot might at his sabre's edge, at the gold dessert-knife she held in her fingers.

'Well, listen then,' he said finally, still the same fine air of indifference.

They fell into attitudes of profound attention, and, fixing their gaze on his face, devoured him with their eyes. Every love story is interesting to a woman; but here, perhaps—who knows?—the chief charm lay for each one of his audience in the thought that the tale he was about to unfold might be her own. . . . They knew him to be too much of a gentleman and too well-bred not to be sure he would suppress all names and, where necessary, slur over indiscreet details; and their conviction of this fact made them so much the more eager to hear the story. They not only desired but, what is more, they hoped—each for a special and particular sop to her own vanity.

Yet this same vanity was on the qui vive to scent a rival in this reminiscence called up as the tenderest in a life that must have been so full of them. The old sultan was going once more to throw the handkerchief . . . that no hand would stoop to pick up, but which the favoured *one* it should have fallen to would silently and gratefully receive into her heart.

Knowing what his fair audience expected, you will now be able to realize the utterly unexpected thunderclap he called down on all those listening heads.

IV

'I have often heard moralists declare—men who have had deep experience of life,' began the Comte de Ravila, 'that the strongest of all our loves is neither the first nor yet the last, as many think, but the second. But in these matters everything is uncertain, and at any rate it was not so with me. . . . What you ask me about, ladies, the story I am about to tell you to-night, dates from the best period of my youth. I was not then what is technically called a "young man", but I was young, albeit I had already, as an old uncle of mine, a knight of Malta, used to say to describe this epoch of life, sown my wild oats.[1] I was in the full vigour of my prime, and I was in full *relations* (to use the pretty Italian phrase) with a woman you all know well, and have all admired. . . .'

At this the look which each of the group simultaneously cast at all the rest, one and all eagerly drinking in the old serpent's honeyed words, was a thing to have seen—for, indeed, it is indescribable.

'The woman in question', Ravila went on, 'had every element of "distinction" you can imagine, in every sense of the word. She was young, rich, of noble name, beautiful, witty, and artistic—simple, too, and unaffected, with the genuine unaffectedness to be found only in well-bred circles, and not always there—to crown all, without another thought or inspiration but to please me, to be my devoted slave, at once the fondest of mistresses, and the best of comrades.

'I was not, I have reason to believe, the first man she had loved. . . . She had given her affections once before—and it was not to her husband; but the whole affair had been virtuous, platonic, utopian—the sort of love that practises rather than satisfies a woman's heart, that trains its powers for another and fuller passion, which is bound to supervene ere long. It is prentice love, in fact, something like the *messe blanche* young priests repeat by way of rehearsal, that they may not blunder in the genuine solemn Mass that is to follow. . . . When I came into her life she was only at the "white Mass"; I was her genuine Mass—and she went through it with every circumstance of pomp and ceremony, like a very cardinal.'

[1] *J'avais fini mes caravanes ; caravane* was the word used by the Knights of Malta to designate their periodical filibustering cruises against the Turks.

At this the prettiest smile flashed out on the twelve sweet mouths that listened round, like a circling eddy on the limpid surface of a pool. . . . It was gone in an instant, but entrancing while it lasted.

'She was indeed one in a thousand!' the comte resumed. 'Rarely have I known more real good-heartedness, more gentle compassion, more justness of feeling—and this, even in love, which is, you know, a passion made up of evil as well as good. . . . Nowhere have I seen less manœuvring, or less prudishness and vanity, two things so often entangled in the web of feminine character, like a skein clawed over by a mischievous cat. . . . The cat had no part in her composition. . . . She was what those confounded romance-writers who poison our minds with phrases would call a "simple, primitive nature, complicated and embellished by civilization"; but she had borrowed of it only the pretty luxury of her habits, and not one of those little vices that sometimes seem even more alluring than the luxuries.'

'Was she dark or fair?' suddenly interrupted the duchesse, with a startling directness, tired out with so much metaphysics. . .

'Ah! you miss my point!' exclaimed Ravila keenly. 'Well, I will tell you; her hair was dark, black as the blackest jet, the most perfect ebony mirror I have ever seen flash back the light from a woman's head, but her complexion was fair—and it is by complexion, not hair, you should pronounce a woman brunette or blonde,' added this student of the sex, who had observed women for something else than just to paint their portraits afterwards. . . . 'She was blonde with black hair. . . .'

Each blonde head around the table (alas, only blond-*haired* they!) betrayed an almost imperceptible movement of disappointment. For them clearly the tale had henceforth lost something of its interest.

'She had the ebony locks of Night,' resumed Ravila, 'but crowning the face of Aurora, for indeed her face glowed with a rosy freshness of dawn, as dazzling as rare, that had triumphantly resisted years of Paris life with its hot rooms and artificial light, that burns up so many roses in the flames of its candelabra. *Her* roses seemed but to win a richer hue, so brilliant was the carmine that mantled on cheek and lip! Indeed, this twofold radiance accorded well with the ruby she always wore on her forehead (the frontlet was still in fashion in those days), which, in combination with her flashing eyes, whose very brilliancy made it impossible to distinguish their colour, formed a triangle, as it were, of three bright jewels in her face! Tall, but robust, and even majestic in figure, cut out for the helpmate of a colonel of dragoons—her husband at that time was only a major in the Light Horse—she enjoyed, for all her fine ladyhood, a peasant woman's vigorous health, who drinks in the sun at every pore. And she had all the heat and ardour of the sun in her veins, and in her very soul as well—ever present, and ever ready. . . . But—and this was the strange part of it—this being, so strong and simple and unspoiled, as generous and as pure as the red blood that mantled in her cheeks and dyed her rosy arms, was —can you credit it?—maladroit and awkward in a lover's arms. . . .'

Here one or two fair auditors dropped their eyes, only to raise them again directly with a look of demure mischief in their depths. . . .

'Yes! awkward in this respect as she was reckless in her regard for appearances,' continued Ravila, and vouchsafed no further information on this delicate point. 'In fact, the man who loved her had to be incessantly teaching her two lessons, neither of which she ever really learnt—not to affront needlessly public opinion, a foe that is always under arms and always merciless, and to practise in the intimacy of private life those all-important acts of love that guard passion from dying of satiety. Love she had in abundance, but the art and mystery of its skilled exponents were beyond her ken. . . . She was the antipodes of most women, who possess the latter qualifications to perfection, but of the other not a whit. Now to comprehend and apply the cunning maxims of the *Il Principe*, you must be a Borgia to begin with. Borgia comes first, Machiavelli second; one is the poet, the other the critic. No Borgia was she, but just a good woman in love, as simple-minded, with all her monumental beauty, as the little maid in the rustic picture who tries to take up a handful of spring water from the fountain to quench her thirst, but in her trembling haste lets it trickle away every drop between her fingers, and stands there an image of embarrassment and confusion. . . .

'Yet in a way the contrast was piquant and almost delightful between this embarrassed awkwardness and the grand, passion-fraught personality of the woman, who would have deceived the most acute observer when seen in society—who knew love, and even love's bliss, but had not the faculty to pay back half of what she received. Only, unfortunately, I was not artist enough to be content with this mere delight of contrast; hence now and again displays on her part of disquiet, jealousy, and even violence. But all this jealousy, disquiet, violence, was swallowed up in the inexhaustible kindness of her heart at the first sign of pain she thought she had inflicted—as awkward at wounding as she was at caressing! Tigress of an unknown species, she fondly imagined she had claws, but lo! when she would show them, none were to be found within the sheath of her beautiful velvet paws. Her very scratches were velvet-soft!'

'What is the man driving at?' whispered the Comtesse de Chiffrevas to her neighbour. 'This surely cannot be Don Juan's proudest triumph!'

All these complex natures could not understand such simplicity, and remained incredulous.

'Thus we lived,' Ravila went on, 'on terms of friendship, now and then interrupted by storms, yet never shipwrecked, a friendship that, in the little village they call Paris, was a mystery to none. . . . The marquise—she was a marquise . . .'

There were three at the table, and raven-locked too. But they made no sign. They knew only too well it was not of them he spoke. . . . The only velvet about the trio was on the upper lip of one of the three—a lip bearing a voluptuous shadowing of down, and for the moment, I can assure you, a well-marked expression of disdain.

'. . . And a marquise three times over, just as pashas may be pashas of three tails,' continued Ravila, who was getting into the swing of his narrative. 'The marquise was one of those women who have no idea of hiding anything, and who, if they had, could never do it. Her daughter even, a child of thirteen, for all her youth and innocence, saw only too clearly the nature of the feeling the mother had for me. I know not which of our poets has asked what the girls think of us, the girls whose mothers we have loved. A deep question I often put to myself when I caught the child's inquisitive gaze fixed black and menacing upon me from the ambush of her great, dark eyes. . . . A shy reserved creature, she would, more often than not, leave the drawing-room when I entered and, if obliged to remain, would invariably station herself as far away from me as possible; she had an almost convulsive horror of my person—which she strove to hide in her own bosom, but which was too strong for her, and betrayed itself against her will by little almost imperceptible signs. I noticed every one. The marquise, though anything but an observant woman, was for ever warning me: "You must take care, dearest, I think my girl is jealous of you..'

'But I was taking much better care all the while than she was.

'Had the little girl been the Devil himself I would have defied her to decipher my game. . . . But her mother's was as clear as day. Everything was visible in the rosy mirror of her beautiful face, so often troubled by passing clouds! From the strange dislike the girl showed, I could not help thinking she had surprised her mother's secret through some indiscreet burst of feeling, some involuntary look fraught with excess of tenderness. I may tell you she was a funny-looking child, quite unworthy of the glorious mould she had issued from, an ugly child, even by her mother's admission, who only loved her the more for it. A little rough-cut topaz—how shall I describe it?—a half-finished sculptor's study in bronze—but with eyes black as night, and having a strange, uncanny magic of their own. Later on . . .'

But here he stopped dead, as if regretting his burst of confidence, and fearful of having said too much. . . . Every face once more expressed an open, eager, vivid curiosity, and the countess, with a knowing air of pleased expectancy, actually dropped from between her lovely lips an expressive 'At last!'

'In the earlier days of my liaison with her mother,' the Comte de Ravila resumed, 'I had shown the child all the little fondling familiarities one has with children. . . . I used to bring her bags of sugared almonds; I used to call her my "little witch", and very often, when talking to her mother, I would amuse myself with fingering the curls that hung over her temple—thin, sickly-looking curls, like black tow—but the "little witch", whose big mouth had a pretty smile for everybody else, at once waxed pensive, her little face grew tense and rigid, the wrinkled mask of an overburdened caryatid, and as my hand brushed her forehead, it looked for all the world as though it bore the crushing weight of some vast entablature.

'After a while, meeting invariably the same sullenness and apparent hostility, I took to leaving this sensitive plant alone which drew in its sad-coloured petals so violently at the least touch of a caress. . . . I even left off speaking to her! "She feels you are robbing her", the marquise would say to me. "Her instinct tells her you are appropriating a portion of her mother's love." Sometimes she would add outright: "The child is my conscience, and her jealousy my remorse".

'Once the marquise had tried to question her as to the profound disfavour in which she held me, but she had got nothing out of her but the broken, obstinate, stupid answers you have to drag out with a corkscrew of reiterated questions from a child that prefers not to speak. . . . "Nothing is the matter. . . . I don't know . . ." and so on. Finally, seeing how hard and obstinate the little image was, she had left off questioning her, and turned away in sheer weariness.

'I forgot, by the by, to tell you one thing. The queer child was profoundly religious, in a gloomy, medieval, Spanish, superstitious sort of way. She twined around her meagre little person all kinds of scapularies and stuck on her bosom, which was as flat as the back of your hand, and round her swarthy throat a whole heap of crosses, Blessed Virgins, and Holy Spirits. "You are a free-thinker, you know," the marquise would say to me, "worse luck; perhaps you have shocked her feelings some time with your talk. Be very careful of anything you say before her; and do not add to my sins in the eyes of my child, towards whom I already feel myself so guilty!" Then, later on, the girl's behaviour showing no change or improvement whatever: "You will end by hating the child," the marquise would complain anxiously, "and I cannot blame you". But she was wrong in this; my feeling towards the sullen child was one of simple indifference, when I took the trouble to think of her at all.

'I treated her with the ceremonious politeness usual between grown-up people who do not like each other. I addressed her formally as Mademoiselle, and she returned the compliment with a freezing "Monsieur". . . . She would do nothing when I was there to attract admiration or even notice. . . . Her mother could never persuade her to show me one of her drawings or play a piece on the piano in my presence. If ever I came upon her seated at the instrument practising eagerly and industriously, she would stop dead, get up from the music-stool, and refuse utterly to go on. . . .

'Once only, when there was company, and her mother desired her to play, she consented to take her place at the open keyboard, with a look of being victimized that was anything but propitiating, I can tell you, and began some drawing-room piece with abominably difficult fingering. I was standing by the fireplace, and enfiladed her with my gaze. Her back was towards me, and there was no mirror in front of her in which she could see I was looking at her. . . . All of a sudden her back—she always held herself ill, and many a time her mother would tell her: "If you *will* hold yourself like that, you 'll end by getting consumption"—well, all of a sudden her back straightened as if my look had broken her spine like a bullet; and, slamming down the lid of the piano with a resounding crash, she rushed out of the room. . . . They went to look for her, but for that evening, at any rate, nothing would induce her to come back.

'Well, vain as men are, it would seem their vanity is often blind, and, for all her strange behaviour (and indeed I gave it very little attention), I had never a suspicion of the true feeling the mysterious creature entertained for me. Nor yet had her mother; jealous as the latter was of every woman who entered her drawing-room, in this case her jealousy was as fast asleep as my own vanity. The truth was eventually revealed in a sufficiently startling fashion. The marquise, who could keep nothing from her intimates, told me the story, her face still pale with the fright she had had, though bursting with laughter at the notion of having been frightened at all. In doing so she was ill-advised.'

The word 'ill-advised' the count had marked with just that touch of emphasis a clever actor knows how to throw into his voice when he has a point to make. This was the thread, he was perfectly aware of the fact, on which the whole interest of his story now hung.

The mere hint was enough apparently, for all twelve faces flushed once more with an intensity of emotion comparable only to the cherubim's countenances before the throne of the Almighty! Is not curiosity in a woman's heart as intense an emotion as ever adoration among the angels of God? . . . For his part, he marked them all, those cherub faces (which were a good deal more than mere head and shoulders, though), and, finding them doubtless primed for what he had to say, quickly resumed and went on without further pause.

'Yes, she could not help bursting with laughter, merely to think of it!—so the marquise told me a while after, when she came to relate the story; but she had been in no laughing mood at first!—"Only picture the scene," she began (I will endeavour to recall her exact words); "I was seated just where we are now."

'This was one of those small double sofas known as *dos-à-dos*, of all contrivances in the way of furniture surely the best-designed for a pair of lovers to quarrel and make it up again, without leaving their seats.

'"But you were not where you are now—thank goodness!—when, who do you think was announced?—you would never guess—who but the respected *curé* of Saint-Germain-des-Prés? Do you know him? . . . No, you never go to church, you bad man! . . . So how should you know the poor old *curé*, who is a saint, and who never sets foot inside the doors of any woman in his parish unless it is a question of raising money for his poor or his church? For a moment I thought this was what he had come for now.

'He had prepared my daughter at the proper time for her first communion; and as she went regularly to communion, subsequently, she had retained him as her confessor. For this reason, over and over again since then, I had invited the good priest to dine with us, but always in vain. On entering the room he displayed the greatest agitation, and I read in his usually placid features manifest signs of an embarrassment so extreme and so uncontrollable, I could not set it down to the account of mere shyness. Involuntarily the first words that escaped me were: "Good heavens, Father! What is the matter?"

'"'The matter, dear madame,' he began, '. . . the matter is, you see, before you the most embarrassed man in Europe. For fifty years I have been a minister in God's service, and all that time I have never had a more delicate mission to perform, or one that baffled me more completely to understand. . . .'

'"Then he sat down, asking me to have the door shut against all comers throughout our interview. As you may suppose, all these solemn preliminaries began rather to frighten me. . . .

'"Noticing this, he added: 'Nay! do not be frightened, I beg of you; you will need all your calmness to attend to my story, and to account, to my satisfaction, for the unheard-of circumstance we have to deal with, and which even now I cannot believe authentic. . . . Your daughter, madame, on whose behalf I am here, is—you know it as well as I do—an angel of purity and goodness. I know her very soul. I have held it between my hands since she was a child of seven, and I am convinced she is deceiving herself—through sheer innocence of heart, it may be. . . . But this morning she came to me to avow in confession—you will not believe it, nor can I, but the word must come out—that she was *pregnant*!'

'"A cry escaped me of wonder and incredulity. . . .

'"'I did the very same thing this morning in my confessional,' the priest declared, 'on hearing her make this assertion, accompanied as it was by every mark of the most genuine and terrible despair. I know the child thoroughly; she is absolutely ignorant of the world and its wickedness. . . . Of all the young girls, I confess, she is undoubtedly the one I could most unhesitatingly answer for before God.—There is no more to tell! We priests are the surgeons of souls, and it is our duty to deliver them of shameful secrets they would fain conceal, with hands careful neither to wound nor pollute. I therefore proceeded, with all possible guardedness, to interrogate, question, and cross-question the desperate girl. But, the avowal once made, the fault once confessed—she calls it a crime herself, and her eternal damnation, fully believing herself, poor girl, a lost soul—she thenceforth refused to say another word, maintaining an obstinate silence which she broke only to beseech me to come to you, madame, to inform you of the crime—"for mamma *must* know," she said, "and I shall never, never be brave enough to tell her".'

'"You may easily imagine with what mingled feelings of amazement and anxiety I listened to the *curé* of Saint-Germain des-Prés. I was just as sure as he was, surer, in fact, of my little girl's innocence; but do not the innocent sometimes fall, out of very innocence? . . . And what she had told the confessor was not in the nature of things impossible. . . . I did not believe it! . . . could not believe it! but still it was not in itself impossible! . . . She was only thirteen, but she was a woman, and the very fact of her precocity had startled me before now. . . .' A fever, a frenzy of curiosity came over me.

'"'I must and will know all!' I cried excitedly to the worthy priest as he stood there listening to me with a bewildered air, plucking his hat to pieces in his agitation. 'Leave me, Father. She would not speak before you; but I am certain she will tell me everything. . . . I am certain I can drag everything out of her. Then we shall understand what is now so utterly incomprehensible.'

'"On this the good priest took his departure. The instant he was gone I sprang upstairs to my daughter's room, not having patience enough to send for her and wait till she came.

'"I found her kneeling—no! not kneeling, prostrate—before her crucifix, pale as death, her eyes dry and very red, like eyes that have wept many bitter tears. I took her in my arms, seated her by my side, and presently on my knees, and told her I could not believe what her confessor had just been telling me was true.

'"But here she interrupted me to assure me with a heart-broken voice and look that it *was* true, what he had said; and at this point, more and more anxious and wondering, I asked her who it was that . . .

'"I left the sentence unfinished. . . . The terrible moment was come! She had her head and face on my shoulder . . . but I could see the blush of shame burning on her neck behind, and feel her shudder. The same leaden silence she had opposed to her father confessor, she now opposed to me. She was impenetrable.

'"'It must be some one very much beneath you, since you are so deeply ashamed? . . .' I said, trying to make her speak in self-exculpation, for I knew she had plenty of pride.

'"But still the same silence, the same burying of her head on my shoulder. This lasted what seemed to me an infinity of time, when suddenly she said, without lifting her head: 'Swear you will forgive me, mother!'

'"I swore everything she asked me, at the risk of perjuring myself a hundred times over—little I cared! I was boiling with impatience—boiling. . . . I thought my skull would burst and let my brains out. . . .

'"'Well, then! it was Monsieur de Ravila,' she whispered, without changing her position in my arms.

'"Oh! the shock of hearing that name, Amédée! At one fell swoop I was receiving full and condign punishment for the great fault of my life, and my heart quailed within me! You are so terrible a man where women are concerned, you have made me so fearful of rivals, that those fatal words of doubt, 'why not?' —so heartrending when spoken of the man you love, yet suspect

—rose involuntarily to my lips. What I felt, however, I had resolution enough left to hide from the cruel child, who had, it may be, guessed her mother's guilty secret.

"''Monsieur de Ravila!' I ejaculated in a tone I feared must betray everything; 'why, you never even speak to him!'—'You avoid him,' I was going to add, for my anger was rising, I felt it was. . . . 'You are surely very deceitful, the pair of you!'—But I refrained: was I not bound to learn the details, one by one, of this vile tale of seduction? . . . I began to question her with an enforced gentleness I thought would have killed me, when she released me from the torture of the rack, saying with perfect *naïveté*:

"''It was one evening, mother. He was in the big arm-chair by the fireside, facing the sofa. . . . He sat there ever so long, then presently got up, and I—I had the misfortune to go and sit down in the same chair after him. Oh! mamma . . . it was just as if I had fallen into a flame of fire. I wanted to get up, but I could not . . . for my heart had stopped beating! and I felt . . . Oh! mamma, mamma, I felt . . . that what hurt me so . . . was a baby! . . .'"'

The marquise laughed, Ravila said, when she told him the story; but not one of the twelve women surrounding the table as much as thought of laughing—nor Ravila either.

'And this, ladies, believe me or not, as you please,' he added by way of conclusion, 'I consider the greatest triumph of my life, the passion I am proudest of having inspired.'

And with this he fell silent—a silence they left unbroken one and all. His auditors were pensive. . . . Had they understood his meaning?

What time Joseph was a slave in the Lady Potiphar's household, he was so handsome, says the Koran, that, in their dreamy state, the women he waited on at table used to cut their fingers with their knives as they gazed at him. But we have travelled far since Joseph's time, and the preoccupations we experience at dessert are not so absorbing nowadays.

'But there, what a consummate idiot, with all her cleverness, your marquise was, to have told you about such a thing!' at last said the duchesse, who condescended to be cynical, but who cut neither her fingers nor anything else with the gold dessert-knife she still held in her hand.

Meantime the Comtesse de Chiffrevas was gazing fixedly

into the depths of a glass of Rhine-wine, a green crystal glass, as profound and mysterious as her own reverie.

'And the little witch?' she asked.

'Oh, she was dead—she died quite young—married to somebody in the country—when her mother told me the story,' Ravila quietly replied.

'But for that . . .' said the duchesse thoughtfully.

Translated by E. Boyd

A SIMPLE HEART

Gustave Flaubert

For fifty years the ladies of Pont-l'Évêque envied Madame Aubain her servant Felicity.

For a hundred francs a year she cooked, and cleaned, sewed, washed, ironed, could harness a horse, fatten up poultry, churn butter; and she remained loyal to her mistress who, all the same, was not an agreeable person.

Madame Aubain had married a fine young fellow without a fortune, who died at the beginning of 1809, leaving her two very young children, and a great number of debts. Then she sold her real estate, except the farm of Toucques, and the farm of Geffosses, whose rents amounted to five thousand francs at the outside, and she quitted the house at Saint-Milaine to settle in another one less costly, which had belonged to her ancestors, and was situated behind the market-place.

This house, covered with tiles, was set between a lane and an alley that gave on the river. Inside, its ground levels were unequal, and were the cause of frequent stumbles. A narrow vestibule separated the kitchen from the living-room, where Madame Aubain passed the whole day, seated near the window casement on a straw-bottomed chair. Against the wainscoting, painted white, were lined up eight mahogany chairs. An old piano carried, under a barometer, a heaped pyramid of wooden and cardboard boxes. Two deep arm-chairs, tapestry covered, flanked the yellow marble mantelpiece in the style of Louis XV. The clock in the middle represented a temple of Vesta—and the whole room smelled slightly musty, for the floor was lower than the garden.

On the first floor there was, first of all, 'Madame's' room, very big, hung with a wallpaper with pale flowers, and containing the portrait of 'Monsieur' in the costume of a *muscadin*. It communicated with a smaller room, where two children's couches were to be seen without their mattresses. Then came the drawing-room, always shut up, and filled with furniture covered with a sheet. Then a corridor led to a study: books and papers filled the shelves of a book-case surrounding with its three sides a large blackwood desk. The two end panels were invisible beneath pen-and-ink sketches, landscapes in body colour, and Audran's engravings, souvenirs of better times and vanished luxury. A dormer window on the second story lighted Felicity's room, looking out on the fields.

She rose with the dawn so as not to miss Mass, and worked without stopping until evening; then, dinner being finished, the dishes put away and the door fast shut, she covered the faggots with ashes, and fell asleep before the hearth, her rosary in her hand. Nobody in her marketing could show more obstinacy. As to her cleanliness, the polish on her saucepans was the despair of other servants. Thrifty, she ate slowly, and gathered up from the table with her fingers the crumbs of the loaf—a twelve-pound loaf, baked specially for her, which lasted twenty days.

All through the year she carried a cotton handkerchief fixed at her back by a pin, a bonnet that hid her hair, grey stockings, a red skirt, and over her bodice an apron with a bib like a hospital nurse.

Her face was thin and her voice sharp. At twenty-five years of age you would have guessed her to be forty. After her fiftieth year she showed no traces of any age at all; and, always silent, upright in carriage, and measured in gesture, she seemed a woman made of wood, functioning automatically.

II

She had had, like any one else, her love story.

Her father, a mason, had been killed in falling from a scaffolding. Then her mother died, her sisters scattered; a farmer took her in, and employed her, while still a little girl, in guarding cows in the fields. She shivered under her rags, drank flat on her stomach the water of the pools, for no pretext at all was beaten, and finally was dismissed for a theft of thirty pence which she had not committed. She took service in another farm, became hen girl there, and, as she pleased her employers, her comrades were jealous of her.

One day in the month of August (she was eighteen then) they took her with them to the fair at Colleville. Straightway she was bewildered, stupefied by the noise of the fiddlers, the lights in the trees, the motley of the costumes, the laces, the gold crosses—this mass of people who leapt simultaneously. She was keeping modestly in the background when a young man, well-to-do in appearance, smoking his pipe, with his two elbows on the pole of a small wagon, came to invite her to dance. He recompensed her with cider, with coffee, with cake, with a scarf, and offered to lead her out again. She did not know what to answer, and wanted to run away. He departed.

Another evening on the road to Beaumont she wanted to pass a big wagon of hay that was going along slowly, and as she brushed past the wheels she recognized Theodore.

At once he spoke of the harvests and the notables of the district, for his father had left Colleville for the farm of Écots, so that now they were neighbours. 'Ah', she said. He added that they were wanting to set him up for himself. Yet he wasn't in a hurry; he was waiting for a wife to his taste. She hung her head. Then he asked her if she was thinking of marriage. She answered, smiling, that it wasn't right to laugh at her. 'But I 'm not, I give you my word!' and with his left arm he encircled her waist: she walked on, held up by his embrace: they went more slowly. The wind was soft, the stars shone, the huge wagon-load of hay swayed before them, and the four horses, dragging their feet, raised the dust. Then, without being told, they turned to the right. He hugged her again. She disappeared into the shadows.

Theodore, the following week, got her to promise to meet him.

They met at the far end of the courtyard, under an isolated tree. She was not innocent, in the fashion of ladies, but common sense and the instinct of honour kept her from yielding. This resistance exasperated Theodore's love so much that in order to satisfy it (or perhaps quite ingenuously) he proposed to marry her. She hesitated to believe him. He swore great oaths.

Soon he admitted something annoying; his parents last year had bought him off conscription; but any day they could take him again. The idea of serving terrified him. This cowardice was in Felicity's eyes a proof of affection; her own redoubled. She stole out at night, and when she got to the meeting place Theodore tortured her with his anxiety and his entreaties.

At last he announced that he would go himself to headquarters to get information, and that he would bring her word on the following Sunday between eleven and twelve at night.

When the moment came she ran to her lover.

In his place she found one of his friends. He told her that she would not see him again. To assure himself from conscription Theodore had married a very rich old woman, Madame Lehoussais, of Toucques.

She gave way to a burst of extravagant grief. She threw herself on the ground, cried aloud, called on the good God, and groaned, all alone in the country till sunrise. Then she went back to the farm, and declared her intention of leaving it, and at the end of a month, having received her wages, she tied all her little belongings in a handkerchief, and went to Pont-l'Évêque.

In front of the inn she asked some questions of a lady in a widow's cap, who happened at the time to be looking for a cook. The girl did not know much, but she seemed so anxious to please and to have so few unreasonable demands, that Madame Aubain finished by saying:

'All right, I 'll take you.'

Felicity a quarter of an hour afterwards was settled in her house.

At first she lived there in a sort of tremor caused by the 'kind of house', and the memory of 'Monsieur' hovering over everything. Paul and Virginia, one aged seven, the other hardly four, seemed to her to be made of precious stuff; she carried them on her back like a horse, and Madame Aubain forbade her to kiss them every minute, and that mortified her. Yet she was happy. The gentleness of the environment had melted her sorrow.

Every Thursday friends came to take a hand at boston-whist. Felicity prepared in advance the cards and the footwarmers. They arrived at eight o'clock very punctually, and went away before the stroke of eleven.

Each Monday morning the second-hand dealer who lodged under the alley spread out his scrap iron on the ground. Then the town was filled with a hum of voices, in which were mingled the neighing of horses, the bleating of sheep, the grunting of pigs, and the dry rattle of traps on the road. About midday, at the height of the market, could be seen on the threshold a tall old peasant, his cap pulled down, his nose hooked, and who was Robelin, the farmer of Geffosses. A short time after it was Liébard, the farmer of Toucques, small, red, fat, wearing a grey jacket and leggings fitted with spurs.

Both of them offered their landlady fowls or cheeses. Felicity invariably baffled their tricks, and they went away full of consideration for her.

On indeterminate occasions Madame Aubain received a visit from the Marquis de Germanville, one of her uncles, ruined by debauchery, who lived at Falaise, on the last morsel of his property. He arrived always at lunch time, with a frightful little dog, whose paws dirtied all the furniture. In spite of his efforts to appear a gentleman, even going so far as to lift his hat every time he said: 'My late father', his old habits got the better of him; he poured out for himself glass after glass, and let out some rather free stories. Felicity would push him outside politely: 'You 've had enough of it, Monsieur de Germanville! We 'll see you another time!' And she shut the door.

She opened it with pleasure to Monsieur Bourais, an ex-solicitor. His white cravat, and his bald head, the frill of his shirt, his wide brown frockcoat, his way of taking snuff, making a circle with his arm, his whole personality produced in her the excitement into which the sight of extraordinary men throws us.

As he managed the estate of 'Madame' he shut himself up with her for hours in monsieur's study: he was always afraid of compromising himself, he had a great respect for the magistracy, and had pretensions to Latin.

To instruct the children in a pleasant fashion he made them a present of a geography with engravings. They represented different scenes in the world, cannibals with feathers in their hair, a monkey carrying off a young lady, Bedouins in the desert, a whale being harpooned, etc.

Paul explained these engravings to Felicity. This, in fact, was all her literary education.

The children's education was taken in hand by Guyot, a poor wretch employed at the Town Hall, famous for his fine handwriting, a man who sharpened his penknife on his boot.

When the weather was clear they would go early in the morning to the farm of Geffosses.

The courtyard is sloping, the house in the middle; and the sea, in the distance, appears like a grey stain.

Felicity took out of her basket slices of cold meat, and they lunched in a room attached to the dairy. It was the only remnant of a pleasure house which had not disappeared. The wall-paper hung in rags, and trembled in the draughts. Madame

Aubain leant forward, overwhelmed with memories: the children did not dare to speak. 'But go out and play', she would say. They decamped.

Paul went up into the barn, caught birds, played ducks and drakes with stones on the pond, or with a stick hit the big casks that resounded like drums.

Virginia fed the rabbits, rushed to gather cornflowers, and the swift motion of her legs showed her little embroidered drawers.

One autumn evening they came back through the meadows.

The moon in its first quarter lit up a part of the sky, and a mist was floating like a veil on the windings of the River Toucques. Oxen, stretched amid the turf, tranquilly watched those four people pass. In the third meadow some of them rose, and formed a circle before them. 'Don't be afraid,' said Felicity, and murmuring a sort of low song she patted the one who was nearest on the spine; he turned round, the others imitated him. But when the succeeding field was crossed a formidable bellowing arose. It was a bull that the fog had concealed. He advanced towards the two women. Madame Aubain was going to run. 'No, no, not so quick!' They quickened their steps all the same, and heard behind them a sonorous breathing coming nearer them. His hoofs, like hammers, beat the grass of the fields; there, he was galloping now! Felicity turned round and tore up with her two hands clods of earth which she threw in his eyes. He lowered his muzzle, shook his horns, and trembled with fury, bellowing horribly. Madame Aubain, at the end of the grass with her two children, was madly seeking how to get over the high bank. Felicity retired steadily before the bull, and continually flung bits of turf that blinded him, while she cried: 'Hurry up, hurry up!' Madame Aubain climbed over the ditch, pushed Virginia up, then Paul, fell several times in trying to climb over the slope, and by dint of courage succeeded.

The bull had driven Felicity into a corner against an opening in the hedge; his slaver sprayed on her face, a second more and he would have gored her. She had time to slip between two bars, and the big beast, quite surprised, stopped short.

This event for many years was a topic of conversation at Pont-l'Évêque. Felicity felt no pride about it, not even considering that she had done anything heroic.

Virginia took up all her time, for she suffered, as a result of her fright, from an affection of the nerves, and Monsieur Pourpart, the doctor, advised sea baths at Trouville.

In those days they were not crowded. Madame Aubain made inquiries, consulted Bourais, and made preparations as for a long journey.

Her luggage went off the night before in Liébard's cart. The next day he brought two horses, one of which had a woman's saddle fitted with a velvet backrest; and on the croup of the second a coat, rolled up, formed a sort of seat. Madame Aubain mounted there behind him. Felicity took charge of Virginia, and Paul straddled Monsieur Lechaptois's donkey, lent on condition they would take great care of it.

The road was so bad that the eight kilometres took two hours. The horses sank up to the pasterns in the mud, and to free themselves made brusque movements with their haunches; or else they stumbled against the hedges; other times they had to jump over them. Liébard's mare, at certain spots, stopped suddenly. Liébard waited patiently until she resumed her walk, and he talked about the people whose estates bordered the road, adding moral reflections to their story. Thus, in the middle of Toucques as they passed under windows surrounded by nasturtiums, he said with a shrug of his shoulders: 'There 's a Madame Lehoussais lives there, who, instead of taking a young husband——' Felicity did not hear the rest: the horses trotted, the donkey galloped; they all went in single file up a path; a gate swung round, two stable boys appeared, they got down beside the dung water on the very threshold of the door.

Mother Liébard, seeing her mistress, was prodigal in demonstrations of joy. She served them a lunch where there was roast beef, tripe, black sausage, a fricassee of chicken, sparkling cider, a fruit tart, and plums in brandy, accompanying the whole with polite observations to madame, who seemed in better health, to mademoiselle, become 'magnificent', to Mr. Paul, grown singularly 'stout'; without forgetting their late grandparents, whom the Liébards had known, being in the service of the family for several generations. The farm had, like them, an old-time character. The beams of the roof were worm-eaten, the walls black with smoke, the tiles grey with dust. An oak dresser carried all sorts of utensils, jugs, plates, pewter, basins, wolf traps, sheep shears; an enormous syringe made the children laugh. Not a tree in the three courtyards but had mushrooms at its base, or in its branches a bunch of mistletoe. The wind had thrown down several. They had sprouted again in the middle, and all were bent under the number of their apples. The thatch roofs, like brown velvet, and all unequal in thickness, resisted the strongest gales. Yet the wagon-shed was falling in ruins. Madame Aubain said she would see about it, and bade them reharness the beasts.

They were half an hour yet before they reached Trouville. The little caravan dismounted to pass the Écores Hill; it was a rock overhanging the ships; and three minutes later, at the end of the quay, they entered the courtyard of the Golden Lamb, Mother David's inn.

Virginia, from the beginning, felt herself more robust, the result of the change of air and the action of the baths. She took them in her chemise, for lack of a bathing costume; and her maid dressed her afterwards in the shed of a customs man who looked after the bathers.

In the afternoon they would go with the donkey past the Black Rocks in the direction of Hennequeville. The path at first rose between land undulating like the lawns of a gentleman's estate, then arrived at a plateau, where alternated pasture ground and cultivated fields. At the edge of the road, among the clusters of reeds, grew holly bushes; here and there a tall dead tree made zigzags with its branches on the blue air.

Almost always they rested in a meadow, with Deauville on their left, Havre on their right, and in front the open sea. It was brilliant in the sunshine, smooth like a mirror, so gentle that its murmur could scarcely be heard. Hidden sparrows chirped, and the immense vault of the sky formed a cover for all. Madame Aubain, seated, would work at her sewing; Virginia beside her, plaited reeds; Felicity pulled up lavender; Paul, who was bored, wanted to go away.

Other times they crossed the River Toucques in a boat, and looked for shells. The low tide left uncovered sea urchins, scallops, jellyfish; and the children ran to catch the puffs of foam that the wind carried up. The sleepy waves, falling on the sand, rolled in along the beach; they stretched as far as eye could see, but on the landward side had for limit the dunes separating it from the Marais, a wide meadow, shaped like a hippodrome. When they were coming back that way Trouville, at the foot of its sloping hillock, grew bigger at each step, and with all its different-sized houses, seemed to spread out in gay disorder.

The days on which it was too hot they did not leave their room. The dazzling brightness outside plastered bars of light between the slats of the shutters. No noise in the village. Down below on the pavement, nobody. This widespread silence increased everything's tranquillity. In the distance the hammers of the caulkers plugged the keels, and a heavy breeze brought a scent of tar.

The principal amusement was the homecoming of the ships. As soon as they had passed the buoys they began to tack. Their sails dropped to two-thirds of the masts; and the foresail swelling like a balloon they came on, gliding in the plashing of the waves, to the middle of the harbour, where the anchor suddenly fell. Then the boat drew up beside the quay. The sailors threw over the edge the quivering fish; a row of carts was waiting, and women in cotton bonnets ran forward to take the baskets and embrace their men.

One of the women one day accosted Felicity, who a little while afterwards came into the room full of joy. She had refound a sister: and Nastasie Barette, wife of Leroux, appeared, holding a baby at her breast, another child clinging to her right hand, and at her left a little fellow with his fists on his hips, and his beret over one ear.

At the end of a quarter of an hour Madame Aubain dismissed her.

They were always to be met hanging about the kitchen, or on the walks they took. The husband did not show himself.

Felicity took a liking to them. She bought them bedclothes, shirts, a cooking stove; evidently they were exploiting her. This weakness irritated Madame Aubain, who, besides, didn't like the familiarities of the nephew, for he talked to her son as to an equal; and, as Virginia had a cough, and the weather was no longer good, she returned to Pont-l'Évêque.

Monsieur Bourais gave her advice on the choice of a school. The one at Caen was considered the best. Paul was sent there, and said good-bye stoutly, pleased to go and live in a house where he would have comrades.

Madame Aubain resigned herself to the separation from her son because it was indispensable. Virginia thought of it less and less. Felicity missed the noise he made. But an occupation came along to distract her. Starting at Christmas, she took the little girl every day to Catechism.

III

When she had made a genuflexion at the door she walked on under the high nave between the double row of chairs, opened Madame Aubain's pew, sat down, and looked all round her. The boys on the right, the girls on the left, filled the stalls of the choir; the priest stood near the lectern; on a stained-glass window in the apse the Holy Ghost hovering over the virgin; another showed her on her knees before the Infant Jesus, and behind the ciborium a group carved in wood represented Saint Michael subduing the dragon.

The priest gave them first a short account of Sacred History. She thought she saw Paradise, the deluge, the tower of Babel, cities in flames, peoples dying, idols overthrown; and she retained from this state of amazement respect for the Most High, and fear of His wrath. Then she wept, listening to the Passion. Why had they crucified Him, this One who loved the children, who fed the multitudes, who cured the blind, and had desired, in His gentleness, to be born amid the poor, on the dung of a stable? Seed time, harvest, the winepress, all the familiar things of which the Gospel speaks, existed in her life; the passage of God had sanctified them; and she loved the lambs more tenderly for love of the Lamb of God, the doves because of the Holy Ghost.

She had trouble in imagining its shape; for it was not only a bird, but besides that, a fire, and at other times a breath. Maybe it was its light that flickered at nights on the edge of the marshes, its breath that pushed the clouds, its voice that made the bells ring sweetly; and she stayed in adoration, enjoying the freshness of the walls and the tranquillity of the church.

As to the dogmas, she understood none of them, did not even try to understand them. The priest discoursed, the children recited, she finished by going to sleep; and woke up suddenly when, as they came out, their wooden shoes clattered on the flagstones.

It was in this way, by dint of hearing it, that she learned the catechism, her religious education having been neglected in her youth; and from that time she imitated all the practices of Virginia, fasting as she did, going to confession with her. On Corpus Christi day together they erected a street altar.

She worried about the first communion in advance. She was in a flutter about the slippers, about the wreath, about the book, about the gloves. With what inner tremblings she helped her mother dress her!

All through the Mass she was in an agony. Monsieur Bourais hid a part of the choir from her; but just in front the flock of girls, wearing their white crowns over their lowered veils, formed as it were a field of snow; and she recognized from afar her dear little one by her dainty neck and contemplative attitude. The bells rang out: heads bent: there was a silence. To an outburst of organ music the choristers and the congregation began to sing the Agnus Dei; then the march past of the boys began; and after them the girls rose. Step by step, and hands joined in prayer, they went towards the altar, ablaze with candles, knelt on the first step, received in turn the wafer, and in the same order returned and knelt in their places. When it was Virginia's turn Felicity bent forward to see her, and with the imagination which true tenderness bestows, it seemed to her that she herself was this child. Virginia's face became her own, her dress clothed her; her heart beat in her breast; at the moment when she opened her mouth, shutting her eyes, she almost fainted.

Next day, early, she presented herself in the vestry so that the priest might give her communion. She received it devoutly, but did not taste the same delights.

Madame Aubain wanted to make her daughter accomplished: and as Guyot could not teach either English or music, she resolved to send her to the boarding school of the Ursulines at Honfleur.

The child made no objections. Felicity sighed, finding madame hard-hearted. Then she thought that her mistress, perhaps, was right. These matters went beyond her province.

Finally, one day, an old van stopped before the door, and from it stepped a nun, who had come to get mademoiselle. Felicity lifted the baggage on to the top, gave injunctions to the coachman, and placed under the seat six pots of jam, and a dozen pears, with a bunch of violets.

Virginia, at the last moment, was shaken by a huge sob; she

embraced her mother, who kissed her on the forehead, repeating: 'Come now, courage, courage!' The steps were drawn up, the carriage set out.

Then Madame Aubain fainted: and in the evening all her friends, the Lormeau household, Madame Lechaptois, *those* ladies Rochefeuille, Monsieur de Houpeville, and Bourais put in an appearance to console her.

The loss of her daughter was at first very grievous. But three times a week she got a letter from her, the other days she wrote to her, walked in her garden, read a little, and in this way filled the emptiness of the hours.

In the morning, from habit, Felicity went into Virginia's room and looked at the walls. She missed not having her hair to comb, her boots to lace, to tuck her in her bed—and not seeing continually her pretty face, not having to hold her hand when they went out together. Not having enough work to do, she tried to make lace. Her fingers were too clumsy and broke the threads. She was good for nothing, could not sleep, to use her own expression was 'a wreck'.

To 'cheer herself up' she asked permission to have a visit from her nephew Victor.

He arrived on Sunday after mass, with rosy cheeks, his chest bare, breathing the odour of the country he had passed through. At once she set his place. They had lunch facing each other: and herself eating as little as possible to keep down the expense, she stuffed him with food to such an extent that he finished by going to sleep. At the first stroke of the bell for vespers she woke him, brushed his trousers, tied his tie, and went to church, leaning on his arm in maternal pride.

His parents charged him always to bring something home, maybe a packet of brown sugar, soap, brandy, sometimes even money. He brought his clothes to be mended, and she accepted this task, glad of the chance which forced him to come back.

In August his father took him with him on the coasting trade.

It was holiday time. The arrival of the children consoled her. But Paul had become capricious, and Virginia was no longer young enough to be spoken to as an equal, and that put a feeling of constraint, a barrier between them.

Victor went in turn to Morlaix, to Dunkirk, and to Brighton. On his return from each voyage he made her a present. The first time it was a box covered with shells; the second a coffee cup; the third a big gingerbread man. He grew handsome, with a good carriage, nice frank eyes, and a little leather cap worn well to the front like a pilot. He amused her by telling her stories mixed with nautical terms.

On Monday, 14th July 1819 (she did not forget the date), Victor announced that he was engaged for a trip and, during the night of the day after next, by the Honfleur steamer, he would go to join his schooner, which was going to sail from Havre quite soon. He would be, maybe, away for two years.

The prospect of such an absence grieved Felicity; and to say another good-bye to him on Wednesday evening, after madame's dinner, she put on her clogs and hurried down the four leagues which separated Pont-l'Évêque from Honfleur.

When she was at the crossroads before the Calvary, instead of taking the path to the left she took the one to the right, lost herself in the yards, and came back on her tracks; the people she accosted advised her to hurry. She walked right round the harbour, stumbled over ropes; then the land dropped before her, lights intersected each other, and she thought herself mad, perceiving horses in the air.

On the edge of the quay others whinnied, terrified of the sea. The tackle that lifted them set them down in a boat where travellers elbowed one another among casks of cider, baskets of cheese, sacks of grain; you could hear hens cackling, the captain was swearing; and a boy was standing leaning on the cathead, indifferent to all that. Felicity, who had not recognized him, screamed 'Victor!' He raised his head; she rushed forward, when the gangway was suddenly pulled back.

The steamer which was towed by women, singing, left the port. Its timbers creaked, heavy waves whipped its prow. The vessel had turned, nobody was seen any longer—and, on the sea silvered by the moon, it made a black spot that steadily paled, sank, disappeared.

Felicity, passing near the Calvary, wanted to recommend to God that which she cherished most. And she prayed a long time, standing, her face bathed in tears, her eyes towards the clouds. The town slept, customs officials walked about, and the water fell without ceasing through the holes of the sluice. Two o'clock struck.

The reception room of the convent did not open before day-break. A delay, quite certainly, would annoy madame; and, in spite of her desire to embrace the other child, she returned. The servant girls at the inn were waking as she entered Pont-l'Évêque.

The poor lad was going to roll about on the waves for months. His former voyages had not frightened her. From England and Brittany people came back; but America, the Colonies, the West Indies, that was to be lost in an uncertain land, at the other end of the world.

From that time on Felicity thought exclusively of her nephew. On sunny days she tormented herself with thirst; when a storm came on she feared the thunder for him. Listening to the wind which howled in the chimney and blew off the tiles, she saw him beaten by the same tempest, at the top of a shattered mast, all his body thrown back under a sheet of foam; or else—souvenirs of the geography engravings—he was devoured by savages, captured in a wood by monkeys, was dying along a deserted seashore. And never did she speak of her anxieties.

Madame Aubain had others for her daughter. The good sisters found that she was affectionate but delicate. The slightest emotion unnerved her. The piano had to be given up.

Her mother required a regular correspondence from the convent. One morning that the postman did not come she was impatient: and she walked about the living-room from her chair to the window. It was really extraordinary! For four days no news.

So that she might find comfort in her example Felicity said to her:

'Look at me, madame: it 's six months since I 've had any!'

'From whom?'

The servant replied gently:

'But—from my nephew!'

'Oh—your nephew!' and, shrugging her shoulders, Madame Aubain went on with her walking as if to say: 'I did not think about him! Moreover, I don't care! a cabin boy, a beggar, a fine business—while my daughter—— Think of it!'

Felicity, although brought up on rudeness, was indignant against madame, then forgot.

It seemed to her quite easy to lose one's head about the little girl's concerns.

The two children had an equal importance; one of her heart-strings united them, and their destinies should be the same.

The chemist told her that Victor's boat had arrived at Havana. He had read the information in a gazette.

Because of the cigars she imagined Havana a country where nothing else was done but smoke, and Victor moving among the niggers in a cloud of tobacco. Could he 'in case of need' come back by land? What distance was it from Pont-l'Évêque? To learn that she asked Monsieur Bourais.

He got his atlas, then began explanations about the longitudes, and he had a fine pedant's smile in face of Felicity's bewilderment. At length with his pocket pencil he showed her the indentations on an oval mark, a black imperceptible point, adding: 'That 's it'. She leaned over the map; this network of coloured lines tired her eyes, without teaching her anything; and, Bourais inviting her to say what was worrying her, she begged him to show her the house where Victor was living. Bourais raised his arms, sneezed, laughed enormously; such ingenuousness excited his joy: and Felicity did not understand the cause of it —she who was expecting, perhaps, even to see a photograph of her nephew, so limited was her intelligence.

It was a fortnight afterwards that Liébard, at the hour when the market was on, as was his custom, came into the kitchen and gave her a letter which her brother-in-law had sent. Since neither of the two know how to read, she had recourse to her mistress.

Madame Aubain, who was counting stitches in her knitting, put her work down beside her, unsealed the letter, trembled, and in a low voice with a serious look:

'It 's bad news . . . you are being told of. Your nephew ——'

He was dead. They told her no more.

Felicity fell on a chair, leaning her head on the wall, and shut her eyes, and her eyelids suddenly grew pink. Then, her head drooping, her eyes fixed, she repeated at intervals:

'Poor little chap! Poor little chap!'

Liébard looked at her, emitting deep sighs. Madame Aubain was trembling slightly.

She proposed to her to go and see her sister at Trouville.

Felicity answered by a gesture that she had no need to go there.

There was a silence. Good old Liébard thought it proper to go away. Then she said:

'It 's nothing to them!'

Her head sank down again; and mechanically she lifted, from time to time, the long knitting-needles on the work-table.

Some women passed in the courtyard with a barrow heaped with dripping linen.

As she saw them through the window panes she remembered her washing; she had soaked it the night before, to-day it had to be rinsed, and she left the room.

Her washboard and her tub were on the brink of the River Toucques. She flung on the bank a heap of chemises, tucked up her sleeves, took up her beating-stick; and the heavy blows she gave were heard in the other gardens alongside. The fields were empty, the wind rippled the river; at the bottom long weeds swept over like the hair of dead men floating in the water. She restrained her sorrow till evening, was very brave; but, in her room she abandoned herself to it, lying flat, face down on her mattress, her eyes in her pillow, and her fists against her temples.

Much later, from Victor's captain himself, she learnt the circumstances of his death. He had been bled too much at the hospital for yellow fever. Four doctors were looking after him at once. He died immediately, and the chief had said:

'Tut, tut, that 's another one!'

His parents had always treated him barbarously. She preferred not to see them again; and they made no advances, either through forgetfulness or the callousness of the wretched poor.

Virginia grew weaker.

Shortness of breath, a cough, a continual fever, and red spots on her cheek-bones revealed some deep-seated affection. Monsieur Pourpart had advised a stay in Provence. Madame Aubain made up her mind to go there, and would have immediately recalled her daughter home except for the climate of Pont-l'Évêque.

She made an arrangement with a man who hired carriages to take her to the convent every Thursday. There is in the gardens a terrace from which you can discern the Seine. Virginia would walk there on her arm, on the fallen grape-vine leaves. Sometimes the sun, shining through the clouds, made her blink her eyelids, when she looked at the sails in the distance, and all the horizon from the château of Tancarville to the lighthouse at Havre. Then they rested in the arbour. Her mother had got a little barrel of an excellent Malaga wine; and, laughing at the idea of being drunk, she would drink two fingers of it, not more.

Her strength improved. The autumn slipped away quietly. Felicity reassured Madame Aubain. But one evening that she had been on an errand in the neighbourhood she met before the door Monsieur Pourpart's gig: and he himself was in the vestibule. Madame Aubain was tying on her hat.

'Give me my footwarmer, my purse, my gloves: be quicker, can't you?'

Virginia had an inflammation of the lungs: it was perhaps hopeless.

'Not yet,' said the doctor, and the two of them got into the carriage under the snowflakes which eddied around. Night was about to fall. It was very cold.

Felicity rushed into the church to light a candle. Then she ran after the gig, which she rejoined an hour later, leaped lightly up behind, where she was holding on by the twisted cords, when a reflection came to her. 'The courtyard is not shut. If robbers get in?' and she got down.

Next day at sunrise she presented herself at the doctor's. He had come in, and gone out again to the country. Then she stayed in the inn, thinking that strangers would bring her a letter. At length at dawn she took the coach to Lisieux.

The convent was situated at the end of a steep lane. About the middle she heard strange sounds, a death knell. 'It 's for other people,' she thought, and Felicity pulled violently at the knocker.

At the end of several minutes slippers dragged along, the door half opened, and a nun appeared.

The good sister said with an air of compunction that 'she had just passed'. At the same time the knell of Saint Leonard's redoubled its peal.

Felicity arrived at the second story.

From the threshold of the room she saw Virginia, stretched on her back, her hands joined, her mouth open, and her head thrown back under a black cross bending towards her, between motionless curtains, less white than her face. Madame Aubain, at the foot of the couch which she clasped with her hands, uttered sobs of agony. The Mother Superior was standing on the right. Three candlesticks on the chest of drawers made red splashes, and the mist whitened the windows. Nuns took away Madame Aubain.

For two nights Felicity did not leave the dead girl. She repeated the same prayers, threw holy water on the sheets, came back and sat down, and looked at her. At the end of the first watch she noticed that the face had got yellow, the lips blue, the nose pinched, the eyes sunk. She kissed them several times, and would not have felt an immense astonishment if Virginia had reopened them: for souls like hers the supernatural is quite simple. She dressed her, wrapped her in her shroud, lifted her into her coffin, placed a wreath on her, spread out her hair. Her hair was fair, of an extraordinary length for her age. Felicity cut off a thick lock, the half of which she slipped into her bosom, resolved never to part with it.

The body was carried back to Pont-l'Évêque, in obedience to the wishes of Madame Aubain, who followed the hearse in a closed carriage.

After the mass they took another three-quarters of an hour to reach the cemetery. Paul walked in front and sobbed. Monsieur Bourais was behind, then the principal inhabitants, the women covered in black mantles, and Felicity. She thought of her nephew, and not having been able to render him these honours, felt an increase of grief as if they were burying him with the other.

Madame Aubain's despair was without bounds.

First she revolted against God, finding Him unjust for having taken her daughter, she who had never done any wrong, and whose conscience was so pure. But no! she should have taken her south. Other doctors would have saved her! She accused herself, wanted to join her, cried out in distress amid her dreams. One dream, above all, obsessed her. Her husband, clad like a sailor, was coming back from a long voyage, and said to her weeping, that he had got orders to take away Virginia. Then they arranged to find a hiding place somewhere.

One day she came in from the garden completely upset. The father and daughter (she pointed out the place) had appeared to her just now, one after the other, and they did nothing; they looked at her.

For several months she remained in her room inert. Felicity lectured her gently; she must keep herself for her son, and for the other, in memory of 'her'.

'Her', took up Madame Aubain, as if awakening, 'oh, yes!

yes! You do not forget her!' An allusion to the cemetery which it had been scrupulously forbidden to mention.

Felicity went there every day.

At four o'clock exactly she passed alongside the houses, climbed the slope, opened the gate, and arrived at Virginia's tomb. It was a little column of rose marble, with a flagstone at the base, and chains around, framing a little garden. The flower-beds were invisible under a coverlet of flowers. She watered their leaves, renewed the sand, knelt down the better to work the earth. Madame Aubain, when she could come there, felt some comfort, a kind of consolation.

Then years slipped by, all alike, and without other episodes than the return of the great feasts: Easter, the Assumption, All Saints. Inside happenings marked the dates which they used for reference later on. Thus in 1825 two glaziers white-washed the vestibule; in 1827 a bit of the roof, falling into the courtyard, almost killed a man. In the summer of 1828 it was madame's turn to provide the sacred bread for Mass. Bourais, about this time, absented himself mysteriously; and the old acquaintances, little by little, passed away; Guyot, Liébard, Madame Lechaptois, Robelin, Uncle Germanville, paralysed a long time ago.

One night the driver of the mail coach announced in Pont-l'Évêque the July Revolution. A new sub-prefect was appointed a few days afterwards; the Baron de Larsonnière, an ex-consul in America, who had living with him, besides his wife, his sister-in-law, with three young ladies, already pretty big. They were seen on their lawn, dressed in floating blouses; they possessed a negro and a parrot. Madame Aubain received a visit from them, and did not fail to return it. When they appeared in the farthest distance Felicity ran to warn her. But one thing was alone capable of moving her, her son's letters.

He could not follow any career, being wrapped up in taverns. She paid his debts; he ran up others; and the sighs which Madame Aubain uttered, knitting near her window, could be heard by Felicity, turning her spinning-wheel in the kitchen.

They took walks together beside the wall where the pears grew; and talked always of Virginia, asking each other if such and such a thing would have pleased her; on such an occasion what would she probably have said?

All her little possessions occupied a press in the room with the two beds. Madame Aubain inspected them as seldom as possible. One summer day she resigned herself to it, and moths flew from the wardrobe.

Her dresses were there in a row under a shelf, on which there were three dolls, hoops, doll's furniture, the washbowl she had used. They took out as well underskirts, stockings, handkerchiefs, and spread them on the two couches before folding them up again. The sun shone on those poor objects, showing up the stains and the folds made by the body's movements. The air was hot and blue, a blackbird chirped, everything seemed alive in a deep sweetness. They found a little plush hat, with long hair, chestnut coloured; but it was all eaten by insects. Felicity claimed it for herself. Their eyes met, filled with tears; finally the mistress opened her arms, the servant flung herself into them; and they clung together, satisfying their grief in a kiss that equalized them.

It was the first time in their lives, Madame Aubain not being of an expansive nature. Felicity was grateful for it, as for a kindness, and henceforth cherished her with an animal devotion and a religious veneration.

The kindness of her heart developed.

When she heard in the street the drums of a regiment on the march she stationed herself before the door with a jug of cider, and offered the soldiers a drink. She looked after the victims of cholera. She protected the Poles; and there was even one of them who declared he wanted to marry her. But they quarrelled: for one morning, coming in from the Angelus, she found him in her kitchen, into which he had made his way, and fixed himself up a dish of meat with vinegar sauce which he was eating quietly.

After the Poles there was old Father Colmiche, an old man, who passed for having done terrible things in '93. He lived on the riverside, in the ruins of a pigsty. Urchins used to peer at him through the chinks in the wall, and threw stones which fell on the wretched bed where he lay, continually shaken by a cold, with very long hair, inflamed eyelids, and on his arm a tumour bigger than his head. She got linen for him, tried to clean out his hovel, had dreams of settling him in the washhouse, without annoying Madame. When cancer knocked him out she bandaged him every day, sometimes brought him cake, put him in the sun on a bundle of hay; and the poor old man, drooling and trembling, thanked her in his feeble voice, fearing to lose her, stretching out his hands when he saw her going off. He died: she had a Mass said for the repose of his soul.

That day a great happiness came to her; just at dinner-time Madame de Larsonnières's negro presented himself, holding the parrot in its cage, with the stand, the chain, and the padlock. A note from the baroness announced to Madame Aubain that, her husband being raised to the prefecture, they were leaving that evening; and she begged her to accept the bird as a souvenir, and in token of her respect.

For a long time he had filled Felicity's imagination, for he came from America, and this word recalled Victor, so much so that she had made inquiries about it from the negro. Once even she had said:

'Madame would like to have it!'

The negro had repeated the remark to his mistress who, not being able to take the bird with her, had got rid of it in this way.

IV

He was called Loulou. His body was green, the tips of his wings rose, his front blue, and his throat golden.

But he had the tiresome mania of biting his stand, pulling out his feathers, spilling the water from his bath. Madame Aubain, whom he bored, gave him for good to Felicity.

She undertook to instruct him. Soon he repeated: 'Nice boy!' 'Your servant, sir!' 'Hail Mary!' He was placed beside the door, and some people were astonished that he did not answer to the name of Jacquot, since all parrots are called Jacquot. He was compared to a goose, to a blockhead: so many dagger blows for Felicity! Strange obstinacy of Loulou not speaking at the time people were looking.

Nevertheless he courted company; for on Sundays, when *those* ladies Rochefeuille, Monsieur de Houpeville, and some new friends—Onfroy the apothecary, Monsieur Varin, and Captain Mathieu—were making up their party at cards, he knocked on the window panes with his wings, and thrashed about so violently that it was impossible to hear oneself.

Bourais's face, no doubt, seemed to him very funny. As soon as he saw him he began to laugh, to laugh with all his might. The peals of his voice rebounded in the courtyard, the echoes repeated them, the neighbours came to their windows laughing too; and so as not to be seen by the parrot, Monsieur Bourais slipped along the wall, hiding his profile with his hat, reached the river, then entered by the garden gate; and the glances he directed at the bird lacked tenderness.

The butcher's boy had snapped his fingers at Loulou, who had ventured to thrust his head into his basket; and since then he had always tried to pinch him through his shirt. Fabu threatened to wring his neck, although he was not cruel, in spite of the tattooing on his arm, and his thick whiskers. On the contrary he had rather a liking for the parrot, wanting, in a jovial mood, to teach him swear words. Felicity, who was frightened at this kind of behaviour, put him in the kitchen. His little chain was taken off, and he moved about the house.

When he came down the stairs he leaned the curve of his beak on the steps, raised his right claw, then the left, and she was afraid that such gymnastics would make him dizzy. He became ill, was not able to speak or eat. There was a growth under his tongue, as there sometimes is in hens. She cured him, tearing out the lump with her nails. Monsieur Paul one day was imprudent enough to puff the smoke of a cigar into his nostrils; another time that Madame Lormeau annoyed him with the end of her sunshade he snapped the ferule off; finally he got lost.

She had put him on the grass to let him refresh himself, went away for a moment; and when she came back, no parrot. At first she looked for him in the bushes, at the water edge, and on the roofs, without heeding her mistress who cried to her: 'Take care. You are mad!' Then she inspected all the gardens of Pont-l'Évêque: and she stopped the passers-by: 'You haven't seen anywhere, by chance, my parrot?' To those who did not know the parrot she described him. Suddenly she thought she distinguished, behind the mill, at the bottom of the slope, a green thing fluttering about. But at the top of the hill, nothing! A pedlar affirmed that he had just met it in Saint-Milaine in Mother Simon's shop. She ran there. Nobody knew what she meant. Finally she came back, worn out, her slippers in rags, death in her soul; and, seated in the centre of the garden seat, near madame, she was recounting all her adventures, when a light weight fell on her shoulder—Loulou! What the deuce had he done? Maybe he had taken a stroll in the neighbourhood.

She had trouble in recovering from it, or rather, she never did recover.

As a result of a chill she got a sore throat; a little after, an ear-ache. Three years after, she was deaf; and she spoke very loud, even in the church. Although her sins might have been broadcast to all the corners of the parish, without dishonouring her, or inconveniencing the world, the priest thought it right to receive her confession only in the vestry.

Illusory buzzings in the ear completely confused her. Often her mistress would say: 'Gracious! how stupid you are!' And she would reply: 'Yes, madame,' looking for something round her.

The little circle of her ideas narrowed still more, and the ringing of the bells, the lowing of the herds no longer existed. All creatures functioned in ghostly silence. One noise alone now reached her ears, the voice of the parrot.

As if to amuse her, he would reproduce the tick-tack of the turnspit, the shrill cry of the fishmonger, the saw of the carpenter who lived opposite: and when the bell rang, imitated Madame Aubain: 'Felicity! the door! the door!'

They had dialogues together; he reeling off to satiety the three phrases of his repertory, and she answering by words without coherence but in which her soul unbosomed itself. Loulou, in her isolation, was almost a son, a lover. He climbed up her fingers, nibbled at her lips, hung on to her neckerchief; and as she bent her forehead, shaking her head as children's nurses do, the big wings of her bonnet and the wings of the bird shook together.

When the clouds gathered and the thunder growled, he would utter cries, recalling perhaps the deluges of his native forests.

The trickling of water excited him almost to delirium: he fluttered about madly, rose to the roof, turned over everything, and went through the window to dabble in the garden; but came back quickly to one of the andirons and, hopping about to dry his wings, showed now his tail, and now his beak.

One morning of the terrible winter of 1837, when she had put him before the hearth because of the cold, she found him dead in the middle of his cage, his head down, his claws in the wire meshing. A congestion had killed him, no doubt. She believed he had been poisoned by parsley; and, in spite of the absence of all proof, her suspicions centred on Fabu.

She wept so much that her mistress said to her: 'Well, then, have him stuffed'.

She asked advice from the chemist, who had always been good to the parrot.

He wrote to Havre. A certain Fellacher undertook the business. But, as the stage coach sometimes mislaid parcels, she resolved to carry it herself as far as Honfleur.

Apple trees bare of leaves, one after another, bordered the sides of the road. Ice covered the ditches. Dogs barked around the farms; and, her hands under her cloak, with her little black wooden shoes and her basket, she walked quickly in the centre of the road.

She crossed the forest, passed Haut Chêne, reached Saint Gatien.

Behind her, in a cloud of dust, and carried away by its own impetus on the hill, a mailcoach at a full gallop rushed on her like a whirlwind. Seeing this woman, who did not get out of the way, the driver stood up on the hood, and the postilion shouted too, while the four horses that he could not hold back went quicker than ever; the two first just grazed her; with a twist of the reins he drew them to the side of the road, but in a temper, raised his arm, and with a full swing, with his big whip, gave her such a lash from stomach to the twist of hair at the nape of her neck, that she fell on her back.

Her first gesture, when she came back to consciousness, was to open her basket. Loulou was not hurt, fortunately. She felt a burning on her right cheek: she raised her hands to it, and they were red. Blood was flowing.

She sat down on a pile of road metal, patted her face with her handkerchief, then she ate a crust of bread, put in her basket by way of precaution, and consoled herself for her wound in looking at the bird.

When she reached the heights of Ecquemauville she saw the lights of Honfleur sparkling in the night like a cluster of stars; the sea, farther off, stretched out vaguely. Then a feeling of faintness stopped her, and the wretchedness of her childhood, the disappointment of her first love, the departure of her nephew, the death of Virginia, like the waves of a tide, returning all at once, and rising to her throat, choked her.

Then she wanted to speak to the captain of the boat, and without telling him what she was sending, she gave him careful orders.

Fellacher kept the parrot a long time. He always promised it for the next week; at the end of six months he announced the shipping of a box, and there was no more question of it. She could only think that Loulou would never come back. 'They 'll have stolen him from me,' she thought.

Finally he arrived—and splendid, upright on the branch of a tree, which was screwed in a mahogany base, one claw in the air, his head sideways, and biting a nut which the birdstuffer had gilded through love of the grandiose.

She shut it up in her room.

This spot, to which she admitted few people, had the look at once of a chapel and a bazaar, it contained so many religious objects and heteroclite things.

A big wardrobe was in the way when one opened the door. In front of the window, overhanging the garden, a round window looked out at the courtyard; a table near the truckle bed bore a water jug, two combs, and a cube of blue soap on a chipped plate. On the walls were seen strings of beads, medals, several Holy Virgins, a holy-water basin of coco-nut; on the chest of drawers covered with a cloth like an altar, the shellbox that Victor had given her: then a watering pot and a balloon, writing exercise books, the geography with engravings, a pair of boots; and on the nail which held up the mirror, hung by its ribbons, the little plush hat. Felicity even pushed this kind of respect so far as to keep one of monsieur's coats. All the old stuff that Madame Aubain did not want any more she took for her room. That was why there were artificial flowers at the side of the drawers, and the picture of the Count of Artois in the recess of the dormer window.

By way of shelf, Loulou was established on a part of the chimney-piece which jutted into the room. Every morning as she waked up she saw him in the light of dawn, and recalled then the days that were gone, insignificant actions, down to their least detail, without grief, full of tranquillity.

Communicating with no one, she lived in the torpor of the sleep-walker. The processions of Corpus Christi day roused her. She went to beg from the neighbours torches and straw matting to embellish the altar set up in the street.

At the church she contemplated steadily the Holy Ghost, and noticed that it had a look of the parrot. The resemblance seemed to her still more noticeable on an Épinal picture, representing the baptism of Our Lord. With its purple wings and emerald body it was really the portrait of Loulou.

Having bought it she hung it in the place of the Count of Artois, so that with the same look she could see them both. They became associated in her thoughts, the parrot becoming sanctified by this union with the Holy Ghost, which became more alive and intelligible in her eyes. The Father, to give utterance to his will, had not chosen a dove, since these beasts have no voice, but rather one of the ancestors of Loulou. And Felicity said her prayers, looking at the picture, but from time to time turned a little to the bird.

She wanted to join the Sisters of the Virgin; Madame Aubain dissuaded her.

An event of some importance took place: Paul's marriage.

After having been at first a notary clerk, then in business, in the Customs, in the Treasury, and having even taken some steps to get into the Water and Forests Department, at the age of thirty-six, suddenly, by a heaven-sent inspiration, he had discovered his real road: the Registry Office. And he had shown such high talents that an auditor had offered him his daughter, promising him his protection.

Paul, become serious minded, brought her to his mother.

She looked down on the customs of Pont-l'Évêque, behaved like a princess, hurt Felicity. Madame Aubain, when she went away, felt relieved.

The following week they learned of the death of Monsieur Bourais, in Lower Brittany, in an inn. The rumour of suicide was confirmed: doubts rose about his honesty. Madame Aubain studied her accounts, and was not long in finding the whole list of his evil deeds; embezzlement of arrears, pretended sales of wood, false receipts, etc.

These acts of baseness afflicted her greatly. In March 1853 she was seized by a pain in the chest; her tongue seemed covered with smoke; leeches did not calm the fever; and on the eighth day she died, being exactly seventy-two years old.

She was considered younger, because of her brown hair, whose folds surrounded her pale face, marked with the smallpox. Few friends mourned her, her way of living had displayed a haughtiness which kept people at a distance.

Felicity wept for her, as masters are not wept for. That madame should die before her upset her ideas, seemed to her contrary to the order of things, inadmissible and monstrous.

Ten days after (the time to rush to Besançon) the heirs arrived;

the daughter-in-law went through the drawers, chose the best of the furniture, sold the rest; then they went down to the Registry Office again.

Madame's chair, her table, her footwarmer, the eight chairs were gone. The place of the engravings was marked by yellow squares on the walls. They had taken away the two little beds, with their mattresses, and in the cupboard none of Virginia's belongings were seen any more. Felicity climbed the stairs, drunk with grief.

The next day there was a notice on the door: the apothecary shouted in her ear that the house was for sale.

She staggered and was obliged to sit down.

What distressed her most was leaving her room—so convenient for poor Loulou. Enveloping him with a look of anguish she implored the Holy Ghost, and contracted the idolatrous habit of saying her prayers on her knees before the parrot. Sometimes the sun, entering through the dormer window, fell on his glass eye, and caused it to shoot out a fine luminous beam, which put her in ecstasies.

She had an income of three hundred and eighty francs, a legacy from her mistress. The garden furnished her with vegetables. As to dresses, she possessed enough of them to clothe her to the end of her days, and she saved light by going to bed at dusk.

She hardly ever went out, so as to avoid the second-hand dealer's shop, where was displayed some of the old furniture. Since her attack of dizziness she limped in one leg, and, her strength diminishing, Mother Simon, ruined in the grocery business, came every morning to cut her wood and to pump her water.

Her eyes grew weaker. The shutters were no longer opened. Many years passed. And the house was not let, nor sold.

In terror lest she should be sent away Felicity did not ask for any repairs. The laths of the roof were rotting. During the whole of one winter, her pillow was damp. After Easter she spat blood.

Then Mother Simon had recourse to a doctor. Felicity wanted to know what was the matter with her. But, too deaf to hear, a single word reached her, 'Pneumonia!' It was one she knew, and she replied quietly: 'Ah, like madame', finding it natural to follow her mistress.

The time for setting up the street altars drew near. The first was always at the foot of the hill, the second before the posthouse, the third about the middle of the road. There were rival factions about that one; and the parishioners finally chose Madame Aubain's courtyard.

Her difficulty in breathing and fever grew worse. Felicity was wretched at doing nothing for the altar. If she had had something to put there at least! Then she thought of the parrot. It was not suitable, the neighbours objected. But the priest granted permission for it; she was so happy that she begged him to accept, when she should be dead, Loulou, her only treasure.

From Tuesday to Saturday, the eve of Corpus Christi, she coughed more frequently. In the evening, her face drawn, her lips stuck to her gums, vomitings made their appearance; and the next day, at daybreak, feeling herself very low, she got them to call the priest.

Three old women surrounded her during the extreme unction. Then she declared that she required to speak to Fabu.

He arrived in his Sunday clothes, ill at ease in this lugubrious atmosphere.

'Forgive me,' she said, with an effort to stretch out her arm, 'I thought it was you who had killed him!'

What was the meaning of gossip like that? To suspect him of a murder, a man like him! and he was indignant, was going to make a row.

'She hasn't her wits, you can see that easily enough.'

Felicity from time to time spoke to the ghosts. The old women went away. Madame Simon had her breakfast.

A little later she took Loulou, and lifting him close to Felicity: 'Come, then! Say good-bye!'

Although he was not a corpse the worms were devouring him; one of his wings was broken, the stuffing protruded from his stomach. But blind now, she kissed him on the head, and pressed him against her cheek. Mother Simon took him, to put him on the street altar.

V

From the grass was wafted up the scent of summer; the flies buzzed; the sun glinted on the river, and warmed the roofs. Mother Simon returned to the room and slept peacefully.

Church bells woke her; people were coming out from vespers. Felicity's delirium dropped. Thinking of the procession, she saw it, just as if she were following it.

All the school children, the choristers, and the fire brigade were marching along the pavements, while in the middle of the road were advancing, first the head beadle, armed with his halberd, the under-beadle with his big cross, the teacher supervising the boys, the nun anxious for her little girls; three of the prettiest, curly-haired like angels, were throwing petals of roses into the air; the deacon with outspread arms conducted the music; and two censer swingers turned at each step to the Holy Sacrament, which, under a dais of flaming red velvet, upheld by four churchwardens, the priest in his fine chasuble was carrying. A crowd of people jostled behind, between the white cloths covering the house walls; and the foot of the hill was reached.

A cold sweat wet Felicity's temples. Mother Simon sponged it with a towel, saying that one day we must all go that way. The murmur of the crowd grew, was very loud for a moment, died away.

A volley shook the window panes. It was the postilions saluting the Monstrance. Felicity rolled her eyeballs, and said, as loud as she could: 'Does he look all right?' tormented by the parrot.

Her death agony began. A rattle, more and more hurried, caused her sides to heave. Bubbles of foam came to the corners of her mouth, and all her body trembled.

Soon the blare of ophicleides was distinguished, the clear voices of the children, the deep voices of the men. All was still at intervals, and the tramp of feet which the flowers muffled made the noise of a flock on the turf.

The clergy appeared in the courtyard. Madame Simon climbed on a chair to reach the round window, and in this way commanded a view of the altar.

Green garlands were hanging on the altar, adorned with a flounce in English point lace. There was in the centre a little box enclosing the relics, two orange trees at the corners, and, all its length, silver candlesticks and porcelain vases, whence sprang sunflowers, lilies, peonies, foxgloves, bunches of hortensias.

This mass of dazzling colours descended in a sloping line from the table to the carpet, trailing on the paving-stones; and rare objects drew the eye. A silver-gilt sugar basin had a crown of violets, earrings in Alençon quartz gleamed in the moss, two Chinese screens displayed their landscapes. Loulou, hidden under the roses, only showed his blue front like a sheet of lapis-lazuli.

The churchwardens, the choristers, the children ranged themselves on three sides of the courtyard. The priest slowly mounted the steps, and placed on the lace his huge, glittering 'Golden Sun'. Everybody knelt. There was a great silence. And the censers, swinging in full flight, slipped on their chains.

An azure vapour rose into Felicity's room. She distended her nostrils, scenting it with a mystic sensuality: then she shut her eyes. Her lips smiled. The beats of her heart slowed one by one, more unsteady each time, more gentle like a fountain that is exhausted, like an echo that disappears; and when she breathed her last breath she thought she saw in the heavens as they opened, a gigantic parrot, flying above her head.

FAMILY LIFE

Guy de Maupassant

The tramcar to Neuilly had just passed Porte Maillot, and now was jogging along the long avenue which leads to the Seine. The little engine, harnessed to its wagon, whistled to clear away all obstacles, spat out its steam, panted like a man out of breath who is running; and its pistons made a hurrying noise of iron legs in motion. The heavy heat of the end of a summer's day fell on the road, from which rose, though no breeze was blowing, a white dust, chalky, opaque, suffocating, and hot, that stuck on the damp skin, filled the eyes, entered the lungs.

People came out to their doors, seeking air.

The windows of the tram were lowered, and all the curtains were fluttering, moved by the rapidity of the course. Only a few passengers were seated inside (for people preferred on a hot day the top, or the platforms). There were fat ladies with over-stuffed dresses, those ladies of the suburbs who replace the distinction they lack by an ill-timed dignity: gentlemen tired of the office, with yellowed faces, their figures stooping, one shoulder a little higher than the other, through long hours of duty bent over tables. Their restless, sad faces told besides of domestic troubles, of incessant demands for money, old expectations definitely disappointed: for all of them belonged to that army of poor out-at-elbow devils who vegetate economically in a mean plaster house, with a flower bed for garden, amid that region of night-soil deposits which borders Paris.

Quite near to the door, a little fat man, his face puffed out, his stomach hanging down between his straddling legs, all dressed in black with a ribbon in his buttonhole, was talking to a tall, thin-faced, untidy fellow, dressed in very dirty white duck, and wearing an old panama hat. The first man spoke slowly with hesitations which made him sometimes seem to stutter: it was Monsieur Caravan, principal clerk at the Admiralty. The other, formerly a medical officer on board a merchant vessel, had finished by setting himself up at the Rond-Point of Courbevoie, where he applied to the wretched population of that spot the vague medical knowledge that was left him after an adventurous life. His name was Chenet, and he got himself called Doctor. Rumours were current as regards his morality.

Monsieur Caravan had always led the normal existence of men in offices. For thirty years he invariably went to his office, every morning, by the same route, meeting at the same time, at the same spots, the same faces of men going to their businesses: and he came back from the office every evening, by the same road, where he found the same faces that he had seen growing old.

Every day, after buying his halfpenny newspaper at the corner of the Faubourg Saint-Honoré, he went to get his two rolls of bread, then he entered the Ministry like a guilty man who is giving himself up as a prisoner: and he gained his desk quietly, his heart full of uneasiness, in the eternal expectation of a reprimand for some bit of negligence that he might have committed.

Nothing had ever come to change the monotonous order of his existence: for no event affected him outside the business of his office, promotions, and increases of salary. Whether he was at the Ministry or whether he was at home (for he had married, without a dowry, the daughter of a colleague), he only spoke of the service. Never did his mind, atrophied by the degrading daily task, have other thoughts, other hopes, other dreams, than those relative to the Ministry. But bitterness always ruined his clerkly satisfaction; the accession of navy pursers, 'tinmen' as they were called on account of their silver stripes, to the posts of under-chief and chief: and each Sunday, at dinner-time, with his wife, who shared his hate, he had a hot argument to prove that it is iniquitous in every respect to give positions in Paris to people bred to the sea.

He was old, now, not having felt his life go by, for without transition school had been continued by the office, and the school supervisors before whom he used to tremble in days gone by, were to-day replaced by his chiefs, whom he feared frightfully. The threshold of those chamber despots made him shudder from head to foot; and from this continual fear he had contracted an awkward way of approach, a humble attitude, and a sort of nervous stutter.

He did not know Paris any more than a blind man could know it, led by his dog, every day, under the same door: and if he read in his halfpenny paper of events and scandals, he saw them as fantastic tales invented at will to amuse petty clerks. An orderly man, a reactionary with no fixed party, but an enemy to 'novelty', he passed over the political events which his newspaper, for that matter, always misrepresented in the paid interests of a cause; and when he walked every evening up the Avenue of the Champs-Élysées, he considered the swelling mob of pedestrians and the rolling tide of vehicles in the fashion of a traveller far from home, who might be crossing distant countries.

Having completed, this very year, his thirty years of obligatory service, he had been given on the first of January, the Cross of the Legion of Honour, which is the reward, in these administrations under military rule, for the long years of wretched servitude (they are referred to as loyal services) of those sad convicts riveted to the green portfolio. This unexpected dignity, giving him a new and high idea of his capacity, had changed his way of life completely. He had since then suppressed his coloured trousers, and his gay-coloured vests, worn black trousers and long frock-coats on which his *ribbon*, very wide, looked better: and, shaven every morning, scrubbing his nails more carefully, changing his linen every two days through a legitimate feeling of propriety and of respect for the national *order* of which he made a part, he had become, in the space of a night, another Caravan, cleansed, majestic, and condescending.

In his own house, he would say 'my cross' on every occasion. Such pride took possession of him that he could not even endure in any one else's buttonhole any ribbon of any sort. He was above all exasperated at the sight of foreign orders, 'which should not be permitted to be worn in France', and he was particularly angry with Dr. Chenet, whom he found every evening in the tramcar, adorned with some sort of a decoration, white, blue, orange, or green.

The conversation of the two men, from the Arc de Triomphe to Neuilly, was, for that matter, always the same: and this day, as on preceding days, they busied themselves first with different local abuses which shocked them both, the Mayor of Neuilly taking it at his ease. Then, as infallibly happened in company of a doctor, Caravan introduced the subject of diseases, hoping in this way to glean some little free bits of advice, or even a formal opinion, if he went about it properly, without letting him see the string on the bait. His mother, for that matter, had been worrying him for some time. She had frequent, prolonged, fainting fits, and although ninety years old, she would not consent to look after herself.

Her great age made Caravan affectionate, and he repeated ceaselessly to Dr. Chenet: 'Do you see many get as far as that?' And he rubbed his hands with pleasure, not because he was greatly concerned perhaps in seeing the good woman live eternally on the earth, but because the long duration of the maternal life was like a promise for himself.

He continued: 'Oh, in my family, we go far. And so I am sure, that apart from accidents, I myself will die very old'. The medical practitioner threw him a pitying look: he considered a second time the reddish face of his neighbour, his greasy neck, his belly falling between his two flabby fat legs, all the apoplectic roundness of an enervated clerk: and, raising with a sweep of his hand his greyish panama hat, he answered sneeringly: 'Not so sure as that, my boy. Your mother is a wizened runt, and you are only a fat mass of flesh'.

Caravan was disturbed and said nothing.

But the tramcar arrived at the station. The two companions got out, and Monsieur Chenet offered a vermouth at the Globe Café, opposite, where both of them were accustomed to go. The proprietor, a friend of theirs, stretched two fingers out to them, which they pressed over the bottles on the counter: and they went to join three domino players who had been sitting there since midday. Cordial words were exchanged, with the inevitable 'What news?' Then the players went on with their game: then they wished them good night. They put out their hands without raising their heads, and each went in to dinner.

Caravan inhabited, near the Rond-Point of Courbevoie, a little house of two stories, whose ground floor was occupied by a barber.

Two rooms, a dining-room, and a kitchen, where the glued chairs were moved from room to room according to requirements, formed all the flat that Madame Caravan spent all her time cleaning, while her daughter Marie Louise, aged twelve, and her son Philip Augustus, aged nine, ran loose in the gutters of the avenue, with all the urchins of the district.

Above him, Caravan had installed his mother, whose greed was celebrated in the neighbourhood, and whose thinness gave rise to the saying that the 'good God' had practised on her her own principles of parsimony. Always in a bad temper, she never let a day pass without quarrels and furious bursts of rage. She apostrophized from her window the neighbours on their doorsteps, the vegetable dealers, the street sweepers, and the street boys, who, to avenge themselves, followed her from afar when she went out, shouting, 'Here 's another guy!'

A small servant-girl from Normandy, incredibly stupid, did the housework, and slept on the second story, near the old lady, for fear of accident.

When Caravan entered his home, his wife, attacked by her chronic malady of house-cleaning, was polishing with a bit of flannel the mahogany of the chairs scattered thinly in the solitude of the rooms.

She always wore thread gloves, adorned her head with a bonnet with many-coloured ribbons perpetually slipping over an ear, and she would repeat, any time that anybody surprised her waxing, brushing, polishing, or washing:

'I am not rich, in my house everything is simple, but cleanliness is my luxury, and that 's just as good a one as any other.'

Gifted with a self-willed, practical good sense, she was in everything her husband's guide. Every evening at table, and later on in their bed, they chatted at length about office business, and although she was twenty years younger than he, he confided in her as in a director of conscience, and followed all her advice.

She had never been pretty: she was ugly now, little and thinnish. The want of skill she showed in dressing had always hidden the feeble feminine attributes, which should artfully have come to light with a well chosen style of attire. Her skirts seemed perpetually twisted on one side: and she scratched herself often, no matter where, with absolute indifference as to who was present, through a sort of mania which was almost a disease.

The only ornament she allowed herself consisted in a profusion of twisted silk ribbons on the pretentious bonnets she was accustomed to wear in the house.

As soon as she saw her husband, she rose, and kissing him on his whiskers: 'Did you remember Potin, my dear?' (this referred to an errand he had promised to do). But he fell aghast on a seat: he had just forgotten it again for the fourth time.

'There 's a fate in it!' he said, 'there 's a fate in it; it 's no use my thinking about it all the day; when the evening comes, I always forget.' But, as he seemed distressed, she consoled him.

'You 'll remember about it to-morrow, that 's all. Nothing new at the Ministry?'

'Yes, great news; still another *tinman* nominated under-chief.'

She became very serious.

'To what office?'

'The Office of Foreign Purchases.'

She got angry.

'In the place of Ramon then, exactly the one that I wanted for you: and what about Ramon? Retired?'

He stammered: 'Retired'.

She got raging angry, and the bonnet slipped on to her shoulder.

'It 's all done for, you see, that old office of yours, nothing to be done in it nowadays. And what 's his name, your purser?'

'Bonassot.'

She took the *Marine Year Book,* which she always had at hand, and looked it up. 'Bonnasot—Toulon—born 1851—cadet-purser 1871, under-purser 1875. Has he been at sea, that fellow?'

At this question Caravan brightened up. A fit of gaiety seized him which shook his stomach.

'Just as Balin has, just like Balin, his chief.' And he added, with a louder laugh, an old joke that all the Ministry found delicious. 'One mustn't send them by water to inspect the Naval Station at Pont-du-Jour, they would be ill on the paddle boats.'

But she remained serious, as if she had not heard; then she murmured, slowly scratching her chin:

'If only we had a Member of Parliament up our sleeve? When the House knows all that goes on there, the Minister will give a jump——'

Shouts broke out on the stair, interrupting her sentence. Marie Louise and Philip Augustus, who were coming back from the gutters, were bestowing on one another, from step to step, kicks and slaps. Their mother rushed out, furious, and taking each by an arm, she flung them into the room, shaking them vigorously.

As soon as they saw their father, they rushed on him and he kissed them tenderly, at length: then, sitting down, he took them on his knees, and chatted with them.

Philip Augustus was a nasty little urchin, ill combed, dirty from head to foot, with a stupid face. Marie Louise was already like her mother, spoke like her, repeating her words, even imitating her gestures. She too said, 'What 's new at the Ministry?'

He answered her gaily.

'Your friend Ramon, who comes to dinner here every month, is going to leave us, little daughter. There 's a new under-chief in his place.'

She raised her eyes to her father, and with the pity of a precocious child, 'That 's another that has been promoted over your head, then?'

He stopped laughing and did not answer; then, to create a diversion, addressing his wife who was now cleaning the windows:

'Mamma's quite well upstairs?'

Madame Caravan stopped rubbing, turned round, set straight her bonnet which had quite got down her back, and, with a trembling lip:

'Oh, yes, talk about your mother! She has played me a nice trick! Just think: Madame Lebaudin, the barber's wife, came up just now to borrow a packet of starch from me, and, as I was out, your mother drove her away, and treated her like a beggar. So I settled her, the old woman! She pretended not to hear, as she always does when you tell her the truth about herself, but she 's no more deaf than I am, believe me; it 's all put on, that; and the proof of it is, that she 's gone up to her room at once without saying a word.'

Caravan, upset, didn't say anything, and the little servant rushed in to announce dinner. Then, by way of letting his mother know, he took a long-handled broom, and hit the ceiling three times with it. Then they went through to the dining-room, and Madame Caravan the younger served the soup while they waited for the old lady. She didn't come and the soup got cold. Then they began quite quietly to eat: then, when the plates were empty, they waited again. Madame Caravan, furious, turned on her husband.

'She 's doing it on purpose, you know. And you always back her up.'

He, very perplexed between the two of them, sent Marie Louise to look for grandma, and sat motionless, his eyes down, while his wife angrily tapped the bottom of her glass with the end of her knife.

Suddenly the door opened, and the child reappeared alone, quite out of breath and very pale. She said very quickly:

'Grandma 's fallen on the floor.'

Caravan, with a bound, got to his feet, and, throwing his napkin on the table, dashed for the stairs, where his heavy, hurried footsteps sounded, while his wife, thinking it an ill-tempered ruse of her mother-in-law's, came along more slowly, shrugging her shoulders in contempt.

The old lady was lying full length on her face in the middle of the room, and when her son had turned her over, she lay there motionless and dried up, with her yellow, wrinkled, tanned skin, and her eyes closed, her teeth clenched, and all her thin body stiff.

Caravan, on his knees beside her, groaned: 'My poor mother, my poor mother!' But the other Madame Caravan, after looking at her for a minute, declared: 'Bah, she 's got another fainting fit, that 's all: it 's just to keep us from our dinner, you may be sure of that.'

They carried the body to the bed, took off all her clothes, and all of them, Caravan, his wife, the servant, began to massage her. In spite of their efforts, she did not regain consciousness. Then they sent Rosalie to get Dr. Chenet. He lived on the quay, near Suresnes. It was a long way: the wait was long. At length he arrived, and after having looked at her, felt her, listened to the old woman's chest, pronounced:

'It 's the end.'

Caravan collapsed on the body, shaken by hurried sobs, and he kissed convulsively the rigid face of his mother, weeping with such abundance that the big tears fell like drops of water on the dead woman's face.

Madame Caravan the younger had a conventional attack of grief, and standing behind her husband, she uttered feeble groans, and rubbed her eyes obstinately.

Caravan, his face swollen, his thin hair disordered, very ugly in his sincere sorrow, stood up suddenly: 'But, are you sure, doctor——are you quite sure?' The practitioner came up quickly, and, handling the body with professional dexterity, like a merchant who is showing off his goods: 'Look, my good man, look at her eye.' He raised the lid and the glance of the old woman reappeared under his finger, not at all changed, with the pupil perhaps a little larger. Caravan felt a blow at his heart, and a shudder ran up his bones.

Monsieur Chenet took the stiff arm, forced the finger to open, and, furious as in the face of someone who contradicted him:

'But look at the hand: I never make a mistake, you can depend upon it!'

Caravan fell back sprawling on the bed, almost bellowing; while his wife, still sniffing, did the necessary things. She brought up a night table, on which she spread a napkin, put on it four candles which she lit, took a branch of box-wood hung up behind the mirror on the mantelpiece, and put it between the candles in a plate which she filled with ordinary water, not having any holy water. But, after a quick reflection, she threw into the water a pinch of salt, imagining doubtless that she was making a sort of consecration in it.

When she had finished the ceremonies which should accompany death, she stood up, motionless. Then the doctor, who had helped her to arrange these objects, said to her in a low voice:

'You must get Caravan away!'

She made a sign of assent, and going up to her husband who was sobbing, still on his knees, she raised him by one arm, while Monsieur Chenet took him by the other.

They set him on a chair, and his wife, kissing his brow, lectured him. The practitioner approved of her arguments, counselling resolution, courage, resignation, all the virtues that we cannot display in devastating misfortune like this. Then both of them took him again by the arms and took him away.

He was crying like a big baby, with convulsive sobs, limp, his arms swinging, his legs soft; and he went down the stair without knowing what he was doing, moving his feet mechanically.

They put him down in the arm-chair he always occupied at table, before his almost empty plate where the spoon was still lying wet in the remains of his soup. And he stayed there without a movement, his eyes fixed on his glass, so stupefied that he sat there even without thinking.

Madame Caravan, in a corner, was talking with the doctor, getting advice about the formalities, asking for all practical information. Finally, Monsieur Chenet, who seemed to be waiting for something, took his hat, and declaring that he hadn't had his dinner yet, made his bow before going out. She cried:

'What, you haven't had dinner? But, stay, doctor, stay with us! What we have is going to be brought in: for you understand that people like us don't have a big meal.'

He refused, excusing himself. She insisted.

'Come now, stay. In such moments one is glad to have friends near one: and then, perhaps, you will persuade my husband to cheer up a little: he has so much need to take courage.'

The doctor bowed, and, putting his hat on a table:

'In that case, I accept, madame.'

She gave orders to a bewildered Rosalie, then she herself sat down to the table, 'to make a pretence at eating', she said, and to keep the doctor company.

The cold soup was brought in again. Monsieur Chenet asked for a second helping. Then appeared a dish of tripe à la Lyonnaise, which shed a perfume of onions, and which Madame Caravan decided to taste. 'It is excellent,' said the doctor. She smiled: 'Isn't it?' Then turning to her husband: 'Take a little of it, then, my poor Alfred, only to put something in your stomach; remember that you 've got to get through the night.'

He handed up his plate obediently, just as he would have gone to bed if they had told him to, obeying everybody without resistance and without reflection.

And he ate.

The doctor, helping himself, emptied his plate three times, while Madame Caravan, from time to time, speared a big bit on the end of her fork, and swallowed it with a sort of studied inattention.

When a salad dish appeared, full of macaroni, the doctor murmured, 'Jove, here 's a good thing,' and Madame Caravan, this time, helped everybody. She even filled the saucers in which the children were messing about, and who, left to themselves, were drinking wine without water, and were already kicking one another under the table.

Monsieur Chenet recalled Rossini's love for these Italian dishes; then suddenly:

'Wait! that rhymes; you could begin a bit of poetry:

"Master Rossini,
Loved macaroni."'

Nobody was listening. Madame Caravan, become reflective all of a sudden, was thinking of the probable consequence of the event: while her husband rolled up little balls of bread which he then put on the table-cloth and looked at, with the expression of an idiot. As a blazing thirst burned his throat, he lifted steadily to his mouth his glass ready filled with wine; and his wits, already upset by the shock and the grief, became vague, and seemed to him to dance in the sudden dizziness of indigestion which was beginning.

The doctor, for that matter, was drinking like a fish, and visibly getting intoxicated; and Madame Caravan herself was undergoing the reaction which follows all nervous shock; was restless, troubled too, though she only drank water, and felt her head rather muddled.

Monsieur Chenet began to tell stories of deaths which seemed funny to him. For in this Parisian suburb, filled with a population from the provinces, you find this indifference of the peasant for death, whether it be his father's or his mother's, this disrespect, this unconscious ferocity, so common in the country and so rare in Paris. He was saying.

'Look, last week, in the Rue des Puteaux, someone calls me: I go. I find the sick man dead, and, near the bed, the family who are quietly finishing up a bottle of anisette bought the night before to satisfy a caprice of the dying man.'

But Madame Caravan was not listening: she was thinking steadily of the inheritance: and Caravan, his brain empty, understood nothing at all.

Coffee was served, which had been made very strong to keep up their morale. Each cup, laced with brandy, caused a sudden flush to rise to their cheeks, and confused the last ideas of those already vacillating minds.

Then the doctor, suddenly getting possession of the bottle of brandy, poured out the *cup-rinser* for all the family. And, without speaking, wrapt in the gentle heat of digestion, possessed in spite of themselves by the animal sense of well-being which alcohol after dinner bestows, they let the sugared brandy, which formed a yellowish syrup at the bottom of their cups, trickle slowly down their throats.

The children had gone to sleep and Rosalie put them to bed.

Then Caravan, obeying mechanically the need for forgetting one's troubles which drives on all the unfortunate, took several more drinks of brandy; and his dull eyes gleamed.

The doctor finally rose to go away; and taking hold of his friend's arm: 'Come on, come with me,' he said. 'A little fresh air will do you good: when a man has troubles, it 's not good to sit still.'

The other obeyed quietly, put on his hat, took his stick, went out: and the two of them, arm in arm, went down towards the Seine under the clear stars.

Perfumed breaths of air were wafted in the warm night, for all the gardens of the neighbourhood were at that season full of flowers, whose scents, asleep through the day, seemed to awake at the approach of night and to exhale their fragrance, mingled with the light breezes that passed in the shade.

The avenue was deserted and silent with its two rows of gas jets in line up to the Arc de Triomphe. But lower down Paris muttered in its red fog. It was a sort of continuous roar to which as in answer came, from the plain afar, the whistle of a train rushing full steam ahead, speeding across the provinces to the sea.

The outside air, striking the two men on the face, startled them at first, shook the doctor's equilibrium, and accentuated in Caravan the dizzy spells which had been overtaking him since dinner. He went on like a man in a dream, his spirit torpid, paralysed, without any vibrant grief, seized by a sort of moral torpor which kept him from suffering, finding even a comfort which the lukewarm exhalations spreading in the night increased.

When they were at the bridge, they turned to the right, and the river swept on to their faces a fresh breath of air. It was flowing, melancholy and quiet, behind a curtain of high poplars; and the stars seemed to swim in the water, moving with the current. A thin whitish mist floating on the bank at the farther side brought a wet scent to their lungs, and Caravan stopped brusquely, struck by this smell of the river which stirred in his heart very old memories.

And suddenly he saw again his mother, long ago, in his childhood, on her knees before their door, down in Picardy, washing in the thin trickle of water which flowed through the garden the heaped up linen beside her. He heard her beating-stick in the quiet silence of the country, her voice crying: 'Alfred, bring me some soap.' And he felt this same flowing scent, this same mist rising from the dripping earth, this marshy vapour whose savour had remained with him, unforgettable, which was coming back to him precisely on this very evening when his mother had just died.

He stopped rigid in another attack of passionate despair. It was like a blaze of light illuminating in a single flash the whole extent of his misfortune; and the encounter with this wandering breeze threw him into the black abyss of irremediable sorrow. He felt his heart torn in pieces by this endless separation. His life was cut in half: and all his youth disappeared, swallowed up in this death. All the 'long ago' was finished: all the memories of adolescence were vanished: nobody any more could speak to him of long-ago things, the people that he had formerly known, his native country, himself, the intimacy of this past life: it was a part of his being that had ceased to exist: it was for the other part to die now.

And the file past of awakened memories began. He saw again 'mamma', younger, dressed in clothes shabby by long use, worn so long that they seemed inseparable from her person; he found her again in a thousand forgotten episodes; with expressions that had been effaced from his memory, her gestures, her intonations, her habits, her whims, her fits of temper, the lines of her face, the movements of her thin figure, all the familiar attitudes that she would take no more.

And, clutching the doctor, he groaned. His flabby legs trembled: all his fat body was shaken by sobs, and he stammered: 'My mother, my poor mother!'

But his companion, still drunk, and dreaming of finishing the evening in haunts that he frequented in secret, was impatient at this sharp attack of sorrow, and made him sit down on the grass by the river, and almost at once left him on the pretext of seeing a patient.

Caravan wept for a long time: then, when he was at the end

of his tears, when all his sufferings had, so to speak, poured out, he experienced again a sense of comfort, of repose, a sudden tranquillity.

The moon had risen; it bathed the horizon in its placid light. The tall poplars towered up, silver in the moonshine, and the mist, on the plain, seemed like floating snow: the river, where the stars swam no more, but which seemed covered with mother-of-pearl, still flowed on, wrinkled by spasmodic gleams. The air was mild, the breeze full of perfume. A feeling of indolence passed over the world in the earth's sleep, and Caravan drank in this mildness of the night: he breathed deep, thinking he felt penetrated to the extremity of his limbs by a freshness, a calm, a superhuman consolation.

All the same he resisted this invasive well-being, he repeated: 'My mother, my poor mother', urging himself to weep by a sort of feeling that a decent man should be weeping; but he couldn't weep any more: and no sadness even forced him to the thoughts which, just a moment before, had made him sob so painfully.

Then he rose to go in, coming back with slow steps, enveloped in the calm indifference of serene nature, and his heart appeased in spite of himself.

When he reached the bridge, he saw the head-lights of the last tramcar ready to set out, and behind it, the lit up windows of the Globe Café.

Then a need came over him of telling somebody about the catastrophe, of exciting pity, of making himself interesting. He put on a mournful face; pushed open the door of the establishment, and advanced to the counter where the proprietor was still on his throne. He counted on producing an effect; everybody would get up, would come to him, with their hands outstretched: 'Tell us, what 's the matter?' But nobody noticed the desolation on his face. Then he leant his elbows on the counter, and clutching his head in his hands, murmured: 'God, God!'

The proprietor looked at him: 'You are ill, Monsieur Caravan?' He answered: 'No, my poor chap, but my mother has just died.' The proprietor let out an absent-minded 'Ah', and as a client at the back of the establishment, was shouting: 'Beer, please', he answered at once in a terrible voice: 'All right, boo-oom! it 's coming!' and rushed to serve him, leaving Caravan stupefied.

At the same table as before dinner, absorbed and motionless, the three domino fiends were still playing. Caravan went up to them in search of commiseration. As none of them seemed to see him, he decided to speak. 'A little while ago', he said to them, 'a great misfortune befell me.'

They raised their heads slightly, all three at the same time, but keeping their eyes fixed on the game they were busy on.

'Yes, what 's happened?'

'My mother has just died.'

One of them murmured: 'Ah, heavens!' with that air of false distress which people who are indifferent assume. Another, finding nothing to say, nodded his head, and produced a kind of mournful whistling. The third went back to his game, as if he had thought: 'That 's all it is'.

Caravan was expecting one of those expressions which are referred to as 'coming from the heart'. Seeing himself received like this, he went away, indignant at their calm in face of a friend's grief, although that grief, at this very moment, was so dulled that he hardly felt it any more.

And he went out.

His wife was waiting for him in her night-gown, seated on a low chair near the open window, and still thinking of the inheritance.

'Take off your things,' she said, 'we 'll have a talk when we are in bed.'

He raised his head, and, indicating the ceiling with his eyes: 'But——up there. Is there anybody?'

'Excuse me, Rosalie is beside her; you 'll go up and relieve her at three in the morning when you 've had a nap.'

At the same time he kept his pants on, to be ready for anything that might happen, tied a handkerchief round his head, then joined his wife who had just slipped between the sheets.

They stayed some time lying side by side. She was thinking.

Her hair, even at that hour, was adorned with a rose coloured bow, hanging over a little towards one ear, as if in consequence of the unconquerable habit of all the bonnets she wore.

Suddenly, turning her head to him:

'Do you know if your mother has made a will?' she said.

He hesitated: 'I—I—I think not. No, there 's no doubt about it: she hasn't made one.'

Madame Caravan looked her husband in the eyes, and in a low stormy voice:

'It 's an insult, don't you know: for here we are for ten years sweating ourselves to look after her, giving her a home, feeding her! Your sister isn't the kind to have done as much for her, nor me either, if I had known how I should be repaid for it! Yes, it 's a blot on her memory! You 'll be telling me she paid for her keep; it 's true, but the care you get from your children isn't paid for with money: it is recognized in your will after you are dead. That 's how honest people behave. And so that 's how I 've been had for my trouble and my bother! Oh, it 's a fine thing! It 's a fine thing!'

Caravan, bewildered, was repeating: 'My darling, my darling! I beg you, I beseech you——'

At length she calmed down, and resuming her everyday tone, she went on: 'To-morrow morning, we 'll have to send your sister word.'

He gave a start.

'That 's true, I hadn't thought of that: as soon as morning comes I 'll send her a telegram.'

But she stopped him like a woman who had foreseen everything. 'No, send it only between ten and eleven, so that we 'll have time to turn round before her arrival. From Charenton to here she 'll need two hours at the most. We 'll say you lost your head. In advising her in the morning, we don't put ourselves under the penalty of the law.'

But Caravan smote his forehead, and with the timid intonation which he always used in speaking of his chief, the very thought of whom made him tremble:

'I 'll have to advise the Ministry too,' he said.

She answered: 'Why advise it? On occasions like this, it is always excusable to have forgotten. Don't advise them, listen to me. Your chief can say nothing, and you 'll put him in a queer fix.'

'Oh, he 'll be in that, yes, and in a fine rage when he doesn't see me coming. Yes, you 're right: it 's a rich idea. When I announce that my mother is dead, he 'll be simply compelled to keep silent.'

And the clerk, highly delighted with this farce, rubbed his hands, thinking of his chief's face, while above him the old woman's body lay beside the sleeping servant-girl.

Madame Caravan became anxious, as if obsessed by a pre-occupation difficult to talk about. Finally she made up her mind.

'Your mother did give you her clock, didn't she, the one with the girl playing at cup-and-ball?'

He racked his memory and answered:

'Yes, yes. She said to me (but it 's a long time ago, it was when she came here), she said to me: "That clock will be for you, if you take good care of me".'

Madame Caravan, her fears at rest, brightened up.

'Then, you know, we must go and get it, because if you let your sister come, she 'll prevent us from taking it.'

He hesitated: 'Do you think so?'

She got angry: 'Certainly I think so; once it 's here who 's going to know? it 's ours. It 's the same with that chest of drawers in her room, the one with the marble top. She gave it to me, to me, one day she was in a good temper. We 'll bring it down at the same time.'

Caravan seemed incredulous.

'But, my dear, it 's a great responsibility.'

She turned on him, furious.

'Oh, is that so! you 're always the same then! You will let your children die of hunger, you will, rather than make the slightest movement. From the minute she gave it to me, that chest of drawers is ours, isn't it? And if your sister isn't pleased, she 'll say so to me, won't she? I don't care a snap of my fingers for your sister. Come on, get up, so that we can carry off at once what your mother gave us.'

Trembling and defeated, he got out of bed, and, as he was pulling on his trousers she stopped him.

'It isn't worth the trouble of dressing. Come on, keep on your pants, that 's enough: as for me, I 'll go just as I am.'

And both of them, in their night attire, set out, climbed the stairs noiselessly, opened the door with every precaution, and entered the room where the four candles, lighted round the plate with the holy box-wood, seemed alone to watch the dead woman in her rigid sleep: for Rosalie, stretched in a chair, her legs sticking out, her hands crossed on her skirt, her head fallen to one side, motionless also, her mouth open, was sleeping, and snoring a little.

Caravan took the clock. It was one of those grotesque objects of which Empire art has produced so many. A young girl in gilded bronze, her head adorned with various flowers, was holding in her hand a cup-and-ball, the ball of which served as a pendulum.

'Give me that,' said his wife to him, 'and take the marble slab of the drawers.'

He obeyed, breathing heavily, and he perched the slab on his shoulder with considerable effort.

Then the couple went away. Caravan stooped under the doorway, began to descend the staircase trembling, while his wife, walking backwards, lighted him with one hand, having the clock under her other arm.

When they were in their own room, she heaved a deep sigh.

'The worst is over,' she said, 'let 's get the rest.'

But the drawers of the chest were quite full of the old woman's clothes. These had to be hidden somewhere.

Madame Caravan had an idea.

'Go and bring up the deal box that 's in the vestibule; it isn't worth two francs: we can easily put it here.'

And when the box arrived they began the removal.

They lifted out, one after the other, the cuffs, the collars, the chemises, the bonnets, all the poor belongings of the old body stretched out there behind them, and arranged them methodically in the wooden box in order to deceive Madame Braux, the other child of the dead woman who would come the next day.

When this was done, they first carried down the drawers, then the bulk of the chest of drawers, taking an end each: and both of them sought for a time in which place it would go best. They decided on the bedroom, opposite the bed, between the two windows.

Once the drawers were in place, Madame Caravan filled it with her own linen. The clock was put on the dining-room mantelpiece, and the couple considered the effect obtained. They were immediately charmed by it.

'That goes very well,' she said.

'Yes, very well.'

Then they went to bed. She blew out the candle, and soon everybody was asleep on both floors of the house.

It was already broad daylight when Caravan opened his eyes. His wits were all muddled when he awoke, and he did not recall what had happened until several minutes had gone. The remembrance struck him like a blow in his heart, and he jumped out of bed, greatly affected, ready to cry again.

He went up very quickly to the room above, where Rosalie was still asleep, in the same position as the night before, having spent the whole night in one long nap. He sent her away to her work, replaced the burnt-out candles, then he looked at his mother, turning over in his mind those imitations of profound thoughts, those religious and philosophical banalities which haunt average intelligences in the face of death.

But as his wife was calling him, he went downstairs. She had drawn up a list of things to do in the forenoon, and she handed him the long list of which he was afraid. He read:

(1) Make the declaration at the Town Hall.
(2) Ask for the doctor to certify death.
(3) Order the coffin.
(4) Call at the church.
(5) The undertakers.
(6) The printers for the invitations.
(7) The lawyer.
(8) The telegraph office to tell the family.

Besides a crowd of small messages.

Then he took his hat and went away.

Now, the news having spread, the neighbours began to arrive and asked to see the dead.

In the barber's shop, on the ground floor, a scene had even taken place on this subject between the wife and the husband while he was shaving a client. The wife, knitting a stocking all the while, murmured: 'Another one less, and a miser she was, there aren't many like her. I didn't like her, it 's true: all the same I must go and see her.'

The husband grunted, soaping the customer's chin all the while.

'There 's a queer notion for you! It 's only women who do that sort of thing. It isn't enough to annoy you in their lifetime, they can't even leave you in peace once they 're dead.'

But his wife, without being at all disconcerted, went on:

'I can't help it: I must go. It 's been on my mind since morning. If I didn't see her, it seems to me I would think about her all my life. But when I 've had a good look at her face, I shall be satisfied afterwards.'

The razor-wielder shrugged his shoulders, and confided to the gentleman whose cheeks he was scraping:

'I ask you now, what ideas they have, those confounded females! It 's not my idea of amusing myself, looking at dead people.'

But his wife had heard him, and she answered without being upset:

'That 's how it is: that 's how it is.'

Then, putting her knitting on the counter, she climbed to the first floor.

Two neighbours had already come, and were talking about the event with Madame Caravan, who was recounting the details.

They took their way to the death-chamber. The four women entered on tiptoe, sprinkling the sheet one after the other with the salted water, knelt down, made the sign of the cross, mumbling a prayer, then got up, their eyes wide, their mouths half open, looked a long time at the body, while the daughter-in-law of the dead woman, a handkerchief to her face, pretended to sob in despair.

When she turned round to go out, she saw, standing beside the door, Marie Louise and Philip Augustus, both of them in their night-gowns, watching curiously. Then, forgetting her feigned grief, she flung herself at them, her hand raised, shouting in a furious voice:

'Will you get out of here, you wretched scoundrels, you!'

Going up ten minutes later with another batch of neighbours, having for a second time scattered box-wood over her mother-in-law, prayed, wept, accomplished all her duties, she found her two children come up again behind her. She whacked them again for conscience' sake; but, the next time, she didn't take any notice, and each time visitors returned, the two urchins always followed, kneeling down too in a corner, and invariably repeating all that they saw their mother do.

At the beginning of the afternoon the crowd of curious women diminished. Soon nobody came any more. Madame Caravan went in to her own house, and busied herself preparing things for the funeral ceremony, and the dead woman remained alone.

The window of the room was open. A torrid heat came in with puffs of dust; the flames of the four candles flickered round the motionless body; and on the sheet, on the face with its closed eyes, on the two stretched-out hands, little flies climbed, came and went, walking about, ceaselessly inspecting the old woman, waiting their coming hour.

But Marie Louise and Philip Augustus had gone out again to wander about the avenue. They were soon surrounded by their comrades, above all by little girls, more wide awake, scenting more quickly the mysteries of life. And they asked like grown-ups:

'Your grandma is dead?'

'Yes, yesterday evening.'

'What 's a dead person?'

And Marie Louise explained, told about the candles, the box-wood, the face. Then a mighty curiosity was roused in all the children, and they too asked to go up to the dead woman's room.

At once, Marie Louise organized a first expedition, five girls and two boys, the biggest, the boldest. She made them take off their shoes so as not to be found out: the troop sneaked through the house and climbed the stairs quickly like an army of mice.

Once in the room, the little girl, imitating her mother, took charge of the ceremonial. She solemnly directed her comrades, knelt, made the sign of the cross, moved her lips, rose up, sprinkled the bed, and while the children in a close packed mass came near, terrified, curious, and delighted, to look at the face and the hands, she began suddenly to pretend to be sobbing, hiding her eyes in her little handkerchief.

Then, consoled by the thought of those who were waiting at the door, she swept off at a run all her visitors in order to bring up another group, then a third, for all the urchins of the neigh-bourhood, down to the little ragged beggars, ran to this new pleasure: and each time she simply imitated her mother with an absolute perfection.

In the long run, she got tired. Another game drew the children to a distance: and the old grandmother remained alone, forgotten completely by everybody.

Shadows filled the room: the quivering flame of the candles made lights and shadows dance on her dry wrinkled face.

About eight o'clock Caravan came up, closed the window and renewed the candles. He came in now in a quiet fashion, already accustomed to consider the corpse as if it had been there for months. He even noticed that no decomposition had set in yet, and he remarked about it to his wife at the moment when she sat down to the table for dinner. She answered:

'Oh, she 's made of wood. She would keep for a year.'

The soup was eaten without saying a word. The children, let loose all day, tired out with fatigue, were dozing on their chairs, and everybody remained silent.

Suddenly the light of the lamp went down.

Madame Caravan at once turned up the wick: but the apparatus gave out a hollow sound, a prolonged gurgling, and the light went out. They had forgotten to buy oil! To go to the grocer's would delay dinner; they looked for candles, but there were no others than those lit in the room above on top of the night table.

Madame Caravan, prompt in her decisions, quickly sent Marie Louise to take two of them, and they waited for her in the darkness.

They heard the little girl's steps distinctly as she climbed the stairs.

Then there was a silence of several seconds: then the child came down again, precipitately. She opened the door, terrified, even more affected than she had been the evening before when she had announced the catastrophe, and she muttered in a stifled voice:

'Oh, papa, grandma 's putting on her clothes!'

Caravan sprang up with such a start that his chair went rolling against the wall. He stammered:

'You say—— What is it you are saying?'

But Marie Louise, strangled by emotion, repeated:

'Grand——grand——grandma 's putting on her clothes. She 's coming down.'

He rushed madly to the staircase, followed by his dumbfounded wife, but opposite the door of the second floor he stopped, shaken by fear, not daring to enter. What was he going to see? Madame Caravan, bolder, turned the handle, and advanced into the room.

The room seemed darker: and, in the centre, a tall thin figure was moving. She was on her feet, the old lady; and in waking from her lethargic sleep, even before consciousness had thoroughly returned, turning on her side and raising herself on an elbow, she had blown out three of the candles which burned near the bed of death. Then, gathering her strength, she had got up to get her clothes. The absence of the chest of drawers had bothered her at first, but little by little she had found her possessions at the very bottom of the wooden box, and had quietly dressed herself. Then, having emptied the plate filled with water, replaced the box-wood behind the mirror, and put the chairs back in their places, she was about to come down when her son and her daughter-in-law appeared before her.

Caravan rushed forward, seized her hands, kissed her, tears in his eyes: while his wife, behind him, repeated with a hypocritical air:

'What a blessing, what a blessing!'

But the old woman, without any sign of softening, without even having the appearance of understanding, stiff as a statue, eyes icy, asked only:

'Is dinner ready now?'

He stammered, losing his head.

'Yes, mamma, we are waiting for you,' and with an immense earnestness, he took her arm, while Madame Caravan the younger seized the candle and lighted them, going down the staircase before them backwards and step by step, as she had done that very night before her husband carrying the marble top.

On arriving at the first floor, she almost fell against some people who were coming up. It was the family from Charenton, Madame Braux followed by her husband.

The wife, tall, fat, with a dropsical stomach that threw her chest back, opened terrified eyes, ready to flee. The husband, a Socialist shoemaker, a little man all hair up to his nose, just like a monkey, murmured without any emotion:

'Well, well, what 's this? She 's resuscitated!'

As soon as Madame Caravan recognized them she made desperate signs to them; then aloud:

'Ah, what 's this! it 's you! What a nice surprise!'

But Madame Braux, dumbfounded, did not comprehend; she answered in an undertone:

'It 's your telegram that brought us. We thought it was the end.'

Her husband, behind her, pinched her to make her stop talking.

He added, with a malicious smile hidden in his thick beard:

'It 's really nice of you to have asked us. We 've come immediately,' making an allusion in this way to the hostility that long had reigned between the two households. Then, as the old lady got to the last steps, he came forward briskly and rubbed against her cheeks the hairy mat which covered his face, and shouted in her ear, because of her deafness:

'Feeling all right, mother? always fit, eh?'

Madame Braux, in her amazement at seeing alive the woman she had expected to find dead, did not even dare to kiss her: and her enormous stomach encumbered all the landing, preventing the others from advancing.

The old lady, uneasy and suspicious, but still without a word, looked at all those people round her: and her little grey eye, hard and scrutinizing, fixed now on one, now on another, full of easily read thoughts that disturbed her children.

Caravan said, by way of explanation:

'She has been rather ill, but she 's all right now, absolutely all right, aren't you, mother?'

Then the old lady, beginning to move again, answered in her broken, as it were far-away, voice:

'It was a swoon: I heard you all the time.'

An embarrassed silence followed; they went into the dining-room; they sat down to a hurriedly improvised dinner.

Monsieur Braux alone had kept his self-possession. His naughty monkey face grimaced, and he launched sentences with a double meaning that visibly disturbed everybody.

But every minute the vestibule bell rang: and Rosalie, all bewildered, came to fetch Caravan, who threw away his napkin, and jumped up.

His brother-in-law even asked him if this was his at-home day. He stammered:

'No, messages, nothing at all.'

Then, as a parcel was brought in, he stupidly opened it, and the invitations to the funeral, black-edged, appeared. Then, reddening up to his eyes, he shut the envelope, and covered it up with his waistcoat.

His mother had not seen it: she was obstinately looking at her clock, whose gilded cup-and-ball was swaying on the mantelpiece. And embarrassment grew amidst an icy silence.

Then the old woman, turning her wrinkled witch's face to her daughter, said, with a flicker of malice in her eyes.

'On Monday, you will bring your little girl! I want to see her.'

Madame Braux, her face lit up, cried: 'Yes, mamma,' while Madame Caravan the younger turned pale and faint with anguish.

All the same, the two men, little by little, began to talk; and they started, apropos of nothing, a political discussion. Braux, upholding the revolutionary and communistic doctrines, gesticulated violently, his eyes alight in his hairy face, shouting:

'Property, sir, is a theft from the worker; the earth belongs to everybody: inheritances are an infamy and a shame!'

But he stopped brusquely, confused like a man who has just said a silly thing: then in a gentler tone:

'But this is not the moment to discuss things like that.'

The door opened: Dr. Chenet appeared. He experienced a second of astonishment, then he regained his countenance and, approaching the old woman:

'Aha, mamma, you 're all right to-day. Oh! I thought you would be, you know! and I was saying to myself just now, climbing the stairs: "I bet the old lady will be on her feet",' and he patted her gently on the back. 'She 's as solid as the Pont-Neuf Bridge: she 'll bury us all, you 'll see.'

He sat down, accepting the coffee that was offered him, and took part in the conversation of the two men, approving Braux's ideas, for he had himself been mixed up in the Commune.

Now the old lady, feeling tired, wanted to go away. Caravan rushed forward. Then she looked him full in the face and said to him:

'You 're going to bring up at once my chest of drawers and my clock.'

Then, as he stammered: 'Yes, mamma,' she took her daughter's arm and disappeared with her.

The two Caravans remained aghast, mute, crushed under an atrocious disaster, while Braux rubbed his hands, sipping his coffee.

Suddenly Madame Caravan, mad with anger, rushed on him, howling:

'You 're a thief, a scamp, a blackguard—— I 'll spit in your face. I 'll——I 'll——' She could find no words, suffocating: but he laughed and went on drinking.

Then, as his wife just then came in, she hurled herself on her sister-in-law, and the two of them, the one enormous with her threatening stomach, the other epileptic and thin, their voices distorted, their hands trembling, launched out full throated on basket-loads of insults.

Chenet and Braux interfered, and the latter, pushing his better half by the shoulders, shoved her outside, crying:

'Out you go, donkey, you 've brayed too much!'

And you could hear them in the road squabbling as they went along.

Monsieur Chenet took his leave.

The Caravans remained face to face. Then the man fell on a chair with a cold sweat on his brow, and murmured:

'Whatever am I going to say to my Chief?'

ON HORSEBACK

GUY DE MAUPASSANT

THE poor couple were living laboriously on the husband's small salary. Two children had been born since their marriage, and the first pecuniary embarrassments had become one of those humble, veiled, shameful poverties, the poverty of a noble family which wants to keep up its rank all the same.

Hector de Gribelin had been brought up in the provinces, in his paternal manor-house, by an old priest who was his tutor. They were not rich, but they rubbed along and kept up appearances.

Then at twenty, they sought for a position for him, and he was entered as a clerk at fifteen thousand francs at the Navy Office. He had run aground on that reef as all those do who are not prepared early for the rough fight for life, all those who see existence through a cloud and are ignorant of contrivances and resistance, in whom there have not been developed since infancy special aptitudes, special faculties, a keen energy for the struggle, all those into whose hands an arm and a weapon have not been given.

His first three years in the office were horrible.

He had found several friends of his family, old people behind the times, and not blessed with much fortune either, who lived in the streets of the nobility, the mournful streets of the Faubourg Saint-Germain: and he had made a circle of acquaintances.

Strangers to modern life, humble and proud, these hard-up aristocrats inhabited the top floors in houses that seemed asleep. From top to bottom of those dwellings, the tenants were titled: but money seemed scarce on the first as on the sixth floor.

The everlasting prejudices, the preoccupation with their rank, the anxiety not to fall from it, haunted these families, formerly brilliant, and ruined by their men-folk's inaction. Hector de Gribelin met in this society a young girl, noble and poor like himself, and married her.

They had two children in four years.

During four years more, this household, harassed by poverty, knew no other distractions than a walk in the Champs-Élysées on Sunday, and some evenings at the theatre, one or two a winter, thanks to free tickets offered by a colleague.

But it happened that, towards spring, a supplementary bit of work was entrusted to the clerk by his chief, and he got an extraordinary fee of three hundred francs.

When he brought home the money he said to his wife:

'My dear Henrietta, we must treat ourselves to something, for example a pleasure trip for the children.'

And after a long discussion it was decided that they would go and have lunch in the country.

'By Jove,' cried Hector, 'once isn't a habit; we will have a carriage for you, the children, and the servant, and I will hire a horse at the riding school. That 'll do me good.'

And all the week they spoke of nothing but the projected excursion.

Every evening, when he came in from the office, Hector would seize his elder son, set him astraddle on his foot, and jogging him energetically up and down, he would say:

'That 's how daddy will gallop next Sunday, on our trip!'

And the little chap, all day long, climbed astride of the chairs and dragged them round the dining-room, crying:

'It 's daddy, riding his horsie.'

And the servant-girl herself looked at her master with admiration, thinking that he was going to accompany the carriage on horseback, and during all the meals, she listened to him talking of riding, recounting his former exploits, at his father's house.

Oh! he had been to a good school, and, once the beast was between his legs, he was afraid of nothing—no, nothing!

He would repeat to his wife, rubbing his hands:

'If they could give me an animal a bit high spirited, I would be delighted. You will see how I ride: and if you like, we will come home by the Champs-Élysées at the time when all the people are coming back from the Bois. As we shall put up a good show, I shouldn't be sorry if we met someone from the Ministry. It doesn't require more than that to make yourself respected by your chiefs.'

On the appointed day, the carriage and the horse arrived at

the same time before the door. He came down at once to examine his mount. He had got understraps sewn to his trousers, and was swishing a riding whip he had bought the night before.

He raised and felt, one after the other, the four legs of the beast, touched the neck, the ribs, the hocks, tried the loins with his finger, opened the mouth, examined the teeth, declared how old it was, and, as all the family came down, he delivered a sort of little theoretical and practical course on the horse in general, and on this one in particular, which he recognized as excellent.

When everybody was nicely placed in the carriage, he verified the girths of the saddle: then raising himself on a stirrup, let himself drop on the animal which began to dance under the weight, and almost unsaddled his rider.

Hector, distressed, tried to calm him.

'Come now, quietly, my friend, quietly.'

Then when the beast who carried him had recovered his tranquillity, and the man who was carried his self-possession, he asked:

'Everybody ready?'

All their voices answered:

'Yes.'

Then he gave the order.

'March!'

And the cavalcade set out.

All their eyes were fixed on him. He trotted in the English fashion, exaggerating the action. Hardly had he fallen into the saddle again, than he rebounded as if to mount into space. Often he seemed about to fall on the horse's neck: and he kept his eyes fixed in front of him, with his face set and his cheeks pale.

His wife, holding one of the children on her knees, and the maid who was carrying the other, went on repeating ceaselessly:

'Look at daddy, look at daddy!'

And the two small boys, intoxicated by the movement, the joy, and the keen air, shouted shrilly. The horse, frightened by this clamour, finished by taking to the gallop, and while the cavalier tried to stop him, his hat rolled on the ground. The coachman had to get off his seat to pick up this headgear, and when Hector had received it from his hands, he addressed his wife from a distance:

'Keep the children from shouting out like that, will you: you 'll have him run away with me!'

They had lunch on the grass in the Vésinet woods, on the provisions stowed away under the seat.

Although the coachman took care of the three horses, Hector got up every moment to go and see if his had everything he wanted: and he stroked him on the neck, giving him bread, cakes, and sugar to eat.

He declared:

'He 's a hard trotter. He even shook me a little in the first few minutes: but you saw that I recovered myself quickly: he recognized his master, he won't forget now.'

As he had resolved, they came home by the Champs-Élysées.

The vast avenue was swarming with carriages. And on the paths the pedestrians were so numerous that you would have said that there were two long black ribbons stretched out from the Arc de Triomphe to the Place de la Concorde. A burst of sunshine illuminated everything, and made the varnish of the barouches, the steel of the harness, the handles of the carriage doors gleam.

A mad love of movement, an intoxication for life, seemed to stir the crowd of people, of carriages, and of horses. And the obelisk rose straight up in a mist of gold.

Hector's horse, as soon as he had passed the Arc de Triomphe, was suddenly seized with a new ardour, and he slipped in and out between the wheels, at a full trot, towards his stable, in spite of all the efforts of his rider to calm him.

The carriage was far away now, far away behind; and then when he was opposite the Palace of Industry, the animal, seeing the coast clear, turned to the right and began galloping.

An old woman in an apron was crossing the road tranquilly. She was exactly in Hector's path, and he was approaching at full speed. Unable to control his beast, he began to cry with all his might:

'Hullo, hullo there!'

She was deaf, maybe, for she peaceably continued on her way until the moment when, struck by the horse's chest, rushing on her like a locomotive, she went rolling ten steps farther, her skirts in the air, after turning three complete somersaults.

Voices cried:

'Stop him!'

Hector, aghast, hung on to the mane and shouted:

'Help!'

A terrible heave made him shoot like a cannon-ball over the ears of his charger, and fall into the arms of a police sergeant who had just flung himself into his way.

In a second, a furious, gesticulating, vociferating group formed round him. An old gentleman especially, an old gentleman wearing a big round decoration and big white moustaches, seemed exasperated. He kept on repeating:

'Good heavens, when you 're as clumsy as that, you stay at home! You don't come killing people in the street, when you don't know how to ride a horse.'

But four men appeared, carrying the old woman. She seemed dead, with her yellow face and her bonnet to one side, all grey with dust.

'Carry that woman to a chemist's,' ordered the old gentleman, 'and let us go to a police station.'

Hector, between two policemen, began his journey. A third held his horse. A crowd followed: and suddenly the carriage appeared. His wife rushed forward, the servant lost her head, the babies squalled. He explained that he 'd be home soon, that he had knocked a woman over, that it was nothing. And his distracted family moved off.

At the police station, the explanation was short. He gave his name, Hector de Gribelin, attaché to the Minister of the Navy, and they awaited news of the injured woman. A policeman, sent to get information returned. She had regained consciousness, but she was suffering frightfully inside, she said; she was a charwoman, aged sixty-five, and called Madame Simon.

When he knew that she wasn't dead, Hector took hope again, and promised to provide for the expenses of her cure. Then he ran to the chemist's.

A crowd was stationed before the door: the old wife, sunk in an arm-chair, was groaning, her hands hanging, her face stupid. None of her limbs were broken, but they feared an internal lesion.

Hector spoke to her:

'Are you suffering much?'

'Oh, yes.'

'Whereabouts?'

'It 's like a fire I have in my innards.'

A doctor came up:

'You are the cause of the accident, sir?'

'Yes, sir.'

'This woman will have to be sent to a nursing home: I know one where they will take her for six francs a day. Would you like me to arrange it?'

Hector, delighted, thanked him, and went back home comforted.

His wife was waiting for him in tears: he calmed her.

'It 's nothing. This Simon woman is better already: in three days it will not show at all. I have sent her to a nursing home. It is nothing.'

Coming out of his office, next day, he went to inquire for Madame Simon. He found her busy eating thick soup with an air of satisfaction.

'Well?' he said.

She answered:

'Oh, my poor sir, there 's no change. I feel almost done for. It 's no better.'

The doctor declared that they would have to wait, a complication might supervene.

He waited three days, then he came back. The old woman, her skin clear, her eyes limpid, began to groan as soon as she saw him.

'I can't move any more, my poor sir, I can't. I 'll be like this till the end of my days.'

A shudder ran up Hector's bones. He asked the doctor. The doctor raised his hands:

'What can I say, sir? I do not know. She howls when we try to raise her. We can't even change the position of her chair, without her uttering heart-rending cries. I have to believe what she tells me, sir: I am not inside her. So long as I have not seen her walk, I have no right to suppose it 's a lie on her part.

The old woman listened, motionless, her eyes cunning.

A week passed: then two weeks, then a month. Madame Simon did not leave her chair. She ate from morning to night, grew fat, talked gaily with the other patients, seemed accustomed to immobility as if it had been the well-earned repose, won by her fifty years of stairs climbed, of mattresses turned, of coal carried from floor to floor, of sweepings and brushings.

Hector, aghast, came every day: every day he found her tranquil and serene, and declaring:

'I can't move, my poor sir, I can't.'

Every evening Madame de Gribelin asked, devoured by distress:

'And Madame Simon?'

And every time he answered with a despairing despondency:

'No change, absolutely none!'

They sent away the servant, whose wages became too great a burden. They economized still more: the whole extra fee was spent.

Then Hector called in four eminent doctors, who met around the old woman. She let them examine her, touch her, feel her, watching them with a shrewd eye.

'She must be made to walk,' said one.

She cried out:

'I can't, my good sirs, I can't.'

Then they seized hold of her, lifted her up, dragged her a few steps: but she slid out of their hands, and collapsed on the floor, emitting such fearful shouts that they put her back on her chair with infinite precautions.

They gave a discreet opinion, concluding all the same that it was impossible that she could go on working.

And when Hector took this news to his wife, she let herself fall on a chair, stammering:

'It would be still better to take her in here, that would cost less.'

He jumped.

'Here, in our home, do you really mean it?'

But she answered resigned to everything now, and with tears in her eyes:

'What can we do, my dear? it isn't my fault——'

THE NECKLACE

GUY DE MAUPASSANT

SHE was one of those pretty, charming girls, born, as if by a mistake of destiny, into a family of clerks. She had no dowry, no expectations, no means of being known, understood, loved, wedded by a rich, distinguished man; and she let herself be married to a petty clerk at the Ministry of Education.

She was simply dressed, not being able to dress richly; but unhappy, like a woman out of her class; for women have no caste or race, their beauty, their grace and their charm serve them for good birth and family. Their native sensitiveness, their instinct for elegance, their subtlety of mind are their only hierarchy, and make girls of the people the equals of the greatest ladies.

She suffered ceaselessly, feeling herself born for every delicacy and every luxury. She suffered from the poverty of her home, from the wretched look of the walls, from the worn-out seats, from the ugliness of the materials. All these things, which another woman of her class would not even have noticed, tortured and distressed her. The sight of the little Breton girl who did her simple housework for her, roused in her desolating regrets and distracted dreams. She dreamed of quiet ante-chambers, padded with oriental hangings, lit by bronze candelabras, and of two tall footmen in knee-breeches, who slept in the wide arm-chairs in the heavy heat of a hot-air stove. She dreamed of big reception-rooms, draped in silks of old time, of fine furniture set out with priceless knick-knacks, and of little dainty drawing-rooms, perfumed, made for five o'clock chats with one's most intimate friends, men known and sought after, whose attentions all the women envied and desired.

When she sat down for dinner, before the round table, covered with a three-days-old tablecloth, opposite her husband who took the lid off the soup tureen, and declared with an air of enchantment: 'Ah! the good old boiled beef and carrots! I don't know anything better than that!' she was dreaming of elegant dinners, of glittering plate, of tapestries that peopled the walls with figures of the days of old and with strange birds amidst a fairy forest: she was dreaming of exquisite food served in marvellous dishes, of whispered compliments listened to with a sphinx-like smile, the while she ate the pink flesh of a trout, or the wings of a grouse.

She had no fine dresses, no jewels, nothing. And she loved those things only, she felt herself made for them. She would have liked so much to please, to be envied, to be seductive and exquisite.

She had a rich woman friend, a comrade of convent days, whom she didn't want to go and see, she suffered so much in coming back. And she would weep for whole days, from sorrow, from regret, from despair, and from wretchedness.

Now, one evening, her husband came in proudly, and holding in his hand a large envelope.

'Here,' he said, 'there 's something for you.'

She tore open the paper quickly and brought out a printed card which bore these words:

'The Minister of Education and Madame Georges Ramponneau request Monsieur and Madame Loisel to do them the honour of coming to spend the evening at the Ministry, on Monday, the 18th January.'

Instead of being delighted, as her husband had hoped, she threw the invitation peevishly on the table, murmuring:

'What do you expect me to do with that?'

'But, my dear, I thought you 'd be glad. You never go out, and this is an opportunity, a fine one. I 've had no end of trouble to get it. Everybody wants one: it is very exclusive, and not many invitations are given to the clerks. You 'll see all the people who hold office there.'

She looked at him angrily, and she declared impatiently:

'What do you expect me to put on to go there?'

He hadn't thought of that; he stammered:

'But the dress you go to the theatre in. I think that 's a very nice one——'

He stopped speaking, stupefied, aghast, seeing that his wife was crying. Two big tears slowly descended from the corners of her eyes to the corners of her mouth; he faltered:

'What 's the matter? What 's the matter?'

But with a violent effort, she had subdued her distress, and she answered in a calm voice, drying her wet cheeks:

'Nothing. Only I have no dress, and consequently I can't go to this reception. Give your card to one of your colleagues whose wife is better got up than I am.'

He was in despair. He tried again:

'See here, Mathilde. How much would it cost to get a suitable dress, which you could use again on other occasions, something very simple?'

She reflected a few seconds, reckoning up the cost, and thinking as well of a sum that she could ask for without an immediate refusal and a frightened exclamation from the thrifty clerk.

'I don't know just exactly, but it seems to me that with four hundred francs I could do it.'

He grew rather pale, for he was laying aside just that sum to buy a gun and treat himself to hunting parties, next summer, on the plains of Nanterre, with some friends who were going to shoot at larks down there, on Sundays.

He said all the same:

'All right. I 'll give you four hundred francs. But try to have a handsome dress.'

The day of the reception was drawing near, and Madame Loisel seemed sad, uneasy, anxious. All the same her dress was ready. Her husband said to her one evening:

'What 's the matter? see here, you 've been in a funny state for three days.'

And she answered:

'I 'm vexed at not having some jewels, not a single stone, nothing to put on me. I shall look dreadfully poverty-stricken. I 'd almost rather not go to this affair.'

He took her up:

'You can wear real flowers. It 's very fashionable this season. For ten francs you can have two or three magnificent roses.'

She was not convinced.

'No. There 's nothing more humiliating than to look poor among rich women.'

But her husband cried out:

How silly you are! Go and find your friend, Madame

Forestier, and ask her to lend you some jewels. You 're friendly enough with her to do that.'

She uttered a joyous cry.

'That 's true. I hadn't thought of that.'

The next day she went to her friend, and told her her trouble.

Madame Forestier went to her glass-fronted wardrobe, took a large jewel box, brought it over, opened it, and said to Madame Loisel:

'Choose for yourself, my dear.'

She saw first bracelets, then a string of pearls, then a Venetian cross, gold, and precious stones, admirably worked. She tried on the ornaments before the mirror, hesitated, could not decide to leave them, to give them up. She asked constantly:

'Have you nothing else?'

'Yes. Look; I don't know what might please you.'

Suddenly she discovered, in a black satin box, a superb string of diamonds. And her heart began to beat with an unmeasured desire. Her hands trembled as she took it up. She fastened it round her throat, on her high dress, and stood in ecstasy before her reflection.

Then she asked, hesitating, full of anguish:

'Could you lend me this, nothing but this?'

'Yes, certainly.'

She flung her arms round her friend's neck, kissed her with abandon, then fled with her treasure.

The day of the reception arrived. Madame Loisel had a triumph. She was prettier than all the other ladies, elegant, gracious, smiling, and mad with joy. All the men were looking at her, asking her name, seeking to be introduced to her. All the attachés of the Ministry were wanting to waltz with her. The Minister noticed her.

She danced madly, with abandon, drunk with pleasure, thinking of nothing, in the triumph of her beauty, in the glory of her success, in a sort of cloud of happiness, made up of all those compliments, all this admiration, all those awakened desires, this victory so complete, and so sweet to a woman's heart.

She left about four o'clock in the morning. Her husband, since midnight, had been asleep in a little deserted room with three other men whose wives were having a good time.

He threw on her shoulders the garments he had brought for going home, modest garments of every day, whose poverty contrasted horribly with the elegance of her ball dress. She felt it, and wanted to flee, so as not to be seen by the other women who were wrapping themselves in rich furs.

Loisel detained her.

'Wait a bit. You 'll catch a cold outside. I 'm going to call a cab.'

But she didn't listen to him, and quickly ran down the staircase. When they were in the street, they couldn't find a cab: and they began to look for one, shouting after the cab-drivers that they saw passing in the distance.

They went down towards the Seine, desperate, shivering. Finally they found on the quay, one of those old night-walking broughams that are not seen in Paris except when night falls, as if they had been ashamed of their wretched appearance during the day.

It took them to their door, Rue des Martyrs, and they climbed wearily up to their flat. It was all over, for her. And he was thinking that he had to be at the Ministry at ten o'clock.

She took off the garments in which she had wrapped her shoulders, before the mirror, so that she could see herself once again in her glory. But suddenly she cried out. She had no longer her string of diamonds round her neck.

Her husband, already half undressed, asked:

'What 's the matter with you?'

She turned to him, distractedly.

'I have—— I have—— I have not got Madame Forestier's necklace.'

He sat up, aghast.

'What? How? It isn't possible.'

And they looked in the folds of her dress, in the folds of her coat, in the pockets, everywhere. They did not find it.

He asked:

'Are you sure you had it still when you left the ball?'

'Yes. I touched it in the vestibule of the Ministry.'

'But if you had lost it in the street, we should have heard it fall. It must be in the cab.'

'Yes. That 's likely. Did you take the number?'

'No. And you, didn't you notice it?'

'No.'

They looked at one another, overwhelmed. Finally Loisel put on his clothes again.

'I am going,' he said, 'to retrace all the walk we did on foot, to see if I shall not find it.'

And he went out. She stayed in her evening dress, without strength to go to bed, collapsed in a chair, without fire, without thought.

Her husband came in about seven o'clock. He had found nothing.

He went to the police office, to the newspapers to offer a reward, to the companies that let out cabs for hire, everywhere, in short, where a glimmer of hope attracted him

She waited all day, in the same state of distraction before this frightful disaster.

Loisel returned in the evening, his cheeks hollowed, pale; he had discovered nothing.

'You must,' he said, 'write to your friend that you have broken the clasp of her diamonds, and that you are having it repaired. That will give us time to turn round.'

She wrote, to his dictation.

At the end of a week they had lost all hope. And Loisel, five years older, declared:

'We must make arrangements to replace this jewellery.'

They took, next day, the box in which it had been contained, and went to the jeweller whose name was inside. He consulted his books:

'It is not I, madame, who sold this necklace: I can only have supplied the case.'

Then they went from jeweller to jeweller, seeking a necklace like the other, searching their memories, ill, both of them, with grief and anguish.

They found in a shop in the Palais-Royal, a string of diamonds that seemed to them exactly like the one they were looking for. It was worth forty thousand francs. They would let them have it for thirty-six thousand.

They begged the jeweller not to sell it for three days. And they made an arrangement that it would be taken back at thirty-four thousand francs if the first string was found before the end of February.

Loisel possessed eighteen thousand francs that his father had left him. He would borrow the rest.

He borrowed, asking a thousand francs from one man, five hundred from another, a hundred francs here, sixty there. He gave promissory notes, made ruinous engagements, had business with usurers, with all the race of money-lenders. He compromised all the rest of his life, risked his signature without even knowing if he could honour it, and, terrified by the anguish of the future, by the black misery which was going to descend on him, by the perspective of all the physical privations, and all the moral tortures, he went to get the new necklace, putting down on the shopkeeper's counter thirty-six thousand francs

When Madame Loisel took back the necklace to Madame Forestier, the latter said to her with an offended expression:

'You ought to have given it back to me sooner, for I might have needed it.'

And she did not open the case, as her friend had feared. If she had perceived the substitution, what would she have thought? What would she have said? Would she have taken her for a thief?

Madame Loisel experienced the horrible life of the poverty-stricken. She made her resolution, moreover, all at once, heroically. This frightful debt had to be paid. She would pay it. The maid was sent away; the flat was given up: an attic was rented up under the roofs.

She experienced the heavy work of a house, the hateful labours of a kitchen. She washed the dishes, wearing out her rosy nails on the greasy pottery and the bottoms of saucepans. She washed dirty linen, shirts, and towels, and hung them out to dry on a rope; she carried the rubbish down to the street every morning, and brought up the water, stopping at each flight to get her breath. And, dressed like a woman of the people, she went to the fruiterer's, the grocer's, the butcher's, with her basket on her arm, bargaining, insulted, defending penny by penny her wretched money.

Every month promissory notes had to be paid, others renewed, time asked for.

Her husband worked in the evening, setting in order a tradesman's accounts, and at night he often made copies at twenty-five centimes a page.

And this life lasted ten years.

At the end of ten years, they had paid back everything, everything, with the usury charges, and the accumulation of superimposed interest.

Madame Loisel seemed an old woman now. She had become the strong rough, hard woman of poor households. Her hair badly dressed, with her skirts uneven, and her hands red, she spoke in a loud voice, washed the floors in a swirl of water. But, sometimes, when her husband was at the office, she would sit beside the window, and she thought of the evening long ago, of that ball where she had been so beautiful and so admired. What would have happened if she had not lost that necklace? Who knows? Who knows? How queer life is, how easily changed! How small a thing it needs to destroy you, or to save you!

Now, one Sunday, when she had gone to take a turn in the Champs-Élysées as a relaxation after the toils of the week, she saw suddenly a lady taking a child out for a walk. It was Madame Forestier, still young, still beautiful, still seductive.

Madame Loisel felt moved. Was she going to speak to her? Why, yes. And now that she had paid she would tell her everything. Why not?

She went up to her.

'Good day, Jeanne.'

The other did not recognize her, and was astonished at being addressed so familiarly by this woman. She stammered:

'But—— Madame! I do not know—— You must have made a mistake.'

'No. I am Mathilde Loisel.'

Her friend uttered a cry.

'Oh, my poor Mathilde! How you 've changed!'

'Yes, I 've gone through very hard days since I saw you: and much distress——and that because of you!'

'Me! How?'

'You remember that necklace of diamonds that you lent me to go to the ball at the Ministry.'

'Yes. Well?'

'Well, I lost it.'

'How? since you brought it back to me.'

'I brought back another just the same. And for ten years we 've been paying for it. You 'll understand that it wasn't easy for us, we who have no money. At last it is done, and I am awfully glad.'

Madame Forestier stood still.

'You say that you bought a diamond necklace to replace mine?'

'Yes. You didn't notice it, eh? They were very alike.'

And she smiled a smile of proud, simple joy.

Madame Forestier, very affected, took her two hands.

'Oh, my poor Mathilde! But mine was imitation. It was worth at the most five hundred francs.'

HAUTOT SENIOR AND HAUTOT JUNIOR

GUY DE MAUPASSANT

I

THE house was half farm, half manor-house, one of those mixed rural dwellings, which used to be almost seigneurial, and which, at the present day, are occupied by big farmers. Before the door the dogs, tied to the apple-trees in the courtyard, barked and howled at the sight of the game-bags carried by the keeper and his boys. In the big kitchen-dining-room, Hautot Senior and Hautot Junior, Monsieur Bermont, the tax-collector, and Monsieur Mondaru, the notary, took a little refreshment, and drank a glass, before going out hunting, for it was the opening day.

Hautot Senior, proud of all his possessions, boasted in advance of the game that his guests were going to find on his land. He was a big Norman, one of those strong, full-blooded, bony men, who can lift apple carts on their shoulders. Half a peasant, half a gentleman, rich, respected, influential, authoritative, he had kept his son, Cæsar Hautot, at school up to the third form, so that he might be educated, and had stopped his studies there for fear that he might turn out a gentleman who didn't care for the land.

Cæsar Hautot, almost as tall as his father, but thinner, was a good sort of son, docile, pleased with everything, full of admiration, respect, and deference for the wishes and opinions of Hautot Senior. Monsieur Bermont, the tax-collector, a little fat man whose red cheeks showed a thin network of violet veins, like the tributaries and tortuous courses of rivers on a geography map, asked:

'And hares—are there any hares?'

Hautot Senior answered:

'As many as you want, especially at the lower end of Puysatier.'

'Where are we to begin?' asked the notary, a gay lad of a

notary, fat and pale, bulging and strapped into a brand new hunting suit, bought at Rouen the other week.

'Well there, at the lower end. We shall drive the partridges into the plain, and beat up above them.'

And Hautot Senior rose. They all imitated him, took their guns from the corners, examined the locks, stamped with their feet to steady themselves in their rather hard shoes, not yet softened by the heat of the blood, then they went out; and the dogs, leaping up at the end of their leads, uttered shrill howls as they pawed the air.

They set out towards the lower ground.

It was a little valley, or rather a big undulation of land of bad quality, that had remained uncultivated for that reason, furrowed by ravines, covered with heather, an excellent game preserve.

The hunters placed themselves at regular distances, Hautot Senior taking the right, Hautot Junior the left, and the two guests in the middle. The keeper and the boys who carried the game bags followed. It was the solemn instant when the first gunshot is expected, when the heart beats a little, while the nervous fingers touch the trigger every instant.

Suddenly it went off, that shot! Hautot Senior had fired. They all stopped, and saw a partridge, detaching itself from a covey that were flying at full speed, fall into a ravine under the thick brushwood. The excited hunter began to run, with great strides, tearing out the reeds that kept him back, and disappeared in his turn into the thicket, in search of the bird he had shot.

Almost at once, a second gunshot was heard.

'Ah, ah, the scoundrel!' cried Monsieur Bermont, 'he 'll have unearthed a hare down there!'

They all waited, their eyes on the heap of branches that the sight could not penetrate.

The notary, making a trumpet with his hands, shouted: 'Have you got them?' Hautot Senior did not answer: then, Cæsar, turning to the keeper, said to him: 'Go and help him then, Joseph. We must keep in line. We shall wait.'

And Joseph, an old trunk of a dry, gnarled man, whose joints all formed protuberances, set out at a quiet pace, and descended the ravine, looking in all the practicable holes with the precautions of a fox. Then suddenly, he called:

'Come on, come on! There 's an accident happened!'

They all ran and plunged into the reeds. Hautot Senior, on his side, unconscious, holding his stomach with his two hands, between which flowed across his cloth vest, torn by the bullet, long trickles of blood on to the grass. Letting go of his gun to seize the partridge lying dead within reach of his hand, he had dropped the weapon, whose second shot, going off with the fall, had shattered his abdomen. They drew him up from the ditch, they took his clothes off, and they saw a fearful wound from which the intestines protruded. Then, after tying it up as well as they could, they carried him home, and awaited the doctor who had been sent for along with the priest.

When the doctor came, he shook his head gravely, and turning to Hautot Junior who was sobbing on a chair:

'My poor boy,' he said, 'this doesn't look too well.'

But when the bandaging was finished, the injured man moved his fingers, opened his mouth, then his eyes, looked before him with troubled, haggard looks, then seemed to search in his memory, remember, understand, and he murmured:

'Jove, that 's the end of it!'

The doctor was holding his hand.

'No, no! Some days' rest only. It won't be anything.'

Hautot went on:

'That 's the end. Shot in the stomach! I know it all right.'

Then suddenly:

'I want to speak to my son, if I have time.'

Hautot Junior, in spite of himself, was crying and repeating like a little boy:

'Daddy, daddy, poor daddy!'

But his father, in a firmer tone, said:

'Come, don't cry any more; it isn't the time for that. I have to speak to you. Sit down there, quite close. It 'll soon be finished, and I 'll be more at ease. The rest of you, leave us alone a minute, please.'

Everybody went out, leaving the son in front of the father.

As soon as they were alone:

'Listen, my son, you are twenty-four. I can talk to you about things. And besides there is not so much mystery about it as we put into it. You know that your mother has been dead these seven years, isn't that true? and I am not more than forty-five years old, seeing that I was married at nineteen. That 's true, eh?'

The son stammered:

'Yes, it 's true.'

'So your mother died seven years ago, and I remained a widower. Well! I 'm not the sort of man who could remain a widower at thirty-seven, isn't that true?'

The son answered:

'Yes, it 's true.'

The father, panting, quite pale, and his face contracted, went on:

'God, but it 's sore! Well, you understand. Man isn't made to live alone, but I didn't want to give your mother a successor, seeing that I had promised her that. So——you understand?'

'Yes, father.'

'So, I took a little lady at Rouen, 18 Rue de l'Éperlan, third floor, second door. I 'm telling you that, don't forget it. But a little lady who has been utterly kind to me, loving, devoted, a real wife, eh? You grasp that, my boy?'

'Yes, father.'

'Well, if I go away, I owe her something. I mean something worth while, which will put her out of the reach of want. You understand?'

'Yes, father.'

'I tell you she 's a fine woman, yes, a really fine woman, and but for you and the memory of your mother, and the house as well where we had lived all three, I would have brought her here, and then married her for sure—— Listen——listen, my boy—I could have made a will—I haven't made one! I didn't want to—for these things shouldn't be written—these things—that 's too big an injury to the legitimate heirs—and, then, that messes everything up—that ruins everybody. Look here, stamped paper isn't needed—never use it. If I am rich, it 's because I never used it in my life. You understand, my son?'

'Yes, father.'

'Listen again, listen hard. Then, I have not made my will—I haven't wanted to—and since I know you, you have a good heart; you are not stingy, or griping, are you? I said to myself that, when my time came, I would tell you all about it, and I would ask you not to forget the little lady: Caroline

Donet, 18 Rue de l'Éperlan, third floor, the second door; don't forget. And then, listen again. Go there immediately when I 'm gone, and then arrange so that she won't need to feel aggrieved at the memory of me. You have money to do it. You can—I am leaving you enough. Listen. Through the week you won't find her. She works with Madame Moreau, Rue Beauvoisine. Go on Thursday, she expects me that day. It 's been my day for six years. Poor little girl, will she cry? I tell you all this because I know you well, my son. These things one doesn't tell to the public, or to the notary, or to the priest. These things exist, everybody knows it, but they aren't talked about, except in case of necessity. Then—no stranger in the secret, nobody but the family, because the family is all in one. You understand?'

'Yes, father.'

'You promise?'

'Yes, father.'

'You swear?'

'Yes, father.'

'I beg you, I beseech you, don't forget. I am set on it.'

'No, father.'

'You will go yourself. I want you to make sure of everything yourself.'

'Yes, father.'

'And then you will see——you will see what she will explain to you. I can tell you no more. Is it an oath?'

'Yes, father.'

'Good, my son. Kiss me. Good-bye. I 'm going to slip off, I 'm sure of it. Tell them to come in.'

Hautot Junior kissed his father, groaning, then, always obedient, opened the door, and the priest appeared, in his white surplice, carrying the sacred oils.

But the dying man had closed his eyes, and he refused to open them again, he refused to answer, he refused to show even by a sign that he understood.

He had spoken enough, this man, he could do no more. Besides, he felt his heart at ease now, he wanted to die in peace. What need had he to confess to the delegate of God, since he had just confessed to his son, who was one of his own family!

He was given the sacrament, purified, absolved, amid his

friends and servants on their knees, without a single movement of his face showing that he was still alive.

He died about midnight, after four hours of shudders that indicated atrocious sufferings.

II

It was Tuesday when he was buried, the hunting having been opened on Sunday. Returned to his house, after having conducted his father to the cemetery, Cæsar Hautot passed the rest of the day in weeping. He hardly slept the following night, and he felt so sad when he woke, that he asked himself how he could go on living.

All day long till evening, however, he thought that to obey his father's last wishes, he ought to go to Rouen next day, and see this girl, Caroline Donet, 18 Rue de l'Éperlan, third floor, the second door. He had repeated, under his breath, as a child does a prayer, this name and this address, an incalculable number of times, so that he would not forget them, and he finished by babbling them indefinitely, without being able to stop or to think of anything at all, his tongue and his mind were so obsessed by these phrases.

The next day, then, about eight o'clock, he told them to harness Graindorge to the tilbury, and set out, at the heavy Norman horse's full trot, on the high road from Ainville to Rouen. He wore on his back his black frockcoat, on his head his tall silk hat, and on his legs his strapped trousers, and he had not chosen, considering the circumstances, to wear on top of his fine suit the blue blouse which balloons out in the wind, protects the cloth from dust and stains, and is taken off quickly on arrival, as soon as you jump out of the carriage.

He entered Rouen just as ten o'clock was striking, stopped as he always did at the Bon-Enfant hotel, Rue des Trois-Mares, submitted to the kiss of the landlord, the landlady, and their five sons, for the sad news was known: then, he had to give details of the accident, and that made him weep; he had to refuse the services of all these people, officious because they knew that he was rich, and even to refuse their lunch, which offended them.

Then, having dusted his hat, brushed his coat, and rubbed up his boots, he began to look for the Rue de l'Éperlan, without daring to make inquiries of anybody, for fear of being recognized and arousing suspicions.

In the end, not finding it, he saw a priest, and trusting the professional discretion of the churchman, he asked information from him.

He had only a hundred yards to go, it was in fact the second road to the right.

Then, he hesitated. Up to that moment, he had obeyed like a brute beast the will of the dead man. Now he felt all upset, confused, humiliated at the idea of finding himself, he, the son, before the woman who had been his father's mistress. All the morality which lies deep in us, heaped up at the bottom of our feelings by centuries of hereditary teaching, all that he had learned since his catechism days about creatures of evil life, the instinctive contempt that every man bears in himself towards them, even if he marries one, all his limited peasant honour, all that stirred in him, held him back, made him blushing and ashamed.

But he thought: 'I promised my father. I mustn't fail'. Then he pushed the half-opened door of the house marked with the number 18, discovered a dark stairway, mounted three floors, saw a door, then another, found the bell rope and pulled it.

The ding-dong that echoed in the neighbouring room, caused a shudder to pass up his body. The door opened and he found himself in front of a very well dressed young woman, dark, with a warm complexion, who looked at him with bewildered eyes.

He didn't know what to say to her, and she, who didn't suspect anything, and who was expecting the other one, did not invite him to come in. They looked at each other so for about half a minute.

At last she asked:

'What do you want, sir?'

He murmured:

'I am Hautot Junior.'

She gave a start, turned pale, and stammered as if she had known him for a long while:

'Mr. Cæsar?'

'Yes.'

'And then?'

'I have something to say to you on behalf of my father.'

She said: 'Oh, my God!' and drew back so that he could enter. He shut the door and followed her.

Then he saw a little boy of four or five who was playing with a cat, sitting on the ground before a stove from which rose the steam of dishes being kept warm.

'Sit down,' she said.

He sat down. She asked:

'Well?'

He did not dare to say more, his eyes fixed on the table set in the middle of the room, with three places set, one of them a child's. He looked at the chair, turned back to the fire, the plate, the napkin, the glasses, the bottle of red wine opened, and the bottle of white wine intact. It was his father's place, back to the fire! He was expected. It was his bread that he saw, that he recognized beside the fork, for the crust had been taken off because of Hautot's bad teeth. Then, raising his eyes, he saw, on the wall, his own picture, the big photograph taken in Paris in the year of the exhibition, the same that was nailed over his bed in his bedroom at Ainville.

The young woman said again:

'Well, Mr. Cæsar?'

He looked at her. A spasm of anguish had made her livid, and she was waiting, her hands trembling with fear.

Then he dared to speak.

'Well, mademoiselle, daddy died on Sunday, opening the hunting.'

She was so overwhelmed that she did not move. After several moments of silence, she murmured in an almost inaudible voice:

'Oh, it 's not possible.'

Then suddenly, tears came to her eyes, and, raising her hands, she covered her face, and began to sob.

Then the boy turned his head, and seeing his mother in tears, howled; then, understanding that this sudden grief came from this unknown man, he rushed at Cæsar, seized his trousers with one hand, and with the other struck his thigh with all his force. And Cæsar remained bewildered, touched, between this woman who was weeping for his father, and this child who was defending his mother. He felt himself overcome by emotion, his eyes swollen by grief, and to save his face he began to speak.

'Yes,' he said, 'the misfortune happened on Sunday morning

about eight o'clock——' And he recounted, just as if she were listening, not forgetting a single detail, telling all the slightest things with a peasant's fondness for minutiæ. And the little boy went on striking him, kicking him this time on the ankles with his feet.

When he came to the moment when Hautot Senior had spoken of her, she heard her name, uncovered her face, and asked:

'Pardon me, I was not following you, I would very much like to know—if it wouldn't bother you to begin again.'

He began again in the same words:

'The misfortune happened on Sunday morning about eight o'clock——'

He told her everything, at length, with pauses, stops, reflections of his own from time to time. She listened greedily, seeing with her woman's nervous sensibility all the sudden twists of fortune that he recounted, and trembling with horror, ejaculating 'Oh, my God!' sometimes. The little boy, thinking her soothed, had stopped hitting Cæsar to take his mother's hand, and he was listening also as if he understood.

When the story was ended, Hautot Junior went on:

'Now we are to make an arrangement together, according to his wish. Listen, I am well off, he has left me property. I don't want you to have any complaints——'

But she interrupted him energetically:

'Oh, Mr. Cæsar, Mr. Cæsar, not to-day. My heart is bleeding—another time, another time. If I accept, listen—it is not for me. No, no, no, I swear it. It is for the boy. Besides, it can be settled on him.'

Then Cæsar, scared, guessed, and stammering:

'Then—it 's his—the boy?'

'Yes, of course!' she said.

And Hautot Junior looked at his brother with a confused, strong, painful emotion.

After a long silence, for she was weeping again, Cæsar, utterly ill at ease, spoke again:

'Well then, Mademoiselle Donet, I 'm going away. When would you like us to speak about it?'

She cried:

'Oh, no, don't go away, don't go away, don't leave me all alone with Émile. I would die of grief. I have nobody any more, nobody except my little boy. Oh! what wretchedness, what wretchedness, Mr. Cæsar! Here, sit down. You are going to talk to me again. You 'll tell me what he did, down there on the farm, all the week.'

And Cæsar sat down, accustomed to obeying.

She drew up, for herself, another chair near his, before the stove where the food was still simmering, took Émile on her knee, and asked Cæsar a thousand things about his father, intimate things in which you could see, in which he felt, without thinking about it, that she had loved Hautot with all her poor woman's heart.

And through the natural association of his rather limited ideas, he came back to the accident, and began to recount it with all the same details.

When he said, 'He had a hole in his stomach you could have put your two fists in', she uttered a sort of cry, and sobbed, and the tears rained again from her eyes. Then, seized by the contagion, Cæsar began to cry too, and as tears always soften the fibres of the heart, he leaned towards Émile, whose forehead was within reach of his mouth, and kissed him.

The mother, catching her breath, murmured:

'Poor little fellow, he 's an orphan.'

'I am too,' said Cæsar.

But suddenly, the practical instinct of the housewife, accustomed to think of everything, awoke in the young woman.

'You have maybe eaten nothing since the morning, Mr. Cæsar?'

'No, mademoiselle.'

'Ah! you must be hungry. You 're going to eat a morsel.'

'No, thanks,' he said, 'I 'm not hungry. I 'm in too great torment.'

She answered:

'In spite of sorrow, we must live. You won't refuse me that! And you will stay a little longer. When you are gone, I don't know what will become of me.'

He yielded, after some more resistance, and sitting with his back to the fire, opposite her, he ate a plateful of the tripe which was crackling on the stove, and drank a glass of red wine. But he did not allow her to uncork the white wine.

Several times he wiped the little boy's mouth, who had smeared all his chin with sauce.

As he rose to go away, he asked:

'When would you like me to come back to speak of our business, Mademoiselle Donet?'

'If it 's all the same to you, next Thursday, Mr. Cæsar. That way I would lose no time. I always have my Thursdays free.'

'That suits me, next Thursday.'

'You will come for lunch, won't you?'

'Oh, as to that, I can't promise.'

'Because it 's easier to talk eating. We 've more time too.'

'Oh, well, all right. Twelve o'clock, then.'

And he went away, after kissing little Émile again, and pressing Mademoiselle Donet's hand.

III

The week seemed long to Cæsar Hautot. He had never been alone, and the isolation appeared intolerable to him. Up to then he had lived beside his father, like his shadow, following him to the fields, surveying the execution of his orders, and when he had left him for some time, he found him again at dinner. They passed every evening smoking their pipes opposite one another, talking of horses, cows or sheep, and the handclasp which they exchanged at waking seemed the exchange of a deep family affection.

Now Cæsar was alone. He wandered through the autumn work in the fields, always expecting to see appear at the edge of the plain the tall gesticulating silhouette of his father. To kill the time, he went over to his neighbours, told the story of the accident to all those who had not heard it, repeated it sometimes to the others. Then, at the end of his occupations and his thoughts, he would sit at the side of the road, and ask himself if this kind of life was going to last a long time.

Often he thought of Mademoiselle Donet. He had found her satisfactory, a gentle, good woman as his father had said—yes, a fine woman, assuredly a fine woman. He was resolved to do the thing in style and to give her two thousand francs income on a capital settled on the child. He even felt a certain pleasure in thinking that he was going to see her again the following Thursday, and arrange that with her. And then the idea of this brother, of this little fellow of five, who was his father's son, worried him, annoyed him a little, and at the same time warmed his heart. It was a kind of family he had there in that little clandestine urchin who would never call himself Hautot, a family that he could take up or leave at his pleasure, but which recalled his father.

So when he found himself on the road to Rouen, on Thursday morning, borne on by the sonorous trot of Graindorge, he felt his heart lighter, more rested then it had been since his misfortune.

When he entered Mademoiselle Donet's flat, he saw the table laid as on the last Thursday, with the sole difference that the crust of the bread had not been cut off.

He grasped the young woman's hand, kissed Émile on the cheeks, and sat down, rather as if in his own house, with his heart full all the same. Mademoiselle Donet seemed to him a little thin, a little pale. She must have wept a great deal. Now her attitude towards him was constrained, as if she had realized what she had not felt the other week under the first shock of her misfortune, and she treated him with an excessive respect, a sad humility, and a touching solicitude, as if to repay him in attention and devotion the kindness he had shown her. They spent a long time over lunch, talking of the business which had brought him. She did not want so much money. It was too much, much too much. She earned enough to live on, but she wanted only that Émile should find a few pennies waiting for him when he grew big. Cæsar stuck to his ground, and even added a present of a thousand francs to her for her mourning.

When he had taken his coffee, she asked:

'You smoke?'

'Yes—I have my pipe.'

He felt in his pocket. Heavens, he had forgotten it! He was just going to get vexed about it, when she offered him a pipe of his father's, shut in a cupboard.

He accepted it, took it, recognized it, stroked it, proclaimed its quality with emotion in his voice, filled it with tobacco and lit it. Then he put Émile astride his leg, and gave him a horseback ride while she cleared the table and shut up in the bottom of the sideboard the dirty dishes, to be washed when he had gone.

About three o'clock he rose regretfully, quite upset at the idea of going away.

'Well, Mademoiselle Donet,' he said, 'I wish you good afternoon, and I 'm delighted to have found you like this.'

She stood still before him, red, very moved, and looking at him, thinking of the other.

'Are we never going to see one another again?' she said.

He answered simply:

'Of course, mademoiselle, if it gives you pleasure.'

'Certainly it does, Mr. Cæsar. Then next Thursday, does that suit you?'

'Yes, Mademoiselle Donet.'

'You 'll come to lunch, surely?'

'But—if you want me to, I shall not refuse.'

'That 's settled, Mr. Cæsar, next Thursday, at twelve o'clock, same as to-day.'

'Thursday, at twelve, Mademoiselle Donet.'

THE DESIRE TO BE A MAN

(*To M. Catulle Mendès*)

VILLIERS DE L'ISLE-ADAM

. . . that Nature might stand up
And say to all the world, 'This was a man!'
SHAKESPEARE: *Julius Cæsar*.

MIDNIGHT struck at the Bourse, beneath a sky crowded with stars. At this period the demands of martial law were still pressing on the citizens, and the waiters of the establishments still illuminated were hurrying to close down in accordance with the curfew regulations.

Along the boulevards, inside the great café, the gaslight butterflies of the chandeliers took quick flight, one by one, into the darkness. From without came the din of chairs being piled in fours on top of the marble tables; it was the psychological moment when every café-proprietor deems it fitting to point, with an arm ending in a napkin, the Caudine Forks of the low door to the last lingering clients.

On that Sunday, the melancholy wind of October was whistling. A few yellow leaves, dusky and rustling, sped past in the gusts, striking the stones, gliding along the asphalt, and then, like bats, vanished into the gloom, evoking as they did so the image of dreary days past beyond recall.

The theatres of the Boulevard du Crime, where during the evening all the Medicis, all the Salviatis, and all the Montefeltres had stabbed each other to their hearts' content, rose up like caverns of Silence, their dumb doors guarded by caryatides. Carriages and pedestrians became fewer as each minute passed. Here and there, the sceptical lantern of a ragpicker was already gleaming, like a phosphorescence given off by the piles of filth over which the creatures wandered.

Beneath a lamp-post at the Rue Hauteville, where the corner is occupied by a café of fairly pretentious appearance, stood a solitary passer-by, tall and of saturnine expression. His chin was clean-shaven, his movements recalled a man walking in his sleep, and on his long hair, turning grey, was set a felt hat of the Louis XIII style. His black gloves rested on an ivory-topped cane, and he was wrapped in an old royal-blue cloak, befurred with doubtful astrakhan. He had stopped, as if in mechanical hesitation to cross the causeway separating him from the Boulevard Bonne-Nouvelle.

Was this belated personage returning to his abode? Had he been brought to this street corner simply by the chance of a nocturnal stroll? It would have been hard to determine from his appearance. But suddenly, to his right, he caught sight of one of those mirrors, narrow and long as his own figure—the sort of public mirrors sometimes attached to the fronts of conspicuous taverns. He halted abruptly, placed himself directly opposite his reflection, and eyed himself with great deliberation from top to toe. Then, suddenly raising his hat with a sweep that recalled its antique mode, he saluted himself with marked courtesy.

His head, thus unexpectedly made visible, allowed one to recognize the famous tragedian Chaudval, originally Lepeinteur, styled Monanteuil, the scion of a very worthy family of St. Malo pilots, whom the mysterious ways of Destiny had led to become a great leading man of the provinces, a top-line name abroad, and a rival (frequently well-matched) of our Frédéric Lemaître.

Whilst he was thus contemplating himself with a sort of stupefaction, the waiters of the café hard by were helping on the overcoats of the last clients and reaching down their hats from the pegs; others were noisily turning out the contents of the nickel money-box and piling a circular heap of the day's coppers on a tray. This startled haste sprang from the ominous presence of two police officers who had suddenly appeared on the threshold and, with folded arms, were intimidating the dilatory proprietor with a cold stare.

Soon the shutters were bolted into their iron rests, with the exception of the mirrored panel, which, by a strange oversight, was omitted in the midst of the general flurry.

Then a deep silence fell over the boulevard. Chaudval alone, heedless of all this desolation, had stayed in his attitude of ecstasy on the pavement at the corner of the Rue Hauteville, in front of the public glass.

This livid, moon-like mirror apparently gave the artist the sensation which he would have experienced had he been bathing in a pond: for Chaudval was shivering.

Alas! we must face it! in this ruthless and mournful crystal, the actor had just unmistakably seen that age was creeping over him.

He observed that his hair, which yesterday had still been only sprinkled with grey, was now turning to silver. So that was the end of it! Farewell to curtain calls and floral tributes! Farewell to the roses of Thalia, to the laurels of Melpomene! There must be an end now, and for ever, with many a hand-shake and tear, to the Ellevious and the Laruettes, to the great style and the easy manners, to Dugazons and *ingénues*!

He must climb hurriedly down from the chariot of Thespis, and watch it pass on into the distance, carrying away his companions. And then—to see the tinsel and the streamers waving from it in the morning sun, even from the wheels, sports of the gladsome winds of Hope, and to watch them dis-appearing at the distant bend of the road, away into the dusk.

Abruptly aware of his fifty years (he was an excellent fellow), Chaudval sighed. A mist passed before his eyes; a kind of wintry fever seized him, and hallucination dilated the pupils of his eyes.

In the end, the haggard fixity of gaze wherewith he plumbed the depths of the providential mirror gave his pupils the faculty of magnifying objects and infusing them with solemnity—a state which physiologists have observed in persons affected by emotion of great intensity.

And so, beneath his eyes with their load of troubled and toneless ideas, the long mirror changed its aspect. Memories of childhood, of the beach and silvery tides, danced in his brain; and the mirror, doubtless on account of the stars, which lent a sense of depth to its surface, gave him at first the feeling of the calm waters of a land-locked bay. Then, expanding further, thanks to the old man's sighs, the glass took on the aspect of the sea and of night, those two ancient friends of hearts stricken by loneliness.

For a time he drugged himself with the vision. But the street lamp overhead, shining red behind him through the cold fog, seemed to him, when it was cast back to the depths of this fearsome glass, like the blood-coloured gleam of a lighthouse, pointing the track of shipwreck to the lost vessel of his future.

He shook off this nightmare, drew himself to the full height of his tall figure, and gave vent to a burst of false and bitter laughter which made the two policemen start, over there under the trees. Fortunately for the artist, the latter imagined it must be some stray drunkard, or some deceived lover perhaps, and continued their official progress without attributing any further importance to the unhappy Chaudval.

'Well, we must face it!' he said simply, in a low voice, like the condemned man, suddenly roused from sleep, who says to the hangman: 'I am at your service, sir!'

And straightway the old actor ventured forth into a monologue, with the stupefaction of mental prostration.

'I have acted prudently enough,' he went on, 'for I asked my good friend Mlle. Pinson (who has access to the Minister, and to his pillow as well) to obtain for me, between two passionate avowals, that post as lighthouse-keeper which my father enjoyed on the ocean coast. And stop! I see now the strange effect that street lamp produced on me in the mirror! It was my underlying thought.—The Pinson will be sending me my authorization, there 's no doubt. And then I shall retreat into my lighthouse like a rat in a cheese. I shall light the way for vessels afar off, away at sea. A lighthouse! It always strikes the note for a good background. I am alone in the world: decidedly, it is the most fitting asylum for my declining days.'

Suddenly Chaudval broke off his reverie.

'Ah, wait a moment!' he said, one hand feeling his chest beneath his cloak. 'That letter the postman brought just as I was coming out—it 's the answer, no doubt? Why, I was just going into the café to read it, and I forgot!—Really, I am breaking up!—Good! Here it is.'

Chaudval had just drawn a large envelope from his pocket.

He opened it, and there fell out a ministerial note which he picked up with feverish haste. He ran his eye through it under the red flame of the lamp-post.

'My lighthouse! My warrant!' he exclaimed. And 'Saved, ye gods above!' he added mechanically, as if from old habit, and in a falsetto so sudden, so different from his own, that he looked all round, imagining there must be some third party at hand.

'Come, keep calm, and . . . be a man!' he went on, after a moment.

But at those words, Esprit Chaudval, originally Lepeinteur, styled Monanteuil, stopped. It was as if he had been turned to a pillar of salt. The word seemed to have paralysed him.

'Eh?' he continued after a silence. 'What was that wish just now?—To be a Man?—And after all, why not?'

He folded his arms, plunged in reflection.

'For nearly half a century now I have been *representing*, I have been *playing*, the passions of others without even experiencing them. For, at bottom, I myself have never experienced anything. I am the likeness of these "others", but only in play, never in earnest! So I'm no more than a shadow? Passion—emotions—real acts—real—these are what constitute a Man properly so-called! Well, age forces me to return into Humanity, so I must needs obtain passions for myself, or some real emotion . . . since that's the *sine qua non* of any claim to the title of Man. There's honest logic for you: it's crammed full of sound sense!—So we must choose to experience something which will best accord with the nature I have at last brought back to life.'

He meditated awhile, and then went on in melancholy tones:

'Love? Too late.—Fame? I've known it.—Ambition? Leave that trumpery stuff to the politicians!'

Suddenly a cry broke from him:

'I've got it!' he said. '*Remorse!* That is something to go with my dramatic temperament.'

He looked at himself in the glass, assuming a face convulsed and contracted as if by some unearthly horror.

'That's it!' he concluded. 'Nero! Macbeth! Orestes! Hamlet! Herostratus! Ghosts—yes! I want to see *true* ghosts! My time's come! Just like all those people who had the luck never to be able to take one step without ghosts beside them.'

He struck his brow.

'But how? I'm as innocent as an unborn lamb.'

And, again pausing, he went on:

'Ah! Don't let that stand in the way! Where there's a will there's a way. I've ample right to become what I ought to be, and at any price. I've a right to my Humanity!—To experience remorse, you must have committed crimes? Well, a fig for crimes! What do they matter, so long as it 's . . . in a good cause?—Yes. . . . Very good!' (And he falls into a dialogue.) 'When?—At once. No putting off till to-morrow!—What crimes?—One only! But a great one, an extravagant, atrocious crime! One to bring all the Furies forth from Hell!—Which shall it be?—The most startling, by heaven! Bravo! I 've got it! A fire! Then I 'll just have time to start my fire—pack my trunks—come back, duly cowering behind the window of a cab—enjoy my triumph amid the horrified crowds—overhear the maledictions of the dying—and catch my westward train with remorse at my heels for the rest of my days! And then I shall be off to hide myself in my lighthouse! Up there in the light! Away out at sea! And consequently the police will never contrive to find me—my crime being disinterested! And I shall breathe my last there, alone.' Here Chaudval drew himself up, improvising a line of Corneille-like splendour:

'*Safe from suspicion by the crime's huge gleam!*

''Tis said.—And now,' concluded the great artist, picking up a cobblestone, and looking round to assure himself that he was alone, 'and now, you shall never reflect any other person!'

And he hurled the stone against the glass, which shivered into a thousand glittering fragments.

This first duty accomplished, Chaudval made off hurriedly—as if satisfied with this preliminary but energetic deed of daring. He hastened towards the boulevards. There, a few minutes later, a carriage stopped at his hail. He jumped into it, and disappeared.

A couple of hours later the leaping flames of an immense conflagration, bursting from great storehouses of petroleum, oils, and matches, were reflected from all the windows of the Temple quarter. Soon the detachments of firemen, rolling and pushing their apparatus, were rushing together from all directions, and the doleful blasts of their trumpets roused with a start all the inhabitants of this populous quarter. Countless hurrying footsteps were clattering on the pavements; the crowd was blocking the great square of the Château-d'Eau and the adjoining streets. In less than a quarter of an hour a body of troops was forming a cordon round the scene of the conflagration. By the blood-red glow of torches, policemen were controlling the floods of humanity in the neighbourhood.

Carriages were caught up, and could move no farther. Every

one was shouting. In amongst the terrible crackling of the fire, distant cries could be distinguished. The victims caught in this inferno were screaming, and the roofs of the houses were crashing in upon them. A hundred families, those of workmen belonging to the blazing factories, were made, alas! penniless and homeless.

But over there, a solitary cab, laden with two large trunks, was standing stationary behind the crowd halted in the square. Inside it was Esprit Chaudval, originally Lepeinteur, styled Monanteuil. And from time to time he drew aside the blind and contemplated his handiwork.

'Oh!' he whispered to himself, 'I feel myself a horror to God and to men!—Yes, that 's it, that really is the touch of a reprobate!'

The good old actor's face was glowing.

'Wretch that I am!' he grumbled. 'What vengeful nights of waking shall I know, beset by the phantoms of my victims! I can feel rising within me the soul of a Nero, burning Rome in an artist's frenzy! Of a Herostratus, burning the temple of Ephesus for love of fame! Of a Rostopchin, burning Moscow for love of country! Of an Alexander, burning Persepolis for the pleasing of his deathless Thaïs!—And I, I am burning for the sake of *Duty*, having no other means of *existence*!—I start a fire because I owe myself to myself! I acquit myself! What a Man I shall be! How I shall taste life! Yes, at last I am going to know what one feels when one is put to the torture!—And those nights I shall pass, nights of delight, of magnificent horror!—Ah!—I breathe again! I am born anew! I exist! And to think I have been an actor! Now, we must make off, with the speed of the lightning: in the gross eyes of mankind, I am no more than food for the gallows! Come, we must lock ourselves into our lighthouse, and enjoy remorse in peace!'

Two days later, in the evening, Chaudval had arrived at his destination and taken possession of his old and deserted lighthouse, situated on our western coast: a flame long unused, on a ruined building, which ministerial compassion had brought back to life for him.

The light itself could hardly be of any use whatever: it was a work of supererogation, a sinecure, a dwelling with a flame on top of it, with which everybody, save for the solitary exception of Chaudval, could dispense.

So the worthy tragedian, having brought thither his bed, some food, and a great mirror in which to study his facial effects, immediately shut himself up in it, away from the threat of any human suspicion.

Around him moaned the ocean, wherein the ancient abyss of the heavens bathed all its starry clarity. He watched the tides flinging themselves against his tower before the gusts of wind, rather as the Stylite could contemplate the sands swirling against his column before the breath of the desert wind.

With every moment that passed, the dreamer forgot his conflagration.—He climbed up and down the stone staircase.

On the evening of the third day, Lepeinteur was seated in his room, sixty feet above the waves, reading once again a Paris newspaper which recounted the story of the great catastrophe of the night before. 'An unknown malefactor had flung a few matches into the petroleum vaults. A phenomenal conflagration, which had kept up the firemen and residents of the neighbouring districts all through the night, had manifested itself in the Temple quarter.'

Close on one hundred victims had perished. Hapless families had been plunged into the direst necessity.

The whole of the square was in mourning, and still smoking.

Nothing was known of the identity of the criminal who had committed this crime; and still less could be imagined as to his motive.

As he read, Chaudval leapt for joy, and rubbed his hands excitedly, exclaiming:

'What a success! What a marvellous criminal I am! Shall I ever be haunted enough? What ghosts I shall see! I knew well that I should become a Man! Ah, the method was a hard one, I 'll admit—but it had to be done! It had to be done!'

And looking again at the Paris paper, Chaudval saw mention of a benefit performance to be given on behalf of the sufferers.

'Ah!' he murmured, 'I ought to have lent the assistance of my talent for the benefit of my victims! That would have been my farewell performance! I would have declaimed *Orestes*. I 'd have been very convincing. . . .'

Thereupon, Chaudval began life in his lighthouse.

And the evenings fell, came one upon the other; and the nights.

One thing happened which stupefied the artist. Something atrocious!

Contrary to all his hopes and anticipations, his conscience gave no murmur of remorse. Not one ghost showed itself! He experienced *nothing—absolutely nothing!*

He could not believe the silence. He could not get over it.

And from time to time he looked in the mirror, but his head had not altered its complacent aspect! In a fury, he rushed to his lantern, and falsified its lights in a glowing hope of sinking some far-off vessel, so as to help, to quicken, to stimulate this mutinous remorse, to awaken the ghost!

Useless toil!

Fruitless attempts! Vain efforts! He experienced *nothing*. Not one menacing phantom did he behold. He no longer slept, so heavily did despair and *shame* weigh him down.—So much so that one night he was stricken in his light-giving solitude by a cerebral congestion, and fell into a fit, wherein he cried aloud, to the sound of the sea, and with the great ocean winds smiting his tower lost there in the infinite:

'Ghosts—for the love of God, ghosts! Let me see just one ghost! *I've well deserved it!*'

The God whom he invoked did not vouchsafe him this grace. And the old actor expired, still proclaiming with all its futile emphasis his great desire to set eyes on the ghosts, *and never once seeing that what he was seeking was simply—himself.*

Translated by HAMISH MILES.

THE FLAX POUNDER

Ernest Renan

The General Hospital, so called because illness, old age, and wretchedness chose it for their meeting place, was an enormous building, covering, like all old constructions, a great deal of space, and lodging a very few people. Before the door was a little pent-roof where, when it was fine, the convalescent, and the able-bodied gathered together. In fact, the hospital did not only house those who were sick; it included also poor folks, handed over to public charity, and even guests who for an insignificant capital lived there in a mean fashion, but without care. All that company used to come, at each ray of the sun, to the shade of the pent-roof, and seat themselves on old straw-bottomed chairs. It was the most lively spot in the little town. As we passed, my friend Guyomar and I, we greeted them and received their greeting: for though we were very young, we were already considered as being in Holy Orders. That seemed natural to us: one thing alone excited our surprise. Although we were too inexperienced to see in it anything that might have been inferred from a knowledge of life, there was among the poor folk at the hospital, one person before whom we never passed without a certain astonishment.

This was an old maid of forty-five, wearing on her head a large hood of a shape impossible to classify. Usually she was almost motionless, with a sombre, distracted air, her eyes lustreless and fixed. When she saw us those dead eyes came to life. She followed us with a strange look, sometimes gentle and sad, sometimes hard and almost ferocious. Turning round, we would find her expression cruel and angry. We looked at each other without comprehension. This interrupted our conversation and threw a cloud over our gaiety. She did not make us precisely afraid. She was considered mad: now, madmen in those days were not treated in the cruel way that administrative custom has invented since. Far from shutting them up, they were allowed to wander about all day. The village of Tréguier had usually a great number of madmen: like all dreamy races, who wear themselves out in the pursuit of an ideal, the Bretons of those parts, when they are not sustained by an energetic will, slip too easily into a state intermediate between drunkenness and madness, which is often only the aberrations of an unsatisfied heart.

The madwoman of the General Hospital spoke to nobody. Nobody gave her a thought; her story was evidently forgotten. She never said a single word to us: but her wild haggard eyes affected us profoundly, disturbed us. I have often thought since of this enigma without being able to explain it. I found the key to it eight years ago when my mother, who had reached the age of eight-five without infirmities, was smitten with a cruel illness which slowly undermined her.

My mother belonged by her sentiments and memories altogether to this old world. She spoke Breton admirably, and knew all the sailors' proverbs, and a crowd of things that no one in the world knows to-day. Everything in her was knit to the people, and her native wit gave a surprising life to the long stories which she told and which she was almost the only one to remember.

One day the conversation turned on the General Hospital. She told me all its history.

'And that madwoman,' I said to her, 'who was usually sitting under the pent-roof, and who frightened Guyomar and me?'

She thought a moment to recollect of whom I spoke, and went on briskly.

'Ah, that woman, my son, was the daughter of the flax pounder.'

'What 's a flax pounder?'

'I have never told you that story. You see, my boy, that isn't understood nowadays: it 's a story of too long ago. Since I have come to this parish of yours, there are things I dare not speak of . . . These country nobility were so respected! I have always considered that they were the real nobles. Ah! if I said that to these Parisians they would laugh. They recognize nothing but their own Paris; I find them fundamentally limited. No, you cannot realize any more how those old country nobles were looked up to, though they were poor.'

She stopped a little while and then went on.

'You remember the little village of Trédarzec, whose steeple we could see from the turret of our house? Less than a quarter of a league from the village, made up at that time almost entirely of the church, the village hall and the parsonage, rose the manor-house of Kermelle. It was a manor-house like so many others, a well-kept farm, old in appearance, surrounded by a long high wall of a beautiful grey colour. The courtyard was approached by a large arched gate surmounted by a tiled roof, at the side of which was a smaller door for everyday use. A dovecot, a turret, two or three well-built windows, almost like church windows, indicated a nobleman's house, one of those old castles which were inhabited before the revolution by a class of people whose character and habits it is nowadays impossible to imagine.

'These country nobles were peasants like the others, but chiefs of the others. In old times there was only one of them in each parish; they were the leaders of the population: no one contested their right, and they were accorded great honour. But already, about the time of the Revolution, they had become scarce. The peasants considered them as the lay chiefs of the parish, as the priest was the ecclesiastical chief. The one who lived at Trédarzec, about whom I am telling you, was a fine old man, tall and vigorous, like a young man, with a frank honest face. He wore his hair long, held up by a comb, and only let it down on Sundays when he was taking communion. I see him still (he used to come to our house at Tréguier), serious, grave, rather sad, for he was the only one of his kind. These petty pedigreed nobility had disappeared for the most part: the rest had long ago gone to live in town. All the countryside adored him. He had a pew set apart for him in church: every Sunday he was seen there, seated in the first row of the faithful, with his old-fashioned attire and his ceremonial gloves, which reached almost to his elbow. At the moment of communion he started at the bottom of the choir, loosened his hair, laid his gloves on a little credence table set ready for him near the screen, and crossed the choir, alone, without abating a jot of his high carriage. Nobody went to the communion table until he was back in his place, and until he had finished pulling on his gauntlets again.

'He was very poor: but he hid it as a duty to his rank. Those country nobility had formerly certain privileges which helped them to live a little differently from the peasants: all that had gone with the times. Kermelle was in very embarrassed circumstances. His rank as a nobleman forbade him to work in the fields: he shut himself up in his house all day, and busied himself behind closed doors with an occupation which did not require open air. When flax is soaked it has to undergo a sort of decortication which only permits the textile fibre to remain. It was this task in which poor Kermelle considered he could engage without loss of dignity. No one saw him: professional honour was saved; but everybody knew it, and as in those days everybody had a nickname, he was soon known in the countryside under the name of the *flax pounder*. This nickname, as usually is the case, took the place of his real name, and it was in this fashion that he was universally designated.

'He was like a living patriarch. You would laugh if I told you what it was with, that the flax pounder supplemented the insufficient remuneration of his poor little trade. People believed that, as chief, he was the depositary of the power of his blood, that he possessed in a high degree the gifts of his race, and that he could, by means of his saliva and the touch of his hands, raise it up when it was weakened. They were persuaded that, to accomplish cures of this kind, an enormous number of quarterings of nobility were needed, and he alone had them. His house was surrounded, on certain days, by people come from twenty leagues round about. When a child was late in walking, with feeble limbs, it was brought to him. He moistened his finger in his saliva, traced this anointing on the child's loins which were thereby strengthened. What do you expect? People had faith in those days: men were so simple and so good! For nothing in the world would he have expected payment, and since the people who came, were too poor to pay the debt in money, they would offer him as a present a dozen eggs, a bit of fat bacon, a handful of linen, a basketful of potatoes, a pat of butter, some fruit. He accepted. The town nobility jeered at him, but they were very wrong. He knew the countryside: he was the soul and the incarnation of it.

'At the time of the Revolution, he emigrated to Jersey: one doesn't quite see why; certainly no one would have done him any harm, but the nobility of Tréguier said to him that the king commanded it, and he went away with the others. He returned early, found his old house, which no one had wanted to occupy, in the state he had left it. At the time of the indemnities people tried to persuade him that he had lost something, and that there was more than one good reason for putting in a claim. The other nobles were annoyed at seeing him so poor, and would have liked to give him a hand; this simple soul did not enter into the arguments that they put before him. When they asked him to declare what he had lost. "I had nothing," he said, "I couldn't have lost anything." Nobody succeeded in getting any other answer from him, and he remained poor as before.

'His wife died, I think, in Jersey. He had a daughter, who was born about the time of the emigrations. She was a fine looking, big girl (you have only seen her withered); she had nature's own sap, a splendid complexion, pure strong blood. She ought to have been married young, but it was impossible. These bankrupt little nobles of a little town who are good for nothing, and who are not worth a quarter of the old country nobility, would have nothing to do with her for their sons. His principles prevented him from marrying her to a peasant. The poor girl stayed thus, hung up like a soul in torment. She had no place here below. Her father was the last of his race, and she seemed wantonly cast on the earth, and could find there no corner to shelter in. She was good tempered and docile. She was a beautiful body, almost without a soul. Instinct in her was everything. She would have been an excellent mother. In default of marriage, she should have been made a nun: rules and austerities would have calmed her: but it is probable that the father was not rich enough to pay the dowry to the church, and his position did not allow of his making her a lay sister. Poor girl! cast into the wrong road, she was condemned to perish there.

'She was born upright and good, she had never any doubt as to her duty: she had no other fault than that of having blood and veins. No young man of the village would have dared to be indiscreet with her, so much her father was respected. The feeling of her superiority kept her from turning to the young peasants: for them, she was a lady: they did not think of her. The poor girl lived thus in an absolute solitude. There was nobody in the house except a young boy of twelve or thirteen, a nephew of Kermelle, whom the latter had received into his house, and whom the vicar, worthy man that he was, taught what he knew: Latin.

'The church was the sole diversion of the poor child. She was pious by nature, although too little intelligent to understand anything of the mysteries of our religion. The vicar, a good priest, very attached to his duties, had for the flax pounder the respect which was his due; the hours which were left over from his breviary and the cares of his ministry, were passed at the latter's house. He educated the young nephew; for the girl he had those reserved manners which our Breton ecclesiastics have with "persons of the sex" as they call them. He greeted her, asked how she was getting on, but never talked with her if it were not about insignificant matters. The wretched girl fell in love with him deeper and deeper. The vicar was the only person of her own rank that she saw, if it is permissible to talk like that. This young priest was, besides that, a very attractive person. Along with the exquisite modesty which his whole outward appearance breathed, he had a sad, resigned, discreet air. You felt that he had a heart and feelings, but that a principle more lofty dominated them, and was transformed in him to something higher. You know the infinite charm of some of our good Breton ecclesiastics. Women feel that very keenly. This invincible attachment to a vow, which is in its way a homage to their power, emboldens them, attracts them, flatters them. The priest becomes for them a safe brother who has laid aside, because of them, his sex and its joys. Thence springs a sentiment in which is mingled confidence, pity, regret, gratitude. Let the priest marry, and you will destroy one of the most necessary elements, one of the most delicate graduations, of our society. The women will protest; for there is only one thing which a woman sets even above being loved, that is, that importance should be attached to love. Women are never more flattered than in showing them that they are feared. The Church, in imposing chastity as the first duty of its ministers, caresses feminine vanity in its most tender spot.

'So the poor girl was seized with a deep love for the vicar, which soon took possession of her entire being. The virtuous and mystic race to which she belonged does not know the frenzy which overturns obstacles, and which accounts it to have nothing if it has not all. Oh, she was content with really very little. If he should only acknowledge her existence, she would have been happy. She did not ask a look from him: a thought would have sufficed. The vicar was naturally her confessor; there was no other priest in the parish. The customs of the Catholic confessional, so beautiful but so dangerous, strangely excited her imagination. Once a week, on Saturday, it was an inexpressible sweetness for her to be half an hour alone with him, as if face to face with God, to see him, to feel him filling his role of God, to breathe his breath, to undergo the sweet humiliation of his reprimands, of telling him her most intimate thoughts, her scruples, her apprehensions. Yet you must not think that she abused it. Very rarely does a pious woman dare to use the confessional for a love confidence. She may enjoy it greatly; she risks giving herself up to feelings which are not without danger; but the fact that such feelings are always a little mystic, is irreconcilable with the horror of sacrilege. In any case our poor girl was so shy, that the words would have died on her lips. Her passion was a silent, intimate, devouring fire. Feeling like that, to see him every day, him, handsome, young, always busied with his majestic functions, officiating with dignity amid a people bent before him, minister, judge, and director of her own soul! It was too much. The unhappy child's head could not stand it; she lost her way. Disorders, more and more serious, arose in this strong organism which could not tolerate being turned from its path. Her old father attributed to a certain weakness of mind that which was the result of the inner ravages of impossible dreams in a heart which love had pierced from side to side.

'Like an impetuous river which, meeting an insurmountable obstacle, renounces its direct course and twists aside, the poor girl, having no means of telling her love to the man she loved, fell back on trifles. To hold his attention an instant, not to be any chance comer in his eyes, to be allowed to do him little services, to be able to imagine that she was useful to him: that was enough for her. "My God, who knows?" she could say to herself, "he is a man after all: perhaps in his heart he is touched, and is only held back by the discipline of his calling." All these efforts met an iron barrier, a wall of ice. The vicar did not swerve from an absolute coldness. She was the daughter of the man he respected the most; but she was a woman. Oh!

if he had avoided her, if he had treated her roughly, that would have been a triumph for her, and a proof that she had touched his heart; but this uniform politeness, this resolution not to see the most obvious signs of love, was something terrible. He did not reprove her, he did not hide from her: he did not depart from the unshakeable decision he had made of not admitting her existence except as an abstraction.

'At the end of some time, this became a cruelty. Repulsed, desperate, the poor girl fell ill; her eyes wandered, but she kept guard on herself; in its entirety nobody saw her secret, she ate her heart out alone. "What!" she would say to herself, "Shall I not be able to arrest his glance for a moment? He will not admit to me that I exist? I shall be for him, whatever I do, only a shadow, a phantom, a soul, along with a hundred others? His love, that would be too much to desire: but his attention, his looks? To be his equal, he so clever, so near to God, I would know not to lay claim to that: to be a mother by him, oh, that would be a sacrilege: but to be his, to be a Martha to him, the first of his servants, charged with the modest duties which I am quite fit for, and in that way have all in common with him, all, that is to say, his house, that which matters to the humble woman who has not been initiated to higher thoughts, oh, that would be paradise!"

'She stayed whole afternoons motionless, seated in her chair, enchained to this fixed idea. She saw him, imagined herself with him, surrounding him with attentions, looking after his home, kissing the hem of his robe. She repelled those insensate dreams: but, after giving herself up to them for hours, she was pale, half dead. She existed no longer for those who surrounded her. Her father ought to have seen it: but what could the simple old man do against an evil, the very thought of which his honest soul could not conceive?

'Things continued so for perhaps a year. It is probable that the vicar noticed nothing; our priests live in this respect so conventionally, in a sort of resolution not to see anything. This admirable chastity only excited the imagination of the poor child. Love in her case became a cult, a pure adoration, an exaltation. She found thus a relative repose. Her imagination led her towards inoffensive games; she liked to tell herself that she was working for him, that she was busy doing something for him. She was at the stage of dreaming while wide awake, of executing like a somnambulist acts of which she was only half aware. Night and day she had only one thought; she saw herself serving him, caring for him, counting his linen, busy with all the things that were too far beneath him for him to think about. All these chimæras finished by taking shape, and led her to a strange act which cannot be explained except by the state of madness in which she decidedly had been for some time.'

What follows, in fact, will be incomprehensible if one does not keep in one's mind certain traits of the Breton character. What is most peculiar among the peoples of Brittany is their attitude to love. Love among them is a tender, deep, affectionate sentiment, much more than a passion. It is an inner voluptuousness which wears out and kills. Nothing is more unlike the fire of the southern peoples. The paradise they dream of is fresh, green, without transports. No race can count so many deaths from love: suicide is rare: what predominates is slow consumption. The case occurs frequently among the young Breton conscripts. Incapable of finding distraction in vulgar, venal attachments, they succumb to a sort of indeterminate languor. Homesickness is only the outward manifestation: the truth is that love with them is associated in an indissoluble way with the village, the church steeple, the evening angelus-bell, the cherished countryside. The passionate southerner kills his rival, kills the object of his passion. The sentiment we are speaking of kills only him who feels it, and that is why the Breton race is a race that has no difficulty in being chaste: through its fine lively imagination it creates for itself an aerial world which suffices. The true poetry of such a love is the Spring song of the Song of Songs, an admirable poem, much more voluptuous than passionate. 'Hiems transiit: imber abiit et recessit; vox turturis audita est in terra nostra. Surge, amica mea, et veni!' 'For lo! the winter is past, the rain is over and gone; the voice of the turtle is heard in our land. Arise, my love, my fair one, and come away.'

My mother continued thus:

'Everything is at bottom only a great illusion, and what proves it, is that, in many cases, nothing is easier than to dupe nature by mimicry which it cannot distinguish from reality. I shall never forget how the daughter of Marzin, the miller of the Grande Rue, insane too through suppression of the maternal feelings, took a faggot, swaddled it in rags, put a kind of baby's bonnet on it, and then spent days cuddling it in her arms, this fictitious doll, rocking it to sleep, pressing it to her heart, covering it with kisses. When it was put in the evening in a cradle beside her, she rested quietly till next morning. There are instincts for which the outward appearance is sufficient, and which can be lulled by fictions. Thus the poor Kermelle girl succeeded in realizing her dreams, by doing what she dreamed of. What she dreamed of was life in common with the man she loved, and the life that she shared in spirit was naturally not the life of the priest, it was the life of the house. The poor girl was made for the marriage state. Her madness was a sort of domestic madness, a thwarted housewife's instinct. She imagined her paradise realized, in seeing herself keeping the house of the man she loved, and since now she did not distinguish very clearly her dreams from reality, she was led to an unbelievable aberration. What of it? These poor madwomen prove by their disorders the holy laws of nature and their inevitability.

'Her days were spent in hemming linen, and marking it. Now, in her thoughts, this linen was destined for the house she imagined, for this common nest where she would have passed her life at the feet of the man she adored. The hallucination went so far that she marked those sheets, those napkins, with the vicar's initials: nay, often the vicar's initials were mingled with her own. She was clever at these petty woman's tasks. Her needle went in and out, in and out ceaselessly and for delicious hours she sat spinning, wrapped in her heart's dreams, believing that he and she were but one. Thus she duped her passion, and found moments of voluptuousness which satisfied her for days on end.

'The weeks flowed by in this way, in tracing stitch by stitch the letters of the name she loved, marrying it with her own; and this pastime was for her a great consolation. Her hands were always busy for him; these linens sewed by her seemed to be her own self. They would be near him, would touch him, would serve his needs; they would be herself beside him. What joy there was in such a thought! She would be always without him, it is true; but the impossible is the impossible. She would get as near him as was permitted. For a year she savoured thus in imagination her poor little happiness. Alone, her eyes fixed on her work, she was a creature of another world, believing herself his wife in the feeble compass of probability. Hours glided by with a motion slow as her needle: her poor imagination was comforted. And then, she had sometimes some hope: perhaps he would let himself be touched, perhaps a tear would escape him when he discovered this surprise, this mark of so great a love. "He will see how I love him; he will think that it is sweet to be together." Thus she lost herself for days in her dreams, which usually ended in fits of complete prostration.

'At last the day came when the set of linen was complete. What to do with it? The idea of forcing him to accept a set, to be her debtor in something, took possession of her absolutely.

'She wanted, if I dare say so, to steal his thanks, violently to force him to be obliged to her for something. That is what she imagined. It had no common sense in it, it was a trick easily found out: but her reason was asleep, and for a long time now she had only followed the will-o'-the-wisps of her disordered imagination.

'It was the time of the Christmas festival. After the midnight Mass the vicar had a custom of receiving at his vicarage the mayor and the notables of the village, and serving them a light repast. The vicarage was joined to the church. Besides the principal entrance on the village square, it had two exits: one leading to the inside of the vestry, and so putting the church and the priest in communication: the other, at the end of the garden, led into the fields. The manor-house of Kermelle was about a quarter of a league away. To save the young lad who came to take lessons from the vicar a detour, he had been given the key of this back door. The poor possessed girl secured this key during the midnight Mass, and entered the vicarage. The vicar's servant, so as to be able to go to the Mass, had laid the table beforehand. Our mad girl rapidly took off all the linen and hid it in the manor-house.

'When the people came out from Mass, the theft was discovered at once. The excitement was extreme. First of all they were greatly astonished that only the linen had disappeared. The vicar did not want to send his guests away without their repast. At the moment when the embarrassment was most acute, the girl appeared.

'Oh, this time, you will accept our services, sir. In a quarter of an hour our linen will be brought to your house.'

'Old Kermelle added his entreaties, and the vicar agreed, not suspecting, naturally, such a refinement of duplicity in a creature who was supposed to have only the most limited intelligence.

'Next day, they thought over this peculiar theft. There was no trace of house-breaking. The principal door of the vicarage and that of the garden were untouched, shut as they should have been. As to the idea that the key entrusted to Kermelle could have served for the execution of the theft, an idea of this kind would have seemed extravagant; it occurred to nobody. There remained the door of the vestry; it seemed obvious that the theft could only have been accomplished through that. The sacristan had been seen in the church all the time of the service. The vestry-woman, on the other hand, had been absent on several occasions; she had been to the fireplace of the vestry to get charcoal for the censers; she had attended to two or three other little matters: suspicion, then, fell on her. She was an excellent woman; her guilt appeared superlatively improbable: but what was to be done against overwhelming coincidences? People couldn't get away from this reasoning: the thief came in by the vestry door; now the vestry-woman alone could have gone through that door, and it is proved that in reality she did go through it: she admits it herself.

'At that time the idea was too often yielded to that it was right that every crime should be followed by an arrest. That gave a great idea of the extraordinary sagacity of justice, of the promptitude with which it surveyed and the sureness with which it seized on the scent of a crime. The innocent woman was taken away on foot between two policemen. The effect of the police, when they arrived in the village with their glittering arms and their fine leather straps, was immense. Everybody wept; the vestry-woman alone remained calm, and told them all that she was certain her innocence would be brought to light.

'In fact, next day or the day after, the impossibility of the supposition that had been made was recognized. The third day the villagers hardly dared to accost one another. Everybody in fact had the same thought, and did not dare to utter it. This thought seemed to them at once obvious and absurd: it is the flax pounder's key which alone could have been used for the theft. The vicar avoided going out so as not to have to give voice to a suspicion which obsessed him. Up till then he had not examined the linen which had been substituted for his own. His eyes fell by chance on the markings: he was astonished, reflected sadly, could not account for the mystery of the two letters, so impossible was it to divine the queer hallucinations of a poor madwoman.

'He was plunged in the most gloomy thoughts when he saw the flax pounder enter, pulled up to his full height, and paler than death. The old man remained standing, then burst into tears.

'"It is she," he said, "oh! the unfortunate girl! I ought to have watched her more, entered more into her thoughts; but she was always melancholic and she eluded me."

'He revealed the mystery: a moment afterwards, the linen that had been stolen was brought back to the vestry.

'The poor girl, because of her lack of sense, had hoped that the scandal would die down and that she would quietly enjoy her little loving stratagem. The arrest of the vestry-woman and the excitement which followed it spoiled all her plan. If the moral sense had not been as completely obliterated in her as it was, she would have thought of nothing but freeing the vestry-woman; but she scarcely thought of it. She was plunged in a sort of stupor which had nothing in common with remorse. What crushed her was the obvious miscarriage of her attack on the mind of the vicar. Any other mind than that of a priest would have been touched by the revelation of such a violent love. The vicar remained unaffected. He forbade himself to think of the extraordinary episode, and, as soon as he clearly saw the innocence of the vestry-woman, he slept, said his Mass and his breviary with the same calm as on any other day.

'The blunder that had been made in arresting the vestry-woman was seen then in its enormity. Without that the affair could have been hushed up. It had not been a real theft: but, after an innocent woman had spent several days in prison for an act qualified as a theft, it was very difficult to leave the real criminal unpunished. Her madness was not obvious: one must admit that this madness was only an inner thing. Before this, it had not occurred to anybody that Kermelle's daughter was mad. Externally she was like everybody else, except for her almost complete speechlessness. The excuse of mental alienation, then, could be contested: besides, the true explanation was so queer, so unbelievable that they hardly dared to bring it forward. Madness not being alleged, the fact of having let the vestry-woman be arrested, was unpardonable. If the theft had only been a game, the author of the joke ought to have cut it short as soon as a third person was its victim. The wretched girl was arrested and taken to St. Brieuc for the Assizes. She did not emerge a moment from her complete prostration; she seemed out of the world. Her dream was finished: the kind of chimæra that she had cherished for some time and which had sustained her, had fallen flat; it existed no longer. Her state had nothing violent about it; it was a mournful silence; then doctors came and judged her with discernment.

At the Assizes, the case was quickly heard. Not a single word could be drawn from her. The flax pounder entered, upright and firm, his face resigned. He approached the prætorian table, and there laid down his gloves, his cross of St. Louis, his sash.

'"Gentlemen," he said, "I can take them up again only if you tell me to. It is she who has done this, and yet she is not a thief. She is ill."

'The good man burst into tears: he suffocated.

'"That 's enough, that 's enough", was heard from all sides. The solicitor-general showed tact, and without making a speech on a case of erotic aberration, he dropped the accusation.

'The deliberation of the jury was not long either. Every one wept. When the acquittal was pronounced, the flax pounder took his insignia, retired rapidly, taking his daughter with him, and returned to the village by night.

'Amid this public scandal the vicar could not avoid learning the truth on a host of points he had hid from himself. He was not affected by them. The obvious facts about which all the world was talking, he feigned to ignore. He did not ask to be removed, the bishop did not dream of proposing it. One would imagine that the first time he saw Kermelle and his daughter, he felt some emotion. He felt none. He betook himself to the manor-house at the hour when he knew he should meet father and daughter.

'"You have gravely sinned," he said to her, "less by your madness, which God will forgive you, than in letting this very good woman be put in prison. An innocent woman, by your fault, has been treated for several days like a thief. The most honest woman of this parish has been led away by the police in the sight of all men. You owe her reparation. On Sunday the vestry-woman will be in her pew, in the last row, near the door of the church: at the *credo* you will go up to her, and you will lead her by the hand to your seat of honour which she deserves to occupy more than you."

'The poor mad girl did mechanically what was enjoined. She was no longer a being with feeling. After this time the flax pounder and his family were hardly seen any more. The manor-house had become a sort of tomb whence no sign of life was heard to issue.

'The vestry-woman died first. The excitement had been too strong for this simple woman. She had not for a moment doubted Providence; but all that had shaken her. She weakened little by little: she was a saint.

'The old man lived a few years longer, dying inch by inch, always shut up in his house, no longer talking to the vicar. He went to the church, but he no longer sat in his pew. He was so strong that he held out eight or ten years against this mournful agony.

'His walks were limited to taking a few steps under the high lime-trees which shaded the manor-house. Now, one day, he saw on the horizon something unusual. It was the tricolour flag which floated on the church tower of Tréguier: the July Revolution had just taken place. When he learned that the king had gone away, he understood more than ever that he had belonged to the end of a world. The professional duty to which he had sacrificed everything, became objectless: he did not regret being attached to too high an ideal of duty: he did not think that he might have enriched himself like the rest: but he lost faith in everything, except in God. The Carlist party at Tréguier went about repeating everywhere that this would not last, that the legitimate king would come back. He smiled at these foolish predictions. He died soon after, succoured by the vicar, who explained to him this beautiful passage that is read in the Service for the Dead:

'"Be not as the heathen, who have no hope."

'After his death his daughter was left without means of support. An arrangement was come to that she should be placed in the hospital. It is there that you saw her. Now, doubtless she is dead too, and others have occupied her bed in the General Hospital.'

CRAINQUEBILLE

Anatole France

I

In every sentence pronounced by a judge in the name of the sovereign people, dwells the whole majesty of justice. The august character of that justice was brought home to Jérôme Crainquebille, costermonger, when, accused of having insulted a policeman, he appeared in the police court. Having taken his place in the dock, he beheld in the imposing sombre hall magistrates, clerks, lawyers in their robes, the usher wearing his chains, *gendarmes*, and, behind a rail, the bare heads of the silent spectators. He, himself, occupied a raised seat, as if some sinister honour were conferred on the accused by his appearance before the magistrate. At the end of the hall, between two assessors, sat President Bourriche. The palm-leaves of an officer of the Academy decorated his breast. Over the tribune were a bust representing the Republic and a crucifix, as if to indicate that all laws divine and human were suspended over Crainquebille's head. Such symbols naturally inspired him with terror. Not being gifted with a philosophic mind, he did not inquire the meaning of the bust and the crucifix; he did not ask how far Jesus and the symbolical bust harmonized in the Law Courts. Nevertheless, here was matter for reflection; for, after all, pontifical teaching and canon law are in many points opposed to the constitution of the Republic and to the civil code. So far as we know the Decretals have not been abolished. To-day, as formerly, the Church of Christ teaches that only those powers are lawful to which it has given its sanction. Now the French Republic claims to be independent of pontifical power. Crainquebille might reasonably say:

'Gentlemen and magistrates, insomuch as President Loubet has not been anointed, the Christ, whose image is suspended over your heads, repudiates you through the voice of councils and of Popes. Either he is here to remind you of the rights of the Church, which invalidate yours, or His presence has no rational signification.'

Whereupon President Bourriche might reply:

'Prisoner Crainquebille, the kings of France have always quarrelled with the Pope. Guillaume de Nogaret was excommunicated, but for so trifling a reason he did not resign his office. The Christ of the tribune is not the Christ of Gregory VII or of Boniface VIII. He is, if you will, the Christ of the Gospels, who knew not one word of canon law, and had never heard of the holy Decretals.'

Then Crainquebille might not without reason have answered:

'The Christ of the Gospels was an agitator. Moreover, he was the victim of a sentence, which for nineteen hundred years all Christian peoples have regarded as a grave judicial error. I defy you, Monsieur le Président, to condemn me in His name to so much as forty-eight hours' imprisonment.'

But Crainquebille did not indulge in any considerations either historical, political or social. He was wrapped in amazement. All the ceremonial, with which he was surrounded, impressed him with a very lofty idea of justice. Filled with reverence, overcome with terror, he was ready to submit to his judges in the matter of his guilt. In his own conscience he was convinced of his innocence; but he felt how insignificant is the conscience of a costermonger in the face of the panoply of the law, and the ministers of public prosecution. Already his lawyer had half persuaded him that he was not innocent.

A summary and hasty examination had brought out the charges under which he laboured.

II. Crainquebille's Misadventure

Up and down the town went Jérôme Crainquebille, costermonger, pushing his barrow before him and crying: 'Cabbages! Turnips! Carrots!' When he had leeks he cried: 'Asparagus!' For leeks are the asparagus of the poor. Now it happened that on October 20, at noon, as he was going down the Rue Montmartre, there came out of her shop the shoemaker's wife, Madame Bayard. She went up to Crainquebille's barrow and scornfully taking up a bundle of leeks, she said:

'I don't think much of your leeks. What do you want a bundle?'

'Sevenpence halfpenny, mum, and the best in the market!'

'Sevenpence halfpenny for three wretched leeks?'

And disdainfully she cast the leeks back into the barrow.

Then it was that Constable 64 came and said to Crainquebille: 'Move on.'

Moving on was what Crainquebille had been doing from morning till evening for fifty years. Such an order seemed right to him, and perfectly in accordance with the nature of things. Quite prepared to obey, he urged his customer to take what she wanted.

'You must give me time to choose,' she retorted sharply.

Then she felt all the bundles of leeks over again. Finally, she selected the one she thought the best, and held it clasped to her bosom as saints in church pictures hold the palm of victory.

'I will give you sevenpence. That 's quite enough; and I 'll have to fetch it from the shop, for I haven't anything on me.'

Still embracing the leeks, she went back into the shop, whither she had been preceded by a customer carrying a child.

Just at this moment Constable 64 said to Crainquebille for the second time:

'Move on.'

'I 'm waiting for my money,' replied Crainquebille.

'And I 'm not telling you to wait for your money; I 'm telling you to move on,' retorted the constable grimly.

Meanwhile, the shoemaker's wife in her shop was fitting blue slippers on to a child of eighteen months, whose mother was in a hurry. And the green heads of the leeks were lying on the counter.

For the half-century that he had been pushing his barrow through the streets, Crainquebille had been learning respect for authority. But now his position was a peculiar one: he was torn asunder between what was his due and what was his duty. His was not a judicial mind. He failed to understand that the possession of an individual's right in no way exonerated him from the performance of a social duty. He attached too great importance to his claim to receive sevenpence, and too little to the duty of pushing his barrow and moving on, for ever moving on. He stood still.

For the third time Constable 64 quietly and calmly ordered him to move on. Unlike Inspector Montauciel, whose habit it is to threaten constantly but never to take proceedings, Constable 64 is slow to threaten and quick to act. Such is his character. Though somewhat sly he is an excellent servant and a loyal soldier. He is as brave as a lion and as gentle as a child. He knows naught save his official instructions.

'Don't you understand when I tell you to move on?'

To Crainquebille's mind his reason for standing still was too weighty for him not to consider it sufficient. Wherefore, artlessly and simply he explained it:

'Good Lord! Don't I tell you that I am waiting for my money?'

Constable 64 merely replied:

'Do you want me to summons you? If you do, you have only to say so.'

At these words Crainquebille slowly shrugged his shoulders, looked sadly at the constable, and then raised his eyes to heaven, as if he would say:

'I call God to witness! Am I a law-breaker? Am I one to make light of the by-laws and ordinances which regulate my ambulatory calling? At five o'clock in the morning I was at the market. Since seven, pushing my barrow and wearing my hands to the bone, I have been crying: "Cabbages! Turnips! Carrots!" I am turned sixty. I am worn out. And you ask me whether I have raised the black flag of rebellion. You are mocking me and your joking is cruel.'

Either because he failed to notice the expression on Crainquebille's face, or because he considered it no excuse for disobedience, the constable inquired curtly and roughly whether he had been understood.

Now, just at that moment the block of traffic in the Rue Montmartre was at its worst. Carriages, drays, carts, omnibuses, trucks, jammed one against the other, seemed indissolubly welded together. From their quivering immobility proceeded shouts and oaths. Cabmen and butchers' boys grandiloquent and drawling insulted one another from a distance, and omnibus conductors, regarding Crainquebille as the cause of the block, called him 'a dirty leek'.

Meanwhile, on the pavement the curious were crowding round to listen to the dispute. Then the constable, finding himself the centre of attention, began to think it time to display his authority.

'Very well,' he said, taking a stumpy pencil and a greasy notebook from his pocket.

Crainquebille persisted in his idea, obedient to a force within. Besides, it was now impossible for him either to move on or to draw back. The wheel of his barrow was unfortunately caught in that of a milkman's cart.

Tearing his hair beneath his cap he cried:

'But don't I tell you I'm waiting for my money! Here's a fix! *Misère de misère! Bon sang de bon sang!*'

By these words, expressive rather of despair than of rebellion, Constable 64 considered he had been insulted. And, because to his mind all insults must necessarily take the consecrated, regular, traditional, liturgical, ritual form so to speak of *Mort aux vaches*,[1] thus the offender's words were heard and understood by the constable.

'Ah! You said: *Mort aux vaches!* Very good. Come along.'

Stupefied with amazement and distress, Crainquebille opened his great rheumy eyes and gazed at Constable 64. With a broken voice proceeding now from the top of his head and now from the heels of his boots, he cried, with his arms folded over his blue blouse:

'I said "*Mort aux vaches!*"? I? . . . Oh!'

The tradesmen and errand boys hailed the arrest with laughter. It gratified the taste of all crowds for violent and ignoble spectacles. But there was one serious person who was pushing his way through the throng; he was a sad-looking old man, dressed in black, wearing a high hat; he went up to the constable and said to him in a low voice very gently and firmly:

'You are mistaken. This man did not insult you.'

'Mind your own business,' replied the policeman, but without threatening, for he was speaking to a man who was well dressed.

The old man insisted calmly and tenaciously. And the policeman ordered him to make his declaration to the Police Commissioner.

Meanwhile Crainquebille was explaining:

'Then I did say "*Mort aux vaches!*" Oh! . . .'

As he was thus giving vent to his astonishment, Madame Bayard, the shoemaker's wife, came to him with sevenpence

[1] It is impossible to translate this expression. As explained on p. 325 it means 'down with spies', the word spies being used to indicate the police

in her hand. But Constable 64 already had him by the collar; so Madame Bayard, thinking that no debt could be due to a man who was being taken to the police-station, put her sevenpence into her apron pocket.

Then, suddenly beholding his barrow confiscated, his liberty lost, a gulf opening beneath him and the sky overcast, Crainquebille murmured:

'It can't be helped!'

Before the Commissioner, the old gentleman declared that he had been hindered on his way by the block in the traffic, and so had witnessed the incident. He maintained that the policeman had not been insulted, and that he was labouring under a delusion. He gave his name and profession: Dr. David Matthieu, chief physician at the Ambroise-Paré Hospital, officer of the Legion of Honour. At another time such evidence would have been sufficient for the Commissioner. But just then men of science were regarded with suspicion in France.

Crainquebille continued under arrest. He passed the night in the lock-up. In the morning he was taken to the Police Court in the prison van.

He did not find prison either sad or humiliating. It seemed to him necessary. What struck him as he entered was the cleanliness of the walls and of the brick floor.

'Well, for a clean place, yes, it is a clean place. You might eat off the floor.'

When he was left alone, he wanted to draw out his stool; but he perceived that it was fastened to the wall. He expressed his surprise aloud:

'That 's a queer idea! Now there 's a thing I should never have thought of, I 'm sure.'

Having sat down, he twiddled his thumbs and remained wrapped in amazement. The silence and the solitude overwhelmed him. The time seemed long. Anxiously he thought of his barrow, which had been confiscated with its load of cabbages, carrots, celery, dandelion, and corn-salad. And he wondered, asking himself with alarm: 'What have they done with my barrow?'

On the third day he received a visit from his lawyer, Maître Lemerle, one of the youngest members of the Paris Bar, President of a section of La Ligue de la Patrie Française.

Crainquebille endeavoured to tell him his story; but it was

not easy, for he was not accustomed to conversation. With a little help he might perhaps have succeeded. But his lawyer shook his head doubtfully at everything he said; and, turning over his papers, muttered:

'Hm! Hm! I don't find anything about all this in my brief.'

Then, in a bored tone, twirling his fair moustache he said:

'In your own interest it would be advisable, perhaps, for you to confess. Your persistence in absolute denial seems to me extremely unwise.'

And from that moment Crainquebille would have made confession if he had known what to confess.

III. Crainquebille before the Magistrates

President Bourriche devoted six whole minutes to the examination of Crainquebille. The examination would have been more enlightening if the accused had replied to the questions asked him. But Crainquebille was unaccustomed to discussion; and in such a company his lips were sealed by reverence and fear. So he was silent: and the President answered his own question; his replies were staggering. He concluded: 'Finally, you admit having said, "*Mort aux vaches!*".'

'I said, "*Mort aux vaches!*" because the policeman said, "*Mort aux vaches!*" so then I said, "*Mort aux vaches!*"'

He meant that, being overwhelmed by the most unexpected of accusations, he had in his amazement merely repeated the curious words falsely attributed to him, and which he had certainly never pronounced. He had said, '*Mort aux vaches!*' as he might have said, 'I capable of insulting any one! how could you believe it?'

President Bourriche put a different interpretation on the incident.

'Do you maintain,' he said, 'that the policeman was, himself, the first to utter the exclamation?'

Crainquebille gave up trying to explain. It was too difficult.

'You do not persist in your statement. You are quite right,' said the President.

And he had the witness called.

Constable 64, by name Bastien Matra, swore he spoke the

truth and nothing but the truth. Then he gave evidence in the following terms:

'I was on my beat on October 20, at noon, when I noticed in the Rue Montmartre a person who appeared to be a hawker, unduly blocking the traffic with his barrow opposite No. 328. Three times I intimated to him the order to move on, but he refused to comply. And when I gave him warning that I was about to charge him, he retorted by crying: "*Mort aux vaches !*" Which I took as an insult.'

This evidence, delivered in a firm and moderate manner, the magistrates received with obvious approbation. The witnesses for the defence were Madame Bayard, shoemaker's wife, and Dr. David Matthieu, chief physician to the Hospital Ambroise-Paré, officer of the Legion of Honour. Madame Bayard had seen nothing and heard nothing. Dr. Matthieu was in the crowd which had gathered round the policeman, who was ordering the costermonger to move on. His evidence led to a new episode in the trial.

'I witnessed the incident,' he said, 'I observed that the constable had made a mistake; he had not been insulted. I went up to him and called his attention to the fact. The officer insisted on arresting the costermonger, and told me to follow him to the Commissioner of Police. This I did. Before the Commissioner, I repeated my declaration.

'You may sit down,' said the President. 'Usher, recall witness Matra.'

'Matra, when you proceeded to arrest the accused, did not Dr. Matthieu point out to you that you were mistaken?'

'That is to say, Monsieur le Président, that he insulted me.'

'What did he say?'

'He said, "*Mort aux vaches !*"'

Uproarious laughter arose from the audience.

'You may withdraw,' said the President hurriedly.

And he warned the public that if such unseemly demonstrations occurred again he would clear the court. Meanwhile, Counsel for the defence was haughtily fluttering the sleeves of his grown, and for the moment if was thought that Crainquebille would be acquitted.

Order having being restored, Maître Lemerle rose. He opened his pleading with a eulogy of policemen: 'those unassuming servants of society who, in return for a trifling salary, endure fatigue and brave incessant danger with daily heroism. They were soldiers once, and soldiers they remain; soldiers, that word expresses everything. . . .'

From this consideration Maître Lemerle went on to descant eloquently on the military virtues. He was one of those, he said, who would not allow a finger to be laid on the army, on that national army, to which he was so proud to belong.

The President bowed. Maître Lemerle happened to be lieutenant in the Reserves. He was also nationalist candidate for Les Vieilles Haudriettes. He continued:

'No, indeed, I do not esteem lightly the invaluable services, unassumingly rendered, which the valiant people of Paris receive daily from the guardians of the peace. And had I beheld in Crainquebille, gentlemen, one who had insulted an ex-soldier, I should never have consented to represent him before you. My client is accused of having said: "*Mort aux vaches !*" The meaning of such an expression is clear. If you consult *Le Dictionnaire de la Langue Verte* (slang) you will find: "*Vachard*, a sluggard, an idler, one who stretches himself out lazily like a cow instead of working. *Vache*, one who sells himself to the police; spy." *Mort aux vaches !* is an expression employed by certain people. But the question resolves itself into this: how did Crainquebille say it? And, further, did he say it at all? Permit me to doubt it, gentlemen.

'I do not suspect Constable Matra of any evil intention. But, as we have said, his calling is arduous. He is sometimes harassed, fatigued, overdone. In such conditions he may have suffered from an aural hallucination. And, when he comes and tells you, gentlemen, that Dr. David Matthieu, officer of the Legion of Honour, chief physician at the Ambroise-Paré Hospital, a gentleman and a prince of science, cried: "*Mort aux vaches !*", then we are forced to believe that Matra is obsessed, and if the term be not too strong, suffering from the mania of persecution.

'And even if Crainquebille did cry: "*Mort aux vaches !*", it remains to be proved whether such words on his lips can be regarded as an offence. Crainquebille is the natural child of a costermonger, depraved by years of drinking and other evil courses. Crainquebille was born alcoholic. You behold him brutalized by sixty years of poverty. Gentlemen you must conclude that he is irresponsible.'

Maître Lemerle sat down. Then President Bourriche muttered a sentence condemning Jérôme Crainquebille to pay fifty francs fine and to go to prison for a fortnight. The magistrates convicted him on the strength of the evidence given by Constable Matra.

As he was being taken down the long dark passage of the Palais, Crainquebille felt an intense desire for sympathy. He turned to the municipal guard who was his escort and called him three times:

''Cipal! . . . 'cipal! . . . Eh! 'cipal!' And he sighed:

'If any one had told me only a fortnight ago that this would happen!'

Then he reflected:

'They speak too quickly, these gentlemen. They speak well, but they speak too quickly. You can't make them understand you. . . . 'Cipal, don't you think they speak too quickly?'

But the soldier marched straight on without replying or turning his head.

Crainquebille asked him:

'Why don't you answer me?'

The soldier was silent. And Crainquebille said bitterly:

'You would speak to a dog. Why not to me? Do you never open your mouth? Is it because your breath is foul?'

IV. An Apology for President Bourriche

After the sentence had been pronounced, several members of the audience and two or three lawyers left the hall. The clerk was already calling another case. Those who went out did not reflect on the Crainquebille affair, which had not greatly interested them; and they thought no more about it. Monsieur Jean Lermite, an etcher, who happened to be at the Palais, was the only one who meditated on what he had just seen and heard. Putting his arm on the shoulder of Maître Joseph Aubarrée, he said:

'President Bourriche must be congratulated on having kept his mind free from idle curiosity, and from the intellectual pride which is determined to know everything. If he had weighed one against the other the contradictory evidence of Constable Matra and Dr. David Matthieu, the magistrate would have adopted a course leading to nothing but doubt and uncertainty. The method of examining facts in a critical spirit would be fatal to the administration of justice. If the judge were so imprudent as to follow that method, his sentences would depend on his personal sagacity, of which he has generally no very great store, and on human infirmity which is universal. Where can he find a criterion? It cannot be denied that the historical method is absolutely incapable of providing him with the certainty he needs. In this connection you may recall a story told of Sir Walter Raleigh.

'"One day, when Raleigh, a prisoner in the Tower of London, was working, as was his wont, at the second part of his *History of the World*, there was a scuffle under his window. He went and looked at the brawlers; and when he returned to his work, he thought he had observed them very carefully. But on the morrow, having related the incident to one of his friends who had witnessed the affair and had even taken part in it, he was contradicted by his friend on every point. Reflecting, therefore, that if he were mistaken as to events which passed beneath his very eyes, how much greater must be the difficulty of ascertaining the truth concerning events far distant, he threw the manuscript of his history into the fire."

'If the judges had the same scruples as Sir Walter Raleigh, they would throw all their notes into the fire. But they have no right to do so. They would thus be flouting justice; they would be committing a crime. We may despair of knowing, we must not despair of judging. Those who demand that sentences pronounced in Law Courts should be founded upon a methodical examination of facts, are dangerous sophists, and perfidious enemies of justice both civil and military. President Bourriche has too judicial a mind to permit his sentences to depend on reason and knowledge, the conclusions of which are eternally open to question. He founds them on dogma and moulds them by tradition, so that the authority of his sentences is equal to that of the Church's commandments. His sentences are indeed canonical. I mean that he derives them from a certain number of sacred canons. See, for example, how he classifies evidence, not according to the uncertain and deceptive qualities of appearances and of human veracity, but according to intrinsic, permanent, and manifest qualities. He weighs them in the scale, using weapons of war for weights. Can anything be at once simpler and wiser? Irrefutable for him is the evidence of a guardian of the peace, once his humanity be abstracted, and he conceived as a registered number, and according to the categories of an ideal police. Not that Matra (Bastien), born at Cinto-Monte in Corsica, appears to him incapable of error. He never thought that Bastien Matra was gifted with any great faculty of observation, nor that he applied any secret and vigorous method to the examination of facts. In truth it is not Bastien Matra he is considering, but Constable 64. A man is fallible, he thinks. Peter and Paul may be mistaken. Descartes and Gassendi, Leibniz and Newton, Bichat and Claude Bernard were capable of error. We may all err and at any moment. The causes of error are innumerable. The perceptions of our senses and the judgment of our minds are sources of illusion and causes of uncertainty. We dare not rely on the evidence of a single man: *Testis unus, testis nullus*. But we may have faith in a number. Bastien Matra, of Cinto-Monte, is fallible. But Constable 64, when abstraction has been made of his humanity, cannot err. He is an entity. An entity has nothing in common with a man, it is free from all that confuses, corrupts and deceives men. It is pure, unchangeable and unalloyed. Wherefore the magistrates did not hesitate to reject the evidence of the mere man, Dr. David Matthieu, and to admit that of Constable 64, who is the pure idea, an emanation from divinity come down to the judgment bar.

'By following such a line of argument, President Bourriche attains to a kind of infallibility, the only kind to which a magistrate may aspire. When the man who bears witness is armed with a sword, it is the sword's evidence that must be listened to, not the man's. The man is contemptible and may be wrong. The sword is not contemptible and is always right. President Bourriche has seen deeply into the spirit of laws. Society rests on force; force must be respected as the august foundation of society. Justice is the administration of force. President Bourriche knows that Constable 64 is an integral part of the Government. The Government is immanent in each one of its officers. To slight the authority of Constable 64 is to weaken the State. To eat the leaves of an artichoke is to eat the artichoke, as Bossuet puts it in his sublime language. (*Politique tirée de l'Écriture sainte, passim.*)

'All the swords of the State are turned in the same direction. To oppose one to the other is to overthrow the Republic. For that reason, Crainquebille, the accused, is justly condemned to a fortnight in prison and a fine of fifty francs, on the evidence of Constable 64. I seem to hear President Bourriche, himself, explaining the high and noble considerations which inspired his sentence. I seem to hear him saying:

'"I judged this person according to the evidence of Constable 64, because Constable 64 is the emanation of public force. And if you wish to prove my wisdom, imagine the consequences had I adopted the opposite course. You will see at once that it would have been absurd. For if my judgments were in opposition to force, they would never be executed. Notice, gentlemen, that judges are only obeyed when force is on their side. A judge without policemen would be but an idle dreamer. I should be doing myself an injury if I admitted a policeman to be in the wrong. Moreover, the very spirit of laws is in opposition to my doing so. To disarm the strong and to arm the weak would be to subvert that social order which it is my duty to preserve. Justice is the sanction of established injustice. Was justice ever seen to oppose conquerors and usurpers? When an unlawful power arises, justice has only to recognize it and it becomes lawful. Form is everything; and between crime and innocence there is but the thickness of a piece of stamped paper. It was for you, Crainquebille, to be the strongest. If, after having cried: '*Mort aux vaches!*' you had declared yourself emperor, dictator, President of the Republic, or even town councillor, I assure you you would not have been sentenced to pass a fortnight in prison, and to pay a fine of fifty francs. I should have acquitted you. You may be sure of that."

'Such would have doubtless been the words of President Bourriche; for he has a judicial mind, and he knows what a magistrate owes to society. With order and regularity he defends social principles. Justice is social. Only wrongheaded persons would make justice out to be human and reasonable. Justice is administered upon fixed rules, not in obedience to physical emotions and flashes of intelligence. Above all things do not ask justice to be just, it has no need to be just since it is justice, and I might even say that the idea of just justice can have only arisen in the brains of an anarchist. True, President Magnaud pronounces just sentences; but if they are reversed, that is still justice.

'The true judge weighs his evidence with weights that are weapons. So it was in the Crainquebille affair, and in other more famous cases.'

Thus said Monsieur Jean Lermite as he paced up and down the Salle des Pas-Perdus.

Scratching the tip of his nose, Maître Joseph Aubarrée, who knows the Palais well, replied:

'If you want to hear what I think, I don't believe that President Bourriche rose to so lofty a metaphysical plane. In my opinion, when he received as true the evidence of Constable 64, he merely acted according to precedent. Imitation lies at the root of most human actions. A respectable person is one who conforms to custom. People are called good when they do as others do.'

V. Crainquebille submits to the Laws of the Republic

Having been taken back to his prison, Crainquebille sat down on his chained stool, filled with astonishment and admiration. He, himself, was not quite sure whether the magistrates were mistaken. The tribunal had concealed its essential weakness beneath the majesty of form. He could not believe that he was in the right, as against magistrates whose reasons he had not understood: it was impossible for him to conceive that anything could go wrong in so elaborate a ceremony. For, unaccustomed to attending Mass or frequenting the Élysée, he had never in his life witnessed anything so grand as a police court trial. He was perfectly aware that he had never cried: '*Mort aux vaches!*' That for having said it he should have been sentenced to a fortnight's imprisonment seemed to him an august mystery, one of those articles of faith to which believers adhere without understanding them, an obscure, striking, adorable and terrible revelation.

This poor old man believed himself guilty of having mystically offended Constable 64, just as the little boy learning his first Catechism believes himself guilty of Eve's sin. His sentence had taught him that he had cried: '*Mort aux vaches!*' He must, therefore have cried: '*Mort aux vaches!*' in some mysterious manner, unknown to himself. He was transported into a supernatural world. His trial was his apocalypse.

If he had no very clear idea of the offence, his idea of the penalty was still less clear. His sentence appeared to him a solemn and superior ritual, something dazzling and incomprehensible, which is not to be discussed, and for which one is neither to be praised nor pitied. If at that moment he had seen President Bourriche, with white wings and a halo round his forehead, coming down through a hole in the ceiling, he would not have been surprised at this new manifestation of judicial glory. He would have said: 'This is my trial continuing!'

On the next day his lawyer visited him:

'Well, my good fellow, things aren't so bad after all! Don't be discouraged. A fortnight is soon over. We have not much to complain of.'

'As for that, I must say the gentlemen were very kind, very polite: not a single rude word. I shouldn't have believed it. And the '*cipal* was wearing white gloves. Did you notice?'

'Everything considered, we did well to confess.'

'Perhaps.'

'Crainquebille, I have a piece of good news for you. A charitable person, whose interest I have elicited on your behalf, gave me fifty francs for you. The sum will be used to pay your fine.'

'When will you give me the money?'

'It will be paid into the clerk's office. You need not trouble about it.'

'It does not matter. All the same I am very grateful to this person.' And Crainquebille murmured meditatively: 'It 's something out of the common that 's happening to me.'

'Don't exaggerate, Crainquebille. Your case is by no means rare, far from it.'

'You couldn't tell me where they 've put my barrow?'

VI. Crainquebille in the Light of Public Opinion

After his discharge from prison, Crainquebille trundled his barrow along the Rue Montmartre, crying: 'Cabbages! Turnips! Carrots!' He was neither ashamed nor proud of his adventure. The memory of it was not painful. He classed it in his mind with dreams, travels, and plays. But, above all things, he was glad to be walking in the mud, along the paved streets, and to see overhead the rainy sky as dirty as the gutter, the dear sky of the town. At every corner he stopped to have a drink; then, gay and unconstrained, spitting in his hands in order to moisten his horny palms, he would seize the shafts and push on his barrow. Meanwhile a flight of sparrows, as poor and as early as he, seeking their livelihood in the road, flew off at the sound of his familiar cry: 'Cabbages! Turnips! Carrots!' An old housewife, who had come up, said to him as she felt his celery:

'What 's happened to you, Père Crainquebille? We haven't seen you for three weeks. Have you been ill? You look rather pale.'

'I 'll tell you, M'ame Mailloche, I 've been doing the gentleman.'

Nothing in his life changed, except that he went oftener to the pub, because he had an idea it was a holiday and that he had made the acquaintance of charitable folk. He returned to his garret rather gay. Stretched on his mattress he drew over him the sacks borrowed from the chestnut-seller at the corner which served him as blankets and he pondered: 'Well, prison is not so bad; one has everything one wants there. But all the same one is better at home.'

His contentment did not last long. He soon perceived that his customers looked at him askance.

'Fine celery, M'ame Cointreau!'

'I don't want anything.'

'What! nothing! do you live on air then?'

And M'ame Cointreau without deigning to reply returned to the large bakery of which she was the mistress. The shopkeepers and caretakers, who had once flocked round his barrow all green and blooming, now turned away from him. Having reached the shoemaker's, at the sign of l'Ange Gardien, the place where his adventures with justice had begun, he called:

'M'ame Bayard, M'ame Bayard, you owe me sevenpence halfpenny from last time.'

But M'ame Bayard, who was sitting at her counter, did not deign to turn her head.

The whole of the Rue Montmartre was aware that Père Crainquebille had been in prison, and the whole of the Rue Montmartre gave up his acquaintance. The rumour of his conviction had reached the Faubourg and the noisy corner of the Rue Richer. There, about noon, he perceived Madame Laure, a kind and faithful customer, leaning over the barrow of another costermonger, young Martin. She was feeling a large cabbage. Her hair shone in the sunlight like masses of golden threads loosely twisted. And young Martin, a nobody, a good-for-nothing, was protesting with his hand on his heart that there were no finer vegetables than his. At this sight Crainquebille's heart was rent. He pushed his barrow up to young Martin's, and in a plaintive broken voice said to Madame Laure: 'It 's not fair of you to forsake me'.

As Madame Laure herself admitted, she was no duchess. It was not in society that she had acquired her ideas of the prison van and the police-station. But can one not be honest in every station in life? Every one has his self-respect; and one does not like to deal with a man who has just come out of prison. So the only notice she took of Crainquebille was to give him a look of disgust. And the old costermonger resenting the affront shouted:

'Dirty wench, go along with you.'

Madame Laure let fall her cabbage and cried:

'Eh! Be off with you, you bad penny. You come out of prison and then insult folk!'

If Crainquebille had had any self-control he would never have reproached Madame Laure with her calling. He knew only too well that one is not master of one's fate, that one cannot always choose one's occupation, and that good people may be found everywhere. He was accustomed discreetly to ignore her customers' business with her; and he despised no one. But he was beside himself. Three times he called Madame Laure drunkard, wench, harridan. A group of idlers gathered round Madame Laure and Crainquebille. They exchanged a few more insults as serious as the first; and they would soon have exhausted their vocabulary, if a policeman had not suddenly appeared, and at once, by his silence and immobility, rendered them as silent and as motionless as himself. They separated. But this scene put the finishing touch to the discrediting of Crainquebille in the eyes of the Faubourg Montmartre and the Rue Richer.

VII. Results

The old man went along mumbling:

'For certain she 's a hussy, and none more of a hussy than she.'

But at the bottom of his heart that was not the reproach he brought against her. He did not scorn her for being what she was. Rather he esteemed her for it, knowing her to be frugal and orderly. Once they had liked to talk together. She used to tell him of her parents who lived in the country. And they had both resolved to have a little garden and keep poultry. She was a good customer. And then to see her buying cabbages from young Martin, a dirty, good-for-nothing wretch; it cut him to the heart; and when she pretended to despise him, that put his back up, and then . . . !

But she alas! was not the only one who shunned him as if he had the plague. Every one avoided him. Just like Madame Laure, Madame Cointreau the baker, Madame Bayard of l'Ange Gardien scorned and repulsed him. Why! the whole of society refused to have anything to do with him.

So because one had been put away for a fortnight one was not good enough even to sell leeks! Was it just? Was it reasonable to make a decent chap die of starvation because he had got into difficulties with a copper? If he was not to be allowed to sell vegetables then it was all over with him. Like a badly doctored wine he turned sour. After having had words with Madame Laure, he now had them with every one. For a mere nothing he would tell his customers what he thought of them and in no ambiguous terms, I assure you. If they felt his wares too long he would call them to their faces chatterer, soft head. Likewise at the wine-shop he bawled at his comrades. His friend, the chestnut-seller, no longer recognized him; old Père Crainquebille, he said, had turned into a regular porcupine. It cannot be denied: he was becoming rude, disagreeable, evil-mouthed, loquacious. The truth of the matter was that he was discovering the imperfections of society; but he had not the facilities of a Professor of Moral and Political Science for the expression of his ideas concerning the vices of the system and the reforms necessary; and his thoughts evolved devoid of order and moderation.

Misfortune was rendering him unjust. He was taking his revenge on those who did not wish him ill and sometimes on those who were weaker than he. One day he boxed Alphonse, the wine-seller's little boy, on the ear, because he had asked him what it was like to be sent away. Crainquebille struck him and said:

'Dirty brat! it 's your father who ought to be sent away instead of growing rich by selling poison.'

A deed and a speech which did him no honour; for, as the chestnut-seller justly remarked, one ought not to strike a child, neither should one reproach him with a father whom he had not chosen.

Crainquebille began to drink. The less money he earned the more brandy he drank. Formerly frugal and sober, he himself marvelled at the change.

'I never used to be a waster,' he said. 'I suppose one doesn't improve as one grows old.'

Sometimes he severely blamed himself for his misconduct and his laziness:

'Crainquebille, old chap, you ain't good for anything but liftin' your glass.'

Sometimes he deceived himself and made out that he needed the drink.

'I must have it now and then; I must have a drop to strengthen me and cheer me up. It seems as if I had a fire in my inside; and there 's nothing like the drink for quenching it.'

It often happened that he missed the auction in the morning and so had to provide himself with damaged fruit and vegetables on credit. One day, feeling tired and discouraged, he left his barrow in its shed, and spent the livelong day hanging round the stall of Madame Rose, the tripe-seller, or lounging in and out of the wine-shops near the market. In the evening, sitting on a basket, he meditated and became conscious of his deterioration. He recalled the strength of his early years: the achievements of former days, the arduous labours and the glad evenings: those days quickly passing, all alike and fully occupied; the pacing in the darkness up and down the market pavement, waiting for the early auction; the vegetables carried in armfuls and artistically arranged in the barrow; the piping hot black coffee of Mère Théodore swallowed standing, and at one gulp; the shafts grasped vigorously; and then the loud cry, piercing as cock crow, rending the morning air as he passed through the crowded streets. All that innocent, rough life of the human pack-horse came before him. For half a century on his travelling stall, he had borne to townsfolk worn with care and vigil the fresh harvest of kitchen gardens. Shaking his head he sighed:

'No! I 'm not what I was. I 'm done for. The pitcher

goes so often to the well that at last it comes home broken. And then I 've never been the same since my affair with the magistrates. No, I 'm not the man I was.'

In short he was demoralized. And when a man reaches that condition he might as well be on the ground and unable to rise. All the passers-by tread him under foot.

VIII. The Final Result

Poverty came, black poverty. The old costermonger who used to come back from the Faubourg Montmartre with a bag full of five-franc pieces, had not a single coin now. Winter came. Driven out of his garret, he slept under the carts in a shed. It had been raining for days; the gutters were overflowing, and the shed was flooded.

Crouching in his barrow, over the pestilent water, in the company of spiders, rats and half-starved cats, he was meditating in the gloom. Having eaten nothing all day and no longer having the chestnut-seller's sacks for a covering, he recalled the fortnight when the Government had provided him with food and clothing. He envied the prisoners' fate. They suffer neither cold nor hunger, and an idea occurred to him:

'Since I know the trick why don't I use it?'

He rose and went out into the street. It was a little past eleven. The night was dark and chill. A drizzling mist was falling, colder and more penetrating than rain. The few passers-by crept along under cover of the houses.

Crainquebille went past the Church of Saint-Eustache and turned into the Rue Montmartre. It was deserted. A guardian of the peace stood on the pavement, by the apse of the church. He was under a gas-lamp, and all around fell a fine rain looking reddish in the gaslight. It fell on to the policeman's hood. He looked chilled to the bone; but, either because he preferred to be in the light or because he was tired of walking he stayed under the lamp, and perhaps it seemed to him a friend, a companion. In the loneliness of the night the flickering flame was his only entertainment. In his immobility he appeared hardly human. The reflection of his boots on the wet pavement, which looked like a lake, prolonged him downwards and gave him from a distance the air of some amphibious monster half out of water. Observed more closely he had at once a monkish and a military appearance. The coarse features of his countenance, magnified under the shadow of his hood, were sad and placid. He wore a thick moustache, short and grey. He was an old copper, a man of some two-score years. Crainquebille went up to him softly, and in a weak hesitating voice, said: '*Mort aux vaches!*'

Then he awaited the result of those sacred words. But nothing came of them. The constable remained motionless and silent, with his arms folded under his short cloak. His eyes were wide open; they glistened in the darkness and regarded Crainquebille with sadness, vigilance, and scorn.

Crainquebille, astonished, but still resolute, muttered:

'*Mort aux vaches!* I tell you.'

There was a long silence in the chill darkness and the falling of the fine penetrating rain. At last the constable spoke:

'Such things are not said. . . . For sure and for certain they are not said. At your age you ought to know better. Pass on.'

'Why don't you arrest me?' asked Crainquebille.

The constable shook his head beneath his dripping hood:

'If we were to take up all the addlepates who say what they oughtn't to, we should have our work cut out! . . . And what would be the use of it?'

Overcome by such magnanimous disdain, Crainquebille remained for some time stolid and silent, with his feet in the gutter. Before going, he tried to explain:

'I didn't mean to say: *Mort aux vaches!* to you. It was not for you more than for another. It was only an idea.'

The constable replied sternly but kindly:

'Whether an idea or anything else, it ought not to be said, because when a man does his duty and endures much, he ought not to be insulted with idle words. . . . I tell you again to pass on.'

Crainquebille, with head bent and arms hanging limp, plunged into the rain and the darkness.

Translated by WINIFRED STEPHEN.

THE MATCH

CHARLES-LOUIS PHILIPPE

IT was in the course of a journey to Switzerland, at Zürich, on the very evening of his arrival that Henri Létang, in three seconds, was hurled into one of the most terrible adventures that can befall a man.

Henri Létang arrived at Zürich by an evening train. He was driven to his hotel. Being well enough off to travel very comfortably, he had chosen one of those hotels recommended by the guide books as well-conducted establishments, frequented by the right sort of people. He dined downstairs; then, feeling a little tired after the railway journey, went up to his room and, though not sleepy, went to bed. It was a comfortable bed.

Henri Létang was like a great many other people. Of course he had come to Zürich to see the town and before getting there had been quite curious to know it. But on the evening of one's arrival in a town, one's feeling towards it become blunted, or rather, having had time to satisfy themselves, they lapse into a state of repose, merely requiring of the town its continued presence. Henri Létang was lying in a bed in Zürich; the electric lamp which lit his room was the electric lamp of a Zürich room. He had put his cigarette case on his bed-side table. He took out a cigarette from it, put it in his mouth: he was going to smoke it in Zürich. That was sufficient for him.

Having lit his cigarette, he had just thrown away his match when he was seized with an anxiety, or rather a scruple. Might not this burning match, falling on the mat, cause a fire? Henri Létang bent down; he had been right to look: as a matter of fact the match was not yet out. He was going to get up, put on a slipper to crush it underfoot, when suddenly, brutally, he no longer needed to perform the act.

Clearly apparent, with all four fingers and thumb bunched up, a hand hidden under the bed emerged, rose, then descended, pressed on the match and extinguished its flame.

At first our brain appreciates only what our eyes have indicated to it. The first thought that seized Henri Létang related to the very action which he had just seen accomplished. When you place your hand on a burning object you risk getting burnt. How had the owner of the hand managed to avoid that? Henri Létang said to himself that of course this man had wet his fingers with his saliva.

It was probably, then, after the lapse of time he required to reason this out, that Henri Létang could say to himself:

'There is a man under my bed!'

Then slowly, word by word, this thought came to him:

'He is waiting till I am asleep to kill and rob me.' When he had understood, weighed, in some sort, touched each of the words of this thought, Henri Létang could not have any other. All his ideas were replaced by a frightful silence which, suddenly entering the room, filled it and became a much more terrible inmate of it even than he who was under the bed, waiting for his hour. It hit Henri Létang like a blow on the head. It was like awakening from a long sleep. He remembered a thing which he had long forgotten. He said to himself:

'Ah yes, it 's time. I 'd forgotten that I must die some day.'

And when he swallowed his saliva, he was surprised by the atrocious taste it had, a taste which seemed as if it must forever remain in his throat.

'I am going to be murdered to-night!'

It was as if he already had in his gullet the taste of his own corpse. He could not stand it.

Sometimes, gently, not to arouse attention, fearing he knew not what, if he made a noise, with every precaution he was capable of, he made his head pivot round on his neck and, avidly casting a glance round, looked at the articles of furniture in the room. There was a sideboard which he did not recognize, a wardrobe, a table. Some chairs which he counted and which were four in number. He almost did not notice a sofa. But no article of furniture came to his aid.

It took quite ten minutes before the idea of fatality could make way for that of violent despair. Good God! why was this happening to him? Why at this moment was he in Zürich? Without—for that purpose—interrupting his journey in Switzerland, he could have been in Basle, in Geneva, in Schaffhausen, towns where no one runs any danger. Life is stupid. Why was he in this room? He could have been in the one next door. Above all, before going to bed, why hadn't he thought of glancing underneath it?

'Oh! I 've made a fine mess of it!' he said to himself.

He struggled with himself as well as he could. First of all, to defend himself, all he could find was the sad thoughts that come to the human creature about to be killed in error.

'But I 've done nothing', he wanted to shout to himself, for the idea of death in us is invincibly associated with that of punishment.

No, he had done nothing. He was innocent. He felt the whole extent, the profundity of his innocence. And he was a very good man. He was so good that he was not even angry with the bandit who, hidden under his bed, wished *him* so much evil. Yes, he might have been angry with him. But, of course, the man did not know him. He wanted to shout to him:

'It 's me, Henri Létang, whom you are going to kill! You 're making a mistake, one doesn't kill people like me.'

He felt capable of becoming his friend. It is for want of money that people adopt the profession of crime. Henri Létang had money. He thought of saying to this man:

'Listen! I know that you are under my bed. Don't do me any harm and I will give you everything I possess. I 'll even give you more. You don't know who I am; you do not even know what I 'm capable of. If everything I have on me is not enough for you, look here; I make you a promise: I 'll go back to Paris and once there, I 'll send you any sum you like to fix.'

Poor comrade lying under the bed! Henri Lêtang no longer dared to be angry with him for fear of arousing his wrath. He was even grateful to him for not making any noise and for having attracted his attention only by that silent gesture of the hand on the match.

But soon something happened which may be called an event. Henri Létang was at this stage in his reflections when brusquely at the moment when he least expected it, a sudden, irresistible warm kindly pity invaded him.

It took him by the throat, it entered his mouth, he felt it flowing, he was filled with it. He did not know how it had come. He nearly shouted:

'My God! I am saved!'

He took plenty of time so as to be sure of success, he regulated every detail; he fixed the exact spot where he would place his feet. He even said to himself that he would put his left hand on the copper knob of his bed. Everything was ready, there was nothing to fear. Now——

Henri Létang sat up, and first of all imitated those persons who are accustomed to talk aloud when they are alone. He spoke to himself, of course, but above all in such a way as to be heard by all the men who might be hidden in his room. He said:

'What a fool I am, I do believe I 've gone and left my key in the door.'

He rose. Nobody leapt at his throat. The other was doubtless congratulating himself on the thought of having escaped a danger. He had run the risk of seeing someone turn the key in the lock and enter at the moment when he would be committing his crime.

Henri Létang did not hurry, so as not to attract attention. He went to the door; opened it. Good Heavens! a lot he cared about his key! How he shouted! how strong his voice was!

'Help! Murder! Come! Run quick!'

Ten people were round him before he had finished shouting. He shouted more than was necessary.

They found the fellow under the bed. They had to drag him out, for he made no movement to facilitate their task. Once on his feet he was pale with two brilliant eyes. Women struck him. The hotel proprietor had never seen him before. The policemen handcuffed him. When they had taken him away, while he was on his way to prison everybody was still trembling.

LEVIATHAN

Julian Green

He had been waiting five minutes on the quay in front of the *Bonne Espérance,* whose huge prow hid from him the entire estuary. Gamins were playing about him in the piles of coal and the pyramids of barrels. He must have heard their cries and bursts of laughter, but, keeping his head bowed, he did not appear to see anything. He was tall, dressed in a worn coat with enormous pockets into which he had thrust his hands. The rim of his hat was pulled down over his eyes and hid his face. He stood there motionless, a large valise at his feet.

When, finally, one of the crew came to get him, he himself picked up the valise, the weight of which made his wrist tremble, and followed his guide over the narrow gangway to the deck of the vessel. The sailor showed him to his cabin. Once alone, he closed the porthole and screwed it tight, drew across it the little serge curtain, and took off his hat. He was a man of about forty, sad-faced, with regular features and no wrinkles, but his age could be guessed from the discouraged and mistrustful expression in his eyes and from that something in the colour of the skin which shows that youth has passed.

Lifting his valise and setting it upon his berth, he opened it and unpacked his things with the air of a man who is resolved not to remain idle a second and seeks to divert his thoughts by busying himself in a little physical labour.

Toward the end of the day a sailor came and asked him, on behalf of the captain, if he would have dinner in the dining-saloon. He did not answer at once. First he asked at what time the *Bonne Espérance* was weighing anchor. The sailor replied that it would be at eleven o'clock that very night.

'Very well,' he said. 'I shall not dine.'

And he did not leave his cabin.

The next day Captain Suger sent word that he wanted to see him. The captain had all the manners of a perfectly frank person, even to the point of impoliteness. He addressed the man bluntly:

'Sir, you know that I almost never take passengers on this boat. Of course, regulations permit it, but my ship is first of all a freighter. I am making a sort of exception in your favour.'

He stopped as if to give his single passenger time to say a word of thanks. But the man was silent. The captain put his hands in his pockets and raised himself on his toes with a somewhat quizzical expression.

'I shall be obliged to see your papers.'

'I will show them to you if it is necessary,' said the passenger, quietly.

'On board this ship what I want is always necessary,' replied the captain in the same tone.

There was a moment of silence while the man adjusted his eyeglasses, felt in the inside pocket of his coat, and produced his passport, unfolding it. The captain took the document and examined it with the greatest care. He had a fat face in which curiosity put an infinite number of little folds, and eyes which looked at everything with a sort of greediness.

'Funny idea you had to travel on a freighter,' he said at last, handing the passport back to the passenger. 'We take twenty days, you know.'

'I know,' said the man.

And he folded up his passport again.

'Of course, it 's a bit cheaper,' resumed the captain, with a little grimace. 'That 's doubtless the reason why . . .'

He did not complete the sentence, but rose on his toes, appearing to wait, before letting himself drop back on his heels, for the passenger to give him an explanation. But the man remained silent.

'Besides,' said the captain, 'it 's none of my business. . . .'

He gave a shrug of his shoulders and turned his back on the passenger. The man withdrew.

II

In spite of the roughness of the sea, a considerable cargo of raw materials assured the *Bonne Espérance* an almost perfect stability and, under threatening skies, she went her way heavily and slowly, but steadily.

The first days were rather painful for the passenger. He

was nothing of a sailor. One might even doubt, seeing his uncertain step and anxious air, whether he had ever before set foot on a ship's deck. The greater part of the day he remained in his cabin, where he seemed to enjoy himself. Certain men have the faculty of being able to settle down anywhere in such a way that they seem to be permanently located. How they manage it is a mystery; but all they have to do is to change the place of a few things and, in an inexplicable manner, the hotel room where they pass the night appears to have been theirs for a long time and to be a home which they will never leave. There must be something in them opposed to the idea of change which tends to give everything about them a certain aspect of permanence.

It was, perhaps, an instinctive impulse of this kind which made the passenger on the *Bonne Espérance* modify as much as possible the appearance of his cabin. He had thrown over his berth a beige blanket belonging to him, thus hiding the quilt that bore the monogram of the company. He had also removed from the back of the arm-chair the antimacassar which displayed the same monogram embroidered in bright colours. There were a few books on a little shelf originally intended for shoes. Finally, the table was now in a corner which was manifestly not designed to receive it, as was evident from the big bright spot its leg had left on the carpet where it had been before. Where the table was now, a single roll of the boat somewhat more severe than the others would not fail to tip it over, but the traveller had only a limited knowledge of the sea.

Almost at the start of the voyage, torrential rains poured down upon the *Bonne Espérance* with such violence that one would have thought they were intent on making the boat return to port. But was there ever a case of a boat turning back because of rain? The captain laughed at the awful weather.

'You 're the cause of this,' he would say, insolently, to the traveller when they happened to meet in the passageway. Then the tall man would readjust his glasses and give a mirthless laugh resembling a cough. One day the captain remarked, brusquely, in a jocose manner:

'You 're my guest, you know. You will have to take your meals at my table.'

He put his little fat hands behind his back and resumed, in a tone which he intended to be humorous:

'That annoys you, eh?'

The man shook his head in protest.

'Say,' said the captain, abruptly, 'do you ever talk?'

Three days before he would not have risked so familiar and impertinent a question, but, as he gained the high seas, he felt more and more his importance. Such jokes were permissible four hundred miles from the French coast. The man made a sort of grimace in an attempt at a smile and retired with a bow.

From that day on they took their meals at the same table, in a little saloon situated well forward on the boat. Through the large portholes could be seen the whole extent of the restless line of the horizon. A bright, hard light beat in upon the captain and the passenger seated opposite each other at the table.

'Here,' said Suger, throwing himself back in his chair, 'you really feel that you 're at sea. We can't turn our heads without seeing it.'

And he confided to his passenger that, of all the saloons and cabins on the boat, it was the one he liked the best. He was, as it were, born to the sea. He did not like dry land and cities. He enjoyed only the solitude of his ship.

'You think I 'm gay, I suppose, because I joke,' he said. 'In reality, I have the gaiety of melancholy people.' And, as if that confidence deserved another, he looked up abruptly and exclaimed: 'But what about yourself? Tell me about yourself. You 're not saying a word.'

It was true. The man said nothing. He ate in silence, watching the captain through his glasses, nodded his head, but did not speak. Nevertheless, he did not appear to be timid; his eyes had that bold expression characteristic of near-sighted people who take for granted that everybody is acquainted with their infirmity and with their need of staring at people in order to see them clearly. Occasionally, however, something went over his face, but it was too rapid for the captain to think of noticing it. Was it the effect of a sudden indisposition? Suddenly his pupils would grow misty, seem to become larger, and his head would drop. A horrible despair spread over his features, remained a moment, and then disappeared immediately in a contraction of his whole face. It was like a nervous twitch.

Whenever this happened the passenger always took off his eyeglasses and bowed his head a little.

They had reached the dessert and the captain was playing with his knife, balancing it on his forefinger.

'Yes,' he repeated, 'you never say anything. However, I don't despair. A few days more at sea and you 'll be more loquacious.'

The passenger shrugged his shoulders, removed his glasses, and began to wipe them.

'We shall see,' he seemed to say.

Certainly the captain was right. A week on board a freighter, meaning almost complete solitude for a passenger, transforms a man. Even the melancholy cannot resist it. One must speak, become acquainted with someone, make friends, even if it is only to abandon them on arriving at port. But is it not curious that after five or six days at sea a person begins to think less of his destination and tends to forget it entirely in proportion as he approaches it? The monotony of the voyage pervades one and with it the singular idea that what has lasted for so many days can never come to an end. If only there were a moment's diversion, if only one were to pass an island, or to perceive in the distance the last cape of a continent! But nothing comes to interrupt the infinite line of the sea, which is there when one awakes, during meals, and all day long. For a person of nervous temperament, the monotony of the scene is a trial, almost a torture. And so it is that people on board ship turn, as if toward their salvation, to the company of their fellows, even if they have contempt for them, even if they hate them. For they have to live, they have to escape from the consuming boredom of the days, from the sea, and from that leviathan, ever lying in wait, which silently accompanies them.

III

Have I said that the *Bonne Espérance* was going from France to America? It was taking the longest route and shaping its course straight for Savannah. The captain was perfectly contented. For a long time he had been resigned to the sea, availing himself, to break his solitude, of conversations with the sailors or, when there were any, with the passengers. A passenger was a windfall. Like many people of mediocre intelligence who have read a few novels, the captain prided himself on knowing a great deal about what he called psychology, and he amused himself by watching the people about him. He believed he possessed considerable insight into character, and he had no doubt of his ability to find, after a few hours' conversation, the *formula*, to use an expression of which he was fond, of the people he was studying. I will not go so far as to say that he set down his observations in writing, but it would have been in character. When he had given orders to everybody and supervised the working of the ship, a long day remained ahead of him which it was necessary to fill. So the passenger furnished him with a precious diversion. He considered himself fortunate in having him on board, exactly as a geometrician rubs his hands in anticipation before a difficult problem. When he came to think of it, he liked those cold ways, that silence which had irritated him at first, and that reserve which, taking it all in all, prolonged the game and rendered it more interesting.

Meanwhile, the traveller seemed resolved to remain silent. It was evident that the inquisitive looks of the captain displeased him and that he considered the meal hours excessively disagreeable; but he tried to conceal his feelings, and what he revealed was only in spite of himself. If the captain had been as observing as he considered himself, he would surely have guessed that the traveller was afraid of him; but he was following another line of thought and he believed that he was dealing merely with a misanthropic and proud man. Pleased with his discovery, he was at present taxing his ingenuity to ask adroit questions which would flatter the traveller in his vanity and at the same time lead him to confidences concerning himself. These tactics failed, however, just as the captain's brusque manner and precise questions had failed in the first place. The traveller said nothing; the only result was that, when the captain became too insistent, he lowered his head, as one lowers one's head before a squall.

Now the sky was clear and the *Bonne Espérance* seemed to be making better time. The air was mild. Silence reigned, scarcely interrupted by the murmur of the waves as they spread out on either side of the boat's prow. But the traveller did not leave his cabin. There only he seemed at ease. One would have said that he had everything to fear outside that little room, and that, once across the threshold, his life was in danger.

Occasionally sailors passing on the deck saw at one of the port-holes a white face with a hesitant expression. Suddenly frightened, it disappeared immediately.

Faced with the passenger's silence, the captain remained at first taken aback; then he became angry. He had invited this man to his table, he had talked frankly to him as to a friend, an old friend, he had even confided to him several facts concerning his private life; and he had obtained nothing at all in return. Of course, it is interesting to fathom the secrets of a taciturn person by resorting to nothing more than observation and intelligence, but after almost three weeks the captain had had enough. There was something repelling in the passenger's morose face, and his silence was no longer interesting.

IV

The voyage was drawing to its close. Already a seagull, harbinger of approaching land, had alighted on the deck of the boat, only to set off again with the heavy flight of his long curved wings. One day, when the captain rose from the table, he planted himself before his guest, who had said nothing since the beginning of the meal. He raised himself on his toes and fell back again on his heels.

'You know, we arrive the day after to-morrow,' he said.

The man raised his head. The captain's severe expression doubtless frightened him. He made a sort of grimace, took off his glasses, and answered in a voice which was scarcely audible:

'I know.'

He seemed so dejected that the captain's irritation gave way before an impulse of compassion.

'Are you all right?' asked Suger, after a moment. 'You 're not ill?'

The man shook his head.

As the passenger was returning to his cabin, a sudden roll of the boat threw him from the wall which he was using as a support, against one of the ship's boats, suspended in its davits. He threw his arms out convulsively and, clutching the davit ropes, gazed down at the sea with the horrified expression of a man brought suddenly face to face with death.

'Don't be afraid,' cried the captain, who was following him at a distance.

And he went and helped him back to his cabin.

That day passed like the others, except for the fact that the captain asked fewer questions than usual. He had evidently become resigned to a silence which no effort of his could break and he even seemed, by an impulse of good nature which did him honour, to be trying to be more agreeable to the passenger than he had been up to that time. Was it because the really dejected expression of the traveller aroused his pity? At times the captain looked at him out of the corner of his eye and shook his head sadly. The traveller ate very little and spent most of his time bent over his plate, rubbing his knees unceasingly with the palms of his hands. From his high-buttoned frock-coat and his poor but neat appearance, one might have taken him for a teacher.

The last day broke on a hazy but calm sea and, when the two men sat down at the table together for the last time, the sky was radiant; the gusts of cool air had a perfume in which one might imagine one already distinguished the delicious odour of earth and trees.

'Well,' said the captain, pouring out wine for his guest, 'let 's part good friends. Let 's drink to each other's health.'

The man seemed dazed and in anguish. He raised his glass and held it in the air for a moment. Then he suddenly let it fall to the tablecloth and to the floor.

'I have something to tell you,' he murmured.

He grew pale and repeated what he had said in a louder tone, as if he were afraid that the captain had not heard him. The latter seemed overcome with surprise and joy.

'Well,' said he, laughing, 'didn't I tell you? I knew that you would end by talking. I know the sea!' And he gave a sonorous laugh in which a certain embarrassment was noticeable. 'Compose yourself,' he continued, seeing that the traveller was trembling. 'You can tell me anything, you know. I 'm a perfect father confessor.'

Then the traveller put both hands on the table and bowed his head in the attitude of a person collecting his thoughts. And he told his story.

When he had finished, the captain said:

'Well?'

'Well, that 's all,' answered the passenger.

'What!' exclaimed Suger. 'That 's why you left the country? You 're crazy. You were unmolested in France. . . .'

'I was not easy in my mind.'

'You might as well have been. No one suspected you.'

The traveller shook his head.

'Come,' resumed the captain, 'there must be something else. That just barely constitutes a crime!'

At these words the traveller raised his eyes quickly and looked at the captain. Beads of perspiration stood out on his temples. Abruptly he struck the table with his clenched fist and exclaimed:

'Everything I have just told you is false! I have deceived you. I am not a criminal!'

'Then why the devil did you tell me all that?' asked the captain.

'Because you forced me to. You look at me continually, you ask me all sorts of questions, you are like a detective on the track of a murderer. I said the first thing that came into my mind.' He struck the table once more with his fist and cried out, in a choking voice: 'I was afraid. You frightened me. I am going to America on business. I am not a murderer at all.'

The captain shrugged his shoulders tranquilly and smiled.

'Yes, you are,' said he. 'But you have nothing to fear from me. I shall not talk.'

The traveller bowed his head and his glasses dropped upon the table. At the same moment the call of a siren rent the air and someone up forward cried:

'Land, ho!'

The captain rose from his chair with a bound and took a rapid glance through a porthole.

'Land, ho!' he cried in his turn. Then he added, 'Many thanks. I saw it ten minutes ago.'

And he left the saloon with an important air.

He went down the little companionway leading to the deck and called out orders to sailors who were passing. Birds were circling about the smokestack, uttering wild cries. On the horizon a line darker than the water indicated America.

Then the captain turned toward the dining-saloon, the six portholes of which could be seen above him, and, putting his hands up to his mouth, he shouted, joyfully:

'Ho, there! Passenger! We are arriving!'

But already for some minutes the traveller had been dead.

Translated by C. Bruerton.